A PERFECT STRANGER

The advent of the Second World War changes everything and when Tom Phillips proposes to Ruth Madiewsky during seven days' leave, Ruth says yes, despite being only twenty. After all, who knows if they'll ever see each other again? A year goes by and there's no news from Tom. Ruth is forced to get on with her life and finds herself enjoying attention from another. It is this temptation which threatens to alter Ruth's life for ever and, when the war is finally over, she finds the battle for her own personal freedom and safety has just begun...

A PERFECT STRANGER

A PERFECT STRANGER

by

Victor Pemberton

Magna Large Print Books

Long Preston, North Yorkshire,
BD23 4ND, England.

British Library Cataloguing in Publication Data.

Pemberton, Victor
    A perfect stranger.

    A catalogue record of this book is
    available from the British Library

    ISBN   0-7505-1967-3

First published in Great Britain in 2002 by Headline Book Publishing

Published in Large Print 2003 by arrangement with
Headline Book Publishing Ltd.

Magna Large Print is an imprint of Library Magna Books Ltd.

Printed and bound in Great Britain by
T.J. (International) Ltd., Cornwall, PL28 8RW

For Christine and Alistair Wilson
with love and affection

Prologue

'*We want the King! We want the King!*' The deafening roar of the thousands of people massed in front of Buckingham Palace burst into a great chorus of ecstatic excitement, high up into the sparkling bright skies of a May afternoon, drifting gloriously above the ravaged streets of London town, which had struggled through the dark clouds of almost six heinous years of war. The elation was infectious; even the pigeon residents of Trafalgar Square had taken up their privileged positions on top of Nelson's column, determined to join in the celebrations of a joyous event which all London, all Britain had been awaiting for so long. It was over! The war in Europe was over! No more drabness, no more belt-tightening, no more crowding into tiny Anderson shelters in the back yard or sleepless nights on a cold tube station platform. It was over! The war was over! Now it was time for everyone to share their feelings of ecstasy and relief with the royal family, that same royal family who, like their beleaguered subjects, had stayed behind in London, facing up to the relentless nightly aerial onslaught by the Luftwaffe. And it was time also to thank the man who had symbolised their determination not to give in to the bullying of a terrifying German dictator. '*Winnie!*' they all chanted in Whitehall over and over

11

again. *'We want Winnie!'* For the time being, however, the clamouring pleas for their hero went unheeded, for the Prime Minister, Winston Churchill, was too preoccupied with the important task of preparing his speech that would inform the nation in a radio broadcast at three o'clock that afternoon that the war in Europe would officially end at midnight.

Ruth Madiewsky had never seen the King before – not in person, that is. However, she had once seen his wife when, at the height of the Blitz, she came to visit the people who had been bombed out of their homes near where Ruth lived in North London. She remembered how the colour of the Queen's pastel blue hat and dress had stood out against the smouldering debris, and how she had smiled that sweet, comforting smile at those poor souls who had lost everything they had possessed. But now both the King and Queen had appeared on the Palace balcony; she had at last seen them in person, even if they were only tiny figures in the distance. Despite the fact that she was half-Polish, a landmark occasion like this made Ruth feel more British than ever. 8 May 1945. This was going to be a date which Ruth was going to remember for the rest of her life – for more reasons than one.

The victorious strains of 'Land of Hope and Glory' swept through the crowds at least a dozen times, their deliriously happy voices constantly swelling in a highly emotional crescendo. Ruth's slight frame swayed to and fro with them, arms stretched high above her head, waving in time to the mass chorus. With hardly enough space to breathe, she could feel the heat emanating from the bodies pressed against her all around, but even in the great excitement of the moment, being hugged and kissed by complete strangers sent an uneasy shiver of foreboding throughout her entire body. However, despite the throbbing weight inside her stomach, she enjoyed being dragged time and again into one of the many ecstatic groups of revellers who had linked arms to do one frenzied 'Knees Up, Muvver Brown' after another, to the accompaniment of boisterous yelling and clapping from everyone around. Only after the final appearance on the Palace balcony of the King, in naval uniform, together with his beaming Prime Minister who had earlier addressed the nation on the wireless, the Queen in her favourite powder blue, Princess Elizabeth in ATS uniform, and her young sister Princess Margaret, did Ruth finally take the opportunity to join the exhausted stream of crowds who were slowly drifting back towards the nearest Tube station at Trafalgar Square.

It was still light when Ruth emerged from the depths of Holloway Road tube station. The main road outside was practically at a standstill, for it had been completely overwhelmed by the surging crowds who were determined to carry on the Victory in Europe celebrations right through the night. The air positively reeked of beer, and as she slowly made her way back home to nearby Jackson Road, hordes of well-oiled revellers frequently attempted to drag her into one of the many 'knees-ups' that were going on around the crackling flames of the many roadside bonfires. In Jackson Road itself the street-party was in full swing, and it was clear that for this one special night of the year at least, none of the excited throng of kids were going to be forced into their beds until they dropped with exhaustion, which for the time being looked most unlikely. The road had been blocked from end to end all day so that trestle tables could be set up for the neighbourhood kids' tea-parties, but the left-overs of Spam sandwiches and fruit jellies had now given way to bottles of brown ale, black-market gin and whisky, and dozens of empty, scrunched-up packets of Smith's crisps.

'Poley gel!' called a chesty female voice to Ruth from one of the tables. 'We bin lookin' for yer all day. Where yer been?'

Ruth had hoped to avoid the table where her neighbour Rita Simmons was boozing with a group of other high-spirited women. She hated being called 'Poley' just because she had a Polish mother, especially by someone like Rita, who was the neighbourhood's number one troublemaker. But as she had already been seen, Ruth decided it was too late to make a quick getaway. 'Hallo, Rita,' she replied, as she reluctantly made her way towards the women.

'Come an' sit yerself down,' said Rita, moving her large frame to make room for Ruth on the bench beside her. ''Ave a glass er muvver's ruin.'

'No, thanks, Rita,' said Ruth, declining the large tot of gin one of the other women was already pouring for her. 'I'm all in. I've been up West. I saw the King and Queen – *and* Mr

14

Churchill. They were all on the Palace balcony with the two Princesses.'

'Gawd bless 'em!' croaked Edie Perkins, one of the neighbours, whose face was almost as plush red as the colour of the curlers in her hair.

'Gawd bless ol' Winnie!' bellowed one of the other women in exaltation of the much revered Prime Minister.

They all joined in a quick raucous chorus of 'For He's A Jolly Good Fellow!' during which Ruth was only too aware how Rita was smirking as she took a passing glance at the bulge that Ruth was doing her best to conceal beneath a loose-fitting summer dress. 'Yer mum was out 'ere early on,' Rita said, as soon as the boisterous singing came to an end. 'She come an' 'elped out at the kids' tea-party. Went in when they was lightin' up the bonfires. She's not a one fer company, your mum, is she?'

'I think today's brought back too many painful memories for her,' said Ruth defensively. 'That's why she didn't want to come with me.'

'Can't be easy fer you eivver, can it, ducks?' Rita said knowingly. 'All fings considered.'

Although she knew exactly what Rita was insinuating, she was not prepared to show it. 'What do you mean?' she asked casually.

Rita grinned, 'Oh, you know,' she replied. 'We've all done fings in this war that we're goin' ter 'ave ter put right now it's over – ain't we?'

For one brief moment, Ruth's eyes met the beady ones of her bloated-faced neighbour. 'If you'll excuse me, I'm going to turn in now,' she said. 'Good night, Rita. Good night, everyone.'

15

The other women bid her good night, but were too much on a high to really take in that she was going. All except Rita, who smiled without saying anything.

As soon as Ruth had managed to get away, she slowly eased herself through the crowd of deliriously happy revellers until she was finally able to reach the corner of the nearby cul de sac where she lived. Before she disappeared out of sight, she stopped briefly to take a last look back to where she had just come from. In the distance, she could still see Rita watching her, her sly chubby face glowing red from the flames of the nearest roadside bonfire.

From the moment she entered the house, Ruth could smell the remains of the *flaki* that had been cooking earlier in the kitchen. Tripe had always been one of her mother's favourite dishes; Bella Whitlock's own mother had taught her how to cook it way back before she left her native Cracow in Poland to come to England with Ruth's father Harry Whitlock. The fact that Ruth had always hated the stuff had never deterred Bella, for she was convinced that the more she gave it to her daughter, the more she would, one day, accept that a good tripe stew was not just an acquired taste.

Ruth crept upstairs. Although it was barely past ten o'clock in the evening, it was obvious that it would be quite some time before her mother would get used to the fact that the war was over and that there was now no need to draw the blackout curtains at lighting-up time each evening. On the first floor, she paused outside her mother's bedroom. Pressing her ear gently against the door, she could hear the sound of snoring, a sure sign that her mama was well away. Bella Whitlock had always lived her life in the firm belief that nothing and no one should ever prevent her from getting her full eight hours' sleep, and that clearly included the victory celebrations in the streets outside. But Ruth knew there was more to it than that. For Bella, today was not only a time of celebration; it was a time of looking back to a past that had brought not only joy but a great deal of pain.

The first thing Ruth did as she entered her own bedroom was to draw back the blackout curtains and throw open the windows. It was still light enough to see outside that there was no one in the cul de sac down below, for most of her neighbours were joining in the celebrations in Jackson Road. The 'end house' as the Whitlocks' home was known locally was situated alongside an elevated railway bridge, which throughout the war had not only carried main-line passenger and troop trains, but also been used for the transport of ammunition and weapons. As she stood there Ruth recalled those long nights lying awake listening to the rumble of train wagon wheels as they echoed down from the bridge above, slowly heading off to distant places that she hoped one day she would be able to see for herself.

Despite the distant sound of overjoyed crowds of people belting out all the popular songs that had helped them through the darkest days of the war, the only sounds that Ruth could really hear

17

were those from her own past, and all she could see were three images mirrored in the reflection of herself in the dark glass panes of the window she was now staring into, the three images that had helped to shape her young life so dramatically over the past two years. There she was, Ruth Madiewsky-Whitlock, twenty-two years old, beautiful to so many, with dark brown eyes that matched the colour of her shining shoulder-length hair, a milky-white complexion that seemed to be drained of any colour, which emphasised her high cheekbones and a doleful smile that more often than not was a vain attempt to disguise a nagging anxiety about the way she was living her life. Also reflected in the glass were two male figures, both young men, both in Army uniform, both staring at her.

In one swift movement, she drew the blackout curtains again, turned and went to sit on the edge of her bed, where she kicked off her shoes and lay down. She gently closed her eyes, but in her mind she could still see the faces of those two male images – staring at her, accusing her. She was adrift, floating in a sea of uncertainty. At that moment, she felt a movement in her abdomen, slight at first, but then more determined. She clutched at it. It throbbed, then became motionless again. Over and over again a small voice within kept asking her how she was going to deal with what lay ahead. All the fears were there, the doubts, the recriminations. The war was over, but the battle was about to begin. How did all this happen to her? How could she have *let* it happen?

The answers lay in the past, on that day two

years before, when it all began ... when life for a twenty-year-old girl was the start of something good...

Chapter 1

The smoke from the burnt-out shell of the second-hand clothes warehouse in Shoreditch was still spiralling up in an eerie thin funnel into the balmy air of an early bright June morning. Even though the previous night's attack had been carried out by only three enemy raiders, once again the East End had taken the brunt of the bombing, and the trail of destruction they had left behind was devastating. By the time Ruth had reached the site of the incident to deliver her message to the NFS officer in charge of the team who had fought the blaze, most of the emergency services had already gone, leaving just a few weary fire-fighters to dampen down the last few flames. Ruth was also weary. After a long night trying to manoeuvre her motorcycle through streets littered with glass and rubble, she was more than ready for a cup of welcoming tea and a hot Spam roll from the nearby Fire Brigade mobile canteen. Being a firewoman dispatch rider in the middle of an air raid was quite a responsibility, especially for a girl who was barely twenty years old. But this was 1943, there was still a war on, and everyone had to do their bit.

'I'm afraid there's no mustard left, dear,' said

19

the middle-aged volunteer firewoman canteen server, her tin helmet still strapped firmly under her chin. 'Can't imagine why everyone's got a taste for mustard all of a sudden. Can't bear the stuff m'self. There's still some ketchup left if you'd prefer.'

Ruth smiled back sweetly, but shook her head. 'I'm fine, thanks,' she replied, taking a bite of her Spam roll.

The woman watched her admiringly. 'Don't know how you can do the job you're doing, love,' she said. 'It'd scare the daylights out of me, riding one of those things.'

'It would scare the daylights out of me doing the things *you're* doing,' Ruth countered.

They both laughed. 'Well, let's hope we won't have to do any of this for much longer,' replied the woman. 'When this war's over, I never want to see another one as long as I live.'

Ruth agreed, then moved on to make way for two ARP men who were panting for a cup of tea. She paused awhile to finish eating her roll, squatting down on the remains of a collapsed brick wall, which seemed to be the only part of the building that had survived complete devastation. All around her the debris was still smouldering from the soaking it had had from the myriad hose-pipes that had showered hundreds of gallons of water onto the dilapidated building overnight, and she found it a sad sight to see the remains of sodden dresses, suits, hats, and underclothes that were now abandoned beneath the smouldering rubble. Despite all the activity around her, she felt strangely alone, finding it hard to reconcile the busy, thriving area this must have once been with the bleak wilderness that now surrounded her. However, in one respect life was still going on quite normally, at least as far as one hungry looking sparrow was concerned. 'Oh come on now,' she said to the tiny creature who was perched cheekily on a dislodged brick on the ground in front of her. 'It's been a long night. I'm starved.' The sparrow was clearly not interested in excuses, and stood his ground. With a sigh, Ruth reluctantly pinched off a morsel of her Spam roll, and delicately fed it to her companion.

Whilst this was going on, she didn't notice the group of men nearby who were panicking in a rush towards her, waving and shouting as they came. 'Out! Out! Out!'

Ruth caught sight of them and saw them pointing frantically up towards the remains of an outer wall which was on the brink of collapse high above her. In the split second that followed, she suddenly found herself leapt upon by one of the shouting men and yanked out of the way. With a loud crash, the wall collapsed, only narrowly missing Ruth and the man who had just saved her. Sprawled out on the ground, covered in dust, Ruth found herself surrounded by anxious fire-fighters and emergency workers. To cries of, 'You all right, gel? Blimey, that was close! You okay, Mike?' Ruth gradually emerged from beneath the heavy weight of the man who was lying across her.

Somebody grabbed hold of Ruth's hand and hauled her up. Her hair, face, and uniform were

21

covered in dust, her trousers ripped right down one leg. Dazed and bruised, all she could splutter was, 'What the hell happened?'

'Bloody 'ell, you was lucky!'

'I fawt you'd 'ad it, an' that's fer sure!'

'Nearest fing *I've* ever seen!'

Oddly enough, the chorus of breathless, desperate voices had no effect on Ruth. She was far too busy brushing down her uniform and spitting out dust.

'It was the back wall of the factory,' said the man who had leapt at her. 'We all saw it comin' down. Din't yer 'ear us?'

Ruth snapped back. 'Don't be silly! If I'd heard you, I'd hardly have carried on sitting there, would I?' When she turned round to see who she was talking to, she was surprised to see that, unlike the others, the man was really a boy, about the same age as herself, tall, quite lanky, and the only one amongst the group who was not wearing any kind of uniform.

'I'm sorry,' she said guiltily. 'I didn't hear anything.' She smiled wryly, as she caught sight of the sparrow who had nearly cost her her life. 'I suppose I was too preoccupied.'

A few moments later, the boy walked her back to her motorbike. 'Bit dicey, this kinda work, ain't it?' he suggested, trying to be friendly.

'Don't know what you mean,' replied Ruth, a bit puzzled by his remark.

'A gel ridin' one of these fings,' replied the boy, whose dark brown hair flopped over his forehead the moment he took off his flat cap. 'I'd be a bit nervous of comin' off, 'specially in an air raid.'

Ruth grinned as she climbed onto the saddle of her motorbike. 'Oh, they're no trouble once you get used to them,' she said. 'In fact, I quite enjoy it. Gives me a sense of freedom.' With one foot, it took her several attempts to kick-start the engine into life. When she had finally succeeded, the exhaust spluttered noisily into a series of deafening bangs, which sent a flock of pigeons fluttering in panic into the air. 'Well,' said Ruth, holding out her hand, 'thanks for everything. I can't tell you how grateful I am. It's good to still be alive.'

The young bloke took her hand and smiled. 'Just make sure yer keep it that way, right?'

'Right,' replied Ruth, shaking his hand. For one split second she thought he had been reluctant to let go, but then he had turned away and was making his way back to his mates. 'Thanks again,' she called, as she used the clutch on her handlebar to rev up. With a roar, her motorbike made a hasty retreat from the devastation of Shoreditch, and in a cloud of exhaust fumes headed off at speed towards her home fire-station in Islington.

Whitlock's was a shadow of its former self. Before the war it had been a thriving newsagent and tobacconists shop, a haven for the kids from Hornsey Road School, who made a beeline for the place to buy their sweets or ice-cream on the way home. Everyone referred to the people who ran the shop as 'the Poleys', even though Harry Whitlock wasn't Polish at all. But his wife Bella was, which made their only child, Ruth, half-Polish. No one liked Harry very much, for he was a brusque man and quite often rude, always giving the impression that he didn't trust any customer who entered his shop. Bella was very different, a popular character with the kids, mainly because she often gave them a 'taster' when they came in to buy their penn'th of bull's-eyes or humbugs, but also because she never told them to stop larking around in the shop. To everyone else, Bella was a quiet little woman, who rarely carried on a conversation with any-one, but always managed to smile when she did.

That was in the good old days. Today, it was very different. Ever since Harry had died, just before the war, Bella had had to run the shop virtually single-handed. Ruth had always loathed working in the shop when she was young because of her relationship with her father, which had always been strained, and was the reason why she had always preferred to be known by her mother's maiden name. During the last few years of his life, Harry Whitlock had never approved of what he considered to be Ruth's wild ways, the hours she kept, and the type of boys she mixed with out in the street. These days, however, Ruth did occasionally help her mother out whenever she could, but only when she wasn't on dispatch-rider duty up at the fire-station. Fortunately, Bella did have young Phil and Dave to deliver the early-morning newspapers for her, and in the school holidays they would occasionally help out in the shop, shifting boxes and holding the fort whenever Bella had to pop into the back room for a few minutes or so.

Although the shop had been left to Harry

Whitlock by his own parents after he had returned from a lengthy working trip to Poland in the early 1920s, he and Bella had always rented out the top two floors to the Dappers, a childless, now middle-aged couple; the Whitlocks themselves preferred to live around the corner in the 'end house' beneath the railway bridge in Jackson Road. When Harry died, the Dappers voluntarily increased their rent by five shillings a week after Bella discovered that she had been left huge debts by her husband, who had overstocked the shop quite unnecessarily.

When Ruth came into the shop after her near-fatal collision with the tumbling warehouse wall earlier that morning, her mother was alarmed to see the girl looking thoroughly exhausted and worn out. 'Dear God!' cried Bella, immediately coming out to meet her from behind the counter.

'No need to panic,' said Ruth reassuringly. 'All I need is a smoke and a good bath.'

'But look at you!' exclaimed Bella in her Polish accent that had remained resolutely fractured ever since she had arrived in the country more than twenty years before. 'What happened?' she asked, clasping her hands in horror at her daughter's appearance.

'Stop fussing, Mama,' replied Ruth, quickly avoiding her, and making her way behind the counter. 'I'm perfectly all right. It's all in a night's work.'

'Not for *my* daughter, it's not,' complained Bella. 'A girl like you shouldn't be doing this kind of work – riding motorcycles in the middle of an air raid. It's not right, it's not natural!'

'There's a war on, Mama,' Ruth replied lightly. 'Don't worry, things will be different when it's all over.' She collected a packet of Players Weights from one of the shelves behind the counter, ripped it open, took out a cigarette, and quickly shoved it between her lips.

Bella watched whilst her girl searched for a new box of matches, then lit up. She hated to see Ruth smoking; she hated to see any girl smoking. In her eyes it was a manly thing to do, something of which her own parents back home in Poland would have strongly disapproved. But then everything the girl was doing these days seemed to be so unnecessary, so unfeminine. War or no war, standards, in Bella's mind, were there to be upheld. She blamed it all on Harry. If it hadn't been for his resentment that Bella had never given him a boy, if he hadn't treated his daughter with such contempt, things might have been so different. 'I wish you'd give up this terrible job,' she said, her eyes welling with tears as they had done so many times before. 'Why can't you come and work with me here in the shop? We could have such good times together.'

Ruth drew deeply on her cigarette. 'War isn't about good times, Mama,' she said. She exhaled a thin funnel of smoke from her lungs. 'It's about survival. It's about winning.'

The bell above the shop door tinkled, and a customer came in. It was a fat man in shirt and braces, with sweat streaming down his face, neck, and back. 'They caught a packet up Shoreditch last night,' he panted, making his way straight to the counter, where Ruth had already laid out his usual two-ounce packet of medium brown tobacco. 'We were lucky to miss that one.'

'Not so lucky for others,' replied Ruth, who had known 'Tub' Trinder, the gents' tailor from down the road, since she was a kid.

'I heard two people copped it,' he said. 'In some warehouse or other.'

'Actually it was seven people,' said Ruth, correcting him. 'One of them was a fireman. He had a wife and four children.'

Tub wished he'd bitten off his tongue. 'Why can't I keep my big mouf shut,' he said, collecting his packet of tobacco from the counter. 'Sorry, Rufe.'

'No need to be,' she replied, taking the few coins he was handing her.

Tub made his way back to the door. 'If me an' my missus get fru this bleedin' war,' he said, on the way, 'I'd like ter sell up an' move us out ter the country.'

'The country?' asked Ruth. 'You wouldn't like the country, Tub. You're a hundred per cent town boy.'

Tub stopped at the door, and turned. 'No one's a 'undred per cent *anyfin'*, Rufe,' he said. 'There's always somefin' inside that tells yer ter try somefin' new. You're exactly the same. That's why you're doin' the job you're doin'. I tip my 'at to yer, Rufe. There ain't many 'round like you wiv your guts. But I still fink yer shouldn't be doin' it. Ridin' motorbikes in the air raids ain't no job fer a gel. I just 'ope that boyfriend er yours 'urries up an' makes an 'onest woman of yer! Cheers!'

'If anyone tells me again that riding motorbikes

27

is dangerous,' said Ruth after Tub had left, 'I'll scream!'

'All the same,' said Bella, 'he's right. It *is* a dangerous job, darling. I get so afraid every time you go out.'

Ruth put Tub's coins into the cash till. 'A lot of girls are doing dangerous jobs, Mama. There's not much we can do about it until the war's over.' She looked at her mother, who was standing at the front window, arms crossed, staring gloomily at the road outside. Ruth went over to her, and from behind, slid her arms around her mother's waist. They stood there like that for a moment or so, Bella miles away, Ruth watching their reflection in the shop window. Ruth was glad she had inherited her mama's eyes and high cheekbones, but regretted that, in contrast to her mother who was small and podgy, with a tiny nose that was slightly upturned at the tip, she herself was more like her father – tall and slim, with sharp determined features. Ruth kissed the back of her mother's hair, which was drawn away severely from her face and plaited into a tight bun behind. 'You mustn't worry, Mama,' she said softly. 'Things always come right in the end.'

Without turning, Bella replied solemnly, 'What kind of a mother would I be if I *didn't* worry?'

When Ruth finally left the shop and went home, she found their neighbour Edie Perkins down on her hands and knees scrubbing and whiting the Whitlocks' front doorstep with a piece of pumice stone. Despite her constant air of anxiety and agitation, Edie was a warm-hearted soul, the best

28

kind of neighbour who was always ready to help out in times of need. Ever since Bella had lost her husband and was forced to work in the shop on her own, Edie had turned up trumps. In fact, the cul de sac was a close-knit little community, and although it was officially an extension of Annette Road, the residents in the few houses there considered themselves to be more a part of Jackson Road. And they seemed to be an ultra-clean lot for, despite the war, letterboxes were kept polished, front doorsteps scrubbed, and even the windows, which had frequently been shattered by bomb blast, were always hastily replaced, cleaned, and protective sticky paper gummed back to prevent splintering. Yes, all the three-storey houses were kept in tip-top condition, despite the thick black dust which billowed down every time a passenger or goods train passed over the bridge just above the end houses on each side of the road.

'You're a brick, Edie, you really are!'

Edie beamed when she looked up to find Ruth coming through the front gate, which was now made of timber after the original iron one had been confiscated by the local authorities for munitions at the start of the war. 'Oh, you're welcome, Rufie,' returned Edie, dropping the floor-cloth and scrubbing brush back into her pail. 'I 'ad some time on me 'ands, so I thought it's the least I could do ter 'elp out.' She stood up, and wiped her hands down her apron. In the heat of the morning sun, sweat was streaked across her forehead, and she had to rub it with the back of her hand to stop it from running down her nose and into her eyes. 'Gawd! You look all in,' she said. 'I bet yer've bin up all night again?'

'It *was* a long night,' replied Ruth, who did look all in. Much as she appreciated her good neighbour's kindness, she was desperate to get into the house to have a bath, and get to bed. 'A busy one too.'

'I 'eard,' said Edie, who had lowered her voice as though what she was being told was a State secret. 'Was yer up Shoreditch?'

Ruth nodded.

'Yer poor fing,' sighed Edie, sympathetically. 'They shouldn't expect young gels like you ter do that sort er work.'

Ruth was so tired, all she could bring herself to say was, 'I don't mind the work, Edie – honest I don't.'

Edie wanted to stay there chatting to her; she loved to hear Ruth's lovely clear speaking voice, with its faint hint of an accent picked up from her mum over the years. But even she was sensitive enough to realise that Ruth was dying to go inside, so she quickly replaced the doormat, and stood back to allow the girl to pass. 'Oh, by the way,' she said, as an afterthought, 'I almost forgot. There was a telegram boy here a bit earlier on.'

Ruth stopped putting the key into the front door lock, and turned with a start. 'A telegram boy?'

'I asked 'im ter leave it wiv me, but 'e wouldn't. 'E says they're not allowed to. But 'e's comin' back.'

Ruth was suddenly agitated. 'What time, Edie?'

''E didn't say.' Edie clasped her hand across her mouth. 'Oh Lord!' she cried, only just realising the significance of Ruth, or indeed of anyone, receiving a telegram in wartime. 'Yer don't fink... Oh Lord, Rufe ... it's not your Tom, is it?'

'It's all right, Edie,' said Ruth, quickly opening the door and trying to sound reassuring.

'This war!' Edie growled. 'They keep tellin' us it'll all be over soon – but then this happens!'

Ruth stepped inside. 'It's all right,' she said again, trying hard to put on a brave smile. 'I'm sure it's nothing. Don't you go worrying yourself. I'll see you later.'

'If it's bad news,' called Edie, as Ruth tried to close the door as politely as she could, 'just give me a shout. I'm only next door, remember. I could always go and get Rita across the road...'

Ruth finally managed to close the door. For a brief moment she just stood there, leaning back against the other side of the door, eyes closed, trying to bring her thoughts into focus. *Tom. No, it can't be Tom. It mustn't be, it just mustn't be.*

Her eyes sprang open again. She ripped off her uniform cap, threw it onto a hook on the hall rack, and rushed straight upstairs to her bedroom on the first floor. The room was stifling hot, so the first thing she did was to fling open the window and let some fresh air in. Then she took off all her clothes, and went down naked to the bathroom at the rear of the kitchen on the ground floor. It was a real luxury having a bathroom at all in the house, especially in wartime, when most people had to make do with heating buckets of water on their gas stoves and filling up

31

aluminium baths in their sculleries, but it had at least been one of the few positive things that Ruth's father had done during the last year before he died, for he had done all the conversion and plumbing work himself.

Once she'd lit the gas water geyser and drawn her regulation six inches of hot and cold water, Ruth lay down and stretched out, doing her utmost to cover at least part of her weary body with the measly ration of water she was allowed. Then she used the remains of some scented bath soap her mother had bought her for her twentieth birthday earlier in the year to wash off the sweat and grime of the previous night's work, slowly working it up into a lather on her face. She closed her eyes. In her mind's eye she could see Tom, all togged up in his brand new Army conscript's uniform, tin helmet, gas mask strapped over one shoulder, rifle over the other, a vast soldier's pack on his back. She could see him as clearly as the day she stood on the platform at King's Cross station only a few months before, tears streaming down her cheeks as though she had known him all her life. And although they were both only twenty years old, in some ways she *did* feel as though she had known him all her life, even though it had really been less than a year. Saying goodbye to him as he was leaving for call-up was painful, oh *so* painful. She was convinced that if anything had happened to him, if that telegram was bringing her bad news, she wouldn't know how to cope with it. Damn the war! And damn all those who were responsible for the war! The front door bell rang. Her eyes sprang open.

Her dressing-gown soaked with bathwater, she only just managed to reach the front door in time.

'Wos up wiv you lot then?' growled the petulant telegram boy from the front gate. 'This is the second time I've bin round 'ere wiv this fing.'

'I'm sorry,' Ruth replied, anxiously reaching out for the telegram the boy was again retrieving from his leather dispatch pouch.

'Your name Mad ... somefin' er uvver?' he asked, trying to read the foreign name scribbled on the buff-coloured envelope.

'Madiewsky!' returned Ruth, impatiently.

The boy allowed her to snatch the telegram from his hand. 'Bloody foreigners!' he said cheekily, then cycled off before he got the response he was expecting.

Ruth hurried back inside, and slammed the door behind her. Heart thumping, she ripped open the envelope and read the telegram which was printed on strips of sticky tape:

ARRIVING KINGS CROSS FROM
LEEDS 2.56 STOP CAN'T WAIT
TO SEE YOU STOP TOM STOP

Edie Perkins could hear the howls of delirious joy coming from her next-door neighbour.

King's Cross station was jammed to suffocation. Three troop trains had left for unknown destinations within the past hour, and just as many were due to arrive from different parts of the north, bringing service personnel either back

33

home on leave or to travel on to other London railway stations for journeys to secret transit camps. Despite the heavy raid on the East End the night before, there were plenty of relatives crowding around to meet or bid farewell to their loved ones, which meant that the atmosphere in the choking, steam-filled station was charged with emotion.

Ruth arrived almost half an hour early, only to find that the train Tom was due in on was running over forty-five minutes late. With so many people around, she wondered whether she would be able to meet up with Tom's sister Kate, and their parents, but the more she searched for them, the more hopeless her task became. To pass the time, she joined a long queue in the station café for a cup of tea, but it was bedlam in there with kids yelling and playing tag with each other around the tables, and a tannoy speaker relaying music from Charles Shadwell and his Dance Orchestra on the wireless. The whole place was thick with cigarette smoke. As the temperature outside was in the eighties, the combination of smoke and sweat was too much for her, so she abandoned her attempts to get a cup of tea and made her way through the crowds on the station concourse outside, past Special Constables in tin helmets, all kinds of servicemen and their relatives, dogs on leashes, and wartime posters everywhere carrying sinister messages such as CARELESS TALK COSTS LIVES and IS YOUR JOURNEY REALLY NECESSARY?

Once again she had to join a queue, this time to buy a penny platform ticket from a machine.

Although the train had not yet arrived, the platform was already overflowing with people. Halfway along, a group of young airmen conscripts, who were clearly waiting to take the train out on its return trip, were lined up for inspection by their Sergeant and Warrant Officer. Ruth felt truly sorry for them all, as they struggled to stand to attention with all the heavy equipment they were having to bear across their shoulders. With no sign of either Tom's sister or their parents, she slowly weaved through the waiting passengers, and made her way towards the far end of the platform. There was still fifteen minutes or so to wait before the delayed train was due to appear, which gave her time to ponder over what Tom would look like after being away for the past few months. Would he still look the same, with that lovely round face and perpetually glowing smile? Would he have been allowed to grow his hair a little longer after the way the Army barber had savaged it so badly when Tom was first called up? Most of all, she wondered whether he still felt the same way about her, whether he still meant what he had said when they parted on this very same platform: *'I love yer, Ruth. Don't you ever ferget that.'* Ruth never *had* forgotten it. In fact, she had dreamt about it every night since he had left.

The first sign of the train was the distant shrill sound of its engine whistle. By the time she caught her first glimpse of the engine itself, gliding slowly but effortlessly alongside the platform, Ruth's heart was thumping so hard she could scarcely make out all the faces of the servicemen who were hanging out of every one of the smoke-smudged train windows. She didn't see him, but she did hear his voice. *'Ruth!'* She swung to left and right, then finally picked him out. By then, despite the fact that the train hadn't yet come to a halt, all the carriage doors were flung open, and the platform was immediately invaded by a sea of khaki. Amidst scenes of high emotion, pushing and shoving, yells and shouts, Ruth finally managed to stretch out her hands over the heads of the crowd and clasp Tom's hands. A second later she was engulfed in his arms, their lips pressed tightly together in a passionate embrace. They stayed like that for several minutes, completely oblivious of anything that was going on around them, an island in the middle of a vast ocean. When they finally pulled back to look at each other, Ruth could see that Tom *hadn't* changed, he hadn't changed at all. In fact, he looked stronger, more fresh-faced, more bright-eyed than he had been the last time she had seen him. He tried to say something to her, but not only were they being pushed and shoved by the crowds surging along the platform, the noise made it almost impossible to hear anything that was being said.

'I can't hear you!' yelled Ruth.

Tom shrugged his shoulders and looked puzzled.

Ruth tried again, but louder. 'I said, I can't hear you,' she bellowed. 'What did you say?'

In desperation, he pulled her back to him, and spoke directly into her left ear. 'I said, let's get married.'

This time she heard him loud and clear.

Whitlock's was full of kids. It was like this every day after school hours, and as it was the middle of June and it was stinking hot outside, they were all streaming in with their pennies to buy fizzy drinks, liquorice sticks, and bags of sherbet, harassing poor Bella, and causing as much havoc as they could until they got what they wanted. It was at times like this that Bella missed her husband Harry most of all, for he was the one person who knew how to deal with the kids; one word from him and they'd shut up like an oyster. But that was the past, and Bella knew that if she wanted to carry on the business, then she had to cope the best way she could. Even so, she often told herself, a little help from her own daughter wouldn't come amiss. It took her more than twenty minutes to get rid of the last of the kids, and just as long to clear up the shambles they had left on the newspaper and magazine racks.

'Little perishers!' said Freda Dapper, Bella's lodger from upstairs, as she came into the shop after the last hell-raising boy had cleared off. 'Pity they didn't *all* stay evacuated,' she said acidly. 'It's ridiculous to let them come back.'

'You can't force their parents to send them away,' replied Bella, always aware that Freda's constant snide remarks about children were probably because she had never been able to have any of her own. 'After all, they're flesh and blood.'

Freda snorted indignantly. She was quite a pretty woman, with a lovely flock of natural brown curls, and a clear complexion that many a woman half her age would have died for. In fact, Freda's looks were her greatest asset, and when anyone ever referred to her as the living image of Loretta Young the film star, she immediately pulled off her glasses and glowed with pride. 'I just come down ter see if yer need any help,' she said, looking around. 'It's too hot for yer ter cope all on yer own.'

'I'm all right,' replied Bella, who was lifting heavy crates of empty lemonade bottles into the back room. 'I'm used to this. Anyway, I'll be shutting up shop in an hour or so.'

Freda went to her at the counter. 'If you go on like this, yer know,' she said, 'you'll wear yerself out. Why don't yer ask your Ruth ter give up her job up the fire-station. Her place is here – with her mum.'

Bella was irritated. 'Now don't let's go through all that again, Freda,' she said. 'I've told you before, I don't interfere in Ruth's life. She's old enough to make her own decisions.'

'And what happens when she gets married?'

Bella swung round on her with a start. 'Married? My Ruth?'

'Well, she's got a boyfriend, ain't she? It's only natural she'll want to get married one of these days.'

Bella thought about this for a moment. Ruth had had several boyfriends since she left school, but it had never occurred to her that she might want to keep one for life. 'I think you'll find that, until the war is over,' she replied unconvincingly, 'Ruth won't be thinking about such things.'

Before Freda had a chance to reply, a customer came into the shop.

''Allo,' said the tall, lanky young man, who looked quite smart in a freshly washed white cotton shirt and navy blue trousers. 'Mrs Madiewsky?'

As he seemed to have addressed his question to Freda, she in turn nodded towards Bella.

'Mrs Whitlock,' said Bella. 'Madiewsky is my maiden name.'

'Actually it's yer daughter I'm lookin' for,' said the boy.

Bella exchanged a brief, puzzled look with Freda. 'Ruth?' she asked.

'That's right.'

'I'll go an' make yer a cup er tea,' said Freda, discreetly disappearing into the back room.

'You know my daughter?' asked Bella, after Freda had gone.

'We've met,' returned the boy, who pushed back a lock of long brown hair that kept tumbling down into his right eye. 'They told me where ter find 'er up the fire-station.'

Bella looked at him with deep suspicion. 'Is it anything I can help you with?' she asked.

'Oh no,' returned the boy. 'I was wiv 'er last night – durin' the air raid up at Shoreditch. She'd 'ad a pretty rough time of it. I just wanted ter know if she's all right.'

Bella stared at him without response.

'Anyway,' said the boy, moving uncomfortably from one foot to the other. 'P'raps you'd tell 'er I called. Tell 'er it was Mike.'

'Mike?'

'Mike Buller. She won't know me name, but she'll remember me, all right. At least I 'ope she will!'

He went to the door, and opened it. The bell above him tinkled. 'Nice shop yer've got 'ere, Mrs Whitlock,' he called. 'Very nice indeed.' He left, shut the door behind him, but then immediately opened it again, and peered round. 'Oh by the way,' he called. 'Ruth'll be sorry she missed me. But tell 'er not ter worry. Tell 'er – I'll catch up wiv 'er later.'

Chapter 2

Although Ruth had only met Tom's parents a couple of times, she did like them. This might have had something to do with the fact that, despite their strong Anglican beliefs, they had so far never shown any concern about their son having a girlfriend who was not only half-Polish, but also a Catholic. And when they had all met up at King's Cross station an hour or so before, they seemed to be just as pleased to see her as they were to welcome their son home. Ruth also got on very well with Tom's sister Kate, who was a couple of years younger than her brother, but because of her deeply religious upbringing, was quite old-fashioned in the way she dressed for a girl of her age. She also refused to wear make-up, which in some ways was a pity, for, like her mother Pearl, she had rather a dull skin, which

40

would have benefited from a little pampering. To Ruth, Pearl herself was the perfect mum, always fussing over her family, always cooking and making excellent meals out of sparse wartime rations, and supporting her kids in any way she could; and Tom's father Ken was the most amiable man Ruth had ever met, even if he did sometimes give a somewhat overdone impression of a good churchgoing man. But even though Ruth was very comfortable with the Phillips family, she was none too sure how they would react to the news that Tom had asked her to marry him.

'Bit sudden, isn't it, son?' asked Ken Phillips, eyeing Tom and Ruth sceptically over a cup of tea at the garden table. 'Yer've only known each other five minutes.'

'Come off it, Dad,' replied Tom, who was sitting with his arm around Ruth's shoulders on a bench seat opposite his mum and dad. 'What difference does it matter how long I've known Ruth? As long as we love each other.'

'It makes a lot of difference,' said Ken firmly, retrieving his pipe from an ash-tray on the table in front of him. 'You 'ave ter know a person if you're goin' ter spend the rest of your life with 'em.'

Ruth was embarrassed, and lowered her eyes.

Ken was undeterred. 'Yer mum an' I walked out tergether three years before we called the banns.' He seemed quite oblivious of how ridiculous he looked in the large white hand-kerchief that was tied in a knot over his head to protect him from the fierce rays of the afternoon sun. 'Yer grandfather was a stickler for doin'

41

things the right way,' he said, digging into the stale remains of the tobacco in his pipe bowl with a dead match. 'That's why they were married for over forty years.'

'I hope Ruth an' I will be married longer than that,' retorted Tom. He turned to Ruth and squeezed her shoulders affectionately.

Ken grunted, and scooped the stale tobacco into his ash-tray.

'Mind you,' continued Tom, 'she hasn't said she'll 'ave me yet. I only asked 'er on the platform at King's Cross a couple er hours ago!'

'Oh she will!' cried Kate, after listening with contained excitement to her brother's news. 'Won't you, Ruth?'

Ruth looked across at her and beamed. 'Well, it all depends, doesn't it?'

'On what?' asked Kate, impatiently.

Ken resisted the urge to look up.

Ruth, eyes gleaming, turned to Tom. 'On whether Tom still feels the same way about me when he leaves the Army.'

'Oh, but he will,' insisted Kate, whose delicate, pallid face was suddenly flushed. 'You're mad about 'er, ain't yer, Tom?' she asked. Without waiting for an answer, she continued, 'Yer told me so – before yer went away.'

Both Ruth and Tom laughed.

'Tell me, dear,' asked Pearl Phillips, whose question came right out of the blue. 'What does yer mum fink about all this?'

A bit taken aback, Ruth replied, 'I don't know, Mrs Phillips. I haven't had a chance to tell her yet.'

'She's a French lady or somefin', in't she?'

'*Polish*, Mum,' sighed Tom. 'Ruth comes from a Polish family.'

'*Half*-Polish,' Ruth said, correcting him. 'My mother was born in Poland, but my father was English. He used to work in Poland – for a shipping firm.'

'Oh really?' said Pearl, with a polite but fixed smile. 'Isn't that interestin', Dad?' she said, turning to her husband whom she always addressed as 'Dad' in front of the children.

'He died just before the war,' continued Ruth falteringly. 'He had a long history of heart problems.'

'I'm sorry ter 'ear that,' said Ken Phillips. 'It can't be easy, goin' through life wiv just one parent.'

Ruth immediately picked up on this. 'Oh, my mother's managed perfectly well, Mr Phillips,' she said. 'She works very hard. She's never let me want for anything.'

'I would've thought yer only 'ave the good Lord ter fank fer that?' suggested Ken, wryly.

The expression on Pearl's face showed that she was proud of her husband's comment. 'You must bring yer mum over ter tea one day,' she said, patting Ruth's hand. 'I'm sure we'll get on like a 'ouse on fire.' As an afterthought she added, 'Does she speak English?'

'Don't be daft, Mum,' said Tom. 'Ruth's mum has been in England for years.'

'I was only asking,' retorted Pearl. 'I know plenty of foreign people who've been 'ere fer years an' they still can't speak English.'

43

'As a matter of fact,' Tom countered, 'I know plenty of *English* people who can't speak English!'

Pearl smiled bravely whilst Tom, Ruth and Kate laughed at the joke.

'What about you, Ruth?' asked Kate. 'Can you speak any Polish?'

'Not really. A few words here and there. But I can usually understand what's being said when other people are speaking it. You see, I was born in England. I've never actually been to Poland.'

With his arm around her shoulders, Tom hugged her tight. 'Well, when the war's over,' he promised, with a reassuring smile, 'I'll take yer there.'

Ruth smiled affectionately at him. 'If there's anything left once the Germans have finished with it,' she said.

A few minutes later Tom and Ruth were strolling hand-in-hand through the labyrinth of lush green plants and shrubs in the Phillipses' back garden. Every so often Ruth stopped to admire the myriad fragrant blossoms and the zigzag of stone borders and winding paths that divided the long narrow lawn in two. Ruth marvelled at the loving care Ken and Pearl Phillips had put into what they called 'their little back patch' and the strenuous efforts they had made to create an escape from the ugly sights of war. With the boughs of two apple trees dipping low over the path as she went, Ruth found it hard to believe that she and Tom were not out in the open countryside, but were surrounded by the urban jungle of human habitation. However, when they reached the far end of the garden there was a painful reminder that there was still a war on, for, despite the attempts to disguise the Anderson shelter with as many shrubs and annual blooms as its curved corrugated iron roof could hold, tucking it away in a corner in the bowels of the earth could not disguise the fact that it was there to save lives.

The moment they found a secluded spot out of sight of the house, Tom pulled Ruth to him and kissed her. There was a lot of raw passion in the way he did it, for it had been a long time since they had been together. Ruth loved his lips. She had always loved them from the first time they had met, for they were so full, completely engulfing her own which were in comparison fine and neat. When he eventually pulled away, he looked into her eyes and used the fingers of his right hand to delicately trace the outline of her mouth. Then he kissed her again. 'I want you so much,' he said, his voice no more than a whisper. Then on a sudden impulse he said, 'I don't want to wait a minute longer. Let's get married now!'

Startled, Ruth pulled away. 'Tom!' she cried incredulously.

'Well, why not?' he asked. 'If we love each other, why do we have to wait? I want ter marry yer, Ruth. I want ter marry yer right now.'

'Oh, don't be so ridiculous,' she said. 'How *can* we get married? You're only home on seven days' leave.'

'We can get a Special Licence. We can get married up at Finsbury Town Hall. I've heard it's easy. We can do it within a couple of days.'

45

'No Tom!'

Ruth's firmness took him by surprise. 'Why not?' he asked.

She shrugged. 'We're under age, remember. We both need our parents' consent.'

Tom gave her a puzzled look. 'So why should that be a problem?'

Ruth hesitated, then dropped down onto the small square of turf they were standing on. Troubled, Tom joined her. For a moment they said nothing. In the distance they could hear the traffic racing up and down Camden Road, a sound that competed with the busy chirping of a male blackbird who was distinctly aggrieved to find intruders hanging around near his nest in the adjoining hedge. Tom leaned forward and with one hand raised Ruth's chin. 'Sounds to me as if you're lookin' fer excuses,' he said, looking directly into her eyes.

She smiled affectionately at him. 'We have to be practical,' she said, awkwardly. 'We have to think about your parents.'

Tom pulled his hand away. 'Mum an' Dad?' he asked with a puzzled frown. 'They fink you're marvellous.'

Ruth reached out for his hand and squeezed it tenderly. 'They have convictions,' Ruth said, choosing her words carefully, 'strong religious convictions. They won't find it easy to accept someone like me into the family. I was brought up a Catholic. I may not be a very good one but, as much as I love you, I just can't give it up.'

'Come off it, Ruth,' Tom snapped, pulling his hand away again. 'Nobody's askin' yer ter give up yer religion. And in any case, I'm not asking yer ter marry me family, I'm asking yer ter marry *me!* That's why I'm sayin' let's do it in a Registry Office. That way there'll be no problems with religion – yours or mine.' He looked away, staring aimlessly at the profusion of wild daisies and buttercups that had completely covered the roof of the Anderson shelter. 'Of course, if I don't mean that much to yer...'

Ruth moved round so that she could kneel directly in front of him. Then she kissed him tenderly on his lips. He responded, and they eased themselves back onto the small patch of turf so that they were lying on their backs beneath the broken shadows of an apple tree. She reached for his hand and held on to it. They stayed like that for several moments, the hot rays of the late afternoon sun squeezing through the branches of the tree, dazzling them with streaks of sharp-pointed light, and covering their faces with a gradually deepening red glow. 'D'you remember when we first met?' she asked dreamily, her eyes still fixed firmly on the branches of the tree above them. 'That day on Holloway Road Tube station,' she continued, turning to look at him, 'when you bumped into me on the edge of the platform, and nearly knocked me onto the track?'

Tom was still looking skywards. 'I remember,' he replied, with a grin.

'Was it really an accident?' she asked. 'Or did you do it on purpose?'

'What do *you* think?' he replied, turning to face her.

'I think you did it on purpose.'

'I saved your life,' he said, now with a broad grin. 'And in any case, you didn't seem to mind.'

'That you saved my life?'

'That we got ter know each uvver.'

Ruth smiled. 'No, I didn't mind,' she said. 'I didn't mind at all. In fact, I thought it was a lovely way to meet. It always seems to happen like that in the pictures.'

'Pictures ain't real,' Tom replied laconically.

'No,' she replied. 'But we are.'

Tom stared at her. 'I don't know what that means,' he said, puzzled.

Ruth paused. 'It means that *I'm* willing to take the risk if you are.'

Tom sat up with a start. 'You mean – we can do it? You'll marry me?'

'I'd be very proud to,' she replied.

He suddenly grabbed hold of her, and held her in his arms. 'But not yet,' she said quickly, just as he was about to kiss her. 'Not just yet.'

Tom froze.

'We've got seven days,' she continued. 'Let's see how we get on. Let's see how we can get to know each other.'

He immediately held her at arm's length. 'Get ter know each uvver?' he snapped. 'Bleedin' 'ell, Ruth, we've known each uvver fer munffs.'

'I mean *really* know each other,' she replied. As she looked at his face, all screwed up with irritation and frustration, she noticed for the first time how full it had become in the short time he had been away. His eyes were also more piercing than she had ever seen them, and for one split

48

second, it disturbed her. 'When two people are going to spend the rest of their lives together,' she continued, 'they can't afford to take decisions lightly.' She leaned forward, and held him tight, her head resting on his shoulder, her long brown hair suddenly flowing down over her own shoulders as it became released from the comb and pins that had been bunching it tightly behind her head.

'And seven days is goin' ter make all that much diff'rence, is it?' replied Tom, unimpressed.

'I don't know,' she said quietly in his ear. 'But we can at least give it a try.'

At the other end of the garden, Pearl and Kate were clearing the tea things from the garden table. Above them, Ken Phillips was at a second-floor window of the house, straining to see what his son was up to with the Polish girl at the end of the garden. He didn't like what he saw.

In the sky above, the sun was evaporating behind a thin layer of haze which had been gradually floating in during the last part of the afternoon. The relentless sunshine was now being replaced by an impending gloom. The hot spell was coming to an end. The storm clouds were gathering.

At the 'end house', the gutter hadn't been fixed for years. Consequently, the rain which was pounding hard on the roof was gushing straight down onto the front doorstep below, which Edie next door always did her best to keep clean and sparkling white. Although the blackout restrictions weren't due until well after eleven o'clock, by early evening the thunderstorm had reduced the midsummer light along Annette Road to a dismal glow, leaving Ruth to battle her way along pavements whose gutters were struggling with the rush of fast-flowing water that was desperately trying to reach the nearest drains. Once inside the house, her only thought was to get out of her wet things as quickly as possible for, like so many other people who were out in their flimsy summer clothes, the sudden rainstorm had taken her by surprise. 'I'm home, Mama!' she called, as she rushed up the stairs.

Bella, who had been balancing the shop books in the sitting room, came out into the passage, and followed her daughter up to the girl's bedroom. 'What happened?' she asked, as she watched Ruth pull off her sopping wet dress and underclothes. 'Why didn't you wait somewhere until the storm was over?'

'There was nothing I could do about it,' replied Ruth, briskly drying herself with a towel. 'I got caught when I was walking back from Camden Road.'

Bella was puzzled. 'Camden Road?'

'I went to have tea with Tom and his parents.'

'*Your* Tom?' asked Bella, taken aback. 'He's home?'

'He sent me a telegram – I went to meet him at King's Cross this afternoon. He's got seven days' special leave.'

'*Special* leave?' asked Bella. 'What does *special* mean?'

Ruth put on her dressing-gown and perched on the edge of her bed. 'It means he's being posted somewhere,' she said, drying her hair with the towel, 'and I may not see him again for some time.'

Bella remained in the doorway watching her daughter, understanding the girl's pretence, knowing only too well how this kind of desperate situation was being suffered by women all over the country, their menfolk going away to fight a war from which so many would never return. 'He didn't tell you where?' she asked tentatively.

Ruth stopped drying her hair for a moment, ran her fingers through it, then exchanged a brief glance with her mother. 'I doubt even *he*'ll know that until he's on board a ship somewhere,' she said.

Some time later Ruth, who had changed into her dispatch-rider's uniform, came downstairs to the kitchen where her mother had prepared some hot borsch. Beetroot soup with mint was one of Ruth's favourites, and considering how chilled she felt, she was glad her mother had heated it up. It was hard to believe how, just a few hours before, the temperature had been in the upper eighties, but even in the kitchen it was now cool and damp. Ruth felt a glow of affection for Bella as she watched her pottering around the place, making last-minute additions to the salad dressing she was preparing for supper, and briefly stopping to wipe the top of the old gas cooker which seemed to have been in the family since the year dot. Ruth knew how much her mother loved the kitchen. It was the one room in the house that was fully her own personal domain. She practically lived in it, and would probably

51

even move her bed in there if she had the chance.

'Seven days doesn't seem very long,' she said, as she sat down to join Ruth at the table. 'When you're walking out with someone and there's so little time, there must be a lot of things to talk about.'

Ruth knew her mother was watching her, but she just carried on eating her soup.

'Especially when you have to go riding off on a motorcycle every night.'

Ruth looked up. 'It's my job, Mama,' she said. 'Just like Tom. The war won't stop just because we only have seven days together.'

For a moment or so, they sat in silence, eating their soup. From time to time, Ruth sneaked a look up at her mother, and when she did she felt nothing but affection for her. She also thought to herself that despite how hard her mother worked, it was amazing how young she looked for her age, so much so that some customers in the shop had sometimes taken them for sisters. Ruth took that as a compliment, not only to her mother but to herself as well. Nonetheless, Bella was still her mother – a woman who was brought up by strict Polish-Catholic parents who believed in the traditional way of life, where a girl should grow up under close supervision, find a respectable job, meet a respectable man, marry him in a good Catholic church, then give him as many children as he wanted. So as she watched her mother sipping her hot borsch, Ruth wondered how on earth she was going to explain that she wanted to marry a man in great haste, and in a Register Office, too.

'Mama,' she said suddenly, on an impulse.

Bella looked up.

'Tom's asked me to marry him.'

Bella slowly put down her spoon.

'I haven't really agreed. Not yet.'

Bella looked as though she was shell-shocked.

Ruth put down her soup spoon, then dabbed her lips, which left a dark red stain on her handkerchief. 'We still have a lot of things to talk about,' she explained. 'You remember I told you, he's not a Catholic.'

Bella leaned back in her chair. Until that moment, she had felt quite weary, but Ruth's news had given her fresh energy. 'I've been thinking about that,' she said. 'There are ways round it. I was talking to Father O'Leary, and he said there was no reason why an Anglican can't convert. It happens all the time. It just needs a little bit of discussion between both parties.'

'Mama,' said Ruth, leaning towards her. 'Tom wants to get married in a Registry Office.'

Bella stifled a gasp with her hand.

'If you agree, if his parents agree, he wants me to marry him before he leaves for duty.'

Bella's eyes were almost bulging out of her head. 'Holy Mother Mary!' she cried, her fingers automatically searching out the small silver cross hanging around her neck.

Ruth stretched across for her mother's other hand, that was still resting on the table. 'Would you hate it, Mama?' she asked sympathetically. 'Would you really hate it?' Her mother was clearly too shocked to answer, so she got up and went to her. 'Of course you would, wouldn't you?' she said, kissing Bella gently on her fore-head. 'But I promise you, I won't do anything until I'm sure.'

'Sure of what?' asked Bella.

'Sure that Tom's the man I want to spend the rest of my life with. At the moment, I think he is, because he's kind, and thoughtful, and he's the only boy I've ever really loved.'

'Is that enough?' asked Bella mournfully.

Ruth hesitated. For one split second she could see Tom in her mind's eye, smiling at her, a smile that had melted her the very moment she had set eyes on him, his rough unshaven face rubbing against her own, leaving a rash, a rash that she had never wanted to disappear, and his large frame engulfing her in a passionate embrace on the platform at King's Cross station just a few hours before. 'I don't know,' she replied. 'But it's a start.' From behind, she put her arms around her mother's shoulders, and hugged her.

Bella waited a moment before saying anything more. But when she did, what she had to say came as a surprise. 'You say that Tom is the *only* boy you've ever been with?'

'You know he is.'

Bella hesitated. 'Then who was this person who came into the shop looking for you today?' she asked.

The kitchen suddenly reverberated to a loud clap of thunder outside. The storm was now right overhead.

By ten o'clock that evening, the sky was so clear it was as though not a drop of rain had fallen.

There wasn't a cloud to be seen, and the sun had made a triumphant reappearance, sinking slowly in the distance behind Highbury Fields, where dozens of kids were playing football on the wet grass, climbing trees, or just loafing around, all of them totally unaware that they were now bathed in the deep red hues of a perfect sunset.

At the nearby fire-station in Upper Street, some of the crews were busily checking their fire-fighting equipment and getting the fire-engines and water pumps ready for the first emergency call of the evening, whilst others were biding their time, fully clothed and stretched out on their beds in the upper-floor dormitory, flipping through copies of the *Star*, *Evening News*, or the *Standard*. After the previous night's random air raid on the East End and parts of North London, everyone hoped they were in for a relatively incident-free night. Fortunately, the raids were coming far less frequently now than they had done up until a few months before, but with regular Allied air attacks now taking place on Berlin and other cities, no one was taking the Luftwaffe's current lull in activities for granted.

Ruth had checked in for duty just before ten o'clock; she went straight up to the female quarters she shared with two other firewomen. The accommodation was little more than a small room with three beds and three lockers, so it was lucky that all three girls got on well together.

'Out with it!' demanded Mavis Miller, who was still in bra and knickers when Ruth came in.

Ruth stopped with a start. 'What do you mean?' she asked.

55

'You're a dark 'orse, you are!' said Mavis, with a broad grin. 'I fawt you 'ad a regular. So wot's 'appened ter poor ol' Tom?'

'I'm sorry, Mavis,' returned Ruth, 'but I don't know what you're talking about.' This wasn't true, of course, for only a short time ago her mother had asked her the same question.

'Oh yes?' said Mavis, stepping into her uniform trousers. She was a year younger than Ruth and always a tease. 'Now pull the uvver one.' She perched on the edge of her bed, and slipped on her shirt. 'Bit of all right if yer ask me. If *you* don't want 'im, I know somebody who does!'

Irritated, Ruth pulled off her uniform cap and dropped it onto the bed. 'Don't want *who*, Mavis?' she asked with a sigh. 'If you could just stop talking in riddles...'

Mavis stopped what she was doing and looked up at her. 'Mike,' she announced with another broad grin. 'Mike Buller. The bloke who come round lookin' for yer.'

Ruth froze. Why was this man, whom she had only met for no more than a few minutes, why was he pursuing her? 'Who gave him my address?' she asked warily.

Mavis took a puff of a half-finished cigarette that was smouldering in a tin-top ash-tray at the side of her bed. 'I fink it was Sweetie,' she replied, unconvincingly, returning the cigarette to the ash-tray.

Ruth didn't believe her. Out of the other two girls who shared the room, 'Sweetie' – whose real name was Hazel Berkeley – seemed to Ruth to be the less likely to divulge that kind of information to a stranger. No, if it was anyone, it was sure to be chatterbox Mavis.

'Why?' asked Mavis, who was doing her best to sound as though she knew very little about it. 'Don't yer like this bloke or somefin'?'

'I hardly know him,' she replied. 'He pulled me out of the way when a wall collapsed at the warehouse in Shoreditch last night.'

'Oh – that's the one, is it?' Mavis got up from her bed, went to a cracked wall mirror, and fluffed up her short auburn hair. 'Yer know,' she said, attempting to change the subject, 'it's munffs since I 'ad a decent perm. Look at it! Got no life in it.' She took a quick glance at Ruth over her shoulder in the mirror. 'Just like me.'

Ruth had to smile. She perched on the edge of her own bed, kicked off her shoes, and lit a cigarette. 'What did he want?' she asked.

Ruth's persistence puzzled Mavis. 'Who?' she asked.

'This man who came looking for me.'

Mavis turned from the mirror. 'Are yer worried about 'im?' she asked, with concern.

Ruth inhaled lightly. 'I do have a chap of my own, you know,' she replied stiffly.

'So do I,' Mavis countered, 'but the Army took 'im, so I reckon 'e belongs more ter them than ter me.' She suddenly felt uncomfortable. 'Look, Ruth,' she said, awkwardly, 'I 'aven't seen Charlie fer nearly a year now. For all I know he's lost in the jungle out in Borneo or some such place. I've got feelin's like anyone else. A gel can't wait for ever.'

'It's not fair to blame Charlie, is it?' said Ruth.

57

'Our chaps didn't ask to be taken off to fight a war. The least we can do is to wait for them.'

'Wait?' asked Mavis, with a sigh. 'Oh I'll wait fer 'im all right. But not for ever. In this war yer could be 'ere terday an' gone termorrow. Before that, I wanna make the best of my life. I'm only human, Ruth. I'm only human.'

Ruth thought about Mavis's words as her motorcycle sped through the darkened streets on her first call of the night: *I'm only human, Ruth.* What did that mean? she asked herself. Did it mean that you had to give up all your principles about being faithful and honest to the man you loved, or did it mean that because there was a war on, you were entitled to live life to the full – which in Mavis's mind clearly meant sleeping around with anyone she wanted. Yes, it was a dilemma, there was no doubt about that. But with her eyes glued to the faint illumination from her masked headlamp on the road ahead, Ruth was convinced that it was a dilemma that didn't apply to someone like herself. As far as she was concerned, if she *did* agree to marry Tom before he left for active duty, then she would remain faithful to him for the rest of her life.

Once she had delivered the message she had been carrying to the headquarters of the London Fire Brigade in the deep basement of the building on the Albert Embankment, Ruth was given an urgent confidential dispatch to take to the number 36 Area fire-station in Fairclough Street, Whitechapel. She estimated that at that time of night, the journey should take no more than ten minutes or so, but the moment she left the building and climbed back onto the saddle of her motorbike, the air-raid siren wailed out from rooftops all over the capital. Within a few minutes, the rumble of ack-ack fire seemed to be drifting in from the eastern suburbs of the city, so she knew she had to get a move on if she was going to avoid the scream of falling bombs. However, by the time she was on her way, the raid was getting closer and closer, and she had to use all her skills and concentration to manoeuvre her way through the winding streets that were littered with jagged pieces of shrapnel. Following the earlier thunderstorm, the roads were wet and slippery, so she also had to use her clutch and brakes carefully to avoid skidding, which was a procedure she had failed several times during her brief period of motorcycle training at a Fire Brigade training school at Willesden when she had been called up a few months before.

'Jesus!' protested Station Officer Ben Curtis once he had read the dispatch Ruth had delivered to him. 'How the hell do they think we're going to get two trailer pumps down to North Woolwich Pier? We've only got four altogether on standby.' As he spoke, the station alarm bell sounded, and within seconds, two of the pump engines and their crews were out on the road heading for the first incident of the night.

Ruth made no comment. Since she had been enrolled into the NFS she had learnt to keep her mouth shut and just get on with her job. Before heading back to her home station, however, she decided to grab a cup of tea in the crew mess room where, to her surprise, she found two of the firemen with whom she had been during the warehouse blaze in Shoreditch.

'Wot's all this then?' asked Nifty Sanders, the younger and more talkative of the two men, who got his name because he was always so quick on his feet when climbing ladders. 'Fawt you'd 'ad enuff of this job after wot 'appened last night?'

'Can't keep away from you, Nifty,' called Ruth, pouring herself a cup of stewed tea. She went to their table and joined them. 'What are you doing here?' she asked. 'Haven't they told you there's an air raid on outside?'

'We're on reserve 'til three o'clock,' said Joe Burnley, with just a casual look up from studying form in a racing newspaper. 'Must say, I could do with a decent night's kip.'

'You're not the only one, mate!' said Nifty. 'An' wot about you, gel?' he asked, offering Ruth a Woodbine. 'No after-effects?'

'From the falling wall, you mean?' she asked, taking the Woodbine. She shook her head. 'Not so far. Although I still feel a bit shell-shocked.'

Nifty was puzzled. 'Say again?'

'Oh, nothing to do with the wall,' said Ruth, as Nifty lit both their fags. 'I'm just curious to know about that bloke.'

'Which bloke?' asked Nifty.

'The one who stopped the wall falling on me.'

The penny dropped. 'Oh,' said Nifty. 'Yer mean Mike. Mike Buller.'

'He's not one of us, is he?' she continued. 'He was in civvies. Who is he?'

60

'Why?' asked Nifty, with a sly grin. 'Took yer fancy, did 'e?'

Ruth ignored Nifty's laugh. She knew from his reputation that he considered himself God's gift to women, and he was always trying to make something out of nothing.

'He went to my mother's shop last night,' said Ruth, pulling on her fag. 'Came looking for me.'

Joe looked up from his paper.

'Did 'e now?' asked Nifty, with one of his lecherous grins. 'An' wot was 'e after, I wonder?'

Joe was more concerned. 'Who gave 'im your address?' he asked.

'I'm not absolutely sure,' she said, 'but I suspect it was one of the girls I share a room with. Have you any idea what he wants?'

'I've got a good idea!' Only Nifty laughed at his own joke.

Once again Ruth ignored him. 'Who is he, Joe?' she asked, anxiously.

'I dunno really,' said Joe. 'All I can tell is that from time ter time 'e turns up outa the blue whenever we get a call-out. I've spoken wiv 'im a coupla times, and he apparently lives wiv 'is grandad up 'Ackney somewhere.'

'Mare Street.'

Ruth turned to look at Nifty.

'Mare Street,' repeated Nifty. 'Work's for the ol' man, 'e says.'

'What kind of business?'

''Aven't a clue.'

'Why hasn't he been called up?' persisted Ruth. 'He looks old enough.'

Nifty shrugged and grinned. 'Yer'll 'ave ter ask

61

'im, won't yer?'

Joe waited for Nifty to leave the room, before he said anything else. 'If you're worried, mate,' he said, lowering his voice, 'why not 'ave a word with your Div Super about 'im. 'E'll soon sort 'im out!'

Ruth gave him a reassuring smile. 'I'm not worried, Joe,' she replied. 'Just curious, that's all. I don't like him following me around. It's a little – unnerving. In any case, whatever he wants he's wasting his time. I've got my own chap, and I can tell you, the way I feel about Tom right now, I intend to keep it that way for a very long time.'

Chapter 3

There wasn't much that Rita Simmons didn't know about the people who lived in Jackson Road, Annette Road, or indeed any other road that was within walking distance of the Victorian terraced house she shared with her husband, Ted. Not that it was easy for Rita to walk anywhere, for she was of such ample proportions that the ground seemed to vibrate every time she passed by. This was a pity, for in her younger days Rita had been a mere wisp of a girl, and quite a good-looker, which was probably the reason why Ted Simmons had taken a fancy to her and subsequently fathered their five boisterous kids. At least, that's what most of her neighbours thought, especially when they themselves so often became the focus of Rita's prying attention. Her status as the neighbourhood busybody had come about during the previous few years, possibly on account of the fact that she had become bored when all her children, now grown up, had left the family nest. The only person who had ever really formed any kind of relationship with her was little Edie Perkins, and that was only because she was careful to agree with everything Rita said. The fact that Edie was a widow also helped, because it meant that Rita had the dominant role in their relationship which, for Rita, was essential. However, the two nuts that she still hadn't cracked were the 'Poleys', who lived in the end house in the Annette Road cul de sac. But it looked as though her chance had come on Saturday evening, for as she sat drinking with Ted and Edie at a table in the saloon bar of the Globe pub in Isledon Road, Ruth came in with Tom. Old Bessie had just finished thumping out her usual medley of popular tunes on the pub's upright joanna which, as always, produced thunderous applause from the Globe's regulars. 'Over 'ere Poley gel!' yelled Rita above the Saturday night din. 'Come an' join us!'

The moment she caught sight of her overweight neighbour, Ruth's heart sank. 'Hello, Mrs Simmons,' she said bravely. 'Hello, Edie, Mr Simmons. This is my friend Tom Phillips.'

Tom nodded politely. 'Evenin', all.'

'Seen *you* before, ain't I, boy?' said Rita, quick as a flash. 'Always comin' an' goin' up the end 'ouse in the cul wiv our Poley, aren't yer?'

'You got good eyesight, Ma,' quipped Tom,

adding mischievously, ''Ow much d'yer pay fer yer telescope?'

The others laughed, but Rita's smile quickly froze.

'Are yer goin' ter join us, Ruth, dear?' asked Edie eagerly.

'You can 'ave my chair,' said Ted Simmons who, despite being a thickset bruiser of a man, had impeccable manners, unlike his wife.

'No, thanks all the same, Mr Simmons,' Ruth replied hastily. 'We can't stay long. This is my only night off, so we're just going to have a quick drink at the counter, then Tom's taking me to the second house at the Finsbury Park Empire.'

'Gert an' Daisy!' exclaimed Edie, whose tiny voice and frame were almost lost in the haze of fag smoke, and the deafening hum of high spirits over at the darts board. 'They're top o' the bill up the Empire this week. Oh, I do love 'em on *Workers' Playtime* on the wireless.'

'So 'ow long you two bin walkin' out now then?' Rita's voice boomed out so loud, some of the regulars turned round to see what was going on.

'Long enuff,' replied Tom loudly and cheekily.

'Long enuff fer wot?' asked Rita, irritably.

'Ah!' Tom grinned, sliding his arm around Ruth's waist and hugging her. 'I bet *you'd* like ter know, wouldn't yer, Ma?'

If looks could kill, Tom would have been struck down in a flash.

'We'll see you later then,' said Ruth. 'Enjoy your evening.' She didn't wait for an answer before practically pushing Tom off through the crowd of drinkers.

'What're yer so nervous of?' asked Tom, the moment they reached the counter.

'Not nervous,' replied Ruth. 'Just very wary. Rita has a very spiteful tongue. She can be quite dangerous.'

'Dangerous?'

'She once caused some mischief between me and my father. I've never been able to prove it was her, but it was very unpleasant at the time.'

Once they'd been served, they made their way out onto the pavement outside, where other drinkers had escaped from the stifling atmosphere inside the pub. The evening sun had brought people out of their houses in the terrace opposite; they were either chatting with their neighbours at their garden gates, or sitting on kitchen chairs by their doorsteps. Although the threat of an air raid was always present, the summer weather had eased the tension, and as long as they were still blessed with daylight and short nights, most people somehow felt safe and secure.

'Finsbury Park Empire!' chuckled Tom, the moment they had found a place to park themselves. 'On a night like this?'

'It was the best excuse I could think of at such short notice,' replied Ruth, whose face was streaked with sweat after just a few minutes struggling to break free from the saloon bar crowd of regulars. 'I wasn't going to hand *you* on a plate to Rita!'

Tom was puzzled. 'Wot d'yer mean?'

'I mean that she can't wait to find out all about

you – if she hasn't done so already. Rita's the number one troublemaker in our neighbourhood.'

'In wot way?'

Ruth leaned her back against the outside wall of the pub. 'I told you how she once caused some mischief between me and my father,' she said, sipping from her glass of shandy. 'It happened one day about a year before he died. Rita went into the shop when neither my mother nor I were there. She got talking to Dad about how I was always running him down to people behind his back, and how I tried to make him sound like a monster who regularly beat me up when I didn't do whatever he wanted me to do.'

'Was it true?' asked Tom. *Did* 'e beat yer up?'

Ruth paused before answering. Nearby, she noticed two small boys sitting on the doorstep of the pub digging into bags of crisps, all the while watching for any sign that their parents inside might have finished their drinks and were ready to go home. 'Yes, he did,' she replied, with some difficulty. 'Not all the time – just occasionally, usually when he'd been drinking. Like a lot of people, he couldn't hold his drink well. It turned him into a madman. But I never talked to anyone about it. Whatever happened between him and me, I kept to myself, I swear to God I did.' She looked up at Tom to see his reaction. 'Do you believe me?' she asked.

Pint glass of bitter in his hand, Tom was leaning against the wall beside her. He turned to look at her. 'She sounds like a cow ter me,' he replied.

'Yes,' said Ruth. 'But do you believe me?'

'Wot d'yer take me for?' he asked. 'Of course I believe yer.' He leaned close and kissed her gently on the cheek. 'But if it's true,' he continued, 'if yer dad *did* do those fings to yer, 'ow come this ol' cow knew?'

Ruth shook her head. 'To this day I still don't know, but when I asked Rita, she looked at me as though I was mad and denied everything.'

'So why d'yer even bother wiv a person like that?, Tom asked. 'I mean, surely yer don't 'ave ter talk ter someone just 'cos she lives in the same neighbour'ood?'

'Tom,' Ruth said emphatically, 'Rita *is* the neighbourhood. I suspect that every street in every city has a Rita like her tucked away somewhere. That sort of person only exists to make trouble. Don't ask me why. All I know is, it took me a long time to convince my father that whatever I thought of him, I would never deceive him.'

Once Tom had returned the empty glasses to the bar, he and Ruth left the pub and moved on, leaving the two small boys snuggled up against each other, fast asleep on the pub doorstep.

As she and Tom strolled hand in hand along Isledon Road in the direction of Finsbury Park, Ruth was only too conscious of how precious time was; she mustn't waste a single minute of it if she was to seriously consider Tom's proposal of marriage before the end of his seven days' leave. It felt so good to be at his side, every so often leaning her head casually on his shoulder as they walked, dreading the fact that this was probably one of the last times she would see him in civilian clothes, his broad frame filling out a sweat-soaked white shirt and grey flannel trousers, a curl of his short brown hair dropping down enticingly onto his forehead. For his part, Tom had come to accept that with the days ticking away, a rush wedding in a Register Office was no longer a practical proposition. Nonetheless, he was still hoping that Ruth would be waiting for him when he returned. 'Yes or no?' he asked her. It was a question he had bombarded her with over the past two days.

Ruth chuckled, smiled, reached up and gave him a quick kiss. 'Give me time,' she said. 'I still don't know you.'

'If I 'ear yer say that once more,' spluttered Tom with an irritated sigh, 'I'll kidnap yer!'

Ruth laughed. 'I want to know *all* about you – what you were like when you were a child, who your friends were, how many girlfriends you've had...'

''Undreds!' joked Tom.

'Liar!' laughed Ruth.

'It's true!' insisted Tom. 'There were so many I had ter fight 'em off!'

'Oh yes?' asked Ruth. 'And what did your father have to say about *that.*'

Ruth's question seemed to sting Tom, and it was fortunate that he had no time to respond before they were suddenly swallowed up by the crowds swarming out into the Seven Sisters Road from the Astoria cinema, where they had just finished watching the early evening showing of *The Mark of Zorro*. It was, in fact, some time later before Tom had the opportunity to answer the question seriously. It came after they had wandered through the main gates of Finsbury Park itself, and settled themselves down on the grass near the old bandstand which had remained virtually unused since the start of the war.

'Yer know, Ruth,' he said, lighting his first fag since they had left the pub, 'my dad's not such a bad bloke really. 'E's got some funny ways, I'll give yer that, but 'e means well.'

Ruth swung him a startled look. 'What are you talking about?' she asked, puzzled. 'I like your father, Tom, you know I do.'

''E's 'ad a 'ard life of it one way an' anuvver,' continued Tom, talking over her. 'If it wasn't fer that gammy foot of 'is, I fink fings would've bin diff'rent. It was becos of that that 'e 'ad ter leave the Merchant Navy. I don't know wot 'appened exactly, but apparently somefin' fell on 'is foot in the kitchens on board when he was a cook. I don't fink 'e'd've ever got married an' 'ad kids if 'e could've stayed on the ships.'

Aware that she might have hurt his feelings, Ruth tried to make light of what she had said earlier. 'You mustn't take things so seriously,' she said, tapping his nose lightly with her finger. 'I was only worried that your dad, being a religious man...'

'Religion's important ter Dad,' said Tom, again talking through her. 'It's wot's kept 'im goin' all these years. When me an' Kate was young, 'e used ter read the Bible to us. I 'ave ter say that I din't know wot most of it was about, but Dad said it was about good an' evil, an' as long as yer kept readin' bits of it out loud ter yerself every day, no harm'd come to yer.'

'That's wonderful, Tom,' said Ruth, a little ill-at-ease. 'So is that what you do? You read from the Bible every day?'

Tom hesitated. 'No,' he said. 'But I respect Dad fer wantin' us ter do so.'

Although Ruth decided not to pursue the subject, it gave her her first real insight into the sort of person Tom was, and it made her realise just how protective he was towards his family. Even so, it troubled her, for as much as she loved Tom, and there was no doubt now in her mind that she *did* love him, she couldn't help wondering which, if she did decide to marry him, of the two relationships would be the most important to him. With this in mind, she stretched out on the grass, rested her head in Tom's lap, and gazed up at the deep blue of a hot evening sky. 'Tom,' she asked, looking up at his face upside down, 'when we get married, would you like to have children?'

'Course!' he said eagerly. 'But not 'til after a coupla years or so.'

'But why?' Ruth asked, sitting up and facing him. 'Why wait that long? I'd like us to try for a child as soon as we get married. I want it to be a girl.'

'A boy!'

'Girl!'

'Boy!'

They both laughed.

'What's so special about a gel?' asked Tom.

Ruth thought about this for a moment. 'A girl is more independent,' she replied. 'When the going gets tough, she knows how to cope better.'

Tom grinned. 'Oh yeh,' he said. 'An' 'ow'd yer work that one out?'

'Personal experience.'

Tom finished the last of his fag, and twisted it into the grass. He glanced around and took note of a family of two adults and three kids who were walking with their floppy black and white mongrel dog. 'I don't fink a gel *needs* ter be independent,' he said, as he watched how the small girl was running on alone ahead of her two young brothers. 'If she's got a feller ter look after 'er, then she ain't got nuffin' ter worry about.'

Ruth pulled a face. 'D'you think that's true?' she asked him sceptically.

'I know it is.' Tom's reply was decisive. 'When a gel gets tergevver wiv a feller, I reckon it's 'er duty ter be loyal to 'im.'

'Loyalty has nothing to do with being in-dependent, Tom. If I love you, which I do, it doesn't mean that I can't have ideas or make decisions of my own.'

Tom slowly shook his head. 'That's not wot I'm sayin', Ruth,' he said. He put his hand under her chin, lifted it, and looked tenderly into her eyes. 'Wot I'm sayin' is that I want *my* gel ter be *my* gel fer the rest of me life. I don't want us ter be in competition, I want us ter be one an' the same person.'

Ruth gave him a huge smile. 'If you mean, will I remain loyal to you whilst you're away,' her eyes scanned every feature of his face, 'then I can assure you that you have absolutely nothing to worry about.'

He smiled back, then kissed her gently on the nose. His response carried more than just wishful thinking. 'I'd better *not* 'ave anyfin' ter worry about,' he replied.

In the distance behind them, the small girl was in floods of tears. The elder of her two brothers had, for one reason or another, just punched her.

Unlike his mate, Dave Smithers, young Phil Gitting hated getting up so early on Sunday mornings. In fact, he hated getting up early any morning, and if it hadn't been for the shilling a week he got for doing his newspaper round at *Whitlock's*, he'd be back where he belonged – tucked up in bed listening to gramophone requests on the BBC Forces wireless programme. Dave was a different kettle of fish. He liked the early mornings, especially during the summer months, for whilst he was pedalling around the back streets on his beloved Raleigh push-bike, it gave him the chance to actually hear the different breeds of birds that greeted him from their concealed positions in the few trees that had survived bomb blast. However, despite the lovely songs coming from the more exotic creatures such as the blackbirds, robins, and thrushes, Dave still preferred the good old sparrows, mainly because they chirped rather than sang, and they were cheeky and daring, a bit like himself.

Today being Sunday, Dave got to the shop bright and early; he found Bella already marking up the day's delivery of newspapers. There was no sign of Phil. Until he actually walked through the front door, no one could ever be quite sure whether Phil would turn up or not. 'Mornin', Mrs Whitlock!' shouted Dave. His voice was still a long way off from breaking.

As always, Bella ignored Dave's hearty greeting. 'Fifteen *Sunday Pictorials*,' she called busily, as the boy approached the counter, 'ten *Chronicles*, five *Sunday Times*, and one copy of the *Daily Worker* for Mr Beale in Benwell Road. Oh – and I've put in one copy of the *Radio Times* for Mrs Dalton in Annette Road. And when you post it through her letterbox, make sure it doesn't tear. I had to refund her for the last one.'

'What about the *News of the World?*' asked Dave, who was already tucking his allocation of newspapers into his satchel.

'Phil is doing the *News of the World* this week,' said Bella, in her most prim Polish accent.

'Why?' complained Dave. 'I like the *News of the World.* They 'ave some smashin' pittures of naked gels on the pages inside.'

Bella's reply was reproving. 'Twelve-year-old boys shouldn't be looking at such things. I shall tell your mother to wash your mouth out with salt!'

The moment her back was turned, Dave did one of his animated mimes of her. As he did so, the bell above the shop door tinkled.

'Sorry I'm late,' called Phil, with a huge yawn. 'Mum wanted a cuppa tea before I left.'

Bella immediately called to him. '*News of the World, Picturegoer, Islington Gazette*, and *North London Press!*'

'Me bike got a puncture,' grumbled Phil, who

73

was a few months older than Dave, and looked as though he'd been up all night.

'Too bad!' replied Bella, mercilessly. 'You'll just have to mend it.'

Phil sighed. Thoroughly miserable, he went straight to the counter to collect the newspapers for his delivery round. 'Okay. Do I 'ave ter do Jackson Road terday?' he asked. 'I 'ate callin' on that fat woman. Every time I go there she's always grumblin' at me 'cos I don't knock on the door before I leave 'er papers.'

Bella turned on him sharply. 'Don't ever call people names like that!' she snapped. 'It's not only rude, it's very hurtful. And if Mrs Simmons wants you to knock on the door first, why can't you?'

Phil snapped back at her. ''Cos she takes ages ter open it!'

'Don't exaggerate,' Bella tutted.

'It's true!' he insisted. 'An' when she does open it, she keeps me standin' there, askin' me all sorts er questions.'

Bella stopped what she was doing, and looked up with a start. '*What* questions?'

Phil exchanged a quick, worried glance with Dave, who had a broad grin on his face. 'All sorts er fings,' he said, sheepishly. ''Bout you – an' – an' your Rufe.'

Bella removed her spectacles and held them on the counter in front of her. 'What *are* you talking about, boy?' she demanded.

'Last week she was askin' me if I knew anyfin' about any of Rufe's pals up the fire-station.'

Bella froze.

74

'I told her I don't know nuffin' 'bout Rufe *or* 'er pals.'

Bella drew close to him. 'Why does she ask you these questions?'

Phil quickly shrugged his shoulders. 'I don't know, Mrs Whitlock! 'Onest ter God I don't! But she's always tellin' me ter keep me trap shut an' not say anyfin' to yer.'

Bella went quiet for a moment, then she put her spectacles on again and returned to what she was doing. 'Take your satchel, Phil,' she said, without giving him even a passing look. 'The first batch is for Eden Grove. When you get back, I'll let you know who's next.'

Phil didn't have to be asked twice. Both he and Dave picked up their satchels and made a rush for the door.

'Dave!'

He stopped dead at the door, and turned.

'I've given you Jackson Road. Leave Mrs Simmons's newspapers on her doorstep.'

Dave nodded, and rushed off.

After the boys had gone, Bella went to the door and locked it. As it was just after six o'clock, she still had a couple of hours before she opened the shop again, so after a casual glance at the headlines of the *Sunday Pictorial*, which reported the King's visit to British troops in North Africa, she went into the back room, where she collected the lukewarm cup of tea which she had made at least twenty minutes before. She sat down in a threadbare armchair to drink it. All around her the room was stacked high with cardboard boxes that contained stock replacements which she had not as yet had time to open. Her mind was too full to think about such mundane matters, not after what that boy had said about Rita Simmons. But why did she even give it a second thought? she asked herself. Everyone knew Rita was a busybody, a nosey-parker, everyone knew that the woman was always out to make trouble. Despite that, however, something was troubling Bella. It was the past. It was her memories of when Ruth was a teenager, when she was known around as a bit of a wildcat; at that time, her daughter had had a succession of boyfriends of the type that no one in their right mind should have been mixed up with. How many times had Ruth been warned about the company she kept? How many times had she fought and argued with her father because she refused to accept that she was doing anything wrong?

Yes, they were the bad old days all right, but that was the past, and Ruth was now a mature young woman whose only thoughts were to marry the young man of her choice, and to settle down and have children of her own. No, everything was perfectly all right. Rita was a trouble-maker; it was she who had sown the seeds of doubt in Bella's mind. Ruth was a good girl, a loyal, devoted girl. One day she would make her Tom a wonderful wife; she would be a wonderful mother. But then those nagging doubts started all over again. Why *did* Ruth never talk about the people she worked with, up at the fire-station? And as she got to her feet again, she suddenly remembered the boy who had come looking for Ruth in the shop a couple of afternoons before.

She resolved not to miss Benediction at church that evening.

Young Dave Smithers did exactly as Bella had told him: he dropped Rita Simmons's copy of the *News of the World* on her doorstep, then made a quick retreat back to his beloved Raleigh. A few minutes later he was on his way again, completing his final few deliveries, then pedalling furiously back along Jackson Road on the return trip to *Whitlock's*, where he would collect the next batch of newspapers for his round. It was hot work even for a twelve year old, so much so that his short navy-blue trousers were sticking to his bottom on the saddle, and the plimsolls he was wearing without socks were saturated with sweat. Whilst he was on the move, he was dreaming up a grand plan to gain some extra cash by collecting old books for salvage. Owing to the wartime shortage of paper, old newspapers were already bringing in a fortune for use as wrapping paper and lots of other things – well, a fortune to Dave, who reckoned he could get a halfpenny a time for each old newspaper he managed to retrieve. He made a mental note to talk it all over with Phil so that they could form their own syndicate and become millionaires.

Halfway along Jackson Road, Dave suddenly found himself being flagged down by a young-looking bloke who, surprisingly in such hot weather, was wearing a white shirt, pale blue striped tie, well-creased grey flannel trousers, and immaculately polished black shoes.

'Could yer tell me where the End 'Ouse is,

son?' he called to the boy.

The bloke's question took Dave by surprise, so much so that he kept on cycling. After what Phil had said about that fat old cow down the road, he wasn't taking any chances. But he became unnerved when the bloke ran alongside him, then out into the road, blocking his path. ''Ere, mister!' Dave objected. 'Wot d'yer fink you're doin'?'

The young bloke gave him a winning, apologetic smile. 'I'm just lookin' fer a friend, that's all,' he explained. 'I've bin told she lives in some place called the End 'Ouse.'

'If she's a friend,' snapped Dave, 'then yer oughta know where she lives.'

Again, the young bloke smiled. 'I just wanna deliver this,' he said, holding up a sealed envelope.

Dave was suspicious. He looked up and down the road, but as it was so early on a Sunday morning, the place was deserted. He tried to cycle on, but with his other hand, the young bloke grabbed hold of Dave's handlebars. ''Alf a crown,' he said, waving the envelope in front of the boy.

Dave's eyes nearly popped out of their sockets.

'Just pop this in the letterbox,' said the bloke. 'Unless yer don't need the cash?'

Need the cash? To Dave, half a crown was a fortune compared to the measly bob a week he and Phil got for their paper rounds. 'Show us!' he demanded bossily.

The bloke grinned, dug into his trouser pocket, took out a half-crown piece, and held it up for

78

Dave to see.

Dave wiped his own hand on his shirt, then grabbed first the half-crown, and then the envelope.

'I take it yer do know where the End 'Ouse is?' the bloke asked, with one hand still hanging on to the handlebars of Dave's bike.

Furious, Dave pulled away, turned the bike around, and without so much as a glance back over his shoulder, pedalled back down Jackson Road.

The young bloke watched him go, taking out a fag from a packet in his back trouser pocket, and lighting up.

Young Dave turned into the Annette Road cul de sac and cycled towards the end house at the side of the railway bridge. When he got there, it took him no more than a few moments to get off his bike, lean it against the low brick wall in front of the house, and then push the envelope through the letterbox. It took only a few more moments for him to get back onto his bike and cycle off as fast as he could back to the shop. He couldn't wait to tell Phil about his stroke of luck.

On the way, Dave raced past the young bloke who had found his way to the corner of the cul de sac. The moment he got there, a train passed over the railway bridge above the end house. He waited for it to pass, drawing on his fag, his young face covered with a glow of satisfaction. Then, after dropping the ample remains of his fag onto the pavement, he crunched it up with the sole of his well-polished shoe, turned, and made his way back to Holloway Road.

Chapter 4

The next three days were idyllic ones for Ruth. Just being in Tom's company was a real tonic, for they spent so much of their time just talking together and enjoying what was turning out to be a perfect summer. It was also fortunate that there had been no real air raids since Tom arrived home, and as she had managed to wangle it with her Station Officer that she could remain on standby duty until Tom's leave was up, Ruth was able to spend practically every minute of every day with her arm around his waist, gazing up into his eyes as though he was some kind of Greek god. And in her eyes that was exactly what he was, for he seemed to possess enormous physical strength as well as the kind of exceptional looks that often turned other female heads. However, despite Tom's obvious kindness and devotion to her, the more Ruth got to know him, the more she felt moments of doubt, an inner feeling that it was his physical attributes that appealed to her most, and not the real love and warmth that she had always craved. But then, every time she was with him, she did feel *something* for him, and always seemed to end up consumed with guilt, as she remembered the brief and sometimes wild relationships she had been involved in during the previous few years.

There were also times, usually when she was

lying alone in bed at night, when she wondered if Tom would ever put their love to the test, and how she would respond if he did. To her surprise, that moment came one evening after they had been to the Savoy cinema in Holloway Road where they had just watched *Waterloo Bridge* – a tender wartime love story starring Vivien Leigh and Robert Taylor. During the film, Ruth began to realise that Tom was restless and showing very little interest in the film; he repeatedly searched for her hand and stroked it sensuously. This was followed by him leaning across and kissing her for long periods, his lips firmly pressed against hers, his tongue gently caressing hers, one hand clasped around her shoulder, pulling her towards him with as much force as he dared. But when his other hand began to creep up between her legs, she panicked. This was not the first time she had found herself in such a situation. But it *was* the first time she had found herself in such a situation with Tom, and it worried her. Tom was not the same as those to whom she had given herself before. *They* were merely part of her desperate attempts to prove to herself that others would find her desirable and be attracted to her. They were boys who made love, but whom *she* could never love. But this was different. She *loved* Tom. At least, that's what she kept telling herself, even if her own instincts were constantly raising questions. Yes, she wanted to spend the rest of her life with him, but how much did she really *know* him? He was moody, and often snapped at her for no reason at all, and she had on more than one occasion been irritated by his de-

81

manding ways. How *much* did she love him? she kept asking herself. How much could she trust him? How much could she trust *herself?* Time and again she was plagued with the thought that if she responded to him in the way she had responded to the others, would she still feel the same way towards him? She couldn't take the risk. 'No, Tom,' she whispered, as she gently eased his hand away from her thigh.

Clearly aroused, Tom froze. 'Why not?' he snapped back sharply, his voice raised louder than a whisper.

Conscious that the people around them might be aware of what was going on, Ruth replied softly, 'Not here, Tom. Not now. Later.'

Later, such as it was, came after they had left the cinema and made their way down Loraine Road, where they eventually lost the rest of the cinema-goers, who dispersed amongst the quiet back streets, leaving others to join late night bus queues or make their way to the Tube station in Holloway Road.

As they turned into Annette Road, Ruth slid her arm through Tom's. She knew he was sulking, but instead of being irritated, it made her feel even more affectionate towards him. 'Don't be hurt,' she said, snuggling up to him as they walked.

''Urt?' he asked, dismissively. 'Why should I be 'urt?'

'I've had a wonderful evening, Tom, really I have,' she said awkwardly. 'But I want to – save myself for you. Can you understand what I'm saying?'

'Wot diff'rence does it make ter me?' he sniffed dismissively, his eyes fixed firmly towards the pavement as they walked. 'If yer don't wanna do it, yer don't wanna do it.'

Ruth brought them both to an abrupt halt. 'Now look,' she said firmly, plonking herself down on the coping stone of a low garden wall in front of one of the terraced houses, 'if we're going to spend the rest of our lives together, the least we can do is to be truthful with each other.'

Tom shrugged, and looked the other way.

Ruth grabbed hold of his hand, and forced him to sit beside her. She waited for two or three people to walk past them, then told him, 'When I say I want to save myself for you, that doesn't mean that I don't *want* you.'

He did not respond, keeping his eyes stubbornly transfixed to the pavement.

Refusing to be ignored, she reached out and pulled his face around towards her. 'The back seat in a cinema is not the place, Tom,' she insisted. 'All those eyes leering, grinning... Peeping Toms...'

'So where *is* the right place, Ruth?' he asked, shooting an irritated look up at her.

'Not *where*, Tom – *when*.'

'When is when?'

'After we're married.'

'Who're you kidding!' he snapped, wrenching his arm away from her. 'Since yer won't even agree ter marry me before I go, this might be the only chance we'll ever 'ave of gettin' tergevver.' He stared her straight in the eyes. ''Ad it occurred ter yer that I might never get back from

83

this war in one piece?'

Ruth drew a sharp, horrified intake of breath. 'Don't say such things, Tom!' she scolded. 'Don't ever say such things.'

'Well it's true, ain't it?' he insisted, undeterred. 'There's a war on. People don't see each uvver fer munffs, sometimes years. 'Ow do we know 'ow long I'll be away. 'Ow do we know if we'll *ever* see each uvver again?'

'Because we love each other, Tom.'

'Then what's wrong wiv–?'

'Because we'd lose respect for each other.'

The light was now fading fast, and as the blackout curtains were being drawn at windows all along the road, that fine line between day and night was now disappearing into myriad long fuzzy shadows. Somewhere behind them, there were the sounds of two wireless sets in different houses competing with each other, one soothing the air with late-night music from Geraldo and his orchestra, the other transmitting a wartime address from the Minister of Home Security in the Coalition Government, Herbert Morrison.

Tom waited a moment, then took a packet of fags out of his back pocket. He pulled out two, put them between his lips, and lit them. 'Gels shouldn't smoke,' he grunted, as he handed one of them to Ruth. 'It's bad for yer.'

Ruth took the fag, and inhaled. 'If it's bad for girls,' she said, exhaling, 'why isn't it bad for boys?'

'We've got stronger lungs.'

'Who said?'

'I dunno,' replied Tom. 'But someone must've.'

There was a pause. They both turned to each other, laughed, and fell into each other's arms.

'Oy!' A woman's shrill voice suddenly bellowed out to them from an upstairs window of the house they were sitting in front of.

Both of them turned to look.

'Ain't yer got no 'omes ter go to?' the woman yelled. 'Go on – sling yer 'ooks, I'll 'ave the law on yer! This ain't no bleedin' doss 'ouse!'

The woman's voice only made Ruth and Tom laugh even more. They got up, and with their arms wrapped around each other's waists, they slowly strolled off.

For the first time in a long time, Bella Whitlock decided to close the shop dead on six o'clock. In any case, most of her regulars had already been in to collect their evening newspapers or buy their cigarettes, and once Mrs Burton from the bagwash around the corner had popped in to buy a pencil and a bottle of Tizer, Bella transferred the money from the till to her handbag, and then put on her new yellow straw hat which she had bought in Selby's department store in Holloway Road the day before, especially for her first meeting with Ruth's future mother- and father-in-law later that evening. A little nervous at the prospect, she bustled around, pulling down the door blinds and turning the OPEN card to CLOSED. Then, after quickly tidying around, she switched off the shop light, left, and after briefly checking her reflection in the glass door outside, locked up and moved off.

As it was still rush hour, Holloway Road was

quite busy. People were everywhere, streaming off buses, hurrying home from the Tube station, a surge of exhausted end-of-the-day workers in their sweaty summer clothes, carelessly dodging in and out of the buses and trams as they crossed the big main road in a desperate race to get home to their 'teas' and their loved ones. Bella herself moved briskly on, for although she had plenty of time before she was due to be collected by Ruth at home, she had something important to do first.

When Rita Simmons opened her front door, she was quite taken aback to see who was standing there. ''Allo, Poley!' she said, face beaming. ''Ere's a nice surprise!'

Bella hated being called 'Poley' and her face showed it. 'Can I have a quick word with you, please, Mrs Simmons,' she said unsmilingly. 'It won't take a minute.'

'Blimey!' gasped Rita, who was wearing her usual outsize apron and carpet slippers. 'Don't tell me I ain't paid me paper bill?'

'It's nothing to do with your newspapers, Mrs Simmons,' replied Bella.

Rita stared at her warily. 'Well, at least yer can come in,' she said, standing back to let Bella enter. 'We don't charge in this 'ouse, yer know!'

But Bella stayed put. 'Thank you,' she said coldly. 'It really isn't necessary.'

Rita's expression hardened. 'Oh well,' she said, 'if my place ain't good enuff for yer...'

Aware that she was giving the appearance of being a little haughty, Bella said quickly, 'Well – just for a minute then.'

Rita smiled smugly and stood back to let Bella in. The moment Bella came into the passage she squirmed. The whole place smelt of burnt fish.

'Bloaters,' said Rita proudly. 'Ted loves 'em. Always 'as bloaters on a Wednesday – *when* I can get 'em.' As she led Bella down the rather dingy passage she barked out, 'Ted! We got a visitor!' With Bella at her heel, she went into the back kitchen parlour. 'Come on in, Poley,' she said. 'We don't stand on ceremony in this 'ouse.'

Ted Simmons, Rita's husband, just home from work, was at the kitchen table finishing off his bloater. But the moment Bella entered, he immediately stood up. ''Allo, Mrs Whitlock,' he said, his fingers sticky from picking out bones from his bloaters.

'I'm sorry to interrupt your meal, Mr Simmons,' said Bella, a little flustered.

'No trouble at all,' said Ted, a bit self-conscious in his vest, which exposed a couple of tattoos on both his arms, grease-stained trousers and braces. 'I've finished anyway.' He wiped his lips with the back of his hand. ''Ave a seat,' he said, offering her his chair.

'No, thank you,' Bella replied, declining graciously. 'I only have a few minutes.' But when she caught Rita's disapproving look, she changed her mind.

'See yer later then,' said Ted, making for the door. 'Nice seein' yer, Mrs Whitlock.' And before Bella had a chance to reply, he was gone.

'Don't worry about 'im,' sniffed Rita, removing Ted's plate and empty pint beer tankard from the table where Bella was sitting. ''E's off round the boozer. 'Is second 'ome!'

'Mrs Simmons,' began Bella. But it fell on deaf ears, because Rita had taken some of the dishes from the table out into the adjoining scullery. In the few moments she was sitting there alone, Bella had just enough time to take in the room, which although clean and tidy, was depressingly small and airless. On one side of the wall was a dark varnished dresser which was jammed with framed family snapshots, kids of all shapes and sizes, either clinging to their mum's apron, or pulling silly faces together at their dad's box camera. The mantelpiece over the black polished oven range was much the same, sharing its space with snapshots of the kids grown up, along with boxes of matches and dog-ends that had clearly been left dangling precariously on the edge by Ted. The place also had a stifling smell of freshly washed clothes that were hanging from the ceiling rack, blocking the slightly open fanlight window, and making it difficult for any air to get into the room.

'Now then,' boomed Rita's voice as she came back in from the scullery. 'Wot can I do for yer, mate?'

Bella waited for Rita to plonk her large frame down opposite her at the table. 'I'll be perfectly frank with you, Mrs Simmons,' she said firmly. 'I'd like to know why you are asking my paperboy so many questions.'

Rita did a double-take. 'I beg your pardon?' she asked, immediately straightening up in her chair.

'My boy who delivers,' continued Bella. 'He said you are always asking him questions about me and my daughter. I would like to know why.'

'Your paperboy?' growled Rita, with a look of thunder. 'Wos 'e talkin' about?'

'Philip told me on Sunday that last week you asked him if he knew anything about any of Ruth's friends – the people she works with at the fire-station.'

Rita did a sharp intake of breath. 'Little sod!' she growled.

'Well – is it true?' asked Bella. *'Did* you ask him?'

'Course it ain't true!' replied Rita, opting not to raise her voice for fear of sounding unconvincing. 'Who your daughter mixes wiv is 'er business. I ain't no busybody!'

'From what he says,' Bella went on, 'I gather it's not the first time you've asked him.'

Rita stiffened. 'Then yer'll 'ave ter believe who yer like, won't yer, Poley?' she replied. 'If yer want ter take the word of a snotty-nosed kid, then that's up ter you. I've said ter Ted time an' time again, that little tyke's a real troublemaker.'

Bella was puzzled. 'Phil?' she asked. 'A trouble-maker? But he's only twelve years old! Why should you think such a thing?'

''Cos *all* kids that age are liars,' she insisted, adjusting her hairnet so that it fitted more snugly over her right ear. 'They look like angels, but they play like the devil. *I* should know. I've 'ad five er me own!'

'My Ruth is a good daughter, Mrs Simmons,' Bella said earnestly. 'You should know that she is a great comfort to me. When my husband died, I don't know how I could have coped without her.

Maybe sometimes she – strays a little. But she would never do anything to hurt me.' She leaned forward and stared Rita straight in the eyes. 'I love her very much.'

Rita stretched across and covered Bella's hand. 'Of course yer do, Poley,' she said, with a flashing smile that gave a hint of how lovely she must have looked when she was young. 'An' I admire yer fer it, 'onest I do. I admire yer boaf. I've always 'ad a soft spot fer you an' your gel. You ask Edie Perkins. I've told 'er so dozens er times. I tell yer, it ain't ever mattered ter me where yer come from. It ain't ever mattered ter me that yer ain't one of us. People oughta be judged on *wot* they are, I always say. Wouldn't you agree?'

Bella reluctantly returned Rita's smile, and tactfully withdrew her hand. Try as she might, she didn't believe a word Rita had said, especially when she talked about it not mattering where she, Bella, had 'come from'. As she looked at that strange, larger-than-life creature sitting opposite her, her pretty face inflated by years of domestic drudgery, Bella's mind flashed back to those days before the war when she, her husband Harry Whitlock, and young Ruth had first come to live in Annette Road. It was at a time when the continent of Europe was in turmoil, a time when every foreigner was viewed with great suspicion just in case they turned out to be a German national. And thanks to people like Rita, that is exactly what most of the neighbours in Jackson and Annette Roads had been given to believe about Bella Whitlock and her daughter. Poland, Germany – all the same thing as far as they were

90

concerned. Ignorance wasn't just a prejudice, it was a disease. 'I have to be going,' said Bella, getting up from the table.

Rita placed the palms of her hands on the table in front of her and, with some difficulty, eased herself up. 'I'm sorry yer can't stay,' she said. 'Since the kids left 'ome, I don't get much company. Sometimes I get sick ter deff of starin' at these four walls.'

Whilst she was making her way down Jackson Road, Bella thought a lot about Rita's parting remark. It didn't explain why the big woman was trying to stir up gossip about Ruth, but it did at least give Bella a clue as to why Rita was the kind of person she had become.

Pearl Phillips and her daughter Kate had set out a wonderful supper table. They had worked hard all afternoon to make sure that things were just right for their first meeting with Ruth's mother, Bella Whitlock, and, considering there was a war on, the cold meal looked absolutely delicious. The boiled ham was a particular favourite of Bella's, and when she saw thick slices of it arranged beautifully on a serving plate decorated with sliced cucumber, spring onions, and spiked tomatoes, she was tempted to let Ruth down by making a grab for as much of it as she could possibly pile onto her plate. However, good manners prevailed, and she was content to watch her future son-in-law Tom eat as much ham as he could, together with massive helpings of Pearl's home-made potato salad, tinned sardines, and a bowl of well-dressed iceberg lettuce, all accompanied by thick slices of freshly baked bread which had been spread with generous portions of butter. Bella was overwhelmed by it all, particularly since she had been given to believe that she had merely been invited to have drinks with the Phillips family. 'Real butter!' she exclaimed, as she took her first delicate nibble of bread. 'What a treat after so much margarine.'

'Sometimes it 'elps ter be married to a borough councillor,' said Pearl, with a twinkle in her eye.

Sitting opposite the two women at the parlour table, Ken Phillips was not amused. 'I don't fink yer should be sayin' fings like that, Pearl,' he said, scolding his wife with a reprimanding glare. 'Everyone 'as ter take pot luck in this war.'

Pearl smiled guiltily, and hurriedly returned to eating a slice of beetroot from her plate.

Ruth tactfully changed the conversation. 'Did you know Mr Phillips is a marvellous gardener, Mother?' she said. 'You should just see all the things he grows in the allotment at the back of his garden.'

'Oh really?' replied Bella, relieved at last to find something to talk about. 'How interesting. You would have got on well with my husband, Harry. We only have a small garden at our house, but he loved to grow all kinds of flowers. His favourites were tulips.'

'Beetroots,' said Ken sullenly.

Bella exchanged a quick puzzled look with Ruth. 'I'm sorry, Mr Phillips?' she asked. 'What did you say?'

'Ken grows beetroots,' said Pearl. 'And lots er uvver fings, er course. Especially 'is runner beans.

92

They melt in yer mouf.'

'Dad don't only grow flowers, Mrs Whitlock,' said Tom.

'More's the pity,' added Kate. ''E's mainly a vegetable man.'

It took Bella a moment to take it in. 'Oh I see,' she said.

There followed what seemed to both Bella and Ruth an eternity of silence, during which all that could be heard was the sipping of tea and the munching of iceberg lettuce.

Pearl dabbed the beetroot stain from the corner of her mouth before starting up a conversation again. 'So, what do yer fink about our two love-birds then, Mrs Whitlock?' she asked Bella.

Bella shrugged her shoulders. 'I hope they'll be very happy,' she replied.

'Of course they'll be happy!' Kate said enthusiastically, glaring at her brother as though she was demanding him to be so. 'If yer ask me, 'e's bloomin' lucky ter find someone like Ruth.'

'Well, no one's askin' *you!*' teased Tom, engaging in his usual brotherly banter with her. 'It's about time yer found someone of yer own – *if* anyone'll take yer!'

Before Kate could come back at him, Ken Phillips intervened. 'So what's Poland like, Mrs Whitlock?' he asked, sizing her up as he stirred his tea.

Bella shrugged again. 'I've no idea,' she replied bitterly. 'I haven't been there in years. The last time I was in Poland, it was not occupied by a foreign army.'

Phillips realised he had touched on a sensitive

issue. 'Which part d'yer come from?' he asked.

'Do you know Poland?' asked Bella.

Phillips smiled weakly, and shook his head.

'I come from a place called Cracow,' Bella told him. 'It's in the south-east of the country – not so far from the border with Czechoslovakia.'

'Oh goodness!' cried Pearl. 'Isn't that where 'Itler marched in?'

'Don't be daft, Mum!' sighed Kate. ''Itler's marched in everywhere.'

'That's why the war started,' said Tom, helping himself to another slice of ham. ''Cos Chamberlain gave 'Itler an ultimatum.'

'I think war would have come whatever Mr Chamberlain may have done,' said Bella quietly. 'The Nazis are ruthless. They want nothing less than an empire of their own.'

'*We* have an empire,' said Pearl, straightening up in her chair proudly.

'Not like 'Itler, Mum!' sighed Kate, exasperated.

Phillips had finally stopped stirring his tea. He was now not only sizing Bella up, but watching intently every reaction she made to his questions. 'So is that why yer come over ter England?' he asked casually. 'Ter get away from Jerry?'

Bella took a moment to answer. 'No,' she replied with a polite smile. 'I came because my husband wanted me to come. Because he loved me. And *I* loved *him*.'

Under the table, Ruth's foot gently caressed her mother's. 'My father worked in a shipping freight company,' she told them all. 'He was a manager. He spoke the language fluently.'

94

'Funny place ter 'ave a shippin' company,' said Phillips. 'I always fawt Poland was mainly countryside, full er villages.'

'Cracow is a city, Mr Phillips,' said Bella. 'Or it was until the Germans came in. It had a beautiful old town, where many Jewish people lived, a wonderful old castle, and many fine churches. When I was young, I remember the church bells echoing out over the rooftops for Mass on Sunday mornings – so many of them, as though they were singing to each other.'

'Sounds like you're a religious woman then, Mrs Whitlock?'

For a few fleeting moments, Bella had been reliving some precious moments from her childhood. But the man's voice brought her straight back to the supper table, and this oppressive room that seemed to be weighed down with heavy furniture, dark curtains, and pointless knick-knacks that were so different not only from her own taste, but also from the world she had come from and brought with her to England so many years before. 'Yes, Mr Phillips,' she said, with a gentle smile. 'I have my faith.'

Phillips suddenly realised that an uneasy silence had descended upon the room. 'Always a good fing,' he said, trying to lighten the atmosphere.

A little later, Bella and Pearl looked on whilst Ruth and Kate took on Tom and his father at a game of darts in the back garden. The brick wall on which the board had been placed was pitted with holes from years of similar family competitions, and the slate tiled scoreboard had been used so many times the chalk marks were now becoming almost impossible to read. After a while, Pearl suggested that she and Bella go for a stroll down the garden, leaving the darts players to battle it out behind them. It was another of those fine English summer evenings where the air smelt of grass cuttings and bonfires, and the cloudless sky seemed higher and higher, beyond reach, beyond reason. More than once, both women stared up at the evening light, their faces bathed in the early pangs of sunset.

'When yer look up there,' said Pearl, her white hair tinged with crimson, 'it's hard ter believe there's a war on. When it's all over, I shall never be able to trust the sky again. It's been used by so much evil.'

Pearl Phillips's poignant words touched Bella. They revealed a woman with heart and sensitivity. But then, she remembered Ruth telling her that ever since she had first met Pearl, the woman had often shown fleeting glimpses of having her own ideas, independent of her husband's strong-willed opinions.

At the end of the garden, Pearl opened a rather battered looking timber gate which led out into Ken Phillips's small vegetable allotment. 'It used ter be a bit of a rubbish dump,' she said. 'When food rationing came in, it was Ken's idea ter dig it up an' put it ter good use.' She had a glowing look as she led Bella through the carefully raked over lines of huge green cabbages, carrots, spring onions, and all kinds of vegetables. 'It's his pride and joy,' she said. ''E's never 'appier than when 'e's diggin' out 'ere.'

Bella was impressed. 'How wonderful,' she said, 'to have fresh vegetables straight from your own back garden.'

'Yer mustn't take against 'im,' Pearl said, quite out of the blue. ''E don't mean 'alf the fings 'e says, yer know.'

Pearl's sudden change of tack took Bella completely by surprise. 'Take against him?' she asked, puzzled.

'All them questions 'e asked yer,' she said, her face clouding over with anxiety. 'I fink it's just that 'e wants ter be sure in 'is own mind, that's all.'

Bella was still puzzled. 'Sure?' she asked. 'Sure of what?'

Pearl hesitated. 'That Tom's makin' the right decision, I suppose.'

For one brief moment, Bella looked at her. It was the first time she had noticed what a pleasant face Pearl had, not attractive, but pleasant. She estimated that Pearl could have been no more than about fifty years old, and was therefore surprised that her hair was so prematurely white, which only drew attention to her long, pointed features, pallid skin, and pale blue eyes, which were magnified by the powerful lenses of her spectacles. But Pearl's remark had stung her, and she faltered as she answered. 'I suppose,' she said, 'that where their future is concerned, *both* our children should be given the opportunity to make their *own* decisions. Wouldn't you think?'

Pearl bit her lip hard. It was still stained by beetroot juice, which gave them the only colour they had. 'Oh yes,' she said, unconsciously clutching Bella's arm. 'You're absolutely right. But you know what young people can be like. They sometimes make 'asty decisions. Ken believes that wiv somefin' as important as gettin' married, they should take time ter get ter know each uvver.'

'Unfortunately,' replied Bella, who from the corner of her eye had noticed a large snail nibbling into one of the cabbages, 'these days, young people rarely have the luxury of time to get to know each other.'

Pearl's face screwed up. Then she looked at Bella and gradually smiled, as though she had suddenly found someone in whom she could confide. 'After Tom's gone away,' she said, 'if yer should ever feel like... I mean, if yer felt that yer'd like to come an' 'ave a cuppa tea wiv me some time – well, I just wanted yer ter know that – yer'd be most welcome.'

Even on a bright summer's morning, King's Cross station looked dark and grimy. Platform number three was thronged with people, the usual sea of khaki accompanied by family and close friends who were coming to see their husbands and sons off on the daily 11.03 'Special' to wherever the war was taking them. Elderly porters struggled to cope with the mountains of service personnel shoulder packs, NAAFI trolley girls were serving last-minute cuppas to the troops and their distraught families, and flocks of sparrows and pigeons fluttered in and out of the entire proceedings, occasionally swooping low to nip at any crumb of anything that might have dropped onto what little space was left on the crowded platform.

Seven days had swept by Ruth and Tom at such a pace that it hardly seemed possible that they were now back where they had been at the start of Tom's leave. With just five minutes before the train's departure, the two of them, like so many other young couples there, were locked in a tight embrace, their cheeks pressed firmly against each other's, their bodies throbbing with dread and anticipation. They were wishing it was the night before, when the following morning seemed a lifetime away, completely oblivious of the endless farewells of the tearful wives, mothers and sisters who consistently refused to watch the minute hand of the great clock over the station concourse as it raced mercilessly towards the hated appointed time.

After a moment, Tom raised Ruth's chin with his hand and kissed her gently on the lips. 'I intend ter keep yer ter yer word, Miss Madiewsky,' he said, his lips pressed up against her ear. 'Yer've promised ter marry me as soon as I get 'ome remember, so yer'd better be waitin' fer me.' He kissed her ear sensually.

'Depends how long I have to wait,' she answered jokingly.

The look he returned was hard and questioning. 'For ever?' he asked.

'And ever?' she teased.

'And ever!' he replied firmly.

'Ever's a long time.'

'Not in my book it ain't,' he replied. 'Not if yer want someone bad enuff.'

'I do want you, Tom,' she assured him.

'Positive?'

'Positive.'

'You'd better be,' he said unsmilingly. He released his hold on her, then felt in his pocket, and took something out. 'Give us yer 'and,' he said.

'Why?' she replied, puzzled.

With little time now to spare, he reached for her left hand, found the appropriate finger, and slipped an engagement ring onto it.

Ruth looked at the ring, which had a stone that sparkled even in the dim station light. She was overwhelmed. 'Tom!'

'So yer'd better wait,' he said, raising her finger to his lips and kissing the stone. 'Or else.'

Ruth smiled lovingly at him. But, to her surprise, he returned a look that was cold and threatening.

A tannoy announcement boomed out from the speakers above them: *The special train now standing at Platform Three is about to depart. Close the doors, please!* That was immediately followed by the train guard at the rear compartment raising his flag and readying his departure whistle. There was an immediate frantic scramble for all the servicemen passengers to board the train.

With the slamming of compartment doors fracturing the atmosphere and scattering sparrows and pigeons in panic back up into the roof, Ruth and Tom threw themselves into each other's arms, hugged, and kissed as long and hard as they could. Behind them came a chorus of jeers

100

and cheers from his mates, 'Tom! Give it to 'er, mate!' Tom ignored them all, and waited until the final moment, when the train started to pull away, before finally, reluctantly breaking loose from Ruth. He only just managed to prise open one of the compartment doors in time, but the moment he was safely on board, he immediately leaned out of the window and stretched down in a last attempt to kiss her. 'For ever?' he called.

'And ever!' she called back.

'Promise?'

'Promise!'

The train gathered speed.

'You'd better!' he yelled, as Ruth finally abandoned her efforts to keep up with him. 'Or else!'

Her last glimpse of him was of a tiny figure amongst so many other tiny figures peering out of the train as it gradually disappeared out along the clanking railway tracks of North London, heading north towards the unknown.

Ruth waited until the very last minute before turning to leave. By the time she started to walk along the platform back towards the station concourse, most of the weeping relatives had gone, handing the space back to the sparrows and pigeons and railway porters, who were only too pleased to be rid of the exhausting sea of khaki. She came to a halt just beneath the station clock, which showed exactly 11.05. She checked it with her own wrist-watch. Yes, the wretched train had left exactly on time, she cursed to herself. Then she looked at her ring, and the stone sparkled as if in response. It brought a

101

smile, and then her eyes welled up in tears. Oh God, she said to herself, I didn't even have time to tell him that I love him. Then she smiled. Of course she had told him. She had told him many times. But she hoped he believed her, because she meant it. At least – she hoped she had meant it. As she slowly wound her way through the crowds outside the station, all she could hear echoing through her mind were those final parting words, which, for some strange reason, were beginning to worry her:

'For ever?'
'And ever!'
'Or else!'

Chapter 5

Sweetie Berkeley was dying for a smoke. She and Mavis had been on duty all night, Sweetie on the switchboard taking an unusual number of calls after a series of rapid hit and run enemy air raids right across London, and Mavis out with the boys from the Islington Fire District Division, who had been tackling a particularly obstinate blaze caused by an oil bomb in City Road. At daybreak, both girls met up in the station staff canteen with Ruth, who had herself spent the night on her motorbike, racing frantically all over London delivering dispatches to officers in charge of one incident after another. All three looked fit to drop, but once they'd settled down to their first fag and a strong cup of tea, life gradually began to seep back into their weary bodies. However, tired as she was, Sweetie's beady eyes had not failed to miss the stone sparkling on Ruth's engagement finger. 'Come on then!' she said, in her upper-middle-class Canonbury Square voice. 'Let's see it!'

Ruth beamed as she held up the ring for the other girls to see.

'Blimey,' said Mavis, whose face was still streaked with grease from her night's work in City Road. 'It's a diamond!'

Ruth laughed. 'Not quite,' she purred proudly. 'But it's not far short.'

'What are you talking about, sweetie?' said Sweetie, who got her nickname because that's what she called practically everybody. She took hold of Ruth's hand, and looked good and hard at the stone. 'That's a diamond, all right. Not top drawer maybe, but I know one *when* I see one.'

Ruth was taken aback, and joined the others in taking her own look at the 'sparkler'. 'A *real* diamond? But Tom doesn't have that sort of money. At least, I don't think he does.'

'Sounds like a dark 'orse ter me,' said Mavis, who was feeling a bit on the jealous side. ''Is ol' man's on the Council, ain't 'e? I bet *'e's* not short of a bob or two.'

Ruth pulled her hand away. 'I don't think that's true, Mavis,' she said. 'Tom's father's a very nice man, but he's no millionaire.'

'Well, all I can say is I wish Charlie did somefin' like that fer me,' Mavis said sourly. ''E didn't ask *me* ter marry 'im before 'e went away.'

'Would you have done so if he'd asked?' asked Sweetie, with a wink to Ruth.

'Depends on 'ow much 'e wanted first!' quipped Mavis. They all laughed. 'What about you, Rufe?' she asked, with a mischievous grin. ''Ave yer done it wiv Tom yet?'

Ruth did a double-take.

'Oh come on!' said Mavis. 'You know ... bangy-bang!' She laughed out loud.

Embarrassed, Ruth shook her head.

'Why not?' pressed Mavis. 'Din't 'e ask yer?'

Ruth hesitated, lowered her eyes and twisted her half-finished cigarette into the ash-tray. Then she got up. 'See you later,' she said, smiling weakly, and quietly leaving the canteen.

'Wos up wiv 'er?' Mavis asked, as she watched Ruth go.

Sweetie slowly shook her head. 'You know, sweetie,' she said reproachfully, 'you're about as subtle as a pink blancmange.'

Ruth went straight to the women's wash-room, where she took off her tunic, rolled up her shirt-sleeves, and went to the wash-basin, where she took off her engagement ring, put it in her trouser pocket for safety, then ran the water and started to wash her face.

'Tactless as ever!'

Ruth looked up to find Sweetie at the next wash-basin, both of them reflected in the long cracked mirror in front of them.

'The trouble with Mavis,' said Sweetie, taking off her jacket and hanging it on a nearby hook, 'is that she never stops to think what she's saying. To her, being in love means only the number of times she can get a man into bed with her.' She looked in the mirror at Ruth rinsing her face. 'Don't take any notice of her, sweetie,' she said. 'Mavis is a silly girl, but she means no harm.'

Ruth smiled back at her. 'I know,' she replied appreciatively.

Sweetie rolled up her shirt-sleeves and started to wash her hands. 'But one thing I will say,' she said. 'That young man of yours is very lucky to have a girl like you.'

'Oh, I think I'm pretty lucky too, Sweetie,' she said, her face dripping with water.

Sweetie flashed her a warm smile. From the first moment they had met, she had always had plenty of time for Ruth, not only because Ruth was roughly the same age as herself, but because they both had mothers who had been born abroad and who were married to Englishmen. 'I must say, he sounds rather special,' she said.

'He is.'

Sweetie looked at her closely. 'So this is it, is it?' she asked. 'This really is it? You're absolutely convinced that he's the man you want to settle down with for the rest of your life?'

Ruth hesitated briefly. 'Yes,' she replied, with a firm nod. 'Absolutely.'

Sweetie persisted. 'How d'you know?' she asked.

Ruth shrugged. 'I just know,' she replied. 'When I'm with him, he makes me feel secure. He makes me feel wanted. Since I've known him, we seem to have grown so much together. I suppose it's all to do with trust.'

Sweetie shook the water from her hands, then

went to the roller towel to dry them. 'Well,' she said, 'all I can say is, thank goodness you *can* trust him.'

Ruth swung her a startled look. 'Well, of course I can,' she said, somewhat taken aback by such a remark. 'Why shouldn't I?'

'Oh, no special reason,' returned Sweetie. 'It's just that I personally have never trusted *any* man. Men scare me. They always seem to say one thing and mean something quite different. Oh, not just about the obvious, but about their intentions. It's as though they're always trying to hide something from you.'

'I know what you mean,' said Ruth, joining her at the towel, 'but I don't think that's entirely true. In any case,' she added lightly, 'how many men have you been with!'

'Enough,' replied Sweetie, with some irony. 'No,' she said, quickly correcting herself. 'As a matter of fact, I've never actually been with any *real* men. The only ones I've ever known have been boys – just *boys*.'

Ruth waited for her to finish wiping her hands, then pulled down a fresh section of towel and began drying her face. She found it deeply worrying to hear Sweetie talk like this. Although she knew that in her time Sweetie had walked out with a succession of boyfriends, she had always been under the impression that Sweetie was perfectly satisfied with not being tied down to someone until the time was right. So what had gone wrong?

'Still, what does it matter?' sighed Sweetie at the mirror, tidying up her short blonde hair with the tips of her fingers. 'In this war a girl has to learn how to stand on her own two feet. And in any case, I much prefer the company of my *real* friends. At least they listen to you when you want to get something off your chest.'

Ruth came across to her. 'Sweetie,' she said, addressing Sweetie's reflection in the mirror, 'is there something you want to talk about? Because if you do, you do know I'm here – don't you?'

Sweetie smiled gratefully, her eyes sparkling with warmth and affection. 'Thank you, sweetie,' she replied. 'I know.'

They exchanged a smile. But Ruth was not happy. She was not happy at all. Because for the first time, she had suddenly noticed how pale and strained her friend was looking.

On the way home, Ruth came across Edie Perkins. Her neighbour had just been shopping in Holloway Road and was struggling home with a huge string bag of vegetables which she had just bought from Taffy Evans's roadside stall. Since Edie was a widow, Ruth had never really understood why she should want to buy so many vegetables each week, but when she had once asked her the reason, Edie replied, quite perplexingly, that she saw no reason to change the habit of a lifetime. Edie was like that – pint-sized, dithery, illogical to the point of incomprehension, but with a heart of gold.

'I only hope Taffy gives you a good price for all this,' Ruth said, as she took hold of Edie's bag and carried it for her. 'He must have made a fortune out of you over the years.'

'Oh yes,' Edie said proudly, 'Taffy's a good 'un all right. Always knocks somefin' off me King Edwards. An' even if 'e didn't, I'd never go ter anyone else 'cos 'e's good an' 'onest. An' I'm tellin' yer, 'is runner beans is the finest in the 'ole wide world!'

They turned into Jackson Road where someone from the Council was up a ladder cleaning the wick holder of one of the street gas lamps. Most of the residents thought it a bit of a pointless exercise, considering street gas lighting had been banned since the start of the blackout. Nonetheless, maintenance had to go on.

''Ave yer 'eard about Ted Simmons, Rita's 'ubby?' Edie asked, her voice low but very animated. She didn't wait for an answer. 'Brought 'ome by a copper last night. Got legless in the boozer, tried ter pick a fight wiv some navvy.'

'Oh dear,' was all Ruth could say. She hardly knew the man, so what he got up to was of little interest to her.

''E's lucky not ter get charged,' Edie continued, determined to pass on her little bit of local gossip. 'Last time 'e did it, they chucked 'im in the nick ter cool off fer the night. 'E got a warnin' that if 'e caused any more trouble, they'd take 'im up before the Magistrates.'

'Oh dear,' sighed Ruth again. 'It must be very upsetting for his wife.'

'Rita?' sneered Edie. 'That's a good one, that is. I know I shouldn't say it seein' as how she's a mate er mine, but if yer ask me, it's all Rita's fault. She never stops pickin' on the poor man. Nag, nag, nag, do this, do that. They fight like cat an' dog all the time. I tell yer, if I was 'im, I'd've walked out on 'er years ago.'

'But that's very sad, Edie,' said Ruth. 'There must be a reason for all this.'

'Oh, there's a reason all right!' sniffed Edie, struggling to keep her voice down as she revealed how she was smugly in the know. 'It's becos of Eric – 'er middle boy.'

If Ruth had shown no interest before, by now she was riveted.

Edie drew as close as she could. ''E's not Ted's, yer know.'

Ruth's eyes were popping out of her head. 'He's not?'

'Oh no!' Edie looked around to make quite sure they could not be overheard. 'Some years ago, Rita 'ad a bit of a ding-dong wiv a commercial traveller – a really good-lookin' Jewish man named Markstein.'

Listening to Edie's intimate revelations was beginning to make Ruth feel a little uncomfortable. 'I must say,' she said awkwardly, 'it sounds very unlikely.'

Edie shook her head. 'If yer mean becos of the way Rita looks,' she said emphatically, 'I can tell yer that quite a lot er men like fat women. Gives 'em somefin' ter get 'old of. Mind you, Rita weren't always the size she is now. In 'er young days, she was quite a smasher. Anyway...' she lowered her voice even more, 'apparently Ted din't know nuffin' about all this 'til the last of their kids'd left home. She told him one night after 'e got 'ome legless from one of 'is sessions round the boozer one night. Rita's way of gettin'

109

'er own back, I s'ppose. But ter this day, I don't fink the boy 'imself's bin told.' They reached the corner of Annette Road, and turned into the cul de sac. 'Not that it'd make much diff'rence to 'im,' continued Edie, relentlessly. 'Not now 'e's got a missus an' kids of 'is own ter look after.'

Ruth was relieved when they finally reached the front gate of Edie's place. 'Well,' she said, handing over the string bag, 'I suppose every family has a skeleton in their cupboard somewhere. I'm very sorry for Rita, but I'm glad that I don't have to have anything to do with her.'

'That's where you're wrong, Ruth,' said Edie, quite pointedly. 'I don't want ter worry yer, but I reckon yer've got quite a lot ter do wiv 'er.'

Ruth did a double-take. 'What do you mean, Edie?' she asked.

Once again Edie looked around to make quite sure no one was listening. Then, lowering her voice almost to a whisper she said, 'Rita's out ter get yer. Did yer know that?'

Ruth was completely taken aback. 'Get *me?*' she asked.

'She wants ter know all about yer,' said Edie. 'She wants ter make as much mischief for yer as she can.'

'What!' gasped Ruth. 'But why? What have I done to *her?*'

Edie shook her head. 'Yer don't 'ave ter do nuffin' ter cross Rita,' she said, her voice edged with foreboding. 'The way Rita sees it is that you're everyfin' she's ever missed out on in life. She's jealous 'cos you're young, an' yer can go out wiv anyone yer like. She's a sad woman,

110

Ruth, make no mistake about it. She should never've got married an' 'ad all them kids. She more or less told me so once. She said it made 'er feel like a prisoner, an' it's made 'er crafty and spiteful. Rita's trouble is that she don't know 'ow ter cope wiv 'er own life, so she 'as ter make mischief fer uvvers.'

Ruth felt quite numb as she watched Edie go up to her front door and put the key in the lock. 'What will she do, Edie?' she called in a strangulated whisper. 'What's she going to do?'

Edie opened her door, went in and put down her shopping bag in the passage. Then she peered out, and looked towards the end of the cul de sac to make sure that no one could hear her. 'She's keepin' an eye on yer,' she called, quietly. 'Believe me, I *know* – I can always tell. An' when she finds wot she's lookin' fer, mark my words – she'll pounce! Be careful, Ruth. That's all I'm sayin'. Just be careful.' She closed the door.

After Edie had gone, Ruth paused for a moment, unable to take in what she had just heard. Was it true? It seemed so utterly absurd. Was Rita really jealous of her, just because she'd had a rough time in life herself? Could it be as simple as that? Or was there something more sinister to it? She turned, and made her way towards her own front door.

Bella was at the shop, so Ruth had the house to herself for the day. Upstairs in her bedroom, she drew back the blackout curtains, and opened the window. A cool breeze caused the white lace curtains to flutter; it was a welcome relief from the searing heat of the morning, and a rare chance to let some fresh air into the room. She took off all her clothes, and stretched out naked on the bed. After a gruelling night's duty on the road, she just wanted to close her eyes and go straight to sleep, but she was too tired even for that. Once she had cooled off sufficiently, she went to her tunic pocket to collect her packet of cigarettes. She took one out and put it between her lips, but then discovered that her box of matches was empty. Her mother always kept a spare box on the mantelpiece downstairs in the living room, which she used for lighting a candle in front of the small statue of the Madonna. Ruth put on her dressing-gown, and went downstairs.

The living room smelt of damp and decay. Not only had no window been opened in there for months, but the blackout blinds were never raised. In any case, it was one of those unnecessary rooms that so many families seemed only to use on high days and holidays, and this was no exception, for it had not been used since the previous Christmas when Harry Whitlock's favourite cousin Richard and his wife Nora had joined Bella, Ruth, and two of Bella's elderly Polish émigré aunts for a small family get-together.

The unlit cigarette dangling from her lips, Ruth went straight to the blackout blinds and raised them. Then she opened a window, leaned out, and took what she hoped would be a deep breath of fresh morning air, but almost simultaneously, a freight train came rattling across the railway bridge above, sending down a cloud of thick black smoke from its funnel. Ruth immediately pulled her head back in and slammed the window. It was a timely reminder of the reason why her mother always kept the windows closed.

Gradually succumbing to total weariness and exhaustion, she slouched her way across to the mantelpiece and picked up the box of matches which was partly hidden behind the casket containing her father's ashes. She lit her cigarette. But just as she was about to go, she noticed a long white envelope propped up against the small antique chiming clock which hadn't worked for years. She took a closer look at the envelope. On the front was her name, *Ruth*, each letter intriguingly scrawled in an Old-English style. She immediately ripped open the envelope and read the contents. The words were casually handwritten on lined paper from a letter pad:

72 Mare Street
Hackney

Dear Ruth,
Hope you don't mind my writing to you, but ever since we met that night when the wall nearly collapsed on you, I've been thinking about you quite a bit.

Anyway, I just wanted you to know that it was really good meeting you, and I was wondering whether you'd like to meet up again some time – maybe a drink in the pub, or a flick or something. If you like, you could come up here to Hackney one Sunday afternoon, and have tea with me and my grandad. It's not much of a place, but he's a good old boy, and he'd make you feel at home. You've probably

113

heard by now that I've tried to make contact with you several times. Saw your mum. She looks really nice. Must be hard work keeping a shop like that going, especially when you aren't there to help out. Saw your house too. Very nice. What's it like living under a railway bridge?!

Looking forward to hearing from you.
All the best,
Mike (Buller)

PS. If you don't want to answer this, don't worry. I'll quite understand.

In the shop, Freda Dapper was helping Bella to unpack a crate of Tizer, which had been part of the morning's soft drink delivery. Neither was prepared for the sudden appearance of Ruth who came charging in clutching Mike Buller's letter in her hand. 'Mama!' she barked the moment she came through the shop door.

'Ruth!' cried Bella, surprised to see her daughter so early after her night-shift. 'Why aren't you at home fast asleep?'

Ruth was too agitated to let her say anything more. 'Mama,' she called, holding out Mike Buller's letter. 'When did this letter arrive for me? It has no date.'

'Letter?' replied Bella, squinting at the envelope Ruth was waving at her. 'What letter?'

'I found this on the mantelpiece in the sitting room,' said Ruth. 'How long has it been there?'

Freda stood back to allow Bella to collect her reading spectacles from the counter.

'Let me see,' said Bella, putting on her spec-

114

tacles and taking the envelope from Ruth. 'I don't remember seeing it,' she replied.

Ruth snatched the envelope back from her. 'Mama!' she snapped. 'It was on the mantelpiece. How many times have I told you to let me know when I have any letters! The only person who could have put it there was *you*. So when did it arrive? Who delivered it?'

It wasn't the first time that Ruth had spoken to her mother in such a way in front of outsiders, and Bella didn't like it. 'As far as I remember,' she said, haughtily, taking off her spectacles, 'it arrived a few days ago.'

'As far as you remember?' Ruth repeated indignantly.

'My memory is not what it used to be,' countered Bella. 'I found it on the doormat in the hall, and as you weren't there, I must have taken it into the sitting room when I went in to say my morning prayers. I'm very sorry, Ruth. I know I should have mentioned it, but I'm getting very absent-minded these days. In any case, what's all the fuss?'

Ruth took a deep, exasperated breath. 'The letter is from the man who came into the shop looking for me.'

Bella exchanged a disquieted look with Freda.

'He said he's been trying to make contact with me,' said Ruth. 'I should have been told.'

'I remember him,' said Freda, who was so hot the curls on her head were soggy with sweat. 'Good-looking boy. Bit cheeky – but he seemed quite nice.'

'That's not the point!' snapped Ruth. 'If somebody is trying to contact me, I want to know about it. But I don't want him following me around without my knowing about it.' Suddenly aware that she had been rather rude to the poor woman, she calmed herself down, and went to her. 'I'm sorry, Mrs Dapper,' she said guiltily. 'It just annoys me when things are being kept from me.'

'I wasn't aware that anything was being kept from you,' said Bella coldly. 'In any case, what's so special about this person?'

'Special?' Ruth was only too aware that her mother was probing. 'As far as I'm concerned, there's nothing *special* about him.'

'Buller,' said Bella. 'He said his name was Buller.' She went to the front door, which Ruth had left open. 'Apparently, he was with you during the air raid up at Shoreditch.'

Ruth knew what her mother was suggesting, and it irritated her. 'I was with a lot of people that night, Mama,' she said. 'He was just one of many.'

'One of many – who saved your life,' returned Bella wryly. 'Isn't that what you told me?'

Ruth resisted the urge to snap back at her. 'It was hardly saving my life,' she replied with restraint. 'He merely pulled me out of the way of a wall that was about to fall on top of me! But that's hardly a reason for starting a relationship.'

Bella looked up with a surprised start. 'Relationship?' she asked, sceptically. 'Is that what he's looking for?'

'Don't be silly now, please, Mama,' Ruth said huffily. 'I'm going to be married to Tom – or have

116

you forgotten that already?'

Freda was embarrassed by the tiff that was developing between Ruth and her mother. 'I'll go and do some unpacking,' she said nervously, before disappearing into the back room.

Once Freda had gone, Ruth felt free to speak her mind to her mother. 'Mama,' she said tautly, 'I don't know what you're insinuating, but I have no interest in this boy at all.'

Bella shrugged. 'It's your life,' she said, quietly provocative. 'You're old enough to know your own mind. All I'm asking you to do is to be careful. You must know that there are prying eyes in this neighbourhood.'

Ruth exploded. 'Oh, for God's sake, Mama! I haven't done anything wrong! This letter is perfectly harmless. Here – look at it, if you don't believe me.'

Bella refused to take the letter. 'I can't stand around talking,' she said, in an infuriatingly disinterested voice. 'I have work to do.'

Ruth grabbed hold of her mother's arm and prevented her from moving off. 'Can't you understand?' she pleaded, knowing that she had upset her. 'I'm not interested in other people. I have a relationship now. I've found someone that I love very much.' In an attempt to reassure Bella, she moved closer, gently took hold of her hands and held them. 'It's not like before, Mama,' she said softly. 'I've put all that behind me. Believe me – I've changed.'

'I hope so, Ruth,' said Bella, calm and composed. 'I hope so, for your sake – *and* for the sake of the man you're going to marry.'

Ruth's expression tensed. She released her mother's hands, then without another word, turned and made for the door. The moment she got there, however, she found her departure blocked by the huge frame of Rita Simmons, who was just coming in.

''Ello, Poley!' Rita beamed, her grin so broad that it revealed a scanty set of yellow teeth. 'An' where're you off to in such a 'urry? Who is it this time?'

Ruth was not amused by Rita's feeble joke. She merely eased herself past her, and rushed off.

'Blimey!' Rita called to Bella, who had retreated behind the counter. 'Not very friendly, your gel – is she?'

Chapter 6

The only time Ruth had ever been to Mare Street in Hackney was when she had once had to deliver a dispatch to the local Divisional Superintendent after a high explosive bomb had completely destroyed a terrace of houses in one of the adjoining back streets during a particularly heavy night-time air raid. Everything looked very different now. Although there were inescapable signs everywhere that Hackney had suffered greatly during the worst days of the Blitz, there was a determination amongst the people who lived and worked there to ensure that life continued as normal. Of course, the sun made a great deal of difference. It was always easier to suffer beneath the glorious blue of a summer sky than during the drab grey of winter, and from the moment Ruth got off the bus outside the Hackney Empire, the austerity of wartime clothes rationing seemed quite inconsequential, for she immediately felt uplifted by the sight of young girls in their thin home-made summer dresses cut daringly just above the knees, older women in cotton dresses that had clearly been in and out of their bedroom cupboards and wardrobes for years, and men and boys of all ages in open-necked shirts, and well-worn flannel trousers held up by what, in a poor working-class district like this, were probably the only pair of braces they possessed in the whole wide world. As she looked around at the everyday hardships of the people who had remained poor during days of peace as well as in war, Ruth found it hard to imagine how this vibrant corner of East London could have once been such a fashionable place of residence.

It was clear that finding the house she was looking for was going to prove quite elusive. For some reason, she had got it into her head that number 72 Mare Street was going to be somewhere in the direction of the Town Hall, which she had pinpointed on one of her father's old London maps to be in the vicinity of Graham Road. But after she had been walking a good ten minutes or so, it soon became apparent that she hadn't a clue where she was going. Of course matters weren't helped by the fact that so many street signs had either been taken down at the start of the war, or just been obliterated during a night's bombing. Nonetheless, she told herself, surely there had to be some more positive way of finding the place she was looking for?

'Seventy-two, d'yer say?' yelled the cockles and whelks barrow-boy, in his rasping Hackney brogue, in answer to Ruth's enquiry. 'Must be down Jessop way.'

'Jessop?' asked Ruth.

'Jessop Place,' called the barrow-boy, who was in fact on the wrong side of fifty. 'Small turnin' just off the main road. Can't miss it!'

'Is it far to walk,' asked Ruth, 'or should I take a bus?'

'Bus!' The barrow-boy roared with laughter. He had obviously smoked too many fags because his chest sounded like a whistling kettle. 'Blimey, mate,' he croaked, 'young gel like you oughta be ashamed er yerself. Take yer no time at all. Five minutes up terwards the park. Even numbers this side. No time at all!'

Ruth thanked him profusely, but as she moved off, she could hear him bellowing out at her: 'Wot about treatin' yerself to a nice pint er cockles?'

Ruth grinned, and waved back. 'Some other time,' she called. 'And thanks again!'

The barrow-boy waved back, and quickly looked around for his next customer.

Five minutes may mean five minutes to a Hackney barrowboy, but to Ruth it seemed more like half an hour, especially in the sweltering heat of the midday sun. On the way she passed endless little shops, many of which still had windows boarded up after bomb blast, but all of them with the same defiant chalk-marked slogans: *Business As Usual*. On the pavement outside a ladies' dress shop, grandly named *Helena's House of Fashion*, a queue of women of all ages had formed, hoping to use some ration coupons to snap up a pair of desperately needed stockings. Ruth was tempted to join the queue herself, but she had a more pressing matter to attend to.

Number 72 Mare Street turned out to be far more elusive than Ruth could have imagined, for, after number 66, everything seemed to go haywire, with some premises showing no identification at all. By the time the numbers resumed at 78, she was absolutely convinced that the place she was looking for did not exist, and she would have given up the search if it hadn't been for a casual glance up at a street sign, which showed the equally elusive Jessop Place. She had no idea if the kind of establishment she was looking for was a shop or a private residence, but the moment she turned the corner and entered the narrow, cobbled mews, the mystery took on a new twist, for the main door of number 72 Mare Street was not in Mare Street at all, but was in fact tucked away in the dark shadows of Jessop Place itself. Even worse was to come, for when she finally reached the door, she found a discreet notice pinned on the boarded-up windows, which read: *Chapel of Rest, Funeral Director: Cyril Buller*. Ruth's heart sank. Her first inclination was to turn tail and get out of the place as fast as she could, but then she remembered why she had made such an effort to come to the place. Taking a deep breath, she went in.

Death, and rose-perfumed disinfectant. Those were the first smells that greeted her. The sights and smells of death were, of course, nothing new to Ruth, for in the short time that she had been delivering Fire Service dispatches on her motorbike around London, she had seen plenty of it, and she knew only too well that rose-perfumed disinfectant was as good a disguise as any. The dim lights did nothing to relieve the gloom, even though it was clearly unavoidable considering that the windows had been shattered at some time by bomb blast, and had had to be replaced with plywood boards. It also meant that the place was practically airless, which was unbearable on such a hot day. She was also depressed by the atmosphere of false repose, for it recalled for her those difficult days immediately after her own father's death when she had accompanied her mother to their local funeral parlour in Seven Sisters Road to collect his ashes. As she reluctantly looked around the gloomy reception area, she could see flowers in vases everywhere, beautiful summer flowers, great sheaves of them propped up against the wall, all carrying sad little sympathy cards, and all waiting patiently to adorn the next coffin and hearse. Ruth hated the thought of flowers being used in such a way. To her they were living things, and should be allowed to live out their lives just like anything else.

'Good mornin', young lady.' The voice was surprisingly robust for someone who had just made a silent entrance through purple velvet curtains from the Chapel of Rest. 'Allow me ter introduce myself,' he said, in his customary solemn and sympathetic voice. 'My name is Cyril Buller. An' 'ow may I 'elp you on such a lovely day?'

Ruth was about to answer, but then didn't get the chance.

'Yer don't 'ave ter whisper, yer know,' said Cyril, with a mischievous smirk. 'They can't 'ear us!'

Ruth grinned awkwardly. The man was terribly tactless, but she liked him. She was mesmerised by his hairpiece, which was dark brown, and fitted uncomfortably just above his ears.

'Not yer first time, is it?' asked Cyril, with a reassuring smile, and a voice that, no matter how hard he tried, could not disguise the fact that he was born and bred in Hackney.

Ruth shook her head. 'Actually,' she replied, at last managing to get a word in, 'I'm looking for someone. I was given this address... His name's Buller – Mike Buller?'

Cyril's double chins and puffed-up cheeks became distorted into a wry grimace. 'Oh yes?' he said, with a twinkle in his eye. He pinched his nose with two fingers, as though using them in place of a handkerchief. 'I fawt as much. That boy er mine!'

'Is he your son?' Ruth asked.

'Me son!' With total disregard for the solemnity of a funeral parlour, Cyril roared with laughter. 'That's a good 'un, that is! Just wait 'til I tell 'im that one!' Flattered by Ruth's unwitting remark, his hands automatically adjusted his hairpiece. 'Mike ain't got no dad,' he said. 'Ain't got no

123

mum neivver. I'm 'is grandad.'

'Oh I see,' replied Ruth, who wasn't really surprised.

'Not bad fer me age, eh?' purred Cyril, vainly.

'Absolutely,' agreed Ruth. 'But what happened to his parents?'

Cyril frowned. 'Mike's dad was my son. 'Erbert – lovely boy, mad on every sport yer could fink of. When young Mike was just five years old, 'Erbert got drowned divin' off Soufend Pier. Knocked 'is 'ead on a lump er stone on the sea-bed. One in a million chance.'

'Oh, how tragic,' said Ruth. 'I'm so sorry.'

'As fer 'is mum,' continued Cyril bitterly, 'well, she soon met up wiv someone else an' did a moonlight flit wiv 'im. Seems she din't want no kid 'angin' round 'er. In any case, Mike's bin far better off wiv me.'

'I'm sure he has,' said Ruth. Although she found it useful to glean this first-hand information about Mike Buller, she was more interested in gaining access to the boy. 'I was wondering,' she asked tentatively, 'if it would be possible for me to have a few words with your grandson. Is he around, by any chance?'

'Young Mickey?' asked Cyril. 'Yes, course 'e is! 'E works fer me, so 'e'd better be! Well, 'e will be 'til 'e gets 'is papers. Cryin' shame wot they do to our boys these days – draggin' 'em off when they're in the middle of learnin' a good trade. Why don't yer just nip out the back? 'E's gettin' ready fer one of our new customers.'

Ruth shivered and hesitated.

Cyril grinned. 'Don't worry,' he said, with a

124

mischievous twinkle in his eye. 'Young Mickey don't work wiv the stiffs. 'E's on the boxes. 'E's a chippie – an' a darn good 'un at that! Foller me.'

He came out from behind the reception counter, and Ruth followed him back into the mews outside. 'Can't keep up wiv the business these days,' groaned Cyril. 'Yer should've bin 'ere durin' the Blitz. My Chapel er Rest couldn't cope wiv 'em all – in an out er this place like a dose er salts! Yer'll find young Mickey in the workshop back there,' he said, pointing to what looked like an old shed at the back of the building. 'Tell 'im from me ter get a move on wiv that box. I've got anuvver customer comin' in at 'alf-past two!'

Then Cyril disappeared back inside the funeral parlour, leaving Ruth to make her own way to the shed at the bottom of the mews. When she got there, she found the doors wide open, so she peered in to see several heavy oakwood coffins propped up against the walls, and a carpenter's workshop, where one tall, gaunt-faced man in overalls was just finishing off a newly made coffin with a coat of dark varnish. Ruth's attention was soon drawn to the other man nearby, bare-chested, fag dangling from his lips, who was busily smoothing down the lid of another coffin with a long carpenter's plane.

The older man was the first to notice Ruth standing in the doorway. ''Allo,' he said, sweat pouring down his face. 'We got company.'

The younger man looked round. His face immediately lit up. It was Mike Buller. 'Ruth!' he called. He put down his plane, wiped his hands on his work trousers, then came across to her.

125

'Fanks fer comin'. It's good ter see yer.'

Ruth stiffened. 'Can I have a word with you?' she said curtly. 'In private.'

Mike grinned, and called across to the other man, 'Be right back, Jimbo.'

Jimbo grinned back. 'Take yer time,' he replied.

Ruth allowed Mike to lead her outside. The moment they were on their own, however, she was given no time to say any of the things she'd been churning over in her mind on the way.

'I'm really pleased yer came,' Mike said, looking her up and down. 'Yer look t'rrific.'

'Now look—' Ruth began, trying to fend him off. But for the moment, at least, she couldn't get a word in edgeways.

'Did yer like my letter?' he asked. 'I like writin'. Always 'ave done since I was a kid. Did yer like the way I wrote your name on the envelope? Ancient script they call it. My grandad taught me. It's 'is 'obby. 'E knows all about letterin' an' fings...'

'Mike!'

He was quite taken aback by the way she had shut him up.

Ruth took a deep breath. 'Why have you been trying to make contact with me?' she asked, calmly and reasonably.

Mike shrugged. 'It's not against the law, is it?' he asked, puzzled by the question.

'No,' countered Ruth, 'but harassing someone is. You have no right to go asking for me at my mother's shop. You have no right to come looking for me at my own home.'

'I wasn't 'arassin' yer,' insisted Mike, who

126

looked quite hurt. 'I knew yer wasn't 'ome. I just wanted yer ter 'ave my letter.'

'I don't *know* you, Mike,' Ruth said firmly.

'I don't know you eivver,' replied Mike, 'but I'd like to. Is that such a crime?'

Ruth sighed with frustration. 'Mike,' she said, trying to reason with him, 'I want you to know that I'm very grateful for what you did that night, for saving my life, and – well, for everything. But I've said nothing to you, have I, that's given you any reason to think that–'

'Is there anyfin' wrong,' Mike said, looking directly at her, 'wiv *likin'* someone?'

'You know nothing about me,' retorted Ruth, 'so how can you *like* me?'

'As a matter er fact, I know quite a *lot* about yer,' he replied mischievously. 'More than yer fink.'

Despite her irritation, Ruth found the boy utterly distracting, and it took all her effort not to notice the small beads of sweat, which were slowly trickling down from his forehead onto his perfectly formed cheekbones and lean upper torso. 'Please don't talk like that,' she said unconvincingly. 'You have no right to pursue me. You should not have written that letter to me.'

'I meant every word.'

'Mike, stop it!' snapped Ruth.

'I don't understand,' said Mike, confused. 'Wot don't yer like about me?'

Ruth was beginning to think the boy was either stupid or just plain arrogant. 'Whether I like you or not has nothing to do with it,' she said, 'but your following me around everywhere is a problem for me, and it has to stop. It may interest you to know that when Tom gets home, we're going to get married.'

'An' wot 'appens if 'e *don't* get 'ome?'

Ruth felt a sudden swell of anger. 'Don't you dare say such things to me!' she said, eyes blazing.

Mike seemed genuinely startled by her reaction. 'All I'm sayin' is, yer've gotta be realistic. After all, there's a war on. I'll be getting me own call-up papers soon. Who knows if *I'll* ever get back 'ome again.' He took off his cap, and wiped his forehead with it. 'It's just that, at times like this, I don't fink people should waste the chance ter get ter know each uvver. I mean, let's face it – we're a long time dead, ain't we? But if that's wot yer want, it's okay wiv me.'

Ruth was suddenly aware of how vulnerable he was. 'Mike,' she said, trying not to sound too harsh, 'I'm very grateful for what you did at the warehouse the other day. As a matter of fact, I think you're a – very nice person. But you must realise that I have a life of my own to live, and I must ask you to respect that.' Ruth turned, and was about to move away.

'Yer've got an accent.'

Ruth stopped, and looked at him.

'That's the first time I've noticed it,' said Mike, a faint smile on his face. 'I like it. I really like it. Yer've got a beautiful voice, Ruth. 'As anyone ever told yer?'

Ruth felt a sudden flush.

'Makes yer sound – kind er diff'rent ter all the people I know.'

For one brief moment, Ruth accidentally met his eyes. But she quickly looked away again. 'Goodbye, Mike,' she said recklessly, before going on her way down Jessop Place and, without looking back, disappearing round the corner out of sight.

In Mare Street, Ruth leapt onto the first bus that came along. A few minutes later, her instincts betrayed her, for it was clearly the last thing she had wanted to do.

Father Timothy O'Leary sipped from a glass of Bella's homemade rhubarb wine, and felt the warmth from it flow through his ageing veins. Despite his thick flock of pure white hair, he had such a massive frame that Bella Whitlock had once remarked that he should have been a wrestler rather than a parish priest. Nonetheless, he was a good priest, and someone whom Bella had come to trust over the years, particularly after the traumatic death of her husband, when Ruth had been responsible for having her father's remains cremated, which was in direct contradiction to the teachings of the Roman Catholic Church.

Father O'Leary, an amiable Irishman with a twinkle in his eye and a fondness for a glass of anything from home-made wine to hard liquor, had been parish priest at St Anthony's Church for over twenty-five years, and during that time he had not only come to know his 'children', as he called Catholic parishioners, but had also made five converts from the Anglican faith which, by his reckoning, was 'not a bad score'.

129

However, the prospect of this particular convert was, if Bella was to be believed, going to be a little more complicated than the others.

'But are y'sure this boy of Ruth's,' said Father Tim, in his soft Irish burr, 'is goin' ter be a willin' partner to all this? I mean, has he agreed to give up his Anglican vows ter come over to the opposition?'

Bella sat up straight in her armchair in the sitting room in front of the fireplace, lips pursed with Polish determination. 'If he wants to marry my daughter, then he has no choice,' she replied adamantly.

'Ah!' returned Father Tim. 'But yer see he *does* have a choice, doesn't he, Bella? That's the problem. That's always the problem. Two sides of a fence.' He put his wine glass down on the small table at his side, clasped his knees with both hands, and leaned towards Bella. 'Have yer thought what might happen if the male party concerned wants it the other way around?'

Bella looked puzzled. 'I don't follow you, Father.'

'Suppose he wants our young Ruth to climb over his side of the fence?'

Bella was horrified by such a suggestion. 'Father!' she exclaimed. 'How can you even think of such a thing?'

'Oh, but I can,' replied Father Tim, scratching the back of his head, which was a habit of his. 'I remember taking Jamie Watson through the catechism when *he* wanted to marry Betty Doyle. Kicked up one hell of a fuss, I can tell ye. He said he was the man, and a man's position in life was ter be the dominant partner, and that if Betty Doyle wanted to marry him, she should not expect him ter go back ter school ter learn things that didn't concern him, and that if she wanted a Catholic husband, then she should look else- where. It was terrible, terrible! They finished up gettin' married – God preserve us – in a Register Office! Betty's poor mother and father disowned the girl.'

Bella looked pale and strained. She got up from her chair, and went to look out of the window, which had been opened to allow some air into the room. 'Ruth is going to marry Tom Phillips, Father,' she said solemnly. 'I give you my word on it.' She turned and looked back at him. 'She *has* to.'

The priest's bushy white eyebrows were immediately raised in alarm. 'Oh dear,' he said. 'How far gone is she?'

Bella shook her head. 'No, no – it's nothing like that,' she said, reassuring him as well as herself. 'It's far more difficult than that.' She returned to her chair, and sat facing him. 'I'm sure you know that my relationship with Ruth has not always been ... easy,' she said. 'The trouble is, she never really loved her father, and I never respected her for it. Oh, Harry was partly to blame. Right from when she was old enough to leave school, he watched her all the time. He wanted her to do all the things *he* had never been able to do himself, and when she wouldn't do so, he made her life intolerable. In some ways, I blame myself. I took Harry's part. Ruth had no one to turn to except – except the kind of people we never wanted her

131

to mix with. Just before Harry died, Ruth was in grave danger of getting into trouble – all kinds of trouble. There were boys ... lots of them. Ruth is a very desirable girl, and they were looking for just one thing. I tried talking to her. I told her that taking it out on her father in that kind of way was harmful – harmful not only to us, but to herself. But she wouldn't listen. When he died, she didn't even want to come to his funeral! I hated her for that. However, as you know, she *did* come. But when it was all over, despite knowing how much I wanted Harry to have a good Catholic burial, it was she who persuaded me to have him cremated. I know how distressed you were about that at the time, but she said that it was the right thing to do, that it was far less upsetting than going through a burial service, and that it was probably what her father would have wanted in any case. Unfortunately, I was too upset myself to argue, because Harry was stupid enough not to leave a will. But this hatred Ruth had for her father...' she sighed, and sat back in her chair, 'it made her so bitter, so unlike the sweet person I know she really is. I can't tell you how much all these things have upset me – refusing to take his name, refusing to release his ashes. It's a terrible thing, Father – terrible.'

Father Tim listened in quiet despair.

'And now, Father,' Bella continued, 'I'm even more concerned. Concerned that Ruth may be going back to her old ways. I can't be sure, of course, but – someone came to see her in the shop last week. He said they knew each other. What I don't know is – how well. Ruth says he

isn't a friend, jus
life when there was
ditch, or something lik
ing unnecessarily, but I jus
it.'

'How d'ye know she's not t
asked Father Tim. 'After all, if the
her life, then surely there's no har
meeting again?'

'He wrote her a letter. He left it at the h
when nobody was here.'

Father Tim was watching her carefully. Although he had known Bella a long time, he was
only too aware she could sometimes be a little
heavy-handed when dealing with her daughter.
He also knew that Bella and Ruth had often
quarrelled with each other, especially when it had
anything to do with Ruth's past life, which he had
to agree had often been a cause of great concern.
His mind began racing. Only a year before, Ruth
had become involved with a much older man
with whom she had become absolutely infatu-
ated. He remembered talking to her about it in
the Confessional, and how difficult it had been
for him to make the girl realise that she was
following a dangerous path. He knew, from what
Ruth had told him, that the man had wanted her
for one reason, and one reason alone. He also
remembered the others – the street boys she had
mixed with, and the time two of them had, at her
own admittance, tried to force their attentions on
her. And yet, even though she had turned her
back on those ways, Ruth had never actually
denounced the type of life she had once lived.

stranger
g up her
he told me
loves Tom

sting on the
gether in his
?' he asked.
r,' she replied.
ike you to talk

king his head. 'I
ter and I have a
with each other.

someone who helped save her
a bomb dropped in Shore-
that. Maybe I'm worry-
don't feel good about
llin' the truth?'
boy did save
in their
ouse

Remem̲ barely a child, when I begged her̲ made you to...' He gestured at the casket of ashes on the mantelpiece above him. 'Even though I told her it was a sin in the sight of God, to cremate a living thing that came from the earth, and which should be returned to the earth. I asked her how the ashes of her father's remains could ever rise up to meet his Maker, or how the trumpet would ever be able to sound on the Day of Judgement. It was so sad. She listened, but she never heard.'

Bella leaned forward in her chair. 'Talk to her, Father,' she pleaded. 'Ruth wants to marry Tom, I know she does. All she needs is the chance to start all over again.'

Father Tim sighed deeply. 'I'll try, my dear,' he said. He eased himself up from his chair. Bella got up at the same time. 'But remember, Ruth is her own person. It's not going to be easy.'

'Thank you, Father,' said Bella, as he took both

her hands, and shook them.

'Expect only what you receive, my dear,' he said. 'But I'll try. God knows, I *will* try.'

Ruth had a lot on her mind. After her meeting with Mike Buller in Hackney, she just couldn't understand why she wasn't more angry with him. There was no denying that he was good-looking, with those deep-set sparkling brown eyes, perfectly shaped nose, and dark brown hair that looked good whichever way it fell across his forehead. But then, Tom was just as good-looking, and he was much more rugged and strong than this boy, and she loved Tom, she loved him dearly, and when he came home she was going to marry him, and they were going to settle down and have a family, and she was going to live the sort of life that she had always wanted to live – no wild adventures, no silly mistakes. Yes, she told herself, Tom was her man, and she would wait for him no matter how long the war lasted. And yet there was something about Mike Buller – the sensitive way he talked, the way he could write a letter, and with such beautiful handwriting. He was clearly an interesting person, there was no doubt in her mind about that, but Tom was just as interesting, because he *wanted* her. And by the time she had got off the bus at Highbury Corner, she had dismissed Mike Buller from her mind once and for all.

As she had the whole afternoon free before the start of her evening shift, Ruth decided to enjoy some of the sun on Highbury Fields. When she got there she found hordes of people with the same idea, girls in bathing costumes, or flimsy summer dresses, men stripped to the waist, all stretched out on the vast area of public fields which reached out to Highbury Grove on one side and then right up to Highbury Hill on the way to Finsbury Park in the distance. She strolled slowly past the public swimming pool, which, despite the shortage of water, was crowded with happy revellers, basking in the sunshine, children screeching with delight as they leapt in and out of the shallow end, and nearly everyone sporting red blotches on their faces and bodies from too much sunbathing. As she strolled, Ruth passed the Air Raid Post, almost completely submerged beneath a mountain of sandbags, and the ARP warden himself sweltering in his tin helmet and uniform, only too aware that with hit and run air raids always a possibility, his services could be called on at a moment's notice.

She eventually made her way to a mobile tea canteen, where she joined a long queue which had formed for cold drinks and cups of tea. By this time, her dress was sticking to her back, and she was only too relieved that the queue was winding beneath the shade of a long row of enormous chestnut trees. However, she had only been queuing for a few minutes when something caught her eye some distance away, near the exit to Highbury Crescent and the tall Edwardian houses beyond. In between the throng of strollers, she saw two figures sitting together on a park bench, engaged in what seemed to be a heated argument. One of them was a middle-aged man in naval officer's uniform, the other was Sweetie, and Ruth could see she was in some kind of distress. Ruth immediately abandoned the queue, and hurried across to see what was going on, but before she could get anywhere near, the naval officer stormed off and disappeared in the direction of Highbury Hill. By the time Ruth had reached Sweetie, her young friend was in tears.

'Sweetie!' she called, as she approached.

Sweetie looked up with a start, tears streaming down her cheeks.

'What is it?' cried Ruth anxiously, sitting down beside her on the bench. 'What's happened?'

Embarrassed, Sweetie quickly tried to contain herself. 'It's all right,' she sniffed. 'I'm all right. Nothing to worry about.'

'What are you talking about?' asked Ruth, agitated. 'Just look at you. What's happened? Who *was* that man that was with you?'

'It's nothing, sweetie,' insisted Sweetie, taking a deep breath as she talked. 'I promise you, it's all right.' But the moment she saw Ruth staring at her with such anxiety she could no longer hold back what she was feeling. Covering her face with her hands, she broke down, dropped forward, and buried her head in her lap. 'Oh Christ!' she sobbed. 'I can't bear it! I'm such a bloody, stupid fool!'

Aware that people were watching them from nearby, Ruth put her arm around Sweetie's shoulders, and held on to her. 'It's all right, Sweetie. Everything's going to be all right. Just take your time.'

It took Sweetie several minutes to recover, and when she did her make-up was smudged all over her face. 'I hate him, Ruth,' she said, addressing Ruth by her real name for the first time in ages. 'I can't tell you how much I hate him.'

Using her own handkerchief, Ruth dabbed Sweetie's eyes, and with the tips of her fingers, tidied the unruly lock of hair that had dropped across Sweetie's forehead. 'Tell me,' she said, with calm affection.

Sweetie composed herself, and leaned back on the bench. 'I hardly know him, Ruth,' she said, taking Ruth's handkerchief and using it to wipe her own nose. 'I hardly know the man, and yet I allow him to ruin my life.'

Ruth felt her stomach tense.

'I met him about four months ago,' continued Sweetie, with difficulty. 'Four months – and I don't even know his surname.' She took another deep breath. 'And yet, I trusted him. I really thought that for the first time in my life I'd met someone who cared for me.' She stared out solemnly at the summer crowds bustling around all over the fields. 'It's strange, isn't it?' she said. 'To be my age and to feel that I've already lived an entire lifetime.' She paused a moment, then said quite out of the blue: 'I'm going to have a baby.' Ruth froze.

'Yes, I know,' continued Sweetie, 'absurd, isn't it? To think that someone like me could be so idiotic, so utterly idiotic. I mean, since the war started, you hear this sort of thing all the time, and yet – I never once thought I would fall into the same trap: serviceman home on leave, wants company, wants more than just company, wants what every man needs, every man takes, and every woman – or at least, quite a lot of women – are prepared to give. Why do we have to carry on as though we all only have a day or so to live?' She paused again. 'I can tell you,' she continued, 'the way I feel right now, I only wish to God I did only have a day or so to live.'

Ruth reached out for Sweetie's hand, and squeezed it.

'No, I mean it,' insisted Sweetie. 'I think I can truly say that I was born with a silver spoon in my mouth, anything I wanted just dropped in my lap. And yet – where has it got me? I live a pointless existence. My family have disowned me, they don't care whether I'm alive or dead, I live in a poky flat in a sordid little back street in Islington, and I fall for every male that wants to get me in bed with him. Believe me, it's all very well for me to criticise Mavis for the loose way she lives *her* life, but it's not a patch on me.' She turned and through swollen red eyes, grinned straight at Ruth. 'I'm a hopeless case, sweetie,' she said, with irony. 'Did you know that?'

'You're nothing of the sort,' replied Ruth, grabbing hold of both Sweetie's hands. 'What's happened to you can be put right. Nothing is hopeless. Remember that – nothing is hopeless at all.'

'He doesn't want any part of all this,' replied Sweetie. 'He just thinks I'm a damned fool, an easy lay – that it's my fault that I've got myself into this mess. How d'you deal with someone who hasn't a care for anyone else in the whole world except himself?'

'You stand on your own two feet,' replied Ruth, adding carefully, 'you could – if you wanted – get rid of the...'

'No,' replied Sweetie emphatically. 'You see, I want the child. I want someone I can truly call my own, someone who might one day actually *like* me.'

'Then in that case,' she said, reassuringly, 'you have nothing to worry about. If you want to have the baby, then I'll give you all the support I can.'

Sweetie beamed. 'Thank you,' she said. 'If there's one person in this world I can rely on, I know it's you. But unfortunately it's not quite as simple as that.' Her smile faded, and she looked up at the sun as its golden rays filtered through the glistening leaves of the chestnut trees. 'You see, I may *want* this baby, but if I do have it, I shall probably live to regret it for the rest of my life.'

'But why?' asked Ruth, who found it perplexing to know what Sweetie was getting at. 'There are plenty of women who have a child and no husband. This could be a wonderful new life for you.'

Even before Ruth had finished talking, Sweetie was already shaking her head. 'If only that were true,' she said with deep irony. 'If only that were true. But unfortunately, it's not. You see, I happen to be married already, and here I am – about to have a child by another man.'

Chapter 7

By the autumn of 1943, the war in Europe was taking a decisive turn. British and American planes were bombing targets in Germany on a daily basis, troops of the Eighth Army and its allies had made a landing on the Italian island of Sicily, and by September of the same year, the Italian dictator Benito Mussolini had resigned, leaving Italy itself on the brink of capitulation. However, the war in the Far East continued unabated, and the British troops who were fighting out there against the Japanese under the command of Field Marshal Sir William Slim were struggling against the most appalling living conditions, especially in the steaming hot jungles of Malaya and Thailand. There were rumours that British prisoners-of-war were being savagely ill-treated by their captors, and were beset with debilitating tropical diseases.

These rumours were particularly worrying for Ruth, for even though Tom's constant flow of air-mail letters were all heavily censored, it was perfectly clear to her that he was based somewhere out there in those hostile jungles. Fortunately, most of his letters were very upbeat, and he never stopped referring to the time when he would get home and pick up the threads of his life again with Ruth. But there were times also when Tom's remarks were quite disturbing, for they seemed to carry a warning that if he ever discovered that any man had laid so much as a finger on Ruth whilst he was away, he, Tom, would *have his guts for garters!* That question, however, did not arise, when in the first month of the following year Tom's letters stopped coming, which prompted her to make one of her rare calls on the Phillips family.

''Aven't 'eard from Tom fer nearly a month now,' said Ken Phillips, wrapped up in his heavy navy-blue duffel coat, woollen scarf, flat cap, and gumboots. Saturday afternoons were his favourite time for working on his allotment at the back of his garden; it gave him a chance to get away from the boredom of his job at the Town Hall, and also from the humdrum everyday conversations with his own wife. ''Is mum's gettin' into a bit of a state about it, but I keep tellin' 'er ter keep calm. It's probably the Army post. It's always gettin' 'eld up.'

'I'm not so sure,' replied Ruth, herself wrapped up in a heavy top coat and synthetic fur hat. 'A month is an awful long time not to hear from Tom. He's always written to me at least once a week.'

'You're lucky then,' said Phillips, leaning on his spade. 'Most we ever 'eard was once in a blue moon.' He went back to his digging, which was hard work on such a bitterly cold day, for the watery sun had only just managed to thaw the overnight frost, and the soil was as hard as iron.

Ruth hadn't expected her future father-in-law to be quite so unconcerned about his son's welfare, and she was beginning to wish that Tom's

142

mother Pearl had been home so that she could get a more reasoned response about what they should all do next. 'I was wondering,' she said tentatively, 'whether there was someone in the Army we could telephone or write to. I know everything's top security and all that, but there must surely be someone who can tell us whether Tom is alive or dead.'

Phillips looked up with a start. 'Alive or dead?' he asked, surprised. 'Yer really fink somefin's 'appened to Tom?'

'No, I'm not saying that, Mr Phillips,' Ruth said quickly. 'All I'm saying is that it would put all our minds at rest if we knew why we hadn't heard from him.'

Phillips briefly took off his cap and wiped his forehead with it. 'Well, yer know wot I fink?' He replaced his cap. '*I* fink we're all gettin' worked up over nuffin'. I'll bet yer one or the uvver of us'll get a letter right out of the blue – when we least expect it. And I bet yer it turns out that 'e's bin out on manoeuvres or somefin'. Don't worry, if I know my son, 'e'll write if 'e wants somefin'. Oh yes!'

Again, Ruth thought he was being a bit callous. 'Do *you* ever write to Tom, Mr Phillips?' she asked, quite pointedly.

'*Me?*' asked Phillips, surprised. 'Gawd 'elp us – no! I leave all that stuff ter the missus. In any case, I wouldn't know wot ter say to 'im. I've never bin much of a letter-writer meself. Too much of a chore.' He paused a moment, during which his eyes casually met hers.

Ruth thought his look had lingered too long.

Embarrassed, she quickly looked away.

'Yer know,' said Phillips, watching her carefully, 'you ought ter pop in an' 'ave a cuppa wiv me up at the Town 'All some time. Borough councillors usually work from 'ome, but they let me 'ave a desk up there fer a coupla days each week.' He watched for her reaction. 'You're practically next door at the fire-station, so – wot d'yer say?'

Ruth suddenly felt uncomfortable and tongue-tied. Fortunately she had no need to answer, for Pearl Phillips's voice suddenly called from the garden gate: 'Ruth! Oh thank goodness you came.'

As Ruth went to meet her, Phillips immediately returned to his digging.

'Are you worried too?' asked Pearl, who was wrapped up in a heavy woollen cardigan, head-scarf, and rubber galoshes. 'Yer 'aven't 'eard from 'im, 'ave yer?' she asked anxiously. 'Yer 'aven't 'eard from Tom?'

Ruth shook her head. 'No, I'm afraid I haven't, Mrs Phillips. I was just asking your husband if *you'd* heard?'

'Not a thing. Not for over a month. I'm so worried, Ruth. I'm so worried.'

Ruth thought the poor woman was looking more strained than she had ever seen her. Tom had always said that at the best of times his mother was a bit on the nervous side, but by the looks of her, she had clearly been having sleepless nights.

'They were saying in the greengrocers that the war out East is getting much worse.' Pearl's remarks seemed to be directed at her husband,

144

who was busily breaking down a clump of hard earth with his spade. 'They say the Japanese are far too cruel and strong to beat, and that the war with them could go on for years.'

'Oh, I'm sure that's not true,' said Ruth reassuringly. 'Once the Allies have finished with the Germans, they'll be able to divert all their power against the Japanese.'

'By then it could be too late,' insisted Pearl. 'At least for Tom.'

'Why don't you go and make some tea, Pearl?' said Phillips, without looking up from what he was doing. 'It'll calm yer down.'

Pearl was about to answer him when Ruth gently took hold of her arm, and moved off with her back towards the house. 'I can't help it,' Pearl said, turning to give Ruth an anxious look as they went. 'I've brought two children into this world, and if anything should happen to either of them, I wouldn't know how to cope.'

Ruth slipped a comforting arm around Pearl's waist. 'Don't you worry now, Mrs Phillips,' she said. 'Nothing's going to happen to Tom. I'm sure we'll hear from him any day now.'

Pearl brought them to a halt halfway down the garden. 'I do so want you for my daughter-in-law, Ruth,' she said affectionately. 'You're the best thing that could have ever happened to Tom – and for our family.'

They embraced.

'You mustn't think too badly about Ken, you know,' she said, turning to look back at her husband. 'He may seem uncaring at times, but I can assure you he loves both his children just as

145

much as I do.'

Ruth wasn't so sure. In the short time she had been talking with Ken Phillips, she had found him to be someone who cared little for anyone but himself.

Sweetie was now just over seven months 'gone'. However, once she had been forced to quit the Fire Service before Christmas, her life, thanks in part to Ruth, had taken on a new and more practical direction. It made no difference that she had not heard from her naval officer since the day he had walked out on her in Highbury Fields, because she was determined to have his baby whether he was prepared to support her or not.

Unfortunately, her biggest problem still remained: how to break the news about her pregnancy to the man she had married only a year before, when he finally returned home from the war – whenever that might be. But until that time came, she was content to potter around her small, one bedroom flat on the top floor of a grubby Victorian house near Dalston Junction, earning a few shillings a week sticking labels on envelopes for a mail order company, and another few shillings making cotton table mats on a wooden frame for a local Chinese trader. Life was not exactly hard, but finding fuel for the fireplace, and heaving what felt like a ten-ton weight in her stomach up and down five flights of stairs was proving to be quite a challenge.

'God, Sweetie!' Ruth said the moment Sweetie had opened the flat door to her. 'You're getting to be as fat as a house! When are you going to stop growing?'

'Not until this little brute stops kicking my insides to pieces,' replied Sweetie. 'Feels as though he's going to be a football player.'

Ruth laughed. 'What happens if it's a girl?'

Sweetie hesitated. 'Then perhaps she'll have more consideration for her mother. Which is more than I ever got from my husband.' She went across to the polished, gate-legged table. 'Mind you, it wouldn't be any different if it was Johnston's baby. It's my own fault. I should never have married him, I know that. But I met him soon after I was kicked out by my mother and father. He was a means of escape, I suppose, a shoulder to lean on. Unfortunately, it turned out to be a pretty hard shoulder.'

Sweetie's bitter remark did not go unnoticed by Ruth. The more she thought about the dreadful predicament Sweetie had got herself into, the heavier the feeling inside her own stomach. She took off her topcoat and threw it over the back of a chair. 'Any word from him?' she asked.

Sweetie shook her head. 'Nothing.'

'How long is it now? Two months – three?'

'About two and a half,' replied Sweetie, sitting at the table, which was covered with hundreds of gummed labels waiting to be stuck on just as many envelopes. 'Nothing since that letter in November – for all the good *that* was. All he could write about was the good time we were supposed to have had at that bloody wedding reception with his mates at the pub in Bethnal Green. He got so drunk he doesn't even remember that he fell asleep on me in bed on our so-called wedding night. God! I *must* be mad!'

After warming her hands by the fire, Ruth went across to Sweetie and joined her at the table. 'Have you ever thought about telling him what's happened – in a letter, I mean?'

Sweetie shook her head vigorously. 'No,' she replied adamantly. 'If I owe him anything at all, it's the right to have him told face to face. I may not love the fool, but I did marry him. I like to think there's still a vestige of integrity left in me.'

Ruth sighed anxiously. 'Aren't you worried about how he's going to react?'

'Worried?' asked Sweetie. 'Of course I'm worried. Johnston is a man who never listens to what anyone says but himself. There are no half ways with him. If he wants to beat the living daylights out of me, then I'll just have to put up with it. But I won't lie to him, sweetie. I just won't.'

Johnston. Every time she heard that name, Ruth found it difficult to understand why a wife should want to call her husband by his surname. Why not Derek, or 'dear' or 'darling' – or anything that would show even a modicum of affection? But as she glanced around the poky rented flat, with its appalling lack of any kind of taste, sparse junk furniture, tattered lace curtains, a broken over-head light shade, and a stifling smell of cigarette smoke, she began to realise that affection had never really seemed to play any part in Sweetie's life; for some unknown reason, Sweetie was incapable of giving or receiving it. It was beyond her reach. *Johnston.* Why did she have to fall for a man nearly twenty years older than herself? Why did she *always* fall for men so much older than she was? Was it because she craved protection, someone she could look up to? Was it because her father had never held her in his arms and told her that he loved her just as much as her two elder brothers, whom he admired so much? Or was it really because she had never had anyone to guide her through her life, to show her what was right and wrong, to take an interest in her? *Johnston.* It was a name that Ruth had grown to loathe and despise. Why did she, Sweetie, have to lie about being married to this man, Ruth asked herself? Why did Sweetie never cry out for help?

'Anyway,' said Sweetie, 'we've talked enough about me. What news of Tom? Have you heard from him yet?'

Ruth shook her head. 'Not a word. I went to see his parents today. They haven't heard either.'

'D'you think something's happened to him?'

Sweetie's direct question gave Ruth quite a jolt, and made her face up to what she feared most. 'I don't know,' she replied with a sigh. 'It's the uncertainty that's so hard to deal with. If only someone could tell us where he is, what he's doing, then at least I'd know what he's up against.'

Even for Ruth, who was someone she really cared for, Sweetie's powers of concentration were limited. 'What about Mike, that boy who was becoming a bit of a pain, the one who kept following you around?' she asked, using a damp sponge on the table as she resumed sticking gummed addressed labels to a pile of envelopes.

149

'He's never tried to make contact with you again?'

For some reason or other, the mention of Mike Buller's name made Ruth's heart miss a beat. 'Oh, *him*,' she replied with very little concern. 'No,' she said. 'I suspect he's got his call-up papers by now. I haven't heard a word from him.'

'That's a shame,' said Sweetie. 'I seem to remember you telling me that he was actually quite a nice person.'

Ruth tried not to react. 'Really?' she asked casually. 'Did I say that?'

Sweetie grinned mischievously. 'Uh huh,' she replied.

For one brief moment, Ruth felt uncomfortable. 'Well, he probably is,' she replied casually. 'But Tom's a nice person too, and I happen to love him.'

'Of course, sweetie,' said Sweetie, none too convinced. As she spoke, she felt a sudden sharp pain from the baby kicking inside her. 'Stop it, you little brute!' she gasped, clutching her stomach. 'You just wait. One of these days I'll get my own back on you!'

Ruth laughed. 'Poor Sweetie!' she said.

Sweetie flopped back in the chair until she'd recovered. 'Oh well, I suppose I shouldn't complain. If this little monster is a boy, perhaps Johnston won't make too much of a fuss about it. Anyway, who cares? Live for today, say I. Let tomorrow take care of itself!'

Tub Trinder's shop in Hornsey Road was so small, even his pet moggie Cadger had only just enough room to sit in the window all day. However, no matter how small the premises, Tub Tinder was considered to be one of the best tailors in the district, and during these difficult days of wartime rationing, his services were always on call for repairs to clothes that had seen better days even during the First War. His old Singer sewing-machine had also seen better days, but despite the fact that it had broken down at least a dozen times during the past year or so, and despite the fact that Cadger absolutely loathed the sound of the monster machine, Tub would no more get rid of his 'old faithful' than Cadger would stop growling and hissing at every passer-by who stopped to talk to him through the window from outside.

Edie Perkins was one of Tub's 'regulars'. She freely admitted that if there was one thing she couldn't do properly in this world, it was sewing, so whenever she wanted anything that required a needle and cotton, then Tub's was the place to bring it. On more than one occasion she had brought in a pair of knickers that needed a new elastic waistband; she assured Tub she had washed them thoroughly first. Much to Edie's irritation, he always referred to her knickers as 'passion-killers', and as he was a married man, he wasn't in the least embarrassed by them. Of course Edie also used Tub's place as a pretext for having a bit of a gossip with any other customer who might have been there at the time. Today, she was fortunate enough to find Bella Whitlock there, which gave her the chance to pass on her latest bit of earth-shattering news.

151

Bella was shocked to hear from Edie that Rita Simmons had been rushed off to hospital in the middle of the night a couple of days before. 'How absolutely terrible. What's the matter with her?'

'Pains in 'er stomach was all *I* 'eard,' said Edie. 'Very severe pains,' she insisted, lowering her voice as though she was afraid someone outside might hear her. 'Ted said she must've bin in sheer agony.'

Tub continued writing out a receipt for Bella's order – one of Ruth's skirts which needed a seam replaced. He had never had much time for Rita Simmons, whom he once called 'an ol' cow' to her face after she'd told him that the best tailors were Jews, from which time she vowed never to set foot inside his shop again, to which he duly replied that with her stomach she'd never be able to *get* inside his shop again anyway.

'But there must have been some reason for it?' suggested Bella. 'Was it something she ate – food poisoning perhaps?'

'Who knows?' replied Edie. 'Yer can't get much out of Ted. 'E's very cagey about it all. Anyway, she's 'ome now, no doubt lyin' in bed bein' waited on 'and an' foot by that poor man.'

'Like the Queen er bleedin' Sheba!' quipped Tub, his spectacles dangling on the end of his nose as he completed Bella's receipt.

'That's unkind, Tub,' said Edie, agreeing with every word he said. 'When will my order be ready?' she asked formally, without reference to what her order actually was.

'Can't remember wot yer brought,' he said, rummaging around the mountain of repair work

152

spread all over his tiny counter. 'Oh yes,' he said as he found what he was looking for. 'Emline on one dress, and one lady's bra...'

Embarrassed by Tub's tactlessness, Edie looked away.

'Try Tuesday,' he said.

'Tuesday!' gasped Edie.

'Can't promise though,' said Tub. 'Got all this stuff ter get fru before then.'

Behind her, Cadger growled and hissed at some kids who were making faces at him through the window.

Tub yelled at them. 'Bugger off!' The kids disappeared fast, laughing and screeching as they went.

'Isn't there something we can do for poor Mrs Simmons?' asked Bella. 'It seems a little heartless to just leave her there alone whilst her husband goes off to work every day.'

Edie stiffened. 'Oh, don't you worry about Rita,' she sniffed, haughtily. 'Rita knows 'ow ter take care of 'erself.'

'Yer can say that again,' sneered Tub, handing Bella her receipt. 'All she needs is anuvver mouf-ful er razor blades. She'll soon sharpen up 'er bleedin' tongue agin!'

'Don't go worryin' yerself, Bella dear,' said Edie, ignoring Tub's acid remarks. 'Ted's left me the front door key, so I'll be goin' round ter see 'er meself later on. In any case, after all the fings she's said about your Ruth, yer should just ignore 'er.'

'About Ruth?' she asked, eyes glaring.

Tub quickly retreated to his sewing machine at

the back of the shop.

'Oh, you know wot Rita's like,' said Edie, flustered and wishing she hadn't opened her mouth. 'She's always going on about someone.'

'She has said things about Ruth before,' insisted Bella. 'What is she saying now?'

The way Bella was staring her out was reason enough for Edie to know that she now had to explain what she had just said. 'Rita's bin tellin' people,' she said falteringly, 'only a few people, mind, she's bin tellin' them that now Ruth ain't 'eard from Tom for a while ... she said that ... Ruth...'

'Yes?' demanded Bella. 'Ruth?'

'...is back to 'er ol' tricks again.'

A few minutes later, Bella was striding back towards Jackson Road. She wanted to get to that woman, she wanted to have it out with Rita Simmons once and for all. How dare she blacken Ruth's name in such a way, she fumed to herself over and over again. How *dare* she suggest that Ruth was being unfaithful to the boy whom she had assured Father O'Leary time and time again that she loved. As she turned the corner from Holloway Road into Jackson Road, she had so much anger and malice for Rita that it suddenly made her come to a stop. For several minutes, she stood there, quite still, waiting for the rage to abate. It was bitterly cold, and she could feel the first few drops of freezing drizzle on her face, and see thick black smoke billowing up from chimney pots all along the road. Was it worth it, she asked herself? Several months before, she had already given Rita Simmons a warning about her

154

malicious gossip, but it had clearly made little or no difference at all. Would it make any difference now? Would someone like this *ever* change her ways? No, of course she wouldn't, because she was incapable of doing so. Malicious gossip was a disease, just like TB or diphtheria. Rita Simmons was a sick person; she needed medical attention. No, Bella told herself, her time would come, and when it did, she would be ready for Rita Simmons. With that in mind, she slowly turned, and made her way back to her own shop.

Head covered with a scarf, and wrapped up in a warm winter coat, Ruth entered St Anthony's Roman Catholic Church, which was completely deserted. She went straight to the centre aisle, genuflected, crossed herself, then went to the statue of the Virgin Mary holding Baby Jesus at the front of the right-hand aisle. Once there, she took a half-crown coin from her coat pocket, and dropped it into the collection box. Then she picked out an unlit candle, lit it from one of the other candles already burning there, and placed it into its own holder. After crossing herself once more, she turned and went to the front pew, knelt on a padded cushion and clasped her hands together in prayer. Once she had said the Hail Mary, she spoke directly to the Virgin Mother. 'Dear Holy Mother,' she said, her whispered voice hissing gently in the echo of the ice-cold empty church, 'please intercede on my behalf. In all your heavenly mercy please find Tom, and keep him well and safe. Please let me hear from him. Please let him know that I love him, and will

155

wait for him, and that I long for the day when he can hold me again in his arms. This I beseech you, Holy Mother, in the name of the Father, the Son, and the Holy Ghost. Amen.'

'Amen.'

Ruth's eyes sprang open. She was startled to find Father Tim O'Leary kneeling at her side, hands clasped together in prayer. He crossed himself and opened his eyes, but directed his glance straight ahead towards the Host in the tabernacle. 'I'm sure your prayer will be answered, child,' he said, his soft Irish burr barely audible. 'The Holy Mother recognises the efforts ye've made.'

'I don't want to lose him, Father,' said Ruth. 'It's been over a month since I heard from him. I'm beginning to give up hope.'

'Ah,' said Tim, turning to look at her now, his hands, like hers, still clasped together. 'That you must never do. The day we give up hope, there's nothing left. Faith is God's gift, child. We must never forget that. Let's pray together in silence,' he said, closing his eyes again.

Ruth did likewise, and for a moment or so, they knelt there locked in mutual silent prayer. Eventually, Ruth, eyes still closed, said: 'Father, if anything *were* to happen to Tom, would it be a sin to love again?'

Father Tim hesitated before replying. 'To love is no sin, Ruth,' he said. 'God gives all His children the right to go on living, provided ... provided we're all true to ourselves.'

Ruth opened her eyes. She knew exactly what he meant. When she turned to look at him, he was smiling at her.

'If ye ask me,' he said, with that customary twinkle in his eye, 'you're worrying over nothin'. I'll bet that even by the time ye get home there'll be a letter waitin' for ye, tellin' ye all the things ye want ter hear.'

Ruth smiled back at him, hoping – and praying – that he was right.

They both got up from their kneeling position, and turned to face each other. 'Your mother's very proud of what ye've achieved these last months,' said Father Tim. 'And so am I. Believe me, I know the efforts ye've made. Overcoming the past is always a struggle, but ye've made it – I know ye have.' He walked quietly with her back along the aisle, then brought them both to a halt. 'But don't ferget,' he said softly, 'ye've still got one hurdle ter get over. It's goin' ter take more than prayer ter get one Catholic and one Anglican in the same church together.'

Ruth sighed, and lowered her eyes. 'I know, Father,' she said.

'Think ye can manage it?' he asked. 'No Register Office?'

Ruth grinned. 'I shall try, Father. I shall try very hard.'

Once they had both genuflected and crossed themselves, Ruth took her leave of Father Tim, and left the church. On her way home, she reflected on what Father Tim had been saying to her. If anything were to happen to Tom, would she ever be able to rebuild her life without returning to the past? She had a lot to dwell on, not least her astonishment at finding herself back

157

inside a church again after such a long time away. Could she really return to 'the fold'? Of course, her mother would thank God if she did. For the last few years Bella had constantly begged her daughter to 'come home' again to the Holy Mother, to the time when she was young, when she could believe in the power of faith. Ruth thought a great deal about faith, and how it had saved her mother from total despair when she had lost her husband's baby boy who was stillborn, a secret that she had kept all these years from every living soul. *Faith.* You didn't have to be religious, she told herself, to believe in something that you couldn't actually see. The truth was always out there. She could almost stretch out her hand and touch it.

By the time she had turned into Holloway Road, it gradually dawned on Ruth that it was snowing – nothing too heavy, just a slow sprinkling of flakes that fluttered down and settled gently on her scarf and shoulders. For some reason, it brought a smile to her face, something she hadn't really felt like doing when she first arrived at the church. The main reason, she imagined, was the sight of people rushing to and fro, straining to keep their balance on the slippery pavement, condensation gushing from their noses and mouths, turning a still picture into a very animated one. Father Tim was right – there *was* life out there – lots of it, everywhere she looked, the snow glistening on the pavements, the reds, the blues, the yellows, the greens – all the colours that people wore. Yes, and there was even life in that drab, grey old sky, hovering high

158

above the smoking chimney pots, and now leaking snowflakes faster than her feet could carry her. *Faith*. She couldn't see it, but she knew it was there. And she asked herself again how she could have turned her back on it for so long.

By the time she turned the corner into Jackson Road, her entire body was bending in the rapidly increasing wind that was driving snow straight into her, covering her with a dazzling blanket of white. She could hardly see the road ahead of her, and as she struggled to stay on her feet, she used one hand to shield her eyes from the snow. But as she did so, her eyes suddenly focused on something in the distance, along the now deserted road, something which at first seemed static and unreal, a vision, an illusion perhaps. She strained hard to see what it was that had started to make the blood in her veins start to pump hard, and warmth race through her body. A figure. A man's figure, almost lost in the haze of white, perched on a coping stone on the corner of the cul de sac where Ruth lived. Despite the risk of hurrying in the snow, she found her pace quickening. She was soon slipping and sliding all over the place, but when she finally managed to identify the figure in the distance, in Army uniform, and now getting up to greet her, she found herself yelling out at the top of her voice: 'Tom! Tom!' The figure in the snow opened his arms, and Ruth threw herself straight into them. 'Oh Tom!' she gasped over and over again, laughing and crying, holding him, hugging him. 'I thought you were dead! I thought I'd lost you!'

There was no response from the figure in the snow. Ruth slowly looked up to see a face blood-red with the cold. But it was not a familiar face; it was not the face she had expected to see, had yearned to see.

The face she was staring into was Mike Buller's.

Chapter 8

Rita Simmons stopped peering out from behind her net curtains and went back to bed. The past few minutes had been absolutely wonderful and she felt better already. She still felt very tired, of course – emotionally and physically drained, in fact. That small overdose of aspirin tablets which had landed her in hospital had been a stupid mistake, she kept telling herself. In future she would be much more careful. But what she had seen in the street outside had cheered her up no end. Blinding snow or no blinding snow, she knew perfectly well whom she had seen kissing and cuddling on the corner of Annette Road. So, young Poley was heartbroken, was she? Heart-broken that she hadn't heard from her so-called husband-to-be for over a month? Well, she won't be so heartbroken now, Rita thought to herself with a huge grin on her face, recalling the delectable picture of Ruth and her fancy man enjoying themselves together in the snow.

Rita struggled into bed, settled her head back

160

on the pillows, and closed her eyes. Her face was bathed in a huge self-satisfied smile. She had been right all along. She had always said that as far as that young Polish tart was concerned, there was no smoke without fire. Back to her old ways, back to taking anything in trousers that just happened to come along. Ammunition – Rita had plenty of it now. Just wait until she was up and about again, she said to herself with a deep, contented sigh. Oh yes, she was feeling better now. Much, much better.

The workmen's caff beneath the railway bridge in Holloway Road wasn't used to having strangers in its midst, especially when one of them was a young girl. However, since it was snowing hard outside, and the girl's companion was in the Army, the other customers moved over and left them alone together at one of the few grubby tables left in the small, overcrowded place. Drinking weak tea out of an enamel mug wasn't exactly Ruth's idea of living dangerously, but being seen in public with Mike Buller was. Once they had sat down, it was several minutes before they said anything to each other, for there were far too many winks and nods going on as the middle-aged navvies and labourers speculated on how many times the Tommy had got it up since he got home on leave. Fortunately, they were out of earshot and Ruth was therefore saved the embarrassment of their bawdy remarks, so she merely sipped her tea quietly until the snow-storm had eased off, and most of the workers had left. 'I told you never to make contact with me

161

again,' she said to Mike, the moment it was safe to start talking. 'Do you never listen?'

Sitting opposite her across the table, Mike could only manage a rare, awkward smile. 'I fawt about it,' he said, avoiding her look, and aimlessly rimming the top of his mug with the tips of his fingers. ''Onest ter God, Ruth, I fawt a lot about it, about wot yer said, 'ow yer felt.' He looked up at her. 'But I couldn't 'elp meself. I 'ad ter see yer. I 'ad ter see yer just once more before I go.'

'Go?' asked Ruth. 'Go where?'

'I've got one week's leave,' he replied. 'Off next week. Posting somewhere – dunno where. Somefin' big goin' on – dunno wot – not yet.'

As he lowered his eyes again, Ruth stared at him. There was something different about him. His long brown hair had been given a regulation Army cut which made him look fuller in the face since the last time she saw him, which was no bad thing, for it gave him a less boyish appearance. But there was also something different in his manner, in the way he looked and talked. 'Well, at least Army life appears to suit you,' she said. But the moment she had said it, she wished she hadn't.

Mike shrugged. 'Can't say I enjoy bein' a number,' he replied, 'but I've got some good mates. It'll 'elp when we 'ave ter go over the top.'

Ruth suddenly felt a twinge of guilt. 'Is that likely?' she asked.

He shrugged again. 'If we're ever goin' ter win this war, it'll 'ave ter come, sooner or later.'

Now it was Ruth's turn to feel awkward. Despite the fact that she had done her best to

162

keep this boy out of her life, it nonetheless gave her a sinking feeling to be talking to someone who could soon be risking his life in a foreign land. She quickly took a sip of her tea.

Mike did likewise. 'My grandad don't like the idea very much,' he said. ''E got gassed in the last war. 'E said 'e never wanted any of 'is kin ter go fru wot 'e 'ad ter go fru. It's funny, in't it? 'E don't turn a 'air when 'e 'as ter lay out dead people in their boxes. But when it comes to is own kind, it scares the – it scares 'im rigid.'

Ruth had no answer for that. But she knew how Mike's grandfather must feel. 'Could we go now, please?' she said, getting up from the table. 'The smoke in here is killing me.'

A few minutes later, they were back outside in the Holloway Road. It had stopped snowing, the wind had dropped, and the heavy grey sky was gradually giving way to the first glimmer of winter sunlight. For a few moments, they strolled in silence, up towards the bus stop outside the Northern Polytechnic. Once they got there, Mike first of all looked down towards the Nags Head to see if his bus was coming, and when he saw it wasn't, he turned to Ruth to say what he had really wanted to say.

'Ter tell yer the trufe, Ruth,' he said, 'I didn't mean ter come an' upset yer, I didn't mean ter make a pest er meself.' He put his hands in his Army greatcoat pocket, and gave her a warm, pleading smile. 'The reason I came,' he said, 'was becos' I wanted – becos' I just 'ad ter see yer one last time. It's like I said, I've fawt about yer a lot since I first met yer. Up at the barracks, I've bin goin' ter bed at night, an' before I go ter sleep, it's always *your* face I see...'

Ruth turned away. 'Please don't, Mike,' she begged, starting to walk off.

Mike immediately went after her and blocked her way. 'I came to say goodbye, Ruth,' he said. 'That's all.'

'Goodbye, Mike,' she replied. She tried to make it sound final, but the words didn't come out like that.

Mike stayed put. 'Yer know,' he said, 'when I was a kid, my grandad told me that life goes in a circle. People come, people go, but they always come tergevver again. They don't always know it, er course. Sometimes they pass each uvver in the street wivout knowin'. Sometimes they're on the same bus or tram goin' in the same direction, but gettin' off at diff'rent stops. But it's not always like that. Sometimes they *do* recognise each uvver in the street, sometimes they *do* get off at the same stop. Yer see, nuffin's for ever, Ruth. Nuffin's final. I hope when I get 'ome again, we'll get off the same bus at the same time, and that we'll actually like each uvver, and never want to be parted again.'

Ruth watched and listened to him with awe and disbelief. She found it incredible that someone like him could think and talk in such a way, a way that, when she first met him just a few months before, she would never have thought possible. During those few extraordinary moments, every part of her being wanted to throw her arms around him, to hug him, to embrace him. But as the fantasy disappeared, the reality quickly took its place.

'Mike,' she said tenderly, 'I love someone else. You've got to understand that, you've got to accept it.' She leaned forward, and kissed him softly on one cheek. 'Some things are meant. *This* is meant. Goodbye, Mike. Keep safe.' She turned and walked off.

At that moment, a bus slowly approached, struggling not to skid on the ice and slush. Mike waited just long enough to see Ruth striding off on the slippery pavement in the distance, then he hopped on the bus platform. For a brief few seconds, he stood there, clinging on to the platform rail, leaning out to watch Ruth for as long as he could.

Ruth moved on as fast as her feet would carry her. All her instincts told her to turn and take one last look at the young soldier boy she had left behind. But she couldn't do it. She just couldn't.

Mavis Miller, propped up in a wicker chair in the women's dormitory at the fire-station, was having great trouble with the blue patch. Although she was only using a simple plain loop, the two balls of wool were different shades, which made the patchwork quilt a bit of a shambles. But since it was her contribution to the forthcoming birth of Sweetie's baby, she was soldiering on regardless. 'If anyone 'ad ever told me that one day I'd be knittin' blankets fer a baby, I'd've told 'em ter go an' sod off!' she grumbled, as she dropped yet another loop, the fifth in the same row.

'Well, I think you're doing wonderful work,'

laughed Ruth. 'It's going to be such a great help for Sweetie. Think of all the things she's going to have to get when the baby arrives. And you're so clever to have found all these scraps of wool to do it.'

'Nuffin' ter do wiv me,' Mavis assured her. 'It was all me mum's idea. She just nicked one of me bruvver's old pullovers, a couple of pairs of Dad's old socks, two of her own old cardigans, and a knitted scarf she made fer 'erself years ago. All I can say is, it'd better be bleedin' worf it after all this!'

Ruth laughed, and continued working on her previous day's dispatch reports. Fortunately, there had been very few air raids over recent weeks, and even those were only hit and run attacks by little more than two or three enemy aircraft. Therefore, the two girls had plenty of time to themselves, other than the routine work of fire crew drills, station and fire-engine maintenance, and the constant cleaning and servicing of Ruth's motorcycle. If no one was exactly complacent, there was certainly a feeling amongst the station crews that, apart from a bit of 'mopping up' here and there, the worst of the war was over, which was probably the reason why Sweetie's old job on the switchboard had now been taken over by anyone who happened to be on duty at the time.

'I 'ad a letter from Charlie terday,' said Mavis, putting down her knitting. ''E reckons 'e might be gettin' a bit er leave soon. Mind you, 'e don't say when. All that part's censored. But I 'ope 'e don't come too soon. I'm enjoyin' meself far too

166

much!' She rocked with laughter.

Ruth, perched on the edge of her bed, was not so amused. 'For goodness' sake be careful,' she warned. 'Charlie may not take it too lightly if he finds out what you've been up to whilst he's been away.'

'See if *I* care!' sniffed Mavis, dismissively. ''Ow long am I expected ter wait fer 'im? This war could go on an' on. I bet *'e* ain't bin no saint while 'e's bin away – all them gels in the broffels an' wot 'ave yer!'

'You don't know that, Mavis,' replied Ruth, disapprovingly.

'Oh yes, I do!' insisted Mavis. 'Are you really tellin' me that all them hot-blooded males are goin' ter tie a knot in their wotnots 'til they get 'ome? Not on your nellie!' She got up, and threw her knitting down onto the chair. 'I bet your feller's dipped 'is wick a coupla times too!' She was about to go across to the locker at the side of her bed, when, suddenly realising what she had just said, she came to an abrupt halt. 'Oh Gawd,' she groaned, turning to look at Ruth. 'There I go again – always puttin' me big foot in it!' She went across to Ruth, sat beside her, and put her arm around her. 'I'm sorry, Rufe,' she said sheepishly. 'That was a stupid fing ter say – 'specially when yer 'aven't 'eard from Tom an' all that.' She leaned closer, and spoke with more tender care than she was used to. 'Yer *aven't* 'eard – 'ave yer?'

Ruth shook her head.

Mavis bit her lip. 'Well,' she said, awkwardly, 'don't you go worryin' yerself. I bet yer'll 'ear any moment now. I've 'eard of some fellers who don't write fer munffs on end, not just becos they're no good at writin', but becos they're too bleedin' lazy.' She realized only too well that as far as Ruth was concerned, her words were falling on deaf ears. 'As a matter er fact,' she went on, 'I wouldn't be at all surprised if 'e wasn't already on 'is way 'ome, an' 'e just wants ter catch yer on the 'op – give yer a big surprise. Oh, I can see the 'ole fing – the moment yer set eyes on 'im, yer'll rush straight inter 'is arms, then 'e'll give yer a big, wet juicy kiss, then before yer know it yer'll be settlin' down wiv 'im, the perfect little wife, 'ot meals on the table waitin' fer 'im every night, straight up ter bed...'

Ruth could take no more. She suddenly got up from the bed, and rushed straight out of the room.

Mavis, leaping to her feet, was totally shocked by Ruth's reaction. 'Ruth!' she called. 'What's up? Wot've I done *this* time?'

Upset, Ruth rushed straight down the stone steps leading to the station forecourt, where the main escape doors were left permanently open in case a sudden air raid prompted an immediate call-out. Several of the evening-duty pump crews were already kitted out in their fire-fighting gear, most of them either playing cards to pass the time, or checking out the pumps and engine ladders. Ruth managed to get out through a side door without, she hoped, being seen. It was a bitterly cold evening, and although she was only wearing a thick uniform jumper and trousers, she stood in the dark, leaning against a wall for

168

several minutes to bring herself back under control. All that nonsense Mavis had come out with about men and what they got up to whilst they were away had sickened her. Oh, she knew her friend had meant no harm, but what she had said had sown seeds of doubt in Ruth's mind, and on top of everything else, it was just too much to take. Tragically, however, what she was really finding difficult to accept was the image of herself as the wife of a man she didn't truly love. Why, she asked herself? She could deceive others, but why deceive herself? Hadn't she promised to dedicate her future life to Tom – isn't this what she had assured her mother, the solemn vow she had made to Father O'Leary? Her mind was in turmoil, her stomach tense with guilt. How, she asked herself, could she feel anything for someone she hardly knew, someone who had barged his way into her life in such a crude and untimely way? What was it about Mike Buller that caused her to doubt who and what she really wanted out of life?

As she looked up at the clear night sky, with a crescent-shaped moon glistening white, and stars clinging to the dark like precious jewels, questions came flying fast and furious. But she could answer none of them. All she knew was that she had made her decision, and she owed it to those who loved and trusted her to keep to that decision.

'Wot a diff'rence, eh?'

Ruth immediately recognised the soft-spoken voice of the middle-aged man who had joined her. It was Sub Officer Ben Slater, with whom

Ruth had always got on well, mainly because he was one of the few people she'd met who seemed to be quite content with life.

'When I remember what that sky looked like during the Blitz,' he went on, 'it don't bear thinking about.'

They both stared up at the moon, their faces bathed in a white fluorescent glow. Without saying anything, Ben took a packet of cigarettes out of his jacket pocket, took two out, and offered one to Ruth. She took it, and waited whilst he lit both hers and his with a match. They stared in silence again for a moment, smoke from their fags funnelling up into the night.

Eventually, Ben said, 'It's a funny thing. When I was a kid, the only thing I ever wanted was to be was a fireman. I got so worked up every time one of them pumps came rushing past, bells clanging, men clinging on to the sides for dear life. But now...' he inhaled, and exhaled, 'now, I'd do anything to get out. I've just had enough of it. Still, when the war's over...'

'Why is it that everyone keeps talking about "when the war's over"?' asked Ruth. 'I haven't seen one single thing that tells me that it isn't going to go on for a very long time.'

Ben hesitated before replying. 'You could be right,' he conceded. 'But when the lads *do* start coming home again, you'll feel different.'

'I doubt it,' replied Ruth, coldly.

Ben turned to look at her. 'Bad as that, is it.'

'I don't know, Ben,' replied Ruth, with a sigh. 'What will they find waiting for them when they come home?' she asked. 'Will they get back their old jobs? Will they find their women waiting for them?' She paused. 'Will they find their women still *wanting* them?' she added pointedly.

Ben thought about that for a moment. 'Well, I know what *I* think,' he said. '*I* think the blokes have to take whatever they find. Being away from home so long must be hell for them, but I hope they'll have enough sense to realise that after so long, things could never be exactly the same as when they left. Times change. So do people.'

In the distance, they could hear a tram rumbling along the tracks in Upper Street, and from a nearby pub, the customers getting tanked up for a boisterous rendition of 'Nellie Dean'.

'What happens if they *don't* take whatever they find?' asked Ruth.

'Well, I reckon they'll only make things worse,' Ben replied. 'Same applies to the women they left behind. There's no way they can expect their menfolk to be the same as when they went away. The things blokes have to do in war changes them. It makes them old before their time. It haunts them for the rest of their lives.' He continued with the cigarette fixed between his lips. 'In this job, I live for today, because you never know if there's going to be a tomorrow. I reckon people should follow their own instincts, and do whatever they feel they have to do.'

Ruth listened to what Ben had to say. It made a lot of sense to her. It made her realise that her mind was telling her to do one thing, and her heart to do something quite different. It also made her decide that she could no longer go on doing the things that people expected of her.

171

At that moment, they were taken completely off-guard as the air-raid siren pierced the evening air from the roof of the police station nearby. Simultaneously, the alarm sounded inside the fire-station.

'Blimey!' yelled Ben, rushing off. 'I thought we'd finished all this lark!'

Ruth followed him inside, where the duty crews were already doing a last-minute check of the pumps, and climbing up onto the fire-engines, waiting for the order to get out onto the road. Other crew members, including Mavis, were already sliding down the poles from the upper dormitory, and Ruth leapt up the steps two by two. In the female dormitory, she quickly kitted herself out for her first dispatch duties. It was only a matter of minutes before the approaching sounds of ack-ack fire began to shake the whole place, and by the time Ruth got back downstairs to the station forecourt, the engines and their crews were already turning out onto Upper Street, alarm bells clanging, racing off to their first incident in Essex Road. From the station watchroom, Ruth received a message to go straight to Headquarters to collect her first dispatch.

In New North Road a high-explosive bomb had severely damaged a cinema, and the old building, together with several adjoining shops, small offices, and houses, was burning fiercely. Ruth arrived there to find that the blaze was so intense, pumps had had to be brought in from both Islington and Shoreditch Divisions, and whilst casualties were being transported to the Royal Northern and London Hospitals, a frantic race was on to prevent the flames from spreading any further. To make matters worse, the local pump station had been hit, and the subsequent reduction in water supplies meant that the tanks the fire-fighters were using had to be topped up with water pumped through hose-lines from the nearby Grand Union Canal. It was a race against time, made even more hazardous by the roar of enemy planes overhead, and a deafening barrage of ack-ack guns doing their best to bring the intruders down.

'How the 'ell did they let this lot get through?' yelled an angry Station Officer Pete Curtis, from Whitehall Division, who was in charge of the incident. 'As usual, no one prepared. Thought the bloody war was over!'

Ruth handed him the dispatch she had brought from Headquarters, but before he could read it, a bomb came whistling down nearby, which sent everyone flat on their stomachs to take cover. By the time they were able to get up again, they were all covered in a thick layer of dust, whilst all around them masonry was falling from the damaged buildings.

One young fireman who got up at the same time as Ruth asked her, 'Wos a nice gel like you doin' on a job like this, mate?'

'Same as you – mate!' she countered acidly.

As soon as he had recovered, Curtis yelled out orders in all directions, to as many of his men as could hear him. It was several moments before he was able to open the dispatch Ruth had brought

173

him, but when he read it he nearly blew his top. 'Christ!' he bawled. 'They need us over Hackney!'

Ruth swung round with a start.

''Ow the 'ell can we cope wiv this lot as well as bloody 'Ackney?' Curtis yelled over the mayhem of deadly ack-ack shrapnel tinkling down onto the debris all around them.

'What's happened, sir?' asked Ruth quickly, anxiously. 'Whereabouts in Hackney?'

'Mare Street,' he barked, irritated that he'd been expected to pass on such information to a dispatch-rider. 'Parachute bomb and two Molotovs...' Before he had even finished what he was saying, Ruth was already retrieving her motorbike from the rubble. 'Oy!' he yelled. 'Where d'yer fink *you're* goin'?'

There was no way Ruth could have heard him, for she was already on her way.

Never had Ruth's training been put to the test so formidably as now, for it had provided her with a near-encyclopaedic knowledge of the London roads, especially in the north and east. Still covered in dust from the incident she had just left, her goggles smeared, face smudged and covered with filth, she battled her way through every short-cut she knew, streets littered with glass and rubble, skilfully avoiding the additional hazards of bomb craters, her face constantly illuminated by incendiary fires burning on each side of her as she went. For the first part of the journey, she didn't even stop to consider why it was that she was racing off with such intensity towards an incident that she had not been

174

ordered to attend, but by the time she had found her way to Mare Street from London Fields, that intensity had turned into a frenzied panic.

Mare Street was virtually sealed off, not that any traffic could have passed through, for the whole area was strewn with broken glass and rubble, and emergency workers, together with local residents, were tackling incendiary fires everywhere. Once she had found a clear and secure place to leave the motorbike, she quickly headed off on foot towards Jessop Place. The signs were not good. As she climbed over smouldering timber and piles of fallen masonry, and picked her way carefully through endless lumps of jagged, burning-hot shrapnel, she could see crowds of rescue workers gathered around what looked like a gap in the terrace of shops and small offices, which she remembered as being no more than a stone's throw from the junction of Jessop Place with Mare Street. Soon she was making a wild dash along the great main thoroughfare of Hackney, running, walking, climbing over rubble and glass, desperate to get to Jessop Place as fast as her feet and legs were able to carry her. When she did finally get there, she found it virtually impassable, for access was barred by a huge mountain of debris which had come tumbling down from the top two floors of a nearby florist's shop which had taken the brunt of the blast from the deadly parachute bomb.

Despite warnings from the Special Constabulary, who were doing their best to keep the area clear until the Fire Service was able to get there, Ruth immediately started clambering on hands and knees over a huge smouldering pile of bricks and mortar, until she was finally able to reach the mews on the other side. To her dismay, she was greeted with a scene of total devastation: most of the small, modest dwellings there had been badly damaged, with windows blown in, tiles missing from the roofs and chimney pots blown down, women in nightdresses clutching their bewildered kids who were protected from the cold by blankets hurriedly stripped off beds, and their menfolk frantically tackling incendiary fires with nothing more than hand-operated stirrup pumps. But in the middle of it all, Ruth was astonished to see that not only was Cyril Buller's funeral parlour relatively unscathed, but Cyril himself was there, in pyjamas and an old raincoat, dousing flames in front of the front door with a bucket of sand. 'Mr Buller!' Ruth yelled, as she struggled to get to him through the debris.

Cyril, totally bald without his treasured hairpiece, was astonished by the sight of Ruth. 'Blimey!' he gasped. 'Wot *you* doin' 'ere?'

'Are you all right?' she bellowed, fighting her way through the teams of residents who were tackling the fires. 'Where's Mike?'

The moment she reached him, Cyril, distraught, was shaking his head. 'He went down the workshop,' he replied, incomprehensibly. 'The workshop... I *told* 'im the shop was all right. I told 'im not ter worry about the bleedin' workshop...'

Ruth tore off, heading down the mews, clambering over rubble and the personal belongings that residents had thrown out of their upper floor windows in a frenzied effort to preserve what little they had left in the world. When she finally reached the workshop, she stared in horror. The place was engulfed in flames, timber and half-made coffins burning fiercely, thick black palls of smoke spiralling up towards the bright, crescent moon. For a brief moment she was too shocked to do anything, but then she grabbed the first person who rushed past her, an ARP warden whose face was blood-red from the intense heat.

'Mike?' she called breathlessly. 'Mike Buller?'

The middle-aged man looked at her as though she was mad, and with a shrug, rushed off to join the others.

Totally disorientated, her face pouring with sweat from the workshop inferno, Ruth frantically searched around for someone else to ask – this time an elderly woman being led to safety by a younger one. 'Mike Buller?' Ruth pleaded. *'Please* – have you seen him?'

'Sorry, love,' cried the younger woman, as she helped the frail, older one to get round the treacherous heaps of rubble.

'Mike went inside! I saw 'im!'

Ruth turned with a start to see a small boy in pyjamas and his dad's flat cap, pointing excitedly towards the workshop fire. Ruth clasped a frantic hand over her mouth.

'Are yer sure, Fred?' asked his mum, who grabbed the boy's hand. 'Are yer sure it was Mike?'

The boy nodded adamantly. 'I saw 'im! I saw 'im go in!' His mum exchanged a look of anguish with Ruth, and rushed off quickly with the boy.

Ruth slowly turned to look at the burning inferno that had once been the workshop. As she stood there, too numb to move, the reflection of the flames flickered in her eyes. Despite the intense heat, the sounds were chilling – burning wood spitting and cracking, the individual sheets of old corrugated roof collapsing into the fire, people yelling and shouting all around her, police whistles, the alarm bells of the approaching fire-engines, and the constant overhead barrage of ack-ack fire. In cold shock, she stood there, surrounded by a sea of human misery. She looked directly into the flames, and her eyes welled with tears. The thought that Mike might be caught up in those flames filled her with despair, so much so that tears started to trickle like rivulets down her cheeks. Yes, she told herself, Mike was a nice person, and even though he was little more than a complete stranger to her, the thought that the person who had saved her own life was now lying in that glowing pyre was a cruel act of fate. But the more she stared into those merciless flames, the more she feared the worst. She broke down, weeping openly, consumed with guilt that she had never shown Mike even one moment of kindness. She tried to compose herself, and when she had, she turned, ready to move off. As she did so, however, her eyes immediately settled on the distant silhouette of a figure standing absolutely motionless in the mews. She blinked her wet eyes, and tried to focus. The surrounding flames did what she had so far been unable to do; they illuminated the features of the person she was straining to see – a man – a young man – in

Army greatcoat and knitted woollen cap. She stared hard. What she was looking at seemed to be an apparition, a ghostly silhouette shimmering in the harsh red glow of the burning fires. The figure slowly moved towards her, and when he was finally within a few paces of her, she could see that it was Mike. The relief that he was alive made her want to throw her arms around him. But she resisted the urge, and remained absolutely still.

''Allo, Ruth,' said Mike calmly, his face smudged with smoke from the burnt rubble. 'Fanks fer comin'.'

'Thank God you're alive,' she said. 'When I heard what had happened up here, I – I... Thank God you're alive.'

He moved a step towards her, but she cautiously avoided him.

'For God's sake take care of yourself,' she said. 'Goodbye, Mike.'

'G'bye, Ruth,' he replied, careful not to over-react to the concern she had shown by coming there. Then he watched incredulously, as she carefully passed by him, picked her way over the fallen rubble, and disappeared out of sight into Mare Street.

Chapter 9

The 'little Blitz', as it was now being called, was in full swing. Complacency had given way to a feeling that the war was far from over, and that the authorities had misjudged the enemy's ability to renew their campaign of wanton destruction against the British civilian population. However, as most of the attacks seemed to be taking place during the evening, people decided not to return to the public and private air-raid shelters to spend the night, opting to wait up until after the raid was over before returning to the comfort of their own beds. In fact, apart from the extensive damage caused to homes and places of work, everyday life seemed to continue more or less as normal. Despite police warnings about his aggressive drunken behaviour, Ted Simmons resumed his nightly forays to the boozer, leaving Rita behind to be the sole occupant of their Anderson 'dug-out' in the back yard; Edie Perkins slept on a makeshift bed under her kitchen table and, after a long day's work in the shop, Bella Whitlock was too tired to do anything but get herself a quick meal before turning in for the night, air raid or no air raid.

During the remaining days of Mike Buller's leave, Ruth spent as much time with him as she possibly could. Casting all caution to the wind, she just accepted the fact that if she was ever going to have any peace of mind, then she would have to do what her heart told her. She realised only too well the can of worms she had opened by deceiving Tom, and she also knew that, sooner or later, she was going to have to face up to the consequences, and not only from Tom himself, but also with his family, her own mother, and with Father O'Leary. But for that one week at least, she was prepared to bury her head in the sand, and wallow in the joy of a new and more exciting relationship, a relationship that for both Mike and herself was something more than just physical. However, the first seeds of doubt and anxiety began to emerge during the moment when she stood on the platform at Charing Cross station, hugging Mike in a final passionate embrace, just as she had done when Tom took his leave of her six months or so before. She found it something of a strange experience, a feeling of déjà vu, and no matter how hard she tried to put to the back of her mind the memory of that final embrace with Tom, their parting words were there to haunt her: *'For ever? And ever! Or else...'*

Shortly after Mike Buller's leave had come to an end, Ruth was astonished to receive a surprise visit from Sweetie. Now in her ninth month of pregnancy, Sweetie had never been to the 'end house' before, and felt very pleased that she had managed to find the place all on her own, let alone getting on and off the bus in bitterly cold weather in such a weighty condition. Ruth had hardly got the front door open when she was met with the biggest smile she had seen on Sweetie's face in months.

'He's home!' Sweetie announced, ecstatically.

'Who's home?' asked Ruth.

'Johnston!' Sweetie replied, as Ruth brought her into the narrow front hall and closed the door behind them. 'He's got a week's leave – and guess what?' She could hardly contain her excitement. 'He knows about the baby – and he doesn't mind!'

'What!' cried Ruth, in disbelief.

'Yes, I know it sounds incredible, but it's true, absolutely true. He said these things happen in wartime, and that they can't be helped. He said, if I want to keep the baby, he'll do everything he can to support us.' In her excitement, she threw her arms around Ruth and hugged her. 'Oh sweetie,' she rambled, 'isn't it wonderful! I should have believed you. You knew it would be all right – you said so. Didn't you say so?'

Ruth, totally bewildered by Sweetie's news, knew only too well that she had never said any such thing. 'I think we could do with a strong cup of tea,' was her less than enthusiastic response.

Sweetie followed her into the kitchen, where she eased herself down onto a chair at the table. 'He's changed, sweetie,' she said. 'I can't tell you how much he's changed. When he went away, he was so loud and bossy, but now he's quietly spoken and gentle, and he even told me to take things easy until the baby arrives. I think it's because of where he's been, what he's had to do. He wouldn't tell me too much, but it sounds as though he was part of the Allied landings in Sicily. I suspect he's had rather a bad time of it.'

Ruth, putting on a kettle at the stove, listened with mixed feelings to all the positive things

Sweetie was telling her. But even though it all sounded too good to be true, she was prepared to go along with it – for the present. 'Has he asked you any questions about the other man?' she asked.

'Yes,' replied Sweetie, positively. 'I told him I was going to be truthful with him, and I was. I told him everything about how I met the bloke I'd got involved with, and that I only slept with him because I was feeling lonely and depressed.'

'Did you ask Johnston if he still loves you?' Ruth asked, joining Sweetie at the table.

'Yes,' replied Sweetie, who was getting misty-eyed.

'And what did he say?'

Sweetie paused for breath so that she could give a considered reply. 'He said, he'd never stopped loving me. It was so wonderful, sweetie, so – unexpected. I never thought the day would come when I'd actually hear a man say such a thing to me. I can't tell you the difference it's made to me. I feel as though I've been given a chance to start all over again.' She sighed deeply with such joy and hope. 'Oh, sweetie,' she said, 'I'm such a lucky woman.'

The kettle whistled on the stove, but once Ruth had made the tea and brought two cups and saucers to the table, she felt uneasy when Sweetie said how much she would love it if Ruth would come along to meet Johnston. Was he really such a reformed character? Ruth asked herself. Was it really true that he was so readily prepared to accept Sweetie's admission that she had deceived him?

183

'You'll like him so much, sweetie,' gushed Sweetie. 'I *know* you will. I've told him so much about you, about you and Tom, and what hell you've been going through because you haven't heard from Tom for so long.'

At the mention of Tom's name, Ruth tensed. Here she was, listening to her best friend blossoming like a flower, prepared to be truthful despite all the risks involved, and yet she, Ruth, couldn't even bring herself to tell Sweetie about what had been happening between her and Mike Buller during the previous week.

'He might even be able to help,' said Sweetie.

'Help?'

'Remember, Johnston's a soldier, just like Tom. He knows all about what goes on, the way a soldier thinks when he's under fire, why he can't bring himself to write home. And I bet he can even tell you why the Army post gets delayed.' With Ruth so quiet and withdrawn, Sweetie reached across the table and gently took hold of her hand. 'Come and meet him – *please*, sweetie,' she pleaded. 'I just *know* you'll like him.'

Father Tim O'Leary made slow progress along Holloway Road. Although he still had quite a commanding frame, in recent years he had filled out quite a bit, which made any form of exercise more of a plod than it used to be. It didn't help that it was a terrible winter, and that the temperature was well below zero even though it was only just after three in the afternoon. Nonetheless, in his black trilby hat, dog collar, black suit and wellies, he was still an impressive sight as he struggled through the filthy brown slush from a previous heavy fall of snow that was now turning to ice.

The priest hadn't visited the Whitlocks in their shop for many a moon, not since shortly after Harry Whitlock's death. Unlike many people, Father Tim had always got on well with Harry, and he had never fully understood Ruth's bitterness towards her poor father, even to the point of declining to be known, after the man's death, by her family surname, preferring instead to adopt her mother's maiden name, Madiewsky. But then, to Father Tim's way of thinking, Ruth had always been a complicated child, which was the reason why he was making one of his rare forays into the frozen wastes of lower Hornsey Road.

'Sometimes I wonder why the Holy Father thinks that enduring a harsh winter is good for the soul,' he complained making straight for the small paraffin stove which was the only form of heating in Bella Whitlock's shop.

Bella herself was busy serving a customer at the counter, but Ruth, already in her uniform for her evening shift, carried on tidying up the meagrely stocked stationery section on one of the side racks. Father Tim warmed his hands at the stove, and watched her carefully. He was aware of the cool reaction Ruth had shown him when he walked in, and from the way her mother had been talking about her again, it wasn't hard to understand why. 'Tell me about your young man, Ruth,' he asked, right out of the blue.

Startled, Ruth swung him a look of panic.

Father Tim grinned. He knew he had taken her off-guard. 'Any news yet?' he asked.

Realising that he was referring to Tom, Ruth relaxed. 'No, Father,' she replied, quickly busying herself again.

'How long is it now?'

'I can't even remember,' sighed Ruth. 'Must be nearly three months.'

Father Tim shook his head despairingly. 'I'm sorry to hear that,' he said, unable to offer any real comfort. 'What about the lad's own family? Have they heard from him?'

'I haven't seen them for a while,' returned Ruth, 'but I'm sure they'd have let me know if they had.'

Father Tim knew that Bella was listening to every word they said, whilst at the same time becoming increasingly irritated with the middle-aged customer who was taking so long to pay her for the packet of Woodbines he had just bought. 'I take it you have no idea which part of the world the Army took him off to?' he asked.

'North Africa or the Far East, I presume,' replied Ruth, with a shrug. 'I've no idea really. The Army are never in much of a rush to tell you *anything*, are they?'

'Indeed,' replied Father Tim, with another sigh. 'But yer must keep up your spirits, child,' he said, with just a hint of irony. 'Ye can rest assured that wherever your young man is, Mother Mary is keeping an eye on him.'

'I hope so, Father,' Ruth replied evasively. 'I hope so.' It was becoming increasingly difficult for her to conceal her true feelings.

Bella's customer finally paid for his cigarettes, and left. 'Stupid man,' she grumbled. 'Did you see how long it took him to count his change? He must be a foreigner!'

'Don't be silly, Mother,' said Ruth. 'That's Mr Wilson from Benwell Road. He comes from Yorkshire.'

'Then he should know how to count his change!' insisted Bella, totally oblivious of her own origins.

Behind them, Father Tim chuckled. He had perched himself on the only chair in the shop, and was struggling to pull off one of his wellies. 'Forgive me fer doing this, ladies,' he said, trying to rub some life back into his frozen toes. 'Me poor feet feel as though they've been set in a block of ice.'

'Father!' Bella gasped, noticing the huge hole in the heel of his sock. 'Just look at that sock! You can't go around like that. Give it to me at once!'

Like a naughty schoolboy, Father Tim readily obeyed, pulled off the offending sock, and handed it over to her. Gabbling a reprimand in Polish as she went, Bella quickly disappeared into the back room to fetch a needle and cotton.

Once she had gone, Father Tim got on with the job he had come to do. For several moments, he watched Ruth pottering around the shop, then he got out his pipe and matches from his jacket pocket. 'So,' he said, in his casual Irish brogue, 'you're managin' ter cope, are ye?'

'Cope?' asked Ruth, deliberately busying herself again.

'With all this great worry on your shoulders,' he

replied. 'Sure, it's a terrible thing not to know what's happened to ye loved one, especially,' he turned to look at her, 'especially when ye've both made so many plans fer ye future life together.'

Ruth stopped what she was doing. This was it, she told herself. This was the moment she knew would come, would *have* to come – sooner or later. She finally turned around and looked straight across at him. Their eyes met. Her lips parted and she prepared to tell him about the way she was feeling about Mike Buller. But no matter how hard she tried, the words just wouldn't come. As she watched Father Tim lighting up his pipe, she agonised over why she just couldn't trust herself enough to confess to him what she had done.

'Ye know,' said Father Tim, through a cloud of pipe smoke, 'I once had a cigarette, the only time in my entire life. Hated the wretched thing. It tasted like an old sock – not *my* sock, I hasten ter add!' He chuckled. 'I'll tell ye somethin' else,' he continued. 'When I was a young man, soon after I'd taken the Holy Orders, I committed a sin that's haunted me ter this day.' He swung around on his chair, and looked across at Ruth. 'I fell in love with a girl. Can ye believe it? *Me* – a newly ordained priest, on the threshold of a wonderful holy vocation, and here I was, falling in love with a young girl that I'd known for only a few days. But she was beautiful, Ruth. Oh, I can't even begin ter describe *how* beautiful. Large, violet-coloured eyes, long blonde hair that draped down over her shoulders like a river of light, and a dimple in one cheek that looked just like a pearl

– well, ter me it did.'

The priest took the pipe out of his mouth, and for a moment or so used a burnt match to poke down the smouldering tobacco. 'It was such an odd emotion, Ruth, unlike anything I'd experienced before – like a great lump inside that weighed me down.' He stopped what he was doing, and looked up at her again. 'Fortunately,' he continued, 'the young lady in question didn't feel the same way about me. Yer see, it was all one-sided, a complete infatuation on my part. Anyway, one day, I woke up. It was extraordinary, Ruth, like coming out of a dream. Suddenly, I was back where I really wanted to be, with my feet firmly on the ground, standing before my Maker, before Our Lady, before everything I'd come ter believe in. Since then, I've often thought that the problem was that, despite all the training I'd had for the vocation that I myself had chosen, I was trying to experiment with things that I was just too young to understand. For one fleeting moment, I wasn't a part of my Maker, or Our Lady. I was only *myself*. There's nothing too wrong in that, of course, but the only way I could see clearly was to question *what* I was about, what it was that I *really* wanted from my life. But most of all,' he threw her a warm, caring smile, 'most of all, I wanted to be quite sure that I wasn't going to do something that I'd regret for the rest of my life.'

'Father!' called Bella, as she returned with a large darning needle and cotton, and clasping Father Tim's offending sock on a sock stool. 'I think it's about time you bought yourself a new pair of socks.'

'Ha!' he snorted. 'And would ye like ter tell me, good lady, just *where* ye think I'm goin' ter be findin' the ration coupons fer *that!*'

'You must be Ruth?' The question came from the quietly spoken, middle-aged man who had just opened the street door to Sweetie's upstairs flat.

Ruth had been dreading the thought of meeting the redoubtable Johnston ever since Sweetie had pleaded with her to do so. She didn't exactly know why, for hadn't Sweetie told her how wonderful her Johnston had been when he had heard that she had been unfaithful to him? Ruth's immediate instincts had been of deep suspicion, not because she didn't trust the man – after all, she had never even met him – but because the newspapers these days were always carrying stories about servicemen coming back home on leave and finding a similar situation to Sweetie's, and how they had reacted by brutally beating up their wives and girlfriends. Could Johnston really be so different? Ruth asked herself. 'I hope I'm not intruding?' she asked the man, as he closed the street door behind her.

'Not at all,' replied the man, who gave her a friendly, welcoming smile, which highlighted his steel-blue eyes and thinning brown hair that was beginning to sprout the first signs of grey. 'Any pal of 'Azel's is a pal er mine. Come on up. She's dyin' ter see yer.'

It sounded so odd to Ruth, hearing Sweetie called by her real name, and she gave the man credit for the caring way in which he had said it, albeit in a rough and ready voice. But it still didn't dispel the nagging feeling inside that just wouldn't go away.

'I've told 'er,' the man said, as they climbed the stairs, 'that the first fing I'm goin' ter do when I get 'ome fer good, is ter get 'er out er this place. I'm not 'avin no woman er mine roughin' it up five flights er stairs each day wiv a kid in 'er arms.'

Ruth was beginning to feel more hopeful.

'Oh, sweetie!' cried an overjoyed Sweetie, as she threw her arms around Ruth the moment she entered the dingy top-floor room. 'You're a dear to come. I've been telling Derek all about you.'

'Non-stop!' joked Johnston, who was poking an obstinate fire in the grate.

Ruth was relieved to hear Sweetie using Johnston's Christian name. But most of all, she could hardly believe the change in Sweetie, her eyes so bright and alive, and the way she kept an adoring eye on the man whose homecoming she had feared for so long. 'You look wonderful,' Ruth told her.

'Well, it's nothing to do with me,' insisted Sweetie, who lovingly watched Johnston's every movement. 'He won't let me do a thing. If I even get up to put the kettle on, he practically pushes me back into the chair. And what d'you think of the place?' She spun round excitedly to show off how bright and tidy the room had become.

'I can hardly recognise it,' said Ruth, duly impressed by the way the place had been cleaned up, all neat and tidy, and a bright new lampshade hanging from the ceiling.

'I can't tell you how hard Derek's been working since he got home,' enthused Sweetie. 'Just shows you – a man's touch makes all the difference!' She and Ruth laughed together.

Johnston appeared not to mind being teased. 'Yeah, well don't fink it's always goin' ter be like this,' he said. 'Soon as I get out er the Army, there're goin' ter be a few changes made 'round 'ere. 'Azel Johnston's goin' ter 'ave ter look after me *an'* the kid – yeah, *an'* a few kids er mine besides!'

The look of pure joy that came to Sweetie's face was certainly one step towards helping Ruth warm to the man. But in her mind, Ruth was still not fully convinced. This was a man, a soldier who had just come back from fighting in what must have been a bloody front line battle, to be told that the woman he was married to had not only been sleeping with another man, but was also about to give birth to a child that he, Johnston, was going to have to support. Somehow it just didn't make sense. Could Johnston really forgive and forget so easily?

While the two girls settled themselves down at the table, Johnston found himself a dog-end on the mantelpiece, and lit up.

'Derek,' called Sweetie, 'tell Ruth what you told me about all the problems you have with the Army post.'

'Yeah, that's right,' said Johnston, who talked whilst he was collecting a half bottle of whisky from one of the two small bedside cabinets. ''Appens all the time,' he said, coming across to join them with the whisky and three glass

192

tumblers. ''Aze tells me yer 'aven't 'eard from your bloke fer a bit?'

Ruth nodded.

'Well,' he said, fag in lips, 'if yer'll take my tip, yer won't get too worked up about it. Soon after we landed in Sicily, I remember the Post Unit got a direct 'it. Luckily, nobody copped it, but most of the blokes' letters went up in smoke.' He unscrewed the cap of the whisky bottle, and offered some to Ruth.

Ruth shook her head. 'Not at the moment, thanks,' she said.

'Wot 'appens in a case like that,' continued Johnston, whilst pouring two glasses of neat whisky, 'is that it fouls up the ruddy system fer weeks on end – sometimes munffs. Bloke in my unit got into a real sweat. 'E'd 'ad a letter ter say that 'is place back 'ome'd 'ad a direct 'it in an air raid, and that 'is missus was recoverin' in 'ospital. 'E couldn't get compassionate leave right away, 'cos we was under fire, so the only fing 'e could rely on was ter get a letter back to 'er. I still don't know if she's ever 'eard from 'im.' He handed one of the glasses of whisky to Sweetie, and kept one for himself. 'So I wouldn't get too worried if yer 'aven't 'eard from your bloke,' he said. 'It don't mean that anyfin's 'appened to 'im. It just means that the system's got all buggered up somewhere.'

'See?' said Sweetie effusively, sipping her whisky. 'I told you, sweetie, didn't I?'

Whilst appreciating their concern, Ruth remained unconvinced. What she couldn't admit, however, even to herself, was that although she hoped nothing untoward *had* happened to Tom,

193

she no longer had the same feeling of anxiety about him as she used to. 'Thank you, Johnston,' she replied. 'I'm sure you're right.'

'Derek,' said Johnston, correcting her, sternly.

Ruth could have kicked herself. 'I'm sorry,' she replied, 'Derek.'

Sweetie glowed with relief at the way Ruth and her husband appeared to be getting on so well. 'I need to spend a penny,' she said, putting down her glass and easing herself up from her chair. 'I'll leave you two to get to know each other.'

Ruth and Johnston exchanged a laugh. 'You've made her very happy,' Ruth said to him, after Sweetie had left the room.

'Yer reckon?' he asked.

'You only have to look at her,' Ruth assured him. 'You've been very – understanding.'

'Understandin'?' repeated the man. 'Yeah well, there's not much yer can do in the circumstances, is there?'

Ruth watched him as he took a quick gulp of his drink. Although she had begun to feel relaxed in his company, she could sense how, like so many of the men who had returned home after serving in some of the bloodiest battles of the war, he had a fixed, distant look in his eye, as though he was still living every moment of what he had been through.

'Yer know,' he said, pulling on his fag, 'me an' 'Aze 'ardly knew each uvver before we was married. Yet the moment I met 'er, I knew I wanted ter be wiv 'er more than anyone else in the world. Don't ask me why. I mean, let's face it, we boaf know what a nut-case she is – all that sweetie fing. Mad as a March bleedin' 'are!'

Ruth laughed affectionately. Interestingly, Johnston didn't.

'But the way I felt about it – and still do – is that she 'ad so much go in 'er – no messin' about, straight ter the point, if yer get my meanin'?'

Ruth agreed.

He pulled hard on his fag again, and gulped down more whisky. 'Did she tell yer I'd never bin wiv a gel before?'

Ruth tried not to show that she was taken aback.

'It's true,' he said. 'I know it sounds creepy an' all that, 'specially at my age, but it 'appens ter be true.' He grinned. 'I s'ppose yer could call me a "late developer"!'

Ruth attempted a smile. It didn't come easy.

'Anyway,' continued Johnston, 'when I met up with 'Aze, I suddenly realised wot a chump I've bin all me life. Oh, it's not the sex fing, I mean. It's the bein' tergevver, bein' a couple. Can yer believe it – all that in just a few weeks. Don't seem possible, do it? I mean – gettin' 'ooked on someone yer've only known fer five minutes, an' never wantin' ter let anyone else get a look in.' He pulled hard on his fag, exhaled, then stubbed out what was left of the dog-end in a makeshift ash-tray. 'So, yer can imagine 'ow I felt when I come back an' – well, yer know the rest.' He paused briefly to down the remains of his drink. 'Still, wot can yer do about it? I said ter meself, "Johnston," I says, "if yer want this gel ter be yours fer the rest of yer life, then you're goin' ter 'ave ter take wotever comes along." After all, a kid's a kid

195

– wevver it's someone else's or yer own. The only fing though, is, when I saw 'Aze at that door when I first come in, fer one second – just *one* second, mind – I didn't recognise 'er, didn't know 'er. It was like lookin' at a total stranger. Maybe I looked the same to 'er too, I dunno. But wot I do know is, I won't let 'er down. As far as I'm concerned, she's mine now, an' I won't ever let 'er go.'

Sweetie suddenly made an exuberant return. 'Well?' she said, with the most radiant smile Ruth had ever seen. 'What do you think of my Mr Johnston, sweetie?'

Ruth paused, then went to her. 'I think you're going to be very happy,' she said, hugging her. Then she looked back at Johnston. '*Both* of you,' she said. And she meant it.

That evening, the air-raid siren sounded twice. The first occasion turned out to be something of a damp squib, for the All Clear came almost immediately. But on the second occasion, a trio of enemy aircraft managed to break through the Outer London air defences and cause havoc to a wide area, which included parts of City Road. As expected, Ruth was kept busy conveying dispatches from one incident to another, and although all three aircraft were shot down well before midnight, it was the early hours of the morning before she had managed to get home.

The moment she got into bed, she fell into a deep sleep. She dreamt that she was at Sweetie's wedding, and that the church was packed with families and well-wishers. Sweetie herself was, of course, deliriously happy, and looked absolutely radiant in a stunning full-length wedding dress, the train of which seemed to stretch for the full length of the church aisle. Ruth slept soundly and contentedly, her face beaming with delight as she watched Sweetie revelling in the wedding ceremony. But there gradually came a moment when she started to move restlessly in her sleep, tossing and turning and groaning. Something in her dream was disturbing her. It came at the point when she was just trying to pick out the faces of the bridesmaids, the Best Man, and the rest of the congregation. With the exception of herself, however, she was unable to recognise any of them. Even more disturbing was the moment when she was straining to fight her way through a thin white haze, stretching out her hands in an attempt to touch the face of the man that Sweetie was about to marry. Johnston was at her side, there was no doubt about that. But when she tried to bring the face into focus, she was horrified to see that it was not that of Johnston at all. It was Tom Phillips. She screamed, and sat bolt upright in bed.

'Ruth! Wake up, darling.'

Ruth's eyes sprang open with a start, to find her mother, still in her nightdress, and standing over her. The blackout blinds had not been raised, and the electric light had been switched on. 'Hurry, Ruth!' Bella called, her voice cracked with alarm and anxiety. 'You've got to get up.'

Ruth came to, and rubbed her eyes. 'What's the matter?' she asked, immediately getting out of bed. 'What's happened?'

'There's someone waiting downstairs for you,' replied Bella solemnly. 'It's a policeman.'

The winter sun was just rising over the River Thames in Central London. At London Bridge, there were a few early-morning onlookers, but as the rush hour had not yet started in earnest, the people who were there were still not sure what had been going on.

Ruth got out of the police car which had brought her from the 'end house', and was led down a steep flight of stone steps by the police constable who had called on her at the crack of dawn. The tide itself was out, leaving the muddy riverbank thick with litter, but the first thing Ruth saw as she was helped on her way towards her destination was what looked like two middle-aged people, a man and a woman, well-dressed and heavily wrapped up against the biting cold, staring out at the fast-flowing surface of the water.

As she passed them, they turned briefly to look at her and, instinctively, she refused to acknowledge them. When she finally reached the place where she was being taken, she found a group of solemn-looking uniformed and plain-clothed officers gathered around, but the moment she approached, they stood back to let her see the figure that was stretched out on the shore of the river, covered in a red ambulance blanket. She came to a halt. No one spoke a word, until she drew closer. 'Can I see her?' she asked.

'It's not necessary, miss,' said the soft-spoken plain-clothed police officer who joined her. 'Her

198

parents have already identified her.'

'I'd *like* to see her,' insisted Ruth, quietly but positively.

'Are you sure?'

Ruth nodded.

The officer signalled discreetly to one of his colleagues, and the blanket was pulled back just enough to reveal Sweetie's face.

Ruth crouched down. Everything inside her told her to cry, but the tears wouldn't come. With one hand, she reached out to touch Sweetie's sodden hair, but was tactfully restrained from doing so by the officer. So she contented herself with just staring at the face of the best friend she had ever had; her eyes were closed, her complexion tinged with blue, but she was as smooth and beautiful as a wax doll. *Why?* That was the only question now that dominated her every thought. What was this lovely girl and her unborn child doing here, stretched out by strangers on the cold banks of a cruel and merciless river? It didn't make sense. Only a few hours before, she had been so happy, so full of love and hope. 'What happened?' she asked the officer.

'They were seen on the bridge by a taxi driver,' he replied.

Ruth swung him a shocked look.

'There was some kind of struggle,' the officer went on. 'She was trying to get away.'

'*They?*' repeated Ruth, quite numb.

The police officer gestured further along the riverbank. Ruth turned to look. In the near distance she could see a second figure stretched out in the mud, also covered by a blanket. The moment she saw it, she felt sick. Her eyes returned to the face at her side. It was at peace now, but it should have been so full of life. As the tears finally started to well up in her eyes, all Ruth could hear was that voice, that exuberant, cut-glass voice, so full of love, so full of joy and hope for the future.

'Oh, sweetie,' called the voice. 'I'm such a lucky woman!'

Chapter 10

One week after the Allied D-Day landings in France, which took place on 6 June, 1944, the Germans launched a campaign of aerial terror against London in the shape of the 'doodlebug', or the V1 as it was known officially. Tub Trinder the tailor had his own name for it: 'the plane wiv its arse on fire!' Hitler had been threatening such a weapon for some time, promising the German people that when launched, it would turn the tide of the war at a stroke. In the event, however, although the deadly machine did eventually wreak a considerable trail of death and destruction right the way across London and the southeast of England, Hitler's boast proved to be no more than wishful thinking.

By August, the doodlebug attacks were gradually losing momentum, and once again the long-suffering public decided that the war could not go on for much longer, so much so that Ruth persuaded the Fire Service to release her from her motorcycle dispatch job, which would allow her to take over the shop and look after her mother, who had suffered a series of minor angina attacks. It would also help her to try to put the memory of Sweetie's death behind her. For the past six months, Ruth had gone to hell and back. Ever since that fateful night when she was taken down to the riverbank, she had relived every moment of what had happened time and time again. Despite the verdict of the inquest that Sweetie had been killed by 'unlawful means', and despite the fact that Johnston had not only been responsible for Sweetie's death, but had also been revealed as a deserter who had been on the run for over a year, there were many questions that still plagued Ruth. Why *did* Sweetie have to die when Johnston had convinced her and Ruth that he loved her, that he wanted to care for her, and that he had so many plans for their future life together? What was it that had snapped in the mind of this strange, distant man who, according to his own family, had never harmed anyone or anything in his entire life? How was it that no one had ever discovered the dark side of Johnston's mind, a side shrouded in mystery and fantasy and which had that terrifying capacity to take another person's life? And yet, the more she thought about it, the more she recalled those chilling words Johnston had used about Sweetie when he and Ruth were alone together: *'As far as I'm concerned, she's mine now, and I won't ever let her go.'*

For Ruth, it was all a recurring nightmare. How

201

would she ever be able to erase the memories of that night from her dreams: the early-morning call by the police, who had been informed by Sweetie's landlady how close a friend Ruth was, and where she could be found; being told what had happened, and pleading with the police to let her see Sweetie's body. But most of all, she knew that she would never be able to erase her memories of seeing those two solitary figures at the river's edge that night, and a week later, at Sweetie's funeral. Was it really possible that those two people were actually Sweetie's own parents, who had so brutally detached themselves from her because she refused to conform to their own style and standards of life? What sort of people were they? Ruth had asked herself so many times. How could they be so indifferent, so cold-hearted to their own daughter. Night after night, Ruth defied everything Father Tim had ever taught her. She prayed that Sweetie's parents would burn in hell.

In his own oblique way, however, Father Tim *had* influenced Ruth about the direction she was going in. He had taught her that a moment of infatuation could never be a substitute for a lifetime of love. There was no doubt in her mind that Sweetie's death had caused her to reappraise her brief relationship with Mike Buller. It wasn't easy. Since he went away, she had been inundated with letters from him, sometimes two in one week. And what extraordinary letters they were, some written in the same style of Old English that his grandfather had taught him, some in perfectly controlled handwriting, but every one of them full of interesting news and observations about the men with whom he was serving. After a while, Ruth stopped reading or even opening them. Sweetie's death had given her pause for thought; now she had decided that whatever her feelings might have been for Mike during the brief few moments they had spent together, she could not jeopardise her own safety if, or when, Tom Phillips should ever return home. However, after months of silence, that possibility became even more remote when, during a busy morning in the shop, she received an unexpected visit from Tom's young sister, Kate.

'Mum and Dad have had a letter from the War Office,' said Kate. 'They say Tom's missing, presumed dead, but that it's just possible he might be in a prisoner-of-war camp.'

'Oh my God,' said Ruth. 'Are they sure? Are they absolutely sure?'

'Nothing's absolutely sure in this rotten war,' replied Kate, who was pale and drawn. 'At work I've heard some terrible stories about Japanese POW camps. They say they treat the prisoners like hell. I'd be very surprised if we ever see Tom again.'

'We mustn't think like that, Kate,' replied Ruth. 'We must try and think positively, and just pray that no harm will come to him.'

'Pray?' said Kate sceptically. 'Who do we pray *to*? God's done nothing for me so far, He's done nothing for all the people who've been killed and lost their homes. So why would He help Tom? No, I'll leave Mum and Dad to do all the praying.

They're used to it.'

Kate's bitterness about God and religion took Ruth by surprise. Somehow she had always thought that Kate, although more cultured than her parents, was nonetheless a true and devoted believer – but here she was, rebelling against everything she had been brought up to believe in. 'We all have to have something to cling to,' said Ruth. 'I know it sometimes doesn't make sense when people are being killed day after day, but we have to find the strength from somewhere.'

'You're not in love with Tom, are you?' said Kate, bluntly. 'You're not really in love with him any more?'

Ruth was completely jolted by Kate's frankness. 'That's not a very nice thing to say,' she replied, tersely.

'But it is true – isn't it?' repeated Kate. 'I can tell.'

'I don't know what you mean,' said Ruth, totally bewildered by the girl's question.

'It's the way you don't ask about him the way you used to,' said Kate. 'I just feel that you don't really seem to care about him any more.'

'I don't know how you can say that,' snapped Ruth. 'I hardly ever see you – *or* your parents.'

'That's what I mean,' said Kate perceptively. 'It's been ages since you came up to see us. Mum said it's probably because you've left the Fire Service, and because you're now working in the shop. But I don't believe that.'

'Kate,' said Ruth, calm but firm. 'Please don't say things like that.'

'It's all right,' Kate assured her. 'I *do* understand – honest I do. I mean, you haven't heard from Tom for ages, so why should you hang around waiting for him? In any case, you've got a right to change your mind. If you don't feel anything for him any more – so what? I mean, that's life, isn't it?'

'I don't know what you're talking about,' said Ruth, turning away. She was finding it difficult to counter Kate's shrewdness. 'You're wrong to suggest such things. I care just as much for Tom now as I always have done.' She paused just long enough to stare aimlessly out of the shop window. 'As far as I'm concerned,' she said, 'nothing's changed.'

She turned around to look at Kate. And she knew by the absolute stillness of the girl's reaction that she didn't believe a word Ruth had said.

Rita Simmons trundled along Hornsey Road at a pace that was far too dangerous for her weight, especially in the heat of a muggy August day. But she was too excited to care about the risk of a heart attack; her only purpose was to get to the Globe pub as fast as her tiny legs would carry her. She knew Edie would be there, because this was Saturday lunch-time, and Edie always popped in for a quick pint of stout on her way home from shopping in Seven Sisters Road. And in any case, reckoned Rita, it was very bad for a woman to drink alone in a pub, and Edie would be so delighted to see her, she would undoubtedly want to buy her a glass of 'mother's ruin'.

As it happened, Edie was not alone. She was sharing a table with a gentleman friend, a happy-go-lucky bloke in his sixties, who had a flock of white hair and a full 'tache to match. However, the moment they caught sight of Rita barging her way in through the Public Bar doors, Edie's companion made a quick getaway.

'Yer needn't bovver ter hide yer bit er trousers from me, Edie Perkins!' growled Rita, plonking herself down onto the vacated chair. 'I know all about you an' 'Arold Beaks.'

Edie was outraged. 'Wot *do* you mean, Rita?' she demanded. 'If you're suggestin'... I'll 'ave you know I don't go in – fer wot you're finkin'. I'm a respectable widow!'

'Yes,' sniffed Rita. 'And a bleedin' merry one by the looks er fings! Now shut yer 'ole an' buy me a short. I've got important fings ter discuss wiv yer.'

By the time Edie returned with Rita's usual pink gin and tonic, her dominant friend was ready to assail her with her latest bit of gossip.

'Young Poley,' she spluttered, after gulping down almost half the short in one go. 'Remember wot I told yer about the day I see 'er wiv that soldier boy in the street outside? Munffs ago, on the corner er the Annette cul, in the snow.'

'Oh Rita,' sighed Edie, who had heard this story over and over again.

'Don't yer Rita me!' snapped Rita. 'I've got proof now – positive bleedin' proof. She's 'ad anuvver letter from 'im. It's the fird one in a row.'

'Rita, 'ow d'yer know all this?' groaned Edie.

Rita leaned close, put her finger to her lips, looked around to make sure no one could hear her, and lowered her voice. 'I've seen 'em,' she said.

Edie gasped. 'Yer mean – yer've read Ruth's letters?'

'Not the letters, yer silly cow! The envelopes!'

Edie did a double-take. 'Yer've seen the envelopes?'

Rita gave a self-satisfied nod.

''Ow?'

Before answering, Rita again checked that no one could hear her. 'Stan left his bag wiv me, didn't 'e?' she replied. ''Im an' me always 'ave a nice little chin-wag in the mornin's. Sometimes I give 'im a quick cuppa, just ter wet 'is whistle. Then he leaves me wiv 'is bag fer a few minutes, whilst 'e delivers down our end er the road.'

Edie was listening with awe and horror. Around her, the bar was filling up, and the guv'nor and his missus were pulling up draught ale and bitter as fast as they could do it. 'Rita,' said Edie who was dying to get back to her gentleman friend who was keeping out of sight on the other side of the bar, 'are you tellin' me that you went through the post-bag, and looked through the letters.'

'The *envelopes!*' snapped Rita, haughtily. ''Ow many times do I 'ave ter tell yer?'

'But that's against the law,' said Edie. 'If you was found out, yer'd not only get yerself into trouble, but Postie too.'

'Ter my knowledge,' said Rita, ignoring her friend's warnings, 'young Poley's 'ad about a dozen letters from this bloke. An' plenty more that I ain't seen. Yer can be sure er that!'

Edie was totally flummoxed. She could hardly believe what her so-called friend was telling her. The two of them had always had a love-hate relationship, and to Edie's way of thinking, what Rita was doing now was absolutely terrible. 'But 'ow d'yer know the letters are from who yer say they're from?'

Rita smiled smugly. 'Private Mike Buller. 'Is name's always written on the back of the envelopes, always written in fancy handwritin'. Unless I'm mistaken, Edie, the person she's s'pposed ter be engaged to is a certain Phillips, is she not? Private Tom Phillips?'

Edie felt like shrivelling up inside. She couldn't bear to think what Ruth would do if she found out what Rita had been up to. Even worse, she knew only too well what Rita would do with the information if and when she was ready. 'Yer not – goin' ter say anyfin' ter 'er mum, are yer?' she asked timidly. 'Yer not goin' ter tell Bella Whitlock?'

Rita sat back in her chair, and polished off the remains of her pink gin. 'Wait an' see, Edie,' she said. 'Wait an' see.'

'Yer can't do it,' insisted Edie, daringly. 'It could kill poor Bella. She ain't been feelin' at all well just lately. She's got 'eart problems.'

'She ain't the only one!' snapped Rita.

'But why? Why are yer doin' this?'

Rita leaned forward in her chair. The look she gave Edie was so cold and calculating that Edie sat back in her own chair.

'They've bin 'ere too long, Edie,' she said. 'They ain't our sort. Ever since they come years ago, I've bin sayin' that they ain't got no right to our neck er the woods, 'specially 'er, 'specially that young Poley. Everyone knows wot that one

208

gets up to. She's not our kind, Edie. She's a tart. They've outlived their welcome, she *an'* 'er "'oity-toity bleedin' mama".' She leaned forward and did her best to be heard over the rowdy laughter coming from the darts game on the other side of the bar. 'The sooner they go,' she said, almost manically, 'the better fer all of us!'

On Saturday evening, Ruth got back home to find yet another of Mike Buller's letters waiting for her. Her immediate instinct was to throw it straight into the kitchen dustbin, but just as she was about to do so, she heard her mother calling to her from the sitting room.

When Ruth went in, her mother was sitting at the polished table by the bay window, flicking through old photographs in the family album. The angina attacks had clearly taken a toll on Bella over the past few weeks, for she was looking pale and drawn, and certainly lacked her usual energy. 'How are you feeling, Mama?' Ruth asked, pecking her mother gently on the cheek.

Bella shrugged. 'I'm still here,' she replied.

'Have you taken your tablets today?'

Bella waved her hand dismissively. 'If I take any more tablets, I'll rattle!'

Ruth smiled, and sat opposite her at the table.

'I've been looking at these pictures of the old days,' said Bella, turning a page of the album, 'when your father used to take us down to the sea.' She sighed, wistfully. 'Oh how he loved the sea. You remember how he always said that when he died he wanted to be near the sea?'

'Please, Mother,' said Ruth, turning to look out aimlessly through the lace curtains. 'Don't let's go through all that again.'

'We could take his ashes down to Clacton,' pressed Bella, taking off her spectacles. 'It was Harry's favourite place. He spent hours sitting on that bench on the promenade, just gazing out at the sea rolling onto the beach below, the seagulls swooping over the waves, the brisk cold air beating against his face.' She was suddenly fired with enthusiasm. 'They say the Army have opened up the beaches again. We could go down on the Orange luxury charabanc, and scatter his ashes over the sea.'

Sick to death of hearing the same old pleading from her mother, Ruth turned uncomfortably from one side to another.

'Oh *please*, Ruth!' begged Bella. 'It's not a long journey. We could go and come on the same day.' She leaned forward and tried another of her favourite tactics. 'He *did* love you, Ruth,' she insisted, calmly. 'I know you don't think he did, but he did.'

At breaking point, Ruth sprang to her feet. 'You're talking rubbish, Mama!' she snapped. 'It's always the same. You say these things without thinking!' She went to the fireplace, and stared down into the empty grate. 'You know very well what he thought of me. You know very well that it was a son he wanted – not me.' She looked up at the casket containing her father's ashes on the mantelpiece. She glowered at it. 'As he reminded me so many times, this is *his* home. He paid for it, and it belonged to him.' She

210

addressed the casket as though she were talking to her father direct. 'It's yours. So this is where you must stay.' She turned. 'If you want to take him down to the sea,' she said, calmly but decisively, 'then you must do it yourself.' Aware of the hurt her mother was feeling, she went across to her, and kissed her gently on her forehead. The look in Bella's eyes caused Ruth great anguish. This woman, her own mother, was ill, perhaps very ill; she might even die at any moment. And yet Ruth still couldn't bring herself to do what Bella wanted. 'I'm sorry, Mother,' was all she could say, before turning, and making for the door.

Bella watched her go, but just as Ruth had reached the sitting-room door, she called out in a contemptuous, but very frail voice, 'There's another letter waiting for you on the kitchen table. I imagine you've been expecting it.'

Ruth rejected the temptation to look back, and quietly left the room. For several moments, she leaned back against the closed sitting-room door, her heart thumping hard; she didn't know why, for the conversation she had just had with her mother had taken place so many times before. Once she'd recovered, she went back into the kitchen. Mike's letter was still there on the kitchen table, unopened. For a moment she just stood there staring at it. In one rash move, she grabbed hold of the envelope, ripped it open, and read the contents. Once again, the handwriting was unmistakable, curved and beautiful, sloping into an almost classical slant.

Dear Ruth,
I still miss you. I know I tell you this every time I write, but it's true. I keep wondering how you are, what you're doing, hoping you're taking care of yourself on that b– motorbike, and that the Fire boys are not working you too hard. Be careful, Ruth. If anything happened to you, I don't know what I'd do.

(This part was censored with a thick black mark-out) *but when we get out of here, I'll tell you all about it, especially the night when we* (This again was censored.) *I tell you, some of the blokes I'm with are real nutters. One of them comes from Derby, and the other day he showed me a trick he does with two matchsticks; he shoves them deep in both his ears, then brings them out again from his mouth. Don't ask me how he does it, but at least it gives us something to pass the time when we're lying down here in* (censored).

Got to go now. I hope you're thinking of me as much as I'm thinking of you. Our time together is the only thing I have to cling to. The thought of us being together again will keep me alive, whatever happens. You can bet on it!

Please write to me, Ruth. I have no way of telling whether you're getting my letters, but a few words from you would pep me up no end. Just write to the P.O. address at Aldershot I gave you. It'll find me. It had better!

Feel my kiss.
Your Mike xx

Ruth put down the letter. She had a sinking

feeling deep inside. How *could* she go on ignoring his pleas? A few words was all he asked. Surely that wasn't too much for a soldier facing death to ask? But then she thought again. What would happen if she did write those few words that he craved so much? Wouldn't that be a sign, a signal, that she would be waiting for him when he returned? In another rash movement, she went straight to the dresser, and took out a writing pad and fountain pen from the drawer there. Then she returned to the kitchen table, sat down, and started to write:

Jackson Road, August

Dear Mike,
Thanks for your letter. Thanks for all your letters. I'm glad you're alive and well, and hope you're looking after yourself. Everyone over here worries about our boys – wherever they are, so please be careful.
　Mike, there's something I have to tell you. It's about you and me, and no matter how hard I try to put it off, I can't do so any longer. The fact is, when you get home, I won't be able to see you again. I won't deny that the week we had together was wonderful, and that you are one of the loveliest people I have ever known. But since you went away I've thought things over very carefully, and I've decided that I can't go on deceiving Tom any longer. At the moment, we don't know if he's alive or dead, and that makes things even worse. But what I do know is that I do care for him, and that if he comes back alive and well, I shall marry him.
　Dear Mike, I'm sorry to have to break this news to

213

you, especially at a time like this when you yourself are in such danger, but it has to be done, now, before I can hurt you any more.

Please forgive me. One of these days some lucky girl will catch up with you, and when she does, no one will be more happy for you than me.

Take care, dear Mike. And thank you for everything.

Ruth

Once she had finished writing, she sat back in her chair for a moment, reading through what she had just written. Then she paused for thought, got up, and went back to the dresser drawer to collect an envelope. Again she paused, to glance over the contents of the letter just once more. Then slowly, methodically, she changed her mind, and tore the letter into tiny pieces.

Pearl Phillips was overjoyed to see Ruth. Ever since she had received the news that her son Tom was reported missing and presumed dead, she had gone into a decline. But Ruth's Sunday afternoon visit had given her renewed hope, mainly because Ruth had spent the past hour reassuring her about the number of men she had heard of who had been reported as missing in similar circumstances, but who had eventually turned up safe and well.

'I don't mind if it means that 'e's *not* completely well,' Pearl explained, her eyes glistening with hope for the first time in months. 'If 'e's injured or anythin', I'll take care of 'im. 'E won't 'ave ter worry about a fing in the world.'

Ruth gave her a reassuring smile.

'Wot I can't bear,' said Pearl, her face screwed up with anxiety, 'is the thought that 'e might be dead, or that 'e's rottin' away in some God-forsaken Japanese prisoner-er-war camp. 'E's my boy. I can't bear to fink wot 'e's goin' through.'

Ken Phillips smoked his pipe and looked longingly towards his allotment at the end of the garden. As far as he was concerned, his wife was quite mad. Her 'boy', as she called him, was, in his opinion, obviously dead, and there was nothing in the world anyone was going to be able to do about it.

For her part, Pearl was certainly giving the impression that her mind was not in good shape. Rocking to and fro in her wicker chair in the back garden, she worked hard on the sweater she was knitting for Tom, the needles clicking furiously, an act of faith that her 'boy' would soon be coming back to her. 'When you two get married,' she said, without looking up at Ruth, 'I shall save you lots of money by knitting all your baby clothes. I shall love it so much.'

Ruth caught a sly smirk from Kate, who was standing in the back doorway of the house, arms crossed, gazing quizzically up into the darkening clouds. 'You must show me how to knit some-time, Mrs Phillips,' said Ruth, doing her best to make some kind of sense out of what was increas-ingly becoming an unreal situation. 'I've always wanted to learn how to knit.'

'Mum,' replied Pearl, again without looking up.

Ruth swung a questioning look at Kate, who merely shrugged. 'I'm sorry?' Ruth asked, turning

215

back to Pearl.

'You're going to marry my boy,' replied Pearl, 'so it's time you called me Mum.'

Ruth was confused. How could Pearl expect her to call her Mum when for all she knew, Tom was dead. But as Ruth watched the poor woman knitting for her son, it was becoming clear that in her own troubled mind, Pearl Phillips would only believe what she wanted to believe – that one day Tom would be coming home to settle down with a wife and family of his own.

Having refused a cup of tea, Ken was into his second pint glass of brown ale. 'I don't see the point in it meself,' he said, between puffs of his pipe. 'Why should she call yer Mum when she already 'as a muvver of 'er own?'

'Because we're all going to be one big happy family,' insisted Pearl, looking up for the first time to give Ruth a huge, affectionate smile. 'Isn't that so, love?'

Ruth did her best to smile back, but it was a real effort. There followed another of those end-less silences which she had begun to dread, mainly because it gave her time to dwell on what her future could be like if she did marry Tom Phillips. Did he have a mind of his own, she wondered? Would he be able to stand up to this kind of empty banter? But even more important was whether she, Ruth, would ever be able to spend evenings alone with a man who was so inextricably tied to such a disorientated family as this? The air was thick and humid. She looked for escape up in the sky. The clouds were getting darker by the minute, and she longed for a storm

– anything that would give her an excuse to get home. She got up, and idly strolled down the garden. After a moment or so, she was convinced she felt the first drop of rain, but it turned out to be wishful thinking.

'Yer don't 'ave ter worry, yer know.'

Ruth turned with a start to find Ken Phillips, pipe in mouth, walking alongside her.

'Tom ain't comin' back,' he said. 'She finks 'e is, but 'e ain't. I know wot those words mean: *missin', presumed dead*. They mean we've lost 'im, an' there's no way we're goin' ter get 'im back.'

'We mustn't give up hope, Mr Phillips,' said Ruth, only too aware that after not hearing from Tom for such a long time, it was becoming increasingly possible that he would never be coming back home. 'I'm told the Red Cross is doing wonderful things keeping in touch with the POWs.'

'We 'aven't 'eard a word from the Red Cross,' replied Ken. 'An' I don't expect to. So if I was you, I'd just get on wiv your life, and ferget all about 'im.'

Ruth was flabbergasted. 'Forget him?' she said, the words sticking in her throat. 'How can I forget the man I've promised to marry?'

'Because yer don't want 'im,' returned Phillips. '*I* know that, an' so do you.'

Ruth was so angry, she turned, and started to walk away, but Phillips immediately took hold of her arm.

'Yer know,' he said, 'I've never pretended ter be an educated man, an' I know I don't talk well, but if there's one fing I've learned in life, it's

217

about people, about the way they try to hide fings.'

'I have *nothing* to hide,' insisted Ruth, firmly, but unconvincingly. 'I've promised to wait for Tom, and that's exactly what I intend to do.'

'Is that a fact?' replied Phillips. 'Well, we'll just 'ave ter wait an' see, won't we? Mind you, I don't blame yer. I don't blame yer one little bit. Life moves on, and we all 'ave ter move wiv it.'

Phillips's assumptions utterly repulsed Ruth, and her inclination was to tell him so. But she made a concerted effort to restrain how she felt about him, and the rest of his family. She moved away from him just a few steps, and found herself beneath the same apple tree Tom had asked her to marry him. The apples themselves were already well formed, and it looked as though it would be producing a bumper crop within a month or so. 'I know you're only saying all these things, Mr Phillips,' she said, 'because you're just as heartbroken at not knowing what has happened to Tom as Mrs Phillips. It's so cruel just sitting around waiting for news, hoping and praying.'

'Praying?' asked Phillips. 'Oh yes, I do plenty er that, all right. But not for Tom. I pray for meself, fer Pearl, an' fer Kate. But not fer Tom.'

Ruth was absolutely shocked and taken aback. 'How can you say such things?' she asked. 'Surely you care for him – your own flesh and blood?'

'Care?' asked Phillips. 'Why should I care?'

Ruth stared at him in disbelief. 'Because he's your son, your only son.'

Even as she spoke, Phillips was shaking his

head at her. 'That's where you're wrong, little lady,' he said. 'Tom ain't my son. He never 'as bin, an' 'e never will be.'

Chapter 11

Ruth was so taken aback by Ken Phillips's remark that she wished he hadn't made it. The fact that he didn't seem to care about his son was shameful enough, but to let it be known that Tom wasn't his *own* son was, in Ruth's opinion, a skeleton that should have been kept well and truly locked up in the family cupboard.

They strolled together towards the end of the garden, where Ken stopped to pull back some ivy that was beginning to block the entrance of the Anderson shelter. When he had finished doing that, he rubbed his hands down his grey flannel trousers, regardless of the fact that they were his Sunday best. 'Don't look so shocked, gel,' he said, in response to Ruth's distant gaze. 'This sort er fing 'appens in all sorts er families. Pearl was pregnant when we got married. It's as simple as that.'

'Simple!' spluttered Ruth.

'I didn't know at the time,' continued Ken, with a bit of a chuckle. 'But I soon found out!'

'And – you didn't mind?'

'Mind?' asked Phillips. 'Oh, I minded all right. But what could I do? Call it a day, and kick 'er out of the 'ouse? Yer can imagine wot boaf our families would've felt about *that!* No.' He casually looked around to see if there were any more jobs that needed attending to. 'I made up me mind ter grin an' bear it, ter take on the kid as if 'e was me own, an' then make sure it wasn't too long before she give me one of me own. That's where Kate come in. She's a good gel, that one. We don't always see eye ter eye, mind – but she means well.'

'And Tom?' asked Ruth cautiously. 'Does *he* know you're not his father?'

'Course 'e does,' replied Phillips, without a sign of remorse. 'I always vowed I wouldn't keep somefin' like that from 'im. An' I 'aven't.'

Ruth waited whilst he relit his pipe before asking him, 'What about his real father?'

'Wot about 'im?' replied Phillips, between puffing out clouds of pipe smoke. 'Tom don't know who 'e is, an' neivver do I. It don't make much difference ter Tom, so who cares. All I know is wot Pearl told me, about 'ow all this 'appened on a one night fling. Usual fing – she meets up wiv a feller at a dance 'all, gets all worked up about 'im fer five minutes, gives 'im wot they boaf want, an' then lets 'im drift off inter the night wivout a by yer leave. Romantic, ain't it?'

Ruth could hardly believe what she was hearing. To Phillips, everything was so matter-of-fact, so natural to him, that she just couldn't make sense of his logic – if, in his case, there *was* such a thing. However, for one fleeting moment it did cross her mind that, despite Pearl's capitulation to what looked like a marriage of convenience, what she had done did at least show that when she was young, she must have had quite a mind and a spirit of her own.

They moved off into Phillips's allotment, his pride and joy, his sanctuary. Along with the cucumbers, carrots, and late summer peas, were now two rows of tomatoes, each plant staked, and bulging with glowing red fruit, ripening in the intermittent flashes of afternoon sun.

'Ah!' said Phillips, stooping down to adjust the string on one of the stakes, and addressing the plant as though it was a living human thing which, to him, it was. 'Got yerself in a bit of a mess, 'ave yer, son? Can't 'ave that, can we?' He finished what he was doing, and got up. 'Yer know the funny fing about Pearl?' he said, quite openly. 'Despite the fact that 'alf the time she's round the bend – I still love 'er.' Once again, he wiped his hands down his trousers. 'Mind you,' he said, flicking Ruth a quick, passing glance, 'I won't deny that from time ter time, me own eye's wandered a bit. Wouldn't be 'uman if it didn't, would I? But even though listening ter the silly cow day after day, dronin' on about fings that mean absolutely nuffin', sometimes – when I catch a look at her – just fer a second – that face, those eyes flickin' or starin' – it's then that I remember why I fell in love wiv 'er in the first place.'

As Ruth listened to this man, she gradually came to the conclusion that he might not be quite the kind of person she had taken him for, and that there was far more beneath the surface of this family than she could have possibly imagined. 'But what about Tom?' she asked. 'If you love your wife, why couldn't you love him too?'

'Ah!' retorted Phillips. 'Now that's a diff'rent story. Chalk an' cheese, that's me an' Tom. D'yer know wot 'e once said ter me when I called 'im *son?* 'E said, *"You ain't my farver, so don't call me son."*'

Ruth squirmed. It was painful to see the look on Phillips's face as he told her.

'I don't know why,' continued Phillips, as he puffed his pipe, and leaned on a spade that he'd left in a patch of half-dug soil. 'I've always done me best fer 'im. When 'e was young, I always give 'im the same as Kate – they never wanted fer anyfin'. When 'e joined the Cubs, I bought 'im 'is uniform, same when 'e joined up the Scouts. I give 'im money ter go off wiv 'is mates, I never forced 'im ter come ter church on Sundays if 'e didn't want – an' yet – an' yet, 'e still didn't 'ave no time fer me.' He picked up the spade and cast it like a spear into the hard earth. 'Respect,' he said. 'That's all I ever asked from 'im. But I never got it.'

The anguish in Phillips's voice was more than Ruth could bear, so she slowly turned and made her way back into the garden.

'Ruth.'

Ruth stopped and turned. It was practically the first time she had heard Phillips address her by her proper name.

'There was always two sides ter Tom, yer know,' he said, talking as though the boy was now in the past. 'Part of 'im was the good-lookin' one, full er life, a knock-out wiv the gels, do anyfin' for yer.

222

Then there was the uvver Tom.' He took several deep puffs of his pipe. 'Dark, moody, opinionated, knock yer down as good as look at yer if 'e din't get 'is own way. I once saw 'im in a right ol' temper, when 'e grabbed 'old of 'is mum's 'air an' pushed 'er across the room an' all becos 'e resented the fact that she was spendin' too much time knittin' a cardigan fer me. That was only a couple er years ago, just before 'e went in the Army. I told 'im, if 'e ever raised 'is fist to 'is muvver in my presence again, I'd bash 'is bleedin' brains in.' He looked directly at Ruth, his eyes trying to tell her something that he wasn't actually prepared to put into words. 'I never trusted that boy,' he said quietly. ''E was always two people. Given 'alf a chance, I reckon one of 'em would've killed yer stone dead!'

Ruth stared back at him with deep foreboding, for she realised only too well that this man believed every word of what he had just said.

Edie Perkins came out of her front door and peered up the cul de sac towards Jackson Road. Once she had made quite certain that the coast was clear, she went back inside and reappeared almost immediately with her gentleman friend, Harold Beaks. Not a word was spoken between them as the white-haired man left as quickly and as unobtrusively as he could manage. To Edie's dismay, however, the moment he reached the end of the road, she saw him bump into Ruth as she turned the corner. But he rushed off immediately without stopping.

'Wasn't that Harold Beaks I just passed?' asked

223

Ruth, as she reached Edie's front garden gate.

Edie looked up with a start from pretending to deadhead some roses with her fingers. 'Who?' she asked, surprised.

'Harold Beaks,' repeated Ruth. 'That floor assistant down at Jones' Brothers, in the hardware department.'

'Actually 'e's a floor manager,' replied Edie, grandly, until she realised that she was giving herself away. 'Oh, was that 'im? Wonder wot 'e's doin' down this way?'

Ruth knew exactly what he'd been doing. It wasn't the first time she'd seen Harold sneaking like a cat burglar into Edie's next door. 'Well, he's a very nice man,' she said reassuringly.

Edie glowed. ''Ave yer got a minute?' she asked mysteriously.

'Of course,' said Ruth. 'What's up?'

A few moments later she was sitting in Edie's neat little back parlour, which smelt of carbolic soap and floor polish. In fact, the place was so ultra-clean, Ruth could see her face reflected in the bright yellow linoleum.

'I haven't told a livin' soul wot I'm about ter tell yer,' said Edie, even more mysteriously, as she poured Ruth a small glass of sweet sherry. 'But I've known you since yer was a kid, an' I know yer wouldn't split on me.'

Edie's plot was thickening, and as Ruth took the glass from her, she was becoming more intrigued by the minute. 'Of course I won't, Edie,' she promised.

Edie sat down opposite her at the parlour table. 'I'm courting,' she announced sheepishly.

'Edie!' gushed Ruth.

'Yes, I know,' said Edie, biting her lip nervously. 'It's terrible, isn't it?'

'Terrible? I think it's the most wonderful thing I've ever heard.' Ruth leaned across and squeezed Edie's hand. 'Oh Edie, I'm so happy for you. Is it Harold?'

Edie looked surprised. ''Ow did yer know?'

Ruth grinned. 'Oh, we girls can tell these things,' she replied teasingly. 'He's a very nice man, and so good-looking.'

Edie flushed like a schoolgirl. 'D'yer fink so?' she asked. 'D'yer really fink so?'

'Absolutely,' replied Ruth. 'How long have you been seeing him?'

'Nearly a year now.'

'A year!' Ruth's face lit up. 'Then has he asked you to marry him?'

Edie was taken aback. 'Blimey, no!' she gasped, flustered. 'I couldn't – I wouldn't. Not yet – I'm not ready. I mean, a woman of my age...'

'A woman of your age has every right to do exactly what she wants.'

Edie was shaking her head.

'Why not?'

'Rita.'

Ruth was puzzled. 'Rita?' she asked. 'Mrs Simmons?' Edie nodded timidly.

'What about her?'

Edie slumped back in her chair. 'I'm scared she's goin' ter find out.'

Ruth was thunderstruck. 'Scared?' she growled. 'Of Rita Simmons? Because you're courting?'

Edie took a quick gulp of her own sherry. 'I've

225

always bin scared of 'er,' she said. 'Ever since we first got ter know each uvver. I'm scared of the way she makes fun er me, of the way she tries ter get me ter take sides wiv 'er about everyfin' an' everybody. I've never liked it.'

'Then why d'you let her bully you like this?' asked Ruth.

Edie put down her glass. 'Becos I 'aven't got the guts ter stand up to 'er,' she replied. 'Rita's got a way of takin' yer over, an' never lettin' go.'

'You *mustn't* let her dominate you like this, Edie,' Ruth said. 'You must make up your own mind about things.'

'Easier said than done,' said Edie. She got up from the table, and ambled across to look at a snapshot of her late husband on the mantelpiece. 'Years before Arfur died, 'e once told me that if anyfin' 'appened to 'im, 'e wanted me ter find anuvver feller, an' settle down wiv 'im. 'E said that becos one of us 'as ter go, it's not right ter sit back an' grieve fer the rest of yer life. At the time, I fawt it was a stupid fing ter say. I told 'im there was never goin' ter be anyone else in my life 'cept 'im an' I meant it. But a year or so after 'e died, I *did* meet someone.' Her eyes flicked up to her own reflection in the mirror above the mantel-piece. ''E worked on the Underground, same as Arfur. I'd often seen 'im when I took Arfur 'is sandwiches. 'E was a lovely man, a widower, lost 'is wife a coupla years before I lost Arfur. We walked out tergevver fer nearly a year. 'E asked me ter marry 'im. I said yes. We set a date an' everyfin'. That is, 'til Rita turned up.' She turned around to look at Ruth. 'From the moment she set eyes on 'im, she started workin' on me. She said it was disgustin' that a woman my age should start muckin' around wiv men, and that I was a laughin' stock up Jackson Road, especially since me "leg er trousers" towered above me.'

'Oh Edie,' sighed Ruth in disbelief.

'Every time Rita saw me wiv 'im in the street,' continued Edie, sitting down opposite Ruth again, 'she always made a point er comin' up to us an' makin' cheap jokes. Rita's a coarse woman, she always 'as bin, 'specially when she wants somefin'. An' she *did* want somefin', Rufe. She wanted ter break up my prospects. She wanted ter 'ang on ter me.'

Ruth listened in shocked astonishment as Edie opened up her heart to her. As she sat there in Edie's beautifully cared for parlour, surrounded by mementos of a happy marriage, the early evening sun flooding the room through the overhead fanlight window, she found it hard to believe that anyone could actually bring themselves to inflict so much pain and suffering on such a harmless, worthwhile person as Edie Perkins.

'I love 'Arold Beaks,' Edie said quite suddenly. 'I don't want to lose 'im.'

'Then you mustn't, Edie!' Ruth insisted firmly.

'It's not becos of wot people – becos of wot Rita – might fink it is,' said Edie, awkwardly. 'It's becos I need someone ter share the rest of me life wiv. I need the companionship, to 'ave someone I can talk fings over wiv. I *need* someone I can look after, just like I did wiv Arfur.'

By now, Ruth felt churned up inside. What with

Tom's father, and now Edie, this had been one hell of a day, and she didn't know what more she could say to Edie. She took a sip of sherry. It was so acid she nearly choked.

'The reason I'm tellin' yer all this,' said Edie, 'is becos I don't want the same fing ter 'appen ter you.'

Ruth looked up with a shocked start.

'Rita's found out about you an' that boy who's bin writin' to yer. I can't tell yer 'ow,' said Edie, before Ruth had a chance to answer. 'All I can tell yer is that she knows.'

For a brief moment, Ruth was too stunned to answer. 'How *much* does she know?' she asked.

Edie found it difficult to tell her. 'She's bin goin' on about it fer munffs,' she said, 'ever since she saw yer with that soldier boy. She saw you wiv 'im on the street corner up the road. It was in the middle of a snowstorm or somefin'. She knows it wasn't the boy you was seein' before, the one yer goin' ter marry.'

In despair, Ruth slumped back into her chair.

'I din't want ter tell yer, Rufe, 'onest I din't,' she said, nervously. 'But when Rita told me what she'd done, about all the letters yer've bin gettin' an' everyfin'…'

'*How* does she know about my letters, Edie,' insisted Ruth. 'You *must* tell me.'

Edie shook her head vigorously.

'Why not?' snapped Ruth. 'For God's sake, Edie, this is *my* life we're talking about! For some reason, this woman is carrying on a vendetta against me, and I want to put a stop to it right now!'

In desperation, Edie got up from her chair, crossed her arms, and looked aimlessly up at the fanlight. 'I can't do it, Rufe,' she replied. 'Whatever Rita is, whatever she's done, I can't let 'er get into trouble fer it.'

'But what about *me?*' demanded Ruth, also getting up from the table. 'If you go on protecting this woman, she could go on destroying people's lives for ever.'

Edie turned around slowly. 'Rita's my friend, Rufe,' she said, ruefully. 'I hate wot she's doin', an' I'll do anyfin' I can ter stop 'er. But I won't be responsible fer sendin' 'er ter prison.'

Ruth was bewildered. How could Edie try to protect someone who was determined to wreck so many lives? 'If you feel this way, Edie,' she said, 'why have you told me all this?'

Edie looked up at her. 'Because she wants ter tell yer mum.'

Ruth stared back in disbelief. 'My mother?' she asked. 'Rita wants to tell my mother that I've been seeing another man?'

Edie lowered her eyes. She was fraught with anguish. 'She wants ter tell 'er that yer 'aven't changed yer ways.'

For one brief moment, Ruth allowed what Edie had said to sink in. Then without saying another word, she turned, and made for the door.

'Rufe!' Edie rushed after her into the passage. 'Don't tell Rita!' she pleaded. 'Please don't tell 'er I told yer.'

Ruth swung round impatiently. 'Why not, Edie?' she barked. 'What are you so afraid of?' The moment she looked at Edie's face, so crumpled up, so vulnerable, she softened. 'Look,' she said with quiet understanding, 'Rita Simmons is only a woman. She's only flesh and blood like you and me. But she can cause great pain, great rifts in our lives. If we don't stand up to someone like her, she'll destroy us, Edie – you, me, and everyone she comes into contact with.'

Once again, Edie was slowly nodding her head.

Ruth sighed. 'Why not, Edie?' she asked in desperation. 'Why *can't* you stand up to her, and tell her the truth about herself?'

Edie slowly looked up. 'Becos if I do,' she said, her eyes welling up with tears, 'if I do... Yer don't understand, Rufe. Nobody understands. Yer see, Rita's got problems. She's always 'ad problems. If I tried ter tell 'er some 'ome trufes about 'erself, she'd do 'erself in. She's tried before – an' she'll try again.'

Ruth and her mother were at Sunday evening Benediction in St Anthony's Church. As always, there was a full congregation, and Father Tim, together with the help of his young altar server, was already reciting the *O Salutaris Hostia*. During the Adoration which followed, Ruth's eyes never left the glistening silver monstrance which contained the consecrated Host, hoping for some kind of comfort from a day that had shocked and traumatised her. Earlier, she had considered asking Father Tim to hear her Confession, but once again her nerve had failed her, and she opted instead to accompany her mother to the evening service.

Despite her reservations about the healing

powers of faith and religion, she found a kind of peace within the smooth stone walls of the old Victorian church where, before they were shattered by bomb blast, its four treasured stained-glass windows had embraced the golden rays of the morning sun. As she knelt alongside her mother in a rear pew, Ruth had much to mull over, many answers to search for in her tortured soul. Throughout the service, she had unconsciously caressed Tom's engagement ring on her finger, her thoughts plagued by guilt and indecision. Surely the only way to clear the air was to confess her true feelings, to put a stop to the deceit and the wagging tongues once and for all. Despite all that, however, she just couldn't forget what Edie had told her about Rita Simmons. Was it really possible that there was a weak, vulnerable side to this overbearing woman, a mind that was so at war with itself that it was capable of putting an end to it all?

After the service, Ruth and her mother strolled slowly home, arm-in-arm, along Hornsey Road. Although most of the blackout blinds had already been drawn at the windows of houses on the way, it was still quite light, and the pavements were gradually drying out after a brief thunderstorm late in the afternoon. Ruth was encouraged to see her mother getting a little stronger each day; the pills the doctor had given her were certainly helping to lessen the pain from her angina attacks, and she was altogether more bright in herself. Even so, she was surprised when Bella suggested that, as it was such a fine evening, they should make a slight detour, and go

231

home through the back streets into Seven Sisters Road. There weren't many people around, and those that were were probably on their way home after spending Sunday with friends or relations. Bella quickened her step as they reached the junction at the Nags Head, and grabbing hold of Ruth's hand, led her across the road until they ended up on a bench seat near the bus stop overlooking Holloway Road. 'I used to come here with your father soon after we came back to England,' she said, once they had settled. 'Of course, there was no seat in those days, so we perched on the wall over there by the cinema.'

Ruth turned to look at the old Marlborough cinema just behind them, where the second of two Sunday showings of *The Man in the Iron Mask* was enthralling audiences young and old.

'I always loved the city,' continued Bella. 'Your father much preferred the country and the seaside, but not me. There's something special about the sounds of a city. They bring everything to life – a real heartbeat. It was the same when I was a child in Cracow. I loved walking home from school and looking in all the fine shop windows in the old part of the town, trying to imagine if one day I would ever be able to afford any of the beautiful things I saw. And the delirious smells of freshly baked bread from Mr Rudzski's shop, and of veal stew from the Jewish restaurant on the corner of our street, and people huddled together around the hot sausage and apple stall on the promenade overlooking the Wisla.' She sighed nostalgically.

At that moment a tram rattled to a halt at the

tram stop, allowing a handful of passengers to get off, and even fewer to get on. The tram moved off again, and the passengers dispersed.

'I miss the church bells, don't you?' continued Bella, her eyes constantly scanning the road all around her. 'Sundays in England are never the same without them. They sing to you – like angels.'

Ruth smiled sympathetically at her mother's reflections, without actually agreeing with them. And she felt guilty that at such a moment, the things she remembered most about her childhood were the screaming matches she heard so often between her parents. Was it hypocritical to ignore the bad times when recalling the past? she asked herself. Or was it that she had never understood that in all marriages, a war of words didn't necessarily mean that two people didn't love each other.

'Do you think Tom really *is* dead?'

Ruth swung a startled look at her mother. The question had come out of the blue, and it had stung her.

'I know it's not easy to know,' said Bella, meeting Ruth's eyes, 'especially when you have no definite news. But sometimes, a woman can tell – it's a feeling inside, an instinct.'

Without realising it, Ruth was fingering her engagement ring again. 'I don't know, Mama,' she said quietly. 'I just don't know. I keep hearing the most terrible things about what's going on in those Japanese camps. It's difficult to imagine how anyone can survive the kind of conditions they say the prisoners are having to endure.'

'But do you *want* Tom to come home again?'

Once again Bella's harsh question stung Ruth. 'That's a terrible thing to ask, Mama,' she said reprovingly.

'Not if you know your child is in love with someone else.'

Bella's directness was taking Ruth completely off-guard, and she wasn't prepared for it. 'I don't know what you're talking about, Mama.'

'My eyes are wide open, Ruth,' replied Bella. 'I can't go on pretending that I'm blind. I'm your mother, remember. If you can't talk to me, you can't talk to anyone.' She reached out for Ruth's hand, and gently covered it. 'Tell me about this man.'

Ruth's reaction was still dismissive and non-committal.

'Oh, Ruth,' sighed Bella. 'I'm not a fool. I've seen all those letters arriving week after week. The least you can do is to tell me who he is, where he comes from.'

The late August sun had now set behind Woolworth's department store on the other side of the road, and the light was fading to leave all the many different shops along the Holloway Road bathed in a curious dark-orange glow.

Ruth got up from the bench. 'Let's go home, Mama,' she said. 'It's getting late.' She gently took hold of Bella's arm, and helped her to her feet.

'You know, darling,' said Bella, 'we can be different things to all people, but we have to be truthful to ourselves.'

She hardly had time to get the words from her

234

mouth, when the air was suddenly cracked by a deafening sound which seemed to come from nowhere. Someone shouted, 'There's one coming!' and all eyes instantly turned towards the sky. Within seconds, a doodlebug flying bomb raced into sight high above the rooftops, its rocket-engine shattering the calm of the road below, the sinister blast of flame from its exhaust pipe ripping through the small puffs of darkening clouds above. The menacing machine disappeared as fast as it had come, but as it did so, its engine suddenly shut down. Several people in the road shouted, 'Down!'

Ruth grabbed hold of her mother, and immediately eased them both to the ground, flat on their stomachs. The few moments of heart-stopping silence that followed were now a familiar signal that the explosion was imminent. When it came, the whole road shuddered and shook, windows were shattered all around, and a sudden gust of wind swept along the pavements, sending a discarded newspaper on the bench that Ruth and Bella had been sitting on fluttering up into the air.

As soon as the road had settled down again, and everyone felt safe enough to get up, Ruth helped her mother to her feet. Shaken, their bright summer dresses smudged with dirt, their stockings laddered, they started to make their way back home as fast as they could. But just as they were doing so, someone shouted, 'Anuvver one!'

All eyes again looked upwards, as another burning flame shot across the sky. This time it was heading straight above Holloway Road, the deafening roar of its engines taking it at lightning speed in the same direction as Ruth and her mother were making for.

A few moments later, there was another shattering explosion in the distance, followed by a huge ball of flame, with thick black smoke that spiralled up into the sky, turning a hot summer's evening into a gloomy dark night.

Chapter 12

The two doodlebugs had caused extensive damage to both commercial and residential property. One had come down on a piano warehouse in Camden Town, and the other demolished a row of houses within a stone's throw of Jackson Road. Fortunately, the railway bridge above the 'end house' survived intact, but the cul de sac suffered shattered windows, tiles off roofs, and lumps of plaster that came fluttering down from ceilings everywhere. It was at times like this that the community really came together, and despite the fact that a number of windows had to be boarded up, within a matter of days things were pretty much back to normal. Despite this, however, Ruth decided that the shock of being caught unawares in the street during the flying bomb attack was too much for her mother, and so after a great deal of arguing, Bella finally agreed to go and spend some time with her two elderly Polish aunts, Katya and Glinka, who lived in the countryside just outside Chesterfield.

With her workload now increased, Ruth decided to start closing the shop on Saturday afternoons, giving her time for stocktaking and for coping with any emergencies. She also asked Freda Dapper if she could help out part-time in the shop, which would at least give Ruth time to look after the 'end house', and have some time to herself. Freda was thrilled to get the job; to be paid for chatting to people was more than she had ever dared hope for in her humdrum world, and the excitement of it all gave her a new lease of life.

After what Edie Perkins had told her about Rita Simmons, Ruth made a conscious decision to put Mike Buller from her mind once and for all. Regardless of the fact that Tom was unlikely to return home alive, she felt she owed it to her mother, Tom's family, and everyone else who cared for her, to show restraint and respect until Tom's fate was ascertained beyond reasonable doubt. It helped that, for the past two weeks, she had not received any more letters from Mike, which was making it easier for her to forget all about him. However, that feeling of calm became more difficult to maintain when, on Wednesday afternoon, she received a visit at the shop from her old mate up at the fire-station, Mavis Miller.

'He's come 'ome, Rufe! Charlie's come 'ome! When I saw 'im standin' on the corner outside in Upper Street, I nearly 'ad a fit! Yer should've 'eard the boys in the station when they saw 'im pick me up in the air, and give me one of the most disgustin' kisses I've ever had! Filthy bleedin' lot!'

Ruth found Mavis's exuberance infectious. 'Oh, Mavis!' she roared, laughing. 'That's absolutely wonderful!' She threw her arms around her, and hugged her. 'But what's he doing home?' she asked. 'Where's he been? Is he home for good?'

Mavis did a quick shufty over her shoulder to make sure there was no one else in the shop. ''E's not s'pposed ter say,' she said, lowering her voice to a whisper. 'But 'e says 'e's bin up front somewhere in France. 'E's in the Medical Corps. 'E's come back wiv a shipload er wounded soldiers. But 'e's got ter go back in a coupla days.'

'Oh dear,' said Ruth, with a sigh. 'Did he say if there were a lot of casualties over there?'

Mavis nodded. 'Sounds like it,' she replied guardedly. 'Still, at least I put all me cards on the table.'

Ruth was puzzled. 'What do you mean?' she asked.

'I told 'im I've 'ad a bit of a fling while 'e's bin away.'

'Oh, Mavis,' said Ruth, remembering what had happened to Sweetie. 'Is that wise?'

'Well, 'e's bin no angel eivver,' she replied, haughtily. ''E more or less said as much, wot wiv all them French madams in the broffels. I always know when he's bin up ter somefin' when 'e pinches my bottom. Guilty conscience, that's wot it is!'

Ruth chuckled. But she had to leave Mavis for a moment whilst she served a customer who came in to buy a copy of the *Beano* for her small son. Once they had left, Ruth took down a fresh packet of cigarettes from the shelf, opened it, and offered one to Mavis.

'So do I detect the sound of wedding bells?' asked Ruth, as they both lit up.

'Not 'til the war's over,' replied Mavis, sceptically. 'When 'e comes 'ome fer good, I shall see 'ow fings go. If he looks as though 'e's the settlin' down type, I'll give 'im a chance.'

'And if he isn't?'

Mavis blew out some smoke. 'Plenty more fish in the sea,' she replied, with a grin. For the next moment or so, she wandered around, taking a look at the shop as she watched Ruth, cigarette between her lips, unpacking a small stock of stationery and stacking it on one of the shelves behind the counter. 'Still no word from Tom?' she asked suddenly.

Ruth briefly stopped what she was doing, and took the cigarette out of her lips. 'No,' she replied, with only a passing glance back at Mavis.

'I'm sorry, Rufe,' said Mavis, coming across to her. 'It must be awful not knowin'.'

Ruth nodded.

'I still shouldn't give up 'ope if I was you,' said Mavis. 'I've 'eard of tons er blokes in the Army who've turned up after bein' reported missin' or dead.'

'I know, Mavis,' said Ruth, carrying on with her stacking. 'I know.'

Mavis decided it was a difficult issue for Ruth to talk about, so she decided it was better not to pursue it. 'Wot about the uvver one?' she asked.

239

Ruth immediately stopped what she was doing, and looked up. But she didn't turn.

'*Which* other one?' she asked, warily.

'Mike,' said Mavis, quite unaware that she was treading on dangerous ground. 'Mike Buller. That juicy lookin' bloke that come up to look fer yer at the station that time. The one who kept leavin' messages fer yer. Did 'e ever write to yer again?'

Ruth paused a moment, then carried on stacking. 'No,' she replied, in an effort to sound as disinterested as she possibly could. 'I haven't heard from him in a long time. Hopefully he's found somebody else to harass. Why d'you ask?'

'No reason,' replied Mavis, flicking through a *Picturegoer* magazine on the newspaper rack in front of the counter. 'It's just that Charlie 'appened ter mention that when 'e was talkin' to a bunch er tommies on the 'ospital boat comin' back from France, one of the boys was sayin' as 'ow 'e worked wiv is grandad up 'Ackney way – in an undertaker's parlour.'

'Did Charlie say who this boy was?' Ruth asked, leaving Mavis hardly enough time to answer. 'Did he mention his name?'

A bit taken aback by Ruth's sudden intense interest, Mavis shook her head.

'But he must have said something,' persisted Ruth. 'Surely Charlie wouldn't have talked about this person unless he knew his name?'

'Ruth, there were loads of fellers on that boat,' said Mavis, defensively. 'This bloke was just one of 'em. I only mentioned it becos I remember you tellin' me that the bloke who kept followin'

240

yer around come from 'Ackney, an' that he worked wiv 'is grandad in a funeral parlour.'

Ruth quickly came round from behind the counter. 'Which regiment was he in?' she pressed, impatiently. 'Was it a London regiment?'

'I've no idea, Rufe,' said Mavis, a bit bewildered by Ruth's intense questioning. 'I s'ppose it must be if the bloke comes from 'Ackney. Which regiment was Mike Buller in, then?'

Ruth shook her head. 'I never really asked him.'

'Charlie's a bit *mum's the word* about it, but 'e did say that the RA were one of the first up front, and that ever since D-Day they've bin takin' quite a hammerin'.'

'The RA?' asked Ruth.

'Royal Artillery.'

Ruth bit her lip anxiously.

'Why?' asked Mavis, now burning with curiosity. 'Is Mike a gunner?'

Ruth hesitated. She was deep in thought, trying to recall the time when Mike had talked about the excitement of being assigned to 'the big guns'. 'I don't know, Mavis,' she replied, pulling nervously on her cigarette. 'I just don't know.'

Mavis watched her old mate carefully. Although she wasn't renowned for her tact, this was a moment in which she suddenly felt real concern for Ruth. 'If yer want, I could find out,' she offered, putting a comforting arm around Ruth's waist. 'I could ask Charlie if 'e knows anyfin' more about the bloke. Would yer like me to?'

Ruth looked at her. Her expression was full of unspoken anxiety.

'I'll see wot I can do,' said Mavis, with a

reassuring smile. 'But I'd better warn yer, Rufe,' she continued, her expression changing. 'Yer might not like wot 'e tells me. Yer see, Charlie says that most of the blokes on that ship were in a pretty bad way, terrible wounds an' all sorts er fings. It's more than likely that some of 'em may never lead a normal life again.'

Soon after Mavis had left, Ruth closed the shop for the day, locked up, and made her way by bus straight to Hackney. Although it was a pleasant enough September evening, there were early signs of autumn in the air. In Graham Road on the other side of Dalston Junction, there was a long tail-back of traffic due to a heavy fall of masonry; an Edwardian tenement building, which had been bombed during the 'little Blitz' a few months before, had suddenly collapsed. As it was still light, Ruth decided to get off and walk the rest of the journey, for the weather was still warm and humid with no sign of rain. On the way she passed groups of people filing into the nearest public air-raid shelters, for when the odd doodlebug or so arrived, it brought no prior warning, and survival was now everyone's primary consideration.

Along Mare Street, the blackout blinds were already being drawn. Apart from a few men who were making their way to a local pub, the busy main road was quite deserted, and the sound of a horse and brewery cart rumbling towards the same pub could be clearly heard on the rough stone surface of the road. Further along, Ruth stopped to watch a small platoon of Home

Guard recruits marching off to Victoria Park for night patrol and lookout duties. Despite the fact that most of the men seemed to be quite ancient, she was impressed to see how proudly they marched in well-disciplined formation.

Except for a few boarded-up shop and residential windows, Jessop Place looked much the same as when Ruth had first seen it before the night the parachute bomb had exploded some months before. As she approached Cyril Buller's funeral parlour, she felt a strong urge to carry on to the old workshop at the end of the mews, which reminded her so much of the time she had spent with Mike. But even from the front door of the parlour itself, she could see that the workshop was now nothing more than a burnt-out ruin, a loss to Cyril that would take months to restore. The front door of the parlour was locked and bolted up for the night, but just to the left of it was another door, which she presumed was the entrance to Cyril's flat on the upper floors. There was no bell, and she found the huge iron knocker heavily rusted and very difficult to use, but once she had managed to raise it, she thumped it down as hard as she could. Almost immediately, a top-floor window opened, and Cyril himself appeared. 'Yes?' he bellowed. 'Who are yer?'

Ruth looked up. 'It's me, Mr Buller,' she called. 'Ruth. Mike's friend.'

'Blimey!' gasped Cyril. ''Ang on!' He disappeared briefly, and when he returned he called, ''Ere's the key! Come on up!'

The key tinkled onto the cobblestones as it came hurtling down from Cyril's window. Ruth

243

picked it up, and let herself in. The moment she entered, Cyril turned on the light upstairs, and Ruth found herself at the foot of a narrow flight of stairs, flanked on either side by brown varnished walls. As she climbed, it was an odd sensation to think that on the other side of the righthand wall, several bodies were probably laid out in their coffins, patiently waiting for their final big day.

'One more floor!' called Cyril, who was peering over the top of the banister high above her.

'Okay!' Ruth called back breathlessly.

The moment she reached the top-floor landing, Cyril was waiting to greet her. 'Now here's a turn-up fer the books!' he said, beaming. "Ow are yer, little lady?'

Old Cyril had such an endearing way of welcoming Ruth that she immediately felt at ease. 'I'm fine, Mr Buller,' she said, shaking hands warmly. 'It's good to see you.'

'Come on in an' make yerself at 'ome,' said Cyril, leading her into his back parlour. 'I don't get many visitors these days, 'speshully pretty young gels like you!' He showed her to a comfortable armchair which was covered in a lush red velour. Although it was only September, he had a fire roaring in the grate, and the heat from it was quite overpowering. 'I feel the cold,' he said, warming his hands. 'Gets right in me bones.'

After the rather dreary climb up the narrow, poorly lit stairs, Ruth was pleasantly surprised to find such a bright and cheerful room, and despite the fact that Cyril was a widower and lived on his own, he kept the place spotlessly clean and tidy. His pride and joy, however, was his massive brown varnished dresser, which reached right up to the ceiling and was absolutely bulging with snapshots of his late wife, Daisy, and almost as many of his grandson Mike, right back to his childhood days. There were also knick-knacks of every shape and size, mainly little china figurines such as horses and dogs and cats and tortoises, that he and his wife had collected from their many seaside holidays together over the years. Ruth had hardly settled into the chair before a glass of black market whisky and ginger ale was thrust into her hand. Although she hated the stuff, she didn't want to hurt his feelings, so she sipped it as slowly as she possibly could. 'Your ears must've bin burnin',' he said, settling down in the armchair opposite her. 'I was on the point of comin' down ter pay yer a visit.'

'Really?' asked Ruth, surprised. 'That would have been nice.'

'I've got ter own up,' he replied, tapping the side of his nose as he always did when he wanted to get a point across. 'It wasn't my idea at all. It was Mike's.'

'Mike?' asked Ruth, warily.

''E's bin worried that yer 'aven't written to 'im once since 'e went away. 'E wanted me ter come down ter your neck er the woods an' find out if yer was okay. Our boys out there 'ear rumours about the bombin' an' all that, an' they get all worked up that somefin' might've 'appened to their own kith an' kin.' He leaned forward in his chair. 'D'yer mind if I call yer Rufe?' he asked.

245

'Of course not,' she replied immediately.

'So then, Rufe – *is* everyfin' all right?'

'Perfectly,' she replied.

'So why 'aven't yer written ter 'im?'

Cyril's sudden blunt question made her shift around on her chair uneasily.

'Yer 'aven't 'ave yer?' he asked again. 'Written ter 'im I mean?'

'No,' she admitted, awkwardly.

'Enuff said,' said Cyril, settling back in his chair again. 'Why should yer, if yer don't want ter. That's wot I'm always tellin' Mike. *Don't expect people ter do fings just 'cos you want 'em to*, I'm always tellin' 'im.'

'It's not that I don't want to, Mr Buller,' said Ruth. 'But–'

'Ah!' said Cyril astutely, tapping the side of his nose with his finger again. 'Yer've got someone else.'

Ruth sighed. 'You have a wonderful view from up here,' she said evasively, getting up. She went to look out of the large French windows, which were crossed with protective sticky tape. There were iron railings and a narrow balcony outside, with winding iron steps which led down to the small, but neat back garden below. 'What a lovely little garden,' she said. 'Looks as though you're fond of flowers?'

Cyril joined her. 'Not me,' he replied, with a little chuckle. 'That's Mike. Got real green fingers that boy. Always snippin' and diggin' an' potterin' round down there. It's got out er 'and since 'e went off. When 'e gets back 'ome, 'e's goin' ter 'ave quite a bit er work ter get all that

246

back ter 'ow 'e likes it.'

Cyril opened the French windows, and led her out onto the balcony. There were several potted plants out there, but all needing attention. 'The back door to the Chapel's down there. That's where we take out the customers.'

Ruth threw only a passing glance at the paved path below, which led to what had once been the coffin-making workshop. It was a somewhat macabre reminder that old Cyril and Mike lived above the 'shop'. Then she looked out over the rooftops, past the bomb-ravaged empty spaces and burnt-out buildings, to the vast expanse of green beyond, and in the distance, the shimmering muddy surface of a large lake. 'Is that Victoria Park?' she asked, quickly pouring some of her whisky into one of the potted plants whilst Cyril was looking the other way.

'That's it all right,' replied Cyril. 'I used ter take Mike there nearly every Sunday mornin' when 'e was a kid – watched him play football wiv 'is mates.' For one split second, his eyes became misted over. 'My Billy's out there somewhere.'

Ruth threw him a puzzled, but caring look. 'Billy?'

'My budgie,' said Cyril. ''Ad 'im fer two years locked up in a cage in my parlour. In the summer I used ter bring 'im out here. Yer should've 'eard 'im carryin' on. Natter, natter, natter all day long. But I understood. It was the company 'e needed. All 'is mates flyin' around out 'ere wivout 'im. Wasn't right. Wasn't kind. So I let 'im go.'

Ruth suddenly felt a wave of affection and admiration for the old man. He seemed like someone she could talk to, someone she could trust.

'So,' said Cyril. "Ave yer got someone else?'

His sudden, repeated question took her off-guard. 'I don't know,' she replied. 'I honestly don't know.'

'So why don't yer tell Mike?'

'I *have* told him,' she replied. 'Lots of times.'

He turned and grinned at her. 'Ah!' he said, with another little chuckle. 'Won't take no for an answer, is that it? That's my boy. That's my Mike!'

Ruth was in torment. She was desperate to know if he was going to confirm what Mavis had told her about Mike. 'Mr Buller,' she said.

'Uncle Cyril,' he said, with a twinkle in his eye. 'Everyone calls me that. It's more friendly.'

Ruth smiled, but with difficulty. 'Uncle Cyril,' she said, 'I don't know when you last heard from Mike, but someone told me – Mike may have been injured.'

Cyril's expression changed immediately. 'Wot's that?'

'Someone who came back on a hospital ship – a medical orderly – he says he thinks Mike may be one of the wounded men he talked to on the way home. It's possible he's being kept in an Army hospital somewhere.'

'Wounded?' asked Cyril. 'Wot d'yer mean, *wounded?*'

Ruth shook her head. 'I don't know, Uncle Cyril,' she said. 'But I just think there ought to be some way you could find out.'

'My boy ain't wounded,' he said emphatically.

Ruth did a double-take. 'How do you know?' she asked.

Cyril turned, and looked out distantly towards the park again. 'I just know, that's all. I always know when Mike's in trouble. I *feel* it *'ere*,' he pointed to his forehead, 'an' *'ere*,' he pointed to his chest. 'It's not somefin' yer can explain,' he said, strangely. 'It's just *somefin'*.'

Ruth waited a moment. 'Well,' she said, 'if you *should* hear anything, only *if*, you will let me know, won't you?'

Cyril turned and looked at her. There was a slight breeze, and with one hand he adjusted his toupee. 'It's gettin' chilly out 'ere,' he said, shivering. 'Time ter go in.' He let her go first, and as she did so he said, with a mischievous grin, 'Oh, by the way, fanks fer givin' me plant a drink!'

The following week, Ruth received a visit from Tom's mother, Pearl Phillips. It was the first time Pearl had been to the shop, so Ruth entertained her to a cup of tea in the back parlour, where there was just enough room to sit down amidst the piles of wooden crates and cardboard boxes. 'It was always my dream ter 'ave a little shop er me own,' said Pearl, settling down in a well-used armchair. 'But Ken wouldn't 'ear of it. 'E's always said a woman's place is in the 'ome, lookin' after the *real* breadwinners.'

Ruth certainly didn't agree with that kind of talk, but as Pearl was looking quite frail and vulnerable, she decided not to challenge the point.

'I do so admire yer, Rufe,' said Pearl, her face beginning to show signs of wear far too prematurely for a woman of her age. 'When yer set out ter do somefin', yer always do it. It takes guts ter stand on yer own two feet. I've never bin able ter do it meself – always 'ad ter rely on someone else.' She sipped her tea, then stirred it aimlessly. 'When Tom comes 'ome I intend ter tell 'im all about wot yer've bin up to.'

Ruth looked up with a start. 'Tell him what, Mrs Phillips?' she asked.

'About wot a good girl yer've bin,' replied Pearl. 'About 'ow yer've never given up 'ope that 'e'd come 'ome one day.'

Ruth's heart sank. She found Pearl's confidence quite depressing, especially as she had only just read in the newspapers that morning even more disturbing reports about the ill-treatment of Allied troops in Japanese prisoner-of-war camps in the Far East, and how very few of the prisoners would ever be able to survive such barbaric treatment. Fortunately, she had to leave the room for a few minutes to attend to a customer in the shop. When she came back, she found Pearl powdering her face in a small hand-mirror. Ruth found it a bizarre, unsettling sight, for Pearl's face was already quite colourless, and the powder she was applying was making her face white and ghostly, with her heavy uneven red lipstick making her lips look like a long, thin bleeding slit.

'I want to let you into a little secret,' said Pearl, in a low, intimate voice. 'I'm preparing a big party fer Tom's return.'

Ruth was astonished. 'A party?' she repeated. 'All the people who've known Tom over the years,' continued Pearl. 'Right from back to when 'e was at school. Even some of 'is gelfriends!' She sniggered like a young schoolgirl. 'You wouldn't mind, would yer, Rufe?' she asked, reaching across to cover Ruth's hand with her own. 'They don't mean anyfin' to 'im any more. You're the only gel in 'is life now – everyone knows that.'

As Ruth stared into the eyes of this poor woman, whose face had now been transformed into something quite grotesque, she felt a deep sense of bitterness; this war had torn so many lives apart without mercy. She thought of all those whose homes had been ravaged by the insanity of human conflict, and those who were unable to cope with the trauma of losing their loved ones, and she couldn't help wondering if, in fifty years' time, future generations would even care what sacrifices ordinary people had had to make just to survive, to give their sons and daughters the chance to live their lives in freedom.

'Yer will come to the party, won't yer, Rufe?'

Pearl's voice snapped Ruth out of her innermost thoughts. 'Of course I'll come,' she replied, affirmatively. 'I'll be very proud to come to your party, Mrs Phillips.'

'Mum,' said Pearl. 'Yer still 'aven't called me Mum.'

'Mum,' said Ruth, returning a weak smile, fighting back tears.

'After all,' said Pearl relentlessly, 'if I'm goin' ter be the grandma of yer kids one day, we mustn't

251

be too formal. An' in any case, I like yer, Rufe. The moment Tom brought yer 'ome ter meet us, I liked yer. You're genuine, Rufe. There aren't many gels around these days yer can say that about. These days, they're all out fer wot they can get – anyfin' in trousers, money, a good time. This war's done terrible fings ter young gels. It's made 'em selfish. It's turned 'em inter men – selfish an' just out fer themselves. But you're different, Rufe. You're a gel – a woman. You're someone I can trust.'

Ruth stared at her own lap. She found it impossible to look Pearl in the eyes.

'Well, I must be on me way.' When Ruth glanced up again, she found Pearl easing herself up from her chair. 'If I'm goin' ter get fings organised fer the party,' said Pearl, 'I'm goin' ter 'ave ter start doin' fings. Oh, I know I've got plenty er time, but yer can't organise a big party in five minutes, can yer, Rufe?'

After Pearl had gone, Ruth sat on her stool behind the counter. She felt as though all the life had been drained from her body, her mind, her very soul. What had happened to that poor woman? she kept asking herself. Why did she have to pay so cruelly for the sin of having a child out of wedlock? Pearl Phillips was basically a very kind and sincere person, and the fact that her life had now been torn apart by the illusion that Tom was not only alive and well, but would be coming home soon, was a crushing thought.

Ruth got up from the stool, and went into the back room to clear away the teacups. She longed for Freda Dapper to turn up as soon as possible, for the thought of dealing with any more customers that day was more than she could take. She picked up Pearl's cup and saucer. The cup still had traces of her lipstick around the rim. She quickly returned the cup and saucer to the table. She paused a moment or so, standing there trying to keep her balance with her fingertips. Life was too much to take, she told herself. Tom wasn't coming home, and that's all there was to it. And neither was Mike. They were either dead or severely injured – *both* of them, there was now no doubt in her mind about that. She wanted to scream out loud, she wanted to shout hate at everything and everybody connected with the making of wars. In her anger, she swung around, and kicked out at a pile of empty cardboard boxes, which tumbled over into a heap on the floor. She swung round with a start as she heard the bell above the shop door ring, and breathed a sigh of relief.

'Freda!' she called. Without waiting for a reply, she quickly collected her cardigan and put it on, then grabbed her handbag from the table. 'Just coming, Freda!' she called again, before going out into the shop. 'Thank God you've come!' she said, as she came through the door. 'If I had to wait another moment, I think I'd go stark, raving...' She stopped dead. It wasn't Freda who was waiting for her.

'Hallo, Ruth,' said the young bloke reaching out both his hands to her from the other side of the counter.

It was Mike Buller.

Chapter 13

Victoria Park looked much the same as it had when Ruth first saw it at a distance from old Cyril's balcony high above the funeral parlour in Jessop Place. She and Mike seemed to have been walking for hours, and by the time they finally stopped to rest for a few minutes at the lake's edge, the light was fading, and there was a decided nip in the air. Ever since Ruth had shut up shop for the day two hours before, the couple had done nothing but talk. Over and over again she told Mike how sure she had been that he had been injured, that she might never see him again. And he told her about the hell he had gone through since the Allied landings on D-Day, and how at times he thought that he would never see *her* again. But now, explanations were behind them, and for a few magical moments, they were together again in silence. Stretched out side by side on the damp grass, the red glow from the setting sun on their faces, they stared into each other's eyes and thought of nothing and no one but themselves.

It was several minutes before Mike finally leaned forward and gently kissed her on the lips. 'You don't know how much I've been longing to do that,' he whispered.

Ruth remained silent. All she could do was to stare longingly at him, to sensually outline every feature of his face, the small pimple on the side of his nose, the dark brown eyes and long eye-lashes, the tiny scar on the right-hand side of his chin. Without saying a word, she leaned forward and kissed him. When she pulled away, she said softy, 'This is wrong, Mike. We shouldn't be doing this.'

'Why not?' he asked, puzzled.

'Because of Tom.'

Mike sat up and looked down at her. 'You said he was dead.'

'No, Mike,' said Ruth. 'I said he was missing, *presumed* dead. Until we know for certain what's happened, I think we owe it to Tom's family to be patient.'

'Patient?' groaned Mike, getting up. 'An' wot about me? I'm only 'ome fer ten days.'

Ruth immediately sprang to her feet. 'I know, darling, I know,' she said, sliding her arms around his waist as he lit a cigarette. 'And we'll live every single moment of it that we can, I promise you.' She leaned her head against his chest, and closed her eyes.

'Yer still love 'im, don't yer?' Mike asked. 'That's why yer didn't write ter me.'

'That's not true!' Ruth said quickly. 'I couldn't write to you. If I had, it would have seemed callous at such a time. Don't you understand, Mike?' she pleaded. 'I used to love Tom. At least, I *thought* I did, until I met you – you big chump!' She kissed him again.

'I'm being transferred.'

Mike's sudden announcement caused Ruth to stare anxiously at him. 'Transferred?' she asked.

'What does that mean?'

Mike drew hard on his fag, swallowed quite a lot of the smoke, and exhaled the rest. 'It means the unit's bein' kitted out so's we can be posted somewhere else.'

Ruth felt a sudden panic. 'Somewhere else?' she said. 'But the war's nearly over. It said on the radio that the Allies have entered Germany. Even Monty said so. He said the war would definitely be over by the end of the year.'

'The war in Europe, Ruth,' Mike replied.

It took a moment for the implication to strike home. 'Oh God!' she gasped. 'They're not sending you out East?'

Mike didn't answer.

'But you've only just come back from fighting in France,' she said, in desperation. 'They can't send you out to fight all over again. It's too much for you. It's not fair. Why can't they send some of the others?'

Mike kissed her on the forehead. 'We *are* the others, Ruth,' he said. 'The Japs are gettin' away wiv murder out there, an' we ain't got enuff men on the ground ter tackle 'em.'

Ruth tried to pull away, but he wouldn't let her. 'Don't worry,' he insisted, 'nuffin's goin' ter 'appen ter me. I told yer that before, din't I? An' wot 'appened? I come back, din't I? An' I'll come back again – promise!'

Ruth looked hard at him, then took the fag out of his lips, and put it in her own. 'It's very rude not to offer a girl a cigarette,' she said bravely.

'Gels shouldn't smoke,' he countered.

'That's old-fashioned.'

'I like bein' old-fashioned,' he said. 'It makes me feel like I'm in charge.'

Before Ruth had a chance to come back at him, he kissed her fully on the lips. As he did so, there was a clap of thunder from the sky above, and almost simultaneously a ferocious downpour of rain. They made a wild dash to the nearest tree, and hugged up close together. 'Isn't it supposed to be dangerous to shelter under a tree during a thunderstorm?' she called, trying to be heard above the sound of rain pelting down onto the chestnut leaves above their heads.

'Not when yer wiv me!' returned Mike, as he pulled her so close that their bodies were pressed hard against each other.

It was now quite dark, and the rain pelting down through the trees was soaking their clothes. But they were both quite oblivious of the discomfort, for they spent all their time looking into each other's eyes, and snuggling up. After a while, they kissed, deeply this time. Mike's tongue probed inside Ruth's mouth, and it immediately aroused her. She groaned as she felt his hands sliding up and down her thighs. She wanted to respond, but something held her back. She had done this before, several times, another place, another time, with people that she didn't care for, didn't want to see ever again. She didn't want to make the same mistake now. She had to be certain. She had to be sure. But when he pressed his crutch against hers, and his tongue deep inside her mouth, despite all her reservations, despite all her fears, she knew that she wanted him. Fortunately, she no longer had to make the decision, for they were suddenly blinded by a torchlight, and a hefty man's voice calling out to them from close by.

'That's enough of that, you two!' called the burly Special Constable on wartime park duty. 'Come on now – move along!'

After the deluge of rain the night before, a thin film of mist hovered obstinately over the Holloway Road. However, within an hour of sunrise, a mischievous breeze found its way into the back streets, and by the time it had reached the Annette Road cul de sac it had sent the mist back to wherever it came from.

In the 'end house', Ruth slept late. After spending the evening with Mike, she had not got back home until well after midnight, by which time the only sign of life was two moggies battling it out in her front garden, to the accompaniment of howls that echoed along the length and breadth of the entire neighbourhood. For Ruth, it had been an exhausting day, and she felt emotionally drained. But despite the fact that it felt like a breath of fresh air to see Mike again, she was relieved that she had been saved from making that crucial decision that would have fed fuel to the wagging tongue of Rita Simmons. It would have destroyed her own confidence in herself. In the cold light of day, she knew only too well that letting Mike make love to her at this stage in their relationship would have been a huge mistake. Although she loved him, she could be accused not only of going back to her 'old ways', but also of never having had any intention of being faithful to Tom, a man she had pledged to love *for ever and ever*. It was a dilemma that could only be resolved in time.

She was woken by the sound of someone banging on her street door downstairs. Yawning, stretching, she quickly put on her dressing-gown.

'Yer late!' squealed young Dave Smithers, the shop's newspaper boy, who was standing on the doorstep as Ruth appeared. 'Mrs Dapper says yer ter come round right away!'

'Why?' asked Ruth. 'What's all the fuss?'

'The fuss,' returned the boy, 'is yer shop. It's bin broken into.'

'Oh my God!' gasped Ruth, clasping a hand to her mouth. 'Have they taken anything?'

'Most er the fags,' Dave told her, 'an' a coupla bottles er ginger beer.'

'Ginger beer?' spluttered Ruth, with incredulity.

'Must've bin firsty!' replied the boy cheekily.

By the time Ruth arrived at *Whitlock's*, a police car was already parked outside. Inside, the place looked as though it had been hit by an explosion. 'Vandals, I'd say,' said the police sergeant who, with a Special Constable, was checking the mess as best he could. 'Pros never leave a place like this. They always know what they're looking for.'

Freda Dapper hovered behind the counter. She was in a terrible state. 'I can't understand it,' she said tearfully. 'I just can't understand it. Me an' Sid were wide awake upstairs, an' yet we didn't 'ear a fing. 'Ow could I be so stupid!' With that, she burst into tears.

'There's no one to blame, Freda,' insisted Ruth,

comforting her. 'No one except the pigs who did this. It seems so pointless. Why?' She looked around in despair at the piles of magazines that had been cleared from their racks and just thrown mindlessly to the floor. 'Why are we fighting a war for people who can do this sort of thing?'

'P'raps it was kids,' suggested the Special Constable. 'Yer know 'ow bored they get when they've got nuffin' ter do.'

'Not in the middle of the night, Mack,' said the sergeant. 'Especially with that smell.'

Ruth and Freda exchanged a baffled glance, then watched the two men as they searched around.

'Ah!' called the sergeant, retrieving an empty whisky bottle from beneath the mess. 'I thought as much.' He held the bottle up for the women to see. 'Here's your culprit, ladies!' he called.

Ruth came across to look at the bottle. 'What does it mean?' she asked, puzzled.

'It means you've been broken into by a drunk.'

'Who also has a liking for ginger beer,' added Ruth.

'Clearly a man of taste!' quipped the sergeant.

'I'm afraid 'e's made a bit of a mess over 'ere!' called the constable, from the smashed shop door.

Ruth and the sergeant went across to look. 'Hope you're insured for this lot, miss?' he asked.

'Yes, thank God,' replied Ruth. 'Though it's going to cost a bit to replace some of that damaged stock. Why he only cleared the place of Woodbines and left all the other more expensive brands on the shelves is a mystery to me.'

'Not really, miss,' said the sergeant. 'Drunk or no drunk, looks like this bloke likes to stick to his own brand of fags.'

'Will you be able to catch him?' asked Ruth.

'We'll do our best,' the sergeant told her. 'In the middle of a war, we don't have much time to tackle petty crime. But we'll do our best.'

'Petty crime'? Ruth asked herself. Somebody breaks into your shop, steals a whole lot of cigarettes and practically wrecks the place, and that's a *petty crime?* Thank God when the war's over, she thought. Perhaps then they'll be able to put some of these thugs behind bars.

Once the police had gone, Ruth and Freda set about cleaning up the mess. It took quite some time before Ruth was finally able to convince Freda that she was not personally to blame for not hearing the break-in during the night. But Freda was a sensitive soul, always fretting over the least important things, and if she wanted to blame herself, then nothing in the world was going to stop her from doing so.

By early afternoon, the shop was more or less back to normal, ready to receive the evening deliveries of the *Star*, the *Evening News* and the *Evening Standard*. Most of the customers who came into the shop hardly realised what had happened during the night, for between them Ruth and Freda had replaced everything on the shelves, with the exception of the stock of Woodbines.

'Woodbines and ginger beer,' said Ruth, turning over everything that had happened in her mind. 'Now who do we know who enjoys *that* combination?'

''Opefully, we don't know no one like that,' retorted Freda. 'I'm only relieved that yer din't leave no cash in the till. Yer can bet yer life, 'e'd've 'ad *that!*'

Ruth was mystified by the break-in. As she struggled to come to terms with the unpleasant feeling that a hostile intruder had actually broken into the place where she spent so much of her time alone, the possibility began to dawn that she knew the person involved. It might well be one of their own customers. Once Freda had gone off for the day, Ruth sat on her stool behind the counter, watching out for anyone who might linger too long, looking through the window from outside. Only when Mr Lawson the carpenter had been to board up the shop door and fit a new lock, did she finally feel more secure – for the time being, at least.

At a quarter to seven, Ruth closed up shop for the day. She had reluctantly stayed open beyond her usual time only because she still had a good few evening newspapers left over, but as they were always provided on a sale or return basis, she decided she'd had enough for one day, and just wanted to get home.

September was turning out to be a funny old month, starting out warm and humid, and now wet and windy practically every day. In fact, as she made her way along Hornsey Road, the wind was so blustery that it was difficult to keep her balance, and at the corner of Holloway Road she was greeted by a strong gust which nearly blew

262

her off her feet. When the drizzle suddenly turned to rain, she took shelter beneath the railway bridge on the opposite side of the road to the Tube station. Several other people had the same idea, and as they waited for the first chance to make a dash for it, everyone looked thoroughly miserable. Still, now that the Allied forces had finally managed to remove the launching sites of the dreaded flying-bombs, at least there were no more doodlebug attacks to worry about.

'Can I join yer?'

Ruth nearly jumped out of her skin when she suddenly felt someone link his arm with hers. 'Mike!' she gasped, her face immediately beaming in the dim light beneath the arch. 'What are you doing here? You told me you had to stay home with your grandfather this evening.'

'I changed me mind,' replied Mike, giving her a quick kiss, regardless of who was watching. 'I told 'im you're far better-lookin' than 'im!'

They laughed, and Ruth couldn't resist returning his kiss. But then she became nervous, and the moment the rain had stopped just long enough to move on, they hurried off. On the way, Ruth did her best to tell him what had happened in the shop the previous night. In the howling wind, it wasn't easy for him to make out what she was saying, but what he heard made him angry and concerned. When the rain started pelting down again, he quickly pulled her into the cover of a shop doorway. 'I don't like yer bein' in that shop on yer own,' he said earnestly. 'There are too many nut-cases around these days.'

'I know,' she replied, 'but don't worry, I can

take care of myself. In any case, my mother's coming home in a couple of weeks. If she's feeling better, I'll let her come and sit with me during the afternoons.'

'If anyone lays a finger on you,' Mike said angrily, 'I'll kill 'em!'

Ruth smiled at the way he was being so protective of her. 'That won't be necessary, thank you, darling,' she said. She reached up and stroked the rainwater from his face. 'In fact, we're both in more danger of getting pneumonia than anything else. D'you realise we're always meeting either when it's snowing or in the rain?'

'I don't care 'ow or when I meet yer,' he replied, 'as long as yer there.'

They drew close, and kissed.

'Fish 'n' chips!'

Ruth looked up at him. 'Huh?' she spluttered.

'I feel like fish 'n' chips,' he replied eagerly. 'I aven't 'ad none since I went away. Where can we get some?'

She came back at him in a flash. 'I know just the place!'

Ten minutes later they had joined the queue outside Anderson's fried fish and chip shop in Hornsey Road. As it was Friday night, the queue was quite long, and by the time they had reached the counter inside, they only just managed to get the last two pieces of cod that were left. Mike amused Ruth by smothering both his fish and chips with vinegar, but as they walked along Hornsey Road, she loved watching him picking out one chip at a time from the newspaper, blowing on it, then dropping it with absolute

264

ecstasy into his mouth.

'Let's go home,' she said. 'I don't want to eat fish and chips in the rain.'

He grinned, took hold of her hand, and walked them both at a steady pace towards Annette Road.

In the 'end house', Ruth soon had a fire burning in the sitting-room grate, the first one in ages. Although it was still only September, the house felt damp, and their clothes were soaking wet. Once Ruth had warmed their fish and chips up in the oven, they crouched down on the rug in front of the fire to eat them. Every so often, Mike would take one of his chips, and slowly lower it into Ruth's mouth, and she would do likewise. Once they had finished eating, they snuggled up together, with his arm around her waist, and her head leaning on his shoulder. For several moments, neither spoke a word; they merely gazed into the fire, the flames reflected in their eyes. Ruth was first to speak. 'If anyone had ever told me that I'd fall for someone who made coffins for a living,' she said, softly, 'I'd say they were stark raving mad.'

'An' if anyone 'ad ever told *me* I'd fall fer a gel wiv a Polish accent, I'd've told 'em they were absolutely right!'

They both chuckled, then kissed long and hard. When they parted, Ruth was staring into his eyes. 'You know something?' she said. 'My father's watching us.'

Mike did a double-take.

'He's up there,' she said, with a wry look up at the mantelpiece. 'Watching our every move.'

Mike looked up at the casket containing Harry Whitlock's ashes. 'D'yer fink 'e minds?' he asked.

'Oh yes,' replied Ruth. 'He minds a great deal. Don't you, Papa?' She looked back at Mike. 'He wouldn't like this at all. In fact, he didn't like anything I ever did. That's why I won't let him have his own way.'

Mike was puzzled.

'He'd have wanted his ashes scattered out at sea,' said Ruth. 'But he'll have to wait until I'm ready.'

Mike sat back on his haunches. 'Not much point in takin' it out on someone who's dead, is there?'

Ruth didn't respond right away, but when she did, she lowered her eyes guiltily. 'No,' she replied. She lay down on her back on the rug. 'You know, Mike,' she said, gazing up at him, 'you've got yourself involved with someone who's very mixed-up.'

He lay down next to her on his side, and leaned his chin on his fist. 'So wot's the problem?' he asked, stroking back her hair with his other hand.

'Us.'

Mike carried on stroking her hair. 'Oh – that ol' fing,' he replied.

Ruth sat up and faced him. 'If I don't tell someone soon,' she said, 'I'll go out of my mind.'

'Then why don't you?' he asked.

'Because I haven't got the guts,' she replied. 'The tongues have been wagging about us in Jackson Road for some time, and I don't know how much longer I can keep it to myself.' He was about to say something to her, but she stopped

266

him. 'No, Mike,' she continued. 'It's not as easy as that. You see, it's not only the neighbours, it's my mother, and Tom's family.'

'If 'e's dead, then I don't see that there's any problem.'

'I've already told you,' Ruth said despairingly. 'It's a problem until it's absolutely certain that he *is* dead. I know it's ghastly, but there are times when I even wish he *was* dead. I'm ashamed of myself, but I can't help feeling the way I'm feeling. And yet, I was in love with Tom. At least, I thought I was – until you came along. What happens if I do the same to you as I did to him?'

'But yer 'aven't done nuffin' to 'im,' said Mike, totally confused. 'So why are yer gettin' yerself all worked up?'

Ruth hesitated again before answering. 'Because I'm afraid that what my mother has said might be true. Maybe I *am* going back to my old ways.'

Mike sat up and faced her. 'Old ways?' he asked suspiciously. 'I have a past, Mike,' she said. 'You're not the first boy I've been with.'

Mike stared at her for a moment, then broke into a broad grin. 'Oh, is that all!' he replied. 'Well, let me tell yer somefin'. Believe it or not, yer not the first gel *I've* bin wiv.'

Ruth's expression immediately changed. On the mantelpiece, the carriage clock sounded the hour.

'It 'appens all the time, yer know,' said Mike gently, taking hold of her hands. 'It's not a sin ter 'ave a life before yer meet someone yer really like. I love yer, Rufe, an' you love me, so I don't see

267

wot diff'rence it makes.'

Ruth pondered this for a moment. It was true. For over a year she had felt nothing but guilt for what she had done, for the sins of which everyone had accused her. But no one had ever told her that experience was all part of growing up. Without it, going forward into a stable relationship could be even more difficult. All this time, she had felt like a naughty child, doing things behind Mama's back, doing things that she dared not tell anyone about, not even her own church. 'Mike,' she said on impulse, 'I want to tell Father O'Leary about us. He's the priest at our church.'

'Fine,' nodded Mike. 'Why not?'

'You don't understand,' she said nervously. 'I want *you* to come along with me. I want him to meet you. I want *you* to meet *him*. It's the only way I can break loose from this guilt I'm being throttled with. I want Father O'Leary to know the truth. I want everyone to know the truth that I'm seeing you – and that whatever's happened to Tom, I have the right to love whoever I want.'

Mike thought about this for a moment, then slowly stood up. 'Okay,' he said. 'I'll come an' see yer priest. But I'm warnin' yer, I ain't much on religion, never 'ave bin. I only ever went ter Sunday school. After that, somewhere along the way – I lost it all.'

'I'm not asking you to do it just for me, Mike,' she said, taking hold of his hands. 'I'm asking you to do it for *us*.' She kissed him on the lips, then led his hands onto her breasts.

Mike looked into her eyes and for a moment

allowed his hands to remain where she had left them. Then he took them away, leaned down, and kissed both her nipples through the flimsy material of her damp dress. 'Time ter go 'ome,' he said.

Rita Simmons hated the rain. Every time she went out in it she seemed totally incapable of keeping on her feet, not only because of her massive weight, but because she always insisted on wearing rubber-soled shoes which failed to grip the unwelcoming pavements in wet or icy conditions. But as her husband Ted had come home late from work, it was left to her to struggle along Holloway Road in the rain to buy the Friday night fish and chips. On the way back, she cursed everything and everybody for having to turn out on such a wet evening. The way she felt was not improved when she got home and found Ted with his feet up, smoking a fag and downing a glass of brown ale, and listening to *ITMA* on the wireless. 'Would it be too much ter ask if yer could sit up at the table ter 'ave yer tea?' she asked acidly, immediately turning off the wireless.

As usual, Ted took everything his wife said in his stride. He merely got up from the easy chair, and went to his usual place at the parlour table. Rita slammed one packet of fish and chips in front of him, and sat down with her own at the other end of the table. For several minutes they sat in silence munching their greasy, lukewarm meal from the newspaper it had been wrapped up in. If anyone outside could have seen them, they would have thought they were two complete strangers, no point of contact between them.

It was Rita who finally spoke. 'When yer've finished,' she said, mouth full, without even glancing up at him, 'I want some 'elp ter move that mattress upstairs. I'm sellin' it ter yer cousin Doll.'

Ted flicked a quick look at her. 'Sellin' it?' he asked. 'It was in the kids' room. We don't need it no more, do we?'

'No,' snapped Rita. 'That's why I'm getting rid of it.'

'But we don't 'ave ter *sell* it,' he insisted. 'Not to our own.'

'Doll's not *my* own,' argued Rita. 'And in any case she's never given *us* anyfin'. That cow wouldn't even give yer the pickin's from 'er nose. Besides, we ain't made er bleedin' money.'

Ted lowered his eyes and carried on picking at his fish with his fingers. 'I can't do it ternight,' he muttered.

'Wot's that yer say?' growled Rita.

'I said, I can't do it ternight! I'm goin' round ter 'ave a drink wiv Jim an' the boys.'

Rita slammed down a half-eaten chip. 'Not again!' she barked. 'Yer din't get 'ome last night 'til the early hours.'

'So?' asked Ted cuttingly, glaring at her.

'So it's about time yer spent one night at 'ome wiv yer wife!' demanded Rita, fuming.

'Wot for? To listen ter you snappin' an' snarlin' at me?'

Exasperated, Rita got up from the table and stormed out into the scullery to wash the grease off her hands at the stone sink. When she returned, she went on the attack. 'It may not've occurred to you, Mr Simmons,' she barked, 'but I do 'appen ter be yer wife, the muvver of yer kids. I don't deserve ter be treated like this, sittin' 'ere night after night on me own, wonderin' wot time I shall 'ave the pleasure er seein' me 'usband walk fru that door again. That's *not* wot bein' married's all about.'

'Is that a fact?' replied Ted. 'An' wot is bein' married all about, Rita? Bein' treated as though I'm just a lodger, passin' fru fer a couple er nights.'

'Bein' married is s'pposed ter be about *carin'* fer one anuvver,' said Rita.

Ted looked up at her, and for one split second he could see the girl he had married, the girl with the flashing smile, long brown hair, and sparkling dark eyes, the girl who was proud of the way she dressed, poor though she was, the girl who knew how to *love*. But not any more. As the vision from his past faded, it was replaced with something that he no longer recognised. And he knew only too well that if he looked in the mirror, he would no longer recognise himself either. 'You 'aven't *cared* fer me since the day we met,' he said, wiping his mouth on the back of his hand, and then getting up from the table. With that, he put on his jacket, grabbed his cap from the dresser, and walked out.

Rita watched him go. When she heard the front door slam she felt as though everything inside her stomach was about to collapse. Only then did she wish she hadn't said all those things to him. Yes, he was an uncaring husband all right – thought-less, cruel, and with no idea how easily he could hurt her. But when she turned away from the door, she caught a glimpse of herself in the mirror hanging over the mantelpiece, and she didn't like what she saw. She didn't like it at all. It was then that she smelt something burning. Turning back to the table, she noticed Ted's Woodbine fag smouldering in his old tin-lid ash-tray. She stubbed it out and threw it into the grate. With a sigh, she stumbled her way across to the dresser, and took a bottle of something out of the lower cupboard. She was about to get herself a glass, but decided she couldn't be bothered, so she unclipped the top, and drank straight from the bottle.

Fortunately, the content of the bottle was not alcoholic. It was only ginger beer.

Chapter 14

Edie Perkins stared wistfully at the wedding rings in Samuels' window. In fact, ever since her late husband had died, she had never been able to pass the old-established jeweller's shop in Holloway Road without stopping to take a look at those same trays. Every time she saw the gold glistening in the sun, she went all weak at the knees; it made her feel like a young, blushing bride all over again. But these days, there was more meaning to her visits. For a start, they were

272

becoming more regular; she had even started making detours when she was out shopping in Seven Sisters Road, which was a sure sign that it was not just wishful thinking. In her mind, she had convinced herself that her gentleman friend, Harold Beaks, had every intention of proposing to her, and when he did, when he took her to choose a wedding ring, she wanted to know which one to select. The only trouble was, every time she looked at the trays in the window, she changed her mind. Today, however, was different. It was Saturday morning, and she was out doing the shopping early because, although she was trying her best to keep quiet about it, Harold Beaks was coming to spend the weekend with her.

'So who's the lucky man then, Mrs Perkins?'

Edie nearly had a fit when she turned to find Tub Trinder, the tailor from Hornsey Road, standing at her side. 'Don't know wot yer talkin' about?' she replied haughtily. 'I was lookin' at the brooches. It's my niece in Hoxton's birfday next week. I'm lookin' fer a present for 'er'

'Oh yes?' said Tub, with a mischievous grin. 'Fawt ol' 'Arold 'ad popped the question to you.'

Edie was both outraged – and shocked. ''Arold?' she asked, dismissively. ''Arold who? I don't know who yer referrin' to.'

'Come off it, Edie!' said Tub, teasing her. 'Everyone knows all about you an' 'Arold. The 'ole er Jackson Road's always goin' on about it. At least, the ones who come in my shop do.'

'I don't know *wot* yer talkin' about, Tub Trinder!' She turned to go, and as she did so, she bumped into a small girl.

'Grandad says yer gettin' married,' said the child, who was sucking on a bar of medicated liquorice. To Edie's intense irritation, the child began to sing, *''Ere comes the bride...'*

'Who does *this* belong to?' Edie was never able to have kids of her own and, therefore, despised them – or at least, pretended to do so.

'This is me darlin',' said Tub, picking up the child and giving her a big kiss on the forehead. 'Yer grandad's little darlin', ain't yer?' The child squealed, and tucked her head into Tub's chest. 'She don't mean no 'arm,' Tub said comfortably. 'We saw yer lookin' at weddin' rings, an' I put two and two tergevver.'

'Well yer can't add up!' growled Edie, about to storm off again.

'Not accordin' ter *your* mate!' called Tub.

Edie stopped dead in her tracks. She waited for two people to go past her into the shop. 'An' just who might that be?' she asked icily.

'Who'd'yer fink?' he replied. 'Our Rita – 'Olloway's answer ter Two Ton Tessie! She says it's weddin' bells fer you an' 'Arold – wotever yer say.'

'Is that so?'

'That's not all she said,' continued Tub. 'She reckons the bloke that broke inter *Whitlock's* the uvver night was Rufe's new boyfriend.'

Edie stiffened. 'Wot new boyfriend?'

'I dunno,' replied Tub cunningly. 'I don't listen to gossip meself. Yer'd better ask Rita.'

A few minutes later, Edie left Tub and his granddaughter, heading towards the Nags Head

274

corner. On the way, she passed all the Saturday-morning street-traders who lined the double steps right the way along the kerb. Most of them were regulars, especially those who sold knick-knacks, so she knew them all by name. But she could never pass one particular space without thinking of old Tony, the ice-cream seller. Before the war, this was his spot, where he sold his delicious water-ice cones from a barrow. As Tony was an Italian, she imagined he had been interned for the duration of the war, and often wondered if they would ever see him back on his patch again.

However, after her brief banter with Tub Trinder, there were now other things on Edie's mind, things that would keep her awake at night if she didn't face up to them. Had Rita really found out about Ruth's soldier boy, or was she just bluffing, drawing nasty conclusions as always? Oh yes, Edie knew that the boy was around, for the walls between terraced houses were not thick enough to contain secrets, and she had certainly heard voices in the 'end house' the night before. But breaking into the shop? Why would this boy want to do such a terrible thing? Was he a thief, a crook, who was trying to win over Ruth's confidence? And if it *was* him that broke into the shop, why would he only take a few packets of Woodbines and two bottles of ginger beer? By the time she had reached Seven Sisters Road, Edie had made up her mind what to do.

Thanks to the war, Father Tim O'Leary had to

spend more time in the graveyard of St Anthony's Church than he would have under normal circumstances. This was mainly because his young gardener had been called up at the start of the war, and his assistant had to spend more time on manoeuvres with the Home Guard than attending to the weeds on the graves of the dear departed. Apart from a few loyal parishioners, there was very little help around these days, and this being Saturday, despite the inclement weather, he wanted to make quite sure that the entrance to the church looked its best for all those inevitable wedding group photos that would be taking place that afternoon. But weeding was no easy job for a man of advancing years, and his grunts and groans could be heard quite clearly on the road outside as he knelt on the wet grass struggling to remove several hostile nettles from the late Mrs Ponting's grave.

'Good morning, Father.'

Practically the last person in the world Father Tim expected to see coming up the church footpath was Mrs Whitlock's girl, Ruth. 'Good morning,' he responded, clasping his aching back. 'What a pleasant surprise.'

'I was wondering whether you could spare time for a few words,' said Ruth, who still had her umbrella up after the recent light drizzle. 'I know this is a busy day for you, but I would appreciate it.'

'I'd be delighted,' he replied, easing himself up from his painful kneeling position. 'Any excuse to get away from this terrible job. What can I do for ye?'

Ruth shuffled from one foot to the other. 'There's someone ... I want you to meet,' she said, turning around to indicate Mike, who was waiting just outside the church gates.

When Father Tim looked to see who it was, Mike waved awkwardly at him. 'Ah,' said the priest, raising his eyebrows. 'I think you'd better come into the house. Both of ye!'

Father Tim's house was exactly how Ruth had imagined it. For a start, the place smelt of furniture and floor polish, the imitation Persian rugs were threadbare, the walls desperately in need of new wallpaper, and the furniture heavy and cumbersome. 'I think we'll be more comfortable in the conservatory,' the priest said, leading them out through the sitting room. Pleasant though it must have been in its day, the war had clearly taken its toll of the poor old conservatory, for quite a lot of the glass had been blown out by bomb blast so that the broken windows had to be covered with squares of plywood. Even the indoor plants looked sorry for themselves. 'As ye can see, I do *not* have green fingers!' quipped Father Tim, in his bright Irish brogue. He showed Ruth and Mike to a garden bench made of iron with tatty cushions, and gingerly sat himself down on a garden chair opposite them. As he had now been introduced to Mike, he got down to business straight away. 'So now,' he asked, 'where do we begin?'

'Father,' Ruth said tentatively, 'the last time we met, you suggested that it was about time that I was truthful with myself, and that I started to find out what I really wanted from my life. Well –

I now know.' She flicked a quick glance towards Mike, whose attention was transfixed on the leaves of a particular potted plant on a ledge at his side.

'I see,' said Father Tim, darting a disapproving look at Mike. 'So where does this leave your former attachment? Have ye had any definite news about the fate of the young man in question?'

'We haven't had any news of Tom for a long time,' she said. 'His sister and his father are convinced he hasn't survived.'

'But you've had no official confirmation yet that he *is* actually dead?'

Ruth looked down at her lap, and shook her head.

'And what would ye do if Tom *was* still alive?'

Ruth hesitated before looking up again. 'I'm afraid it wouldn't make any difference.

'I see,' said Father Tim grimly. 'Not a decision you've taken lightly, I hope – considering ye promised to marry the poor chap when he came home?'

'I love Mike, Father,' replied Ruth. 'I didn't plan it this way. It just happened.'

'That's usually the case,' replied Father Tim. 'And what about you, young man?' he asked, turning to Mike. 'How do *you* feel about all this?'

Mike, still preoccupied with the plant he was looking at, didn't reply.

Ruth snapped at him. 'Mike!'

He turned with a start. 'Sorry?' he asked.

'Father O'Leary was just asking how you feel about us getting together?'

'Oh,' replied Mike. 'Sorry about that. I was just

admiring your *Zygocactus truncatus*. But if yer want it ter flower fer Chrissmas, yer ought ter plant it out fairly soon.'

Ruth and Father Tim exchanged an astonished glance. 'I am right, ain't I?' the young man asked. 'It *is* a Chrissmas cactus?'

'You speak Latin?' asked Father Tim, with disbelief.

'Only plants,' shrugged Mike. 'I 'ave enuff trouble speakin' English, but I love plants. Me grandad 'as loads of 'em on is balcony.'

Father Tim grinned, and leaned back in his chair. 'Do you also love this young lady?' he asked.

Mike swung a look at Ruth, and beamed. 'You bet I do,' he replied.

The old priest sighed. 'Then it sounds ter me as though you two have a problem,' he said. He gazed out through one of the few unbroken windows, into his small unkempt garden, and the drab grey stone of the church walls beyond. This was the time when he was expected to offer words of advice, of worldly wisdom – God's wisdom – but as he sat there pondering on the predicament Ruth had found herself in, he felt strangely incapable of knowing what to say to her. And yet, he knew that he had to say *something*, for in one sense he felt that he was taking the place of Ruth's own father.

The few moments of silence lengthened. Just above their heads, a small garden spider was busily attending to his latest catch in his web, a bumblebee that was buzzing frantically, determined to break loose. 'I suppose we all have a need to escape,' he said, as he watched the bee fly away. 'Sometimes we tie ourselves down into impossible situations, without ever thinking of the consequences.' He sat upright in his chair again. 'Tell me, young man,' he said, directly to Mike. 'What would you advise Ruth ter do, if the man she promised ter marry *did* come back home safely again?'

Mike looked to Ruth to help him out. Her look told him what to say. 'I'd tell 'er ter tell 'im the trufe,' he replied.

'That she no longer loves him?' asked the priest. 'That she's in love with another man? You would expect her to say all this to someone who had just come back from the jaws of death?'

Mike shrugged.

'How would yer feel if you yourself had ter cope with such a situation?'

Mike thought hard for a moment. 'I don't know,' he said. 'I s'ppose the same fing could 'appen ter me if an' when I ever get back.'

Ruth saw the priest's incomprehension. 'Mike's being posted out to the Far East, Father,' she explained.

Father Tim's eyes flicked across to Mike again. 'What faith do ye follow, my son?' he asked, after a pause.

Mike thought about this for a moment. 'Faith?' he asked. 'Well, if ye mean religion, the only faith I know is these fings 'ere.' He turned and looked at the plants by his side, and gently fingered the leaf of the young Christmas cactus. 'I know it sounds stupid, but I trust plants more than any-fin' else.' He looked up at the priest and gave him

280

a mischievous grin. 'Maybe it's becos they're the only fings I can talk ter wivout 'em answerin' back!' And with a wistful look out the window, he added, 'They also stop me feelin' sorry fer meself.'

Father Tim waited for Mike to finish, then slowly eased himself out of the chair and stood up. 'Yer know what?' he said, addressing himself to both of them. 'You two don't need me to tell ye what to do. Ye know, the human spirit is stronger than we think. It has a way of persuading ye ter follow your own instincts.' He turned to Mike, and then to Ruth. 'And that's fine,' he added. 'As long as ye don't hurt people on the way.'

Edie could hardly get to Rita Simmons's house quick enough. All the way from Holloway Road her mind was burning with rage about what Tub Trinder had just told her. Even if it meant the end of their friendship, she was determined to have it out with Rita. The very idea that Ruth's new boyfriend could have been the intruder who broke into *Whitlock's* was, in Edie's opinion, a wicked slur. Whatever Ruth's so-called past, she would never take up with a mean, petty-minded crook who would use her in such an underhanded way.

'She's not at 'ome, Ede,' said Ted Simmons, who opened the front doer to her. 'Gone over ter see my cousin Doll.'

'I 'ave ter see 'er, Ted,' said Edie. 'D'yer know 'ow long she'll be?'

'Well, she said she's doin' Spam fritters fer

dinner,' Ted replied, 'so she should be back any minute. If yer want, yer can come in an' wait.'

Edie followed him into the back parlour. As usual, Ted had a fag in his mouth, and was wearing his grubby white vest, trousers and braces, and as he went down the passage he left behind a long thin trail of fag smoke.

'So,' said Ted, the moment Edie had settled down into a chair at the parlour table. 'Wot's this all about? You in trouble or somefin'?'

Edie was cagey in her reply. 'I'd better wait till Rita gets back,' she said. 'I fink she'll know more about it than you, Ted.'

He shrugged. 'I'll see yer later then,' he said, rubbing his unshaved face. 'I've got ter go an' get washed up.' He moved off to the scullery, but stopped briefly at the door. 'Can I get yer anyfin'?' he offered. 'Cuppa tea?'

'No fanks, Ted,' Edie replied. 'I'm all right, fank you.'

Ted left, closing the scullery door behind him.

Now she was alone, Edie settled back in her chair to await Rita's return. The first thing she did was to take out a pocket watch from her coat and compare the time with the alarm clock on the mantelpiece. 'Five minutes slow!' she said to herself of Rita's clock, confident that the watch she was holding, which had belonged to her late husband, had never lost a minute in all the years she had owned it. She put it back in her pocket. Her eyes then flicked up towards the ceiling; Rita had left the clothes she had ironed to air on the rack up there. As always, Edie was strongly critical of Rita's ironing. How many times had she told her to use a really hot iron on her pillowcases? No wonder they were all creased.

Edie's continuing disapproval of everything in the Simmonses' parlour was, however, suddenly distracted by the smell of Ted's dog-end, which he had left burning in the ashtray. She took out her handkerchief, covered her nose, and pushed the ash-tray as far away across the table as she could manage. But then she noticed that there was the remainder of a packet of Woodbines also left behind on the table. She wouldn't have given it another thought, except that when she looked around the room, she noticed four more packets of Woodbines on the dresser, all unopened. She got up from her chair to take a closer look. Alongside the fags were two bottles of ginger beer, one of them empty, the other half-full. For the moment, she didn't attach too much significance to the discovery, for she knew from experience how much Rita liked guzzling back ginger beer from the bottle, which was obviously one of the reasons why she was such a massive size. But then, something worried her. Ruth's shop. Was it *too* much of a coincidence, the combination of Woodbines and ginger beer?

'Sorry about this, Ede,' said Ted, who had returned from the kitchen, razor in hand, his face half-covered with a lather of shaving cream. 'She's probably out gassin' – runnin' someone down, as usual.'

Just as he was about to go back into the scullery again, Edie called to him, 'Ted, 'as Rita mentioned anyfin' ter you about – about Rufe's new boyfriend?'

Ted stopped and turned. 'Who?'

'Ruth,' said Edie. 'In *Whitlock's?*'

Ted hesitated a moment before replying. 'Don't really know 'er,' he said. 'I've only met 'er a coupla times when I've gone in ter get me *Daily 'Erald*. Polish gel or somefin', ain't she?'

'So Rita din't tell yer about the break-in the uvver night?'

Ted froze. 'Break-in?' he repeated.

'Somebody broke inter the shop, an' took an 'ole lot er fags. An' two bottles er ginger beer.'

Ted's eyes immediately darted across to the dresser.

'Apparently, Rita told Tub Trinder that Rufe's got a new boyfriend who's a bit of a crook. She reckons this boy's usin' Rufe ter clean 'er out.'

Quite unconsciously, Ted started to wipe the shaving cream from his face with the back of his hand. The rest of his body had gone quite still.

'If it's true,' continued Edie, pointedly, 'it's goin' ter knock poor Rufe fer six. She doesn't deserve it. She's a good gel, good ter everyone round 'ere.' She paused a moment, then stared directly at him from the other side of the room. 'D'yer know, sometimes, she an' 'er mum let customers go munffs on end wivout payin' their newspaper bills. And I did 'ear say that they've got a tab board in that shop that's as long as yer arm.'

'Excuse me, Ede,' said Ted, quite abruptly. 'I'd better go an' finish my shave.'

The woman watched him disappear quickly back into the scullery. But the look on his face had told her all she wanted to know.

284

Ruth felt as though she was emerging from a huge dark cloud. Although Father Tim hadn't exactly approved of her relationship with Mike, he certainly hadn't condemned it, and the fact that he had told them to *follow your own instincts* was a discreet way of saying that, provided she found a way of telling Tom's family that wouldn't hurt them, she must get on with her life as best she could. During the meeting, Mike had revealed a part of himself that she never knew existed. And she was still reeling from hearing him refer to a plant by its Latin name, when she, who had been brought up a Roman Catholic, could still not adequately pronounce the ancient language of the Matins. However, there was one big dark cloud hanging over her. There was now barely a week to go before Mike's leave came to an end.

That evening, Ruth and Mike went to the Savoy cinema in Holloway Road to see *Casablanca* – a romantic wartime melodrama starring Humphrey Bogart and Ingrid Bergman. Although it wasn't really Mike's cup of tea, at least it gave him the opportunity to snog with Ruth in the back row of the circle, without, that is, going any further than just that – a kiss and a cuddle. Surprisingly enough, it was he who was now taking the initiative by not allowing their relationship to become too intimate, not at least until the situation with Tom had been resolved once and for all. For Ruth, it turned out to be something of a melancholy occasion, since the last time she had come to this very same cinema had been with Tom himself.

When they came out into the street, Ruth suggested that they go and have a drink. This took Mike by surprise, until Ruth assured him that from now on, she didn't give a damn who saw them together, for after talking with Father Tim, she was convinced that her relationship with Mike was nothing to be ashamed of.

'Wot about yer mum?' asked a sceptical Mike, as they strolled hand in hand along Holloway Road towards the Nags Head. 'Wot 'appens when *she* finds out?'

'If Father Tim says it's all right,' Ruth assured him, 'then so will my mother. And if she doesn't, then it's just too bad.'

Mike listened to what she said, but wasn't convinced.

They ended up in the Enkel Arms pub in Enkel Street. It was just before closing time, and the landlord was already calling for last orders. To Ruth's surprise, she found Edie and her gentleman friend, Harold Beaks, sitting at a small table in the corner, but instead of trying to keep out of sight, Ruth grabbed hold of Mike's arm. 'Over here,' she said, leading him straight across to where Edie and Harold were sitting. 'Hallo, Edie,' she said.

'Rufe!' Edie was taken completely by surprise.

'I didn't know you used this pub,' said Ruth. 'I thought you and Rita always went to the Globe?'

Edie was too tongue-tied to answer.

'You must be Mr Beaks?' said Ruth, quite brazenly. 'I'm Ruth Madiewsky from the news-agents in Hornsey Road.'

286

'I'm very pleased ter meet you, Miss Ruth,' said the ultra-polite Harold, who had got up from the table the moment Ruth had approached. 'Edie's told me a great deal about you.'

'I wish I could say the same about you,' she said, with tongue-in-cheek. 'I'm afraid Edie's rather selfishly kept you to herself.'

Harold flicked a shy glance at Edie.

'Oh, by the way,' said Ruth, 'this is my friend, Mike Buller. We've just been to the Savoy and we've had a lovely evening. Mike, this is Edie, my neighbour from next door.'

Edie's mouth was wide open. She just couldn't get over this turnaround by Ruth, the way she was now prepared to bring her relationship with this new boyfriend out into the open.

''Ow-de-do, darlin',' beamed Mike cheekily. 'Just got time fer a drink. Wot'll it be?'

'No, no,' insisted an equally beaming Harold. 'This one's on me.'

'Come on then, mate,' said Mike, putting his arm around Harold's shoulders. 'We'll fight for it over the counter!'

With that, the two men hurried off to buy the drinks before the landlord called Time.

Edie watched them go in absolute bewilderment. 'They don't know wot we want,' she said anxiously.

Ruth sat down beside her. 'Don't worry. They'll get something.'

'I'm amazed,' gasped Edie, once she had come to. 'I can't believe this.'

'What can't you believe?' Ruth asked.

'Yer not afraid – I mean, yer don't care that

287

people know now?'

'Why should I?' replied Ruth. 'I've had enough of hiding in the shadows. This is my life, Edie, and I intend to run it the way *I* want, and not the way others expect. Mike is absolutely wonderful. I never dreamed I could be so happy.'

'Yer said that about the other one,' Edie reminded her, somewhat unkindly.

Ruth sat back in her chair. 'This is different,' she replied.

'Yer still wearing 'is ring.'

Ruth immediately felt for the engagement ring Tom had given her just before he went away. 'I told Mike,' she said guiltily, 'that I wanted to carry on wearing it until I know for certain what's happened to Tom. But I now realise it's not the right thing to do, so I'm sending it back to his mother.'

'An' when yer *do* know wot's 'appened to Tom – wot then?'

This irritated Ruth. 'I do wish people would stop asking me that.'

'Don't get me wrong, Rufe,' Edie said, sheepishly. 'I'm just worried fer yer, that's all. Mike seems such a nice boy.'

Ruth smiled. 'I think your Mr Beaks is pretty nice too,' she said.

'But yer've got ter be careful,' said Edie, lowering her voice.

'Careful?' asked Ruth. 'Careful of what?'

Behind them, some of the last hangers-on in the bar were determined to have their final sing-song, leaving Edie the difficult job of competing with a rousing chorus of 'Any Old Iron?'

Edie drew her chair as close as she could to Ruth. 'Rita's bin puttin' it around that your boy's the one who broke inter the shop the uvver night.'

Ruth was shattered. 'What!'

'She says he's a crook who's bin takin' yer fer a ride, an' that someone should tell the coppers before 'e can do any more 'arm.'

'God in heaven!' bellowed Ruth, leaping up angrily from her seat.

'No, Rufe!' pleaded Edie, grabbing her arm and struggling to pull her down again. 'Yer don't 'ave ter worry. I know your boy din't do it, I know!'

Ruth slowly allowed herself to be eased back into her chair again. 'What are you talking about, Edie?' she asked. 'What are you trying to tell me?'

'I'm trying ter tell yer,' said Edie, now almost whispering into Ruth's ear, 'that there's no way your boy could've broken into the shop – becos *I* know who *did!*'

It was well after midnight when Ruth finally saw Mike off onto his bus in Holloway Road. After leaving the pub, they had strolled quite aimlessly around the darkened streets, arms hugging each other's waists, talking, humming 'As Time Goes By', the haunting song they had heard in the film they had seen earlier, and just relishing the time they were able to spend with each other. For several minutes, they stopped in a dark shop doorway near the railway arch, kissing, fondling each other, their bodies pressed so close together that Ruth could hardly breathe. Oh God! She wanted so much to take him back home to the 'end house'. She wanted so much to give herself to him, to prove that what she felt for him now was real, and would last for ever. But every time she reached the point where she was prepared to risk all and bring her longings to reality, she somehow managed to come back from the brink. When it was finally time for Mike to leave, he was reluctant to get on his bus and let her walk home on her own, but Ruth insisted that they were no more than a few hundred yards from the 'end house', and if he missed his last bus, there wouldn't be another one until the morning.

After she had watched Mike's bus disappear into the distance along Holloway Road, Ruth slowly made her way back home. It was an extremely dark night, for there were low clouds which threatened more rain, and they completely obliterated the September moon. She was glad she had her torch with her, for with the streets still plagued with the curse of the blackout, it wasn't easy to see the pavement ahead of her. On the way, she thought about everything Edie had been telling her, about Rita Simmons's endless obsession with trying to create trouble for her. Over and over again she tried to work out why the woman should want to spread rumours about Mike. She'd never even met him! So what was her reason for creating so much mischief, so much fear? As she crossed over the junction with Hornsey Road and passed beneath the railway arch, Ruth also wondered why Edie Perkins had refused to name the person whom she knew to be responsible for the break-in.

As she turned the corner of Jackson Road,

Ruth's pace quickened. It was the first time she had realised how eerie a London back street could be at dead of night, in the middle of a blackout, no moon, no stars, and despite the fact that there were people in each one of the houses she passed, a feeling of loneliness.

Eventually, she reached the corner of the Annette Road cul de sac, but it was here that she was jolted by an unexpected flash of panic. Coming to an abrupt halt, she suddenly remembered that just before she had locked up Whitlock's that evening, she had left the safe keys on the table in the back parlour. After quickly making sure that she had the key to the front door of the shop in her purse, she turned around, and made off as fast as her feet would carry her.

Despite the dark, she ran practically all the way, and by the time she had reached Hornsey Road there wasn't a person to be seen anywhere. Although the shop was no more than a hundred yards or so from the corner of Holloway Road, it seemed to take for ever to get there. When she did finally reach the front door, she quickly retrieved the key from her purse, and put it into the lock. To her horror, she found the door wasn't locked. Once again she was consumed with blind panic. Suppose there was someone in there, the same person who had broken in before? Suppose she went in, and he did her some harm? She stood back from the door, just staring at it. Call the police. It was the only thing to do. She was on the point of turning away, but stopped. Her mind churned over. *Had* she locked the door when she left earlier that evening, or was she getting absent-minded like her mother?

For several moments she pondered over the predicament she was in. Finally, however, she decided that she was making a great fuss out of nothing. Clearly she had not locked the door, and it was lucky that she had come back in time to put things right. She entered, but left the front door open behind her. She went straight to the electric light switch, but before she could turn it on, someone from behind suddenly clasped a hand over her mouth, and the other over the hand that was trying to turn on the light switch. Terrified, she pulled away, and tried to make for the door, but the intruder was there before her, blocking her escape, and slamming the door behind him. Ruth backed away, and turned her torch beam onto the man's face.

'Oh my God!' she gasped, horrified. 'What are *you* doing here?'

Chapter 15

Ted Simmons tried to shield his eyes from Ruth's torch beam. The moment she had identified him, he had wanted to run, but he now knew that it was too late, and that whatever he tried to say or do from now on, his fate was in her hands. 'I'm sorry, miss, I'm sorry,' was all he could say, over and over again.

Ruth could hardly believe that Rita Simmons's husband could have been so stupid. As she stared at the pathetic figure cowering in the light from her torch, she couldn't be sure if he was a dangerous criminal, or just plain stupid. 'Why, Mr Simmons?' she asked. 'What's happened that's made you do such a thing?'

Ted looked utterly crushed. Wearing only his vest, old dungarees, and well-worn rubber-soled shoes, he turned away.

'What've you taken?' demanded Ruth, as he turned his back on her, lowered his head, and rested both hands on the counter.

'I ain't taken nothing,' he replied, his voice barely audible.

Ruth switched on the light. Fortunately the blackout blinds were still down. 'The other night you cleared my stock of Woodbines,' she said. 'Plus two bottles of ginger beer.'

'I tell yer I ain't taken *nothin'*!' he growled.

Nervous that in the state he was in, he might turn on her, she moved just a few cautious steps towards him. As she did so, he turned around and faced her. To Ruth's astonishment, in his hand he was holding out five packets of Woodbine cigarettes. ''Ere!' he said.

Ruth did not respond. She remained where she was, absolutely shocked and bewildered by the sight of a man she had only ever passed a few words with in her entire life.

'Go on – take them!' insisted Ted. 'They're yours. I took them. Five packets er Woodbines. I smoked one packet, so I've replaced it.' Then he reached into his pocket and took out some coins. 'And 'ere's the money fer the ginger beer.' As Ruth was still too nervous to move, he went up to her. 'It's yours!' he growled, pushing the five packets and the coins at her. 'I'm sorry,' he said, his voice cracking with emotion. 'All I can say is – I'm sorry!'

Ruth took the packets of cigarettes, and watched in disbelief as Simmons turned away, rested his hands on the counter again, and dissolved into tears. Faltering at first, she finally went to him. 'Please, Mr Simmons,' she said, dismayed. 'Let's talk about this.'

'There's nuffin' ter talk about,' he replied, in between sobs. 'I've done it, an' that's all there is to it. This time I've really done it!'

Realising that she had nothing to fear from him, Ruth put the packets of Woodbines down on the counter, then went across to close the door. 'Mr Simmons,' she said gently, placing her hand on his shoulder. 'Ted – please listen to me.'

The man shook his head. He was unable to face her.

'I have no intention of calling the police,' Ruth told him. 'Do you hear what I say?'

Simmons gradually pulled himself together, wiped his eyes with the back of his hand, and turned around to look at her. 'Why would yer do a fing like that fer me?' he asked sceptically.

'Because I want to talk to you,' replied Ruth. 'I want to know why you felt you had to do such a thing, to break into our shop and take something that doesn't belong to you.' She took one step closer to him. 'Was it because of your wife? Was it because Rita *made* you do it?'

Simmons lowered his eyes, then moved away. 'I did it fer Rita – yes,' he said. 'But not becos she

294

asked me ter do it. There are some fings yer can't explain,' he continued, moving aimlessly around the shop. 'Some fings yer do on the spur er the moment wivout stoppin' ter fink why.' He stopped moving around, put his hands in his pockets, flicked a quick glance up at the ceiling, and then back to Ruth. 'Rita – my wife,' he began, 'sometimes, she pushes yer over the edge. It's bin like that fer a long time now. I don't know why she does it, but she does – all the time. Day in, day out, I 'ave ter listen to 'er runnin' people down, plottin' against folk, makin' life a real misery. That's why the kids left 'ome early – all of 'em. They couldn't wait ter find someone an' get out of it. Did yer know, my youngest left 'ome when she was just sixteen – went off ter live wiv a man twice 'er age. I should've put a stop to it, I know – but I refused to. She was far better off away from it all.' He started to move around again. 'An' then there's Eric – my middle one. Well, that's not strictly true. 'E ain't mine. 'E came after she'd 'ad a bit of a ding-dong with a commercial traveller. But I didn't care. I let 'er get on wiv it. You probably fink I'm a bleedin' fool. Well – I s'ppose I am.'

Although Ruth already knew all this, she listened intently.

'But I'll tell yer somefin',' Simmons continued. 'Our family ain't no different from loads of uvvers round the back streets. There are plenty more Ritas where she come from.' Without being conscious of what he was doing, he took a dog-end from behind his ear, and lit it. 'People fink everyone down the streets are always lovey-dovey ter each uvver – one big 'appy family, all stickin' tergevver, 'elpin' each uvver out whenever they're in a jam. Well, it ain't like that, not all the time it ain't. Number sixteen gets pissed off wiv somefin' number seventeen said, number twenty-eight won't talk ter number thirty-seven, number thirty-seven can't bear the sight of forty-two, an' so on an' so on. When people go inter their 'ouses and shut their front doors, that's it! As far as they're concerned, they're tucked away safe an' sound in their own little worlds. From that moment on, they don't want ter know about anyfin' or anybody.' Once again, Ted stopped, and looked back at Ruth. 'An' that's wot Rita can't take. She 'as ter know. She 'as ter know who they are an' wot they're doin', an' if she can't be told, then she'll make it up fer 'erself. That's when the sparks begin ter fly.' He took a deep pull on his dog-end, then went back to Ruth. 'The reason I broke in 'ere the uvver night,' he said, 'was becos I was goin' round the bend listenin' to 'er lyin' an' chunterin' on about people, about the way they looked, the way they talked, the fings they did or didn't do. I 'ad ter do somefin' ter get it out er me system, somefin' that would scare the bleedin' daylights out of 'er. I wanted ter 'umiliate 'er.'

Ruth was about to say something, but he prevented her from doing so.

'Oh I know,' he continued. 'Why didn't I give meself up if I wanted ter do all this to 'er?' His eyes misting up again, he took another deep pull on his fag, and casually looked around the shop. 'It was becos I fawt about *this* place,' he said, with real pain and anguish on his face. 'I fawt about you an' yer mum, an' 'ow I 'ad no right ter do this ter two people who've done more fer the people who live round 'ere than a lot of 'em deserve.' He looked back at her again. 'I also did it becos I didn't want anyone close ter you ter take the blame.'

They were suddenly interrupted by a loud banging on the front door, and a man's voice calling from outside. 'This is the police! Is anyone in there?'

Ruth immediately led Simmons out of sight behind the counter, then called back, 'Coming!' She hurried over to the front door, opened it, turned off the light, and peered out. 'It's all right, Constable,' she said. 'I'm in the middle of stocktaking.'

'At this time er night?' asked the police constable, trying to peer in. 'Don't yer know it's the middle er the night?'

'Don't worry,' replied Ruth. 'I'm sleeping in the back room. I'm perfectly all right.'

As the place was in darkness, the officer took Ruth's word for it, and quickly withdrew. 'Well, don't stay up too late, miss,' he joked. 'Yer won't be up in time ter get our mornin' papers!'

'Good night, Constable!' Ruth called. 'Thank you!' She closed the door, locked it, but left the light off. 'Are you there?' she whispered to Simmons in the dark. There was no reply, so she felt her way back to the counter and collected her torch. When she turned it on, there was no sign of Simmons, but the parlour door was wide open. And when she went to check the back door, she found that the bolt had been slipped, and that door too was wide open. Simmons had gone.

Sighing, Ruth quietly closed and bolted the door again. She turned off her torchlight, and for a brief moment just stood there, alone in the dark, turning over in her mind all the extraordinary things Simmons had just told her. Although she felt a sense of despair, at the same time she felt that there was hope, hope that somewhere among the back streets of this huge city there were more people like Simmons, people who were prepared to take risks in order to knock sense into those who had none themselves.

The following morning Ruth got up bright and early. It was Sunday morning, and despite the fact that she had spent much of the night in the shop, she didn't want to be late for Mike when she went to Hackney to meet him for a walk in Victoria Park that morning, before going on to have a midday meal in Jessop Place with Cyril.

The journey up to Hackney seemed to take for ever; the Sunday bus service was always beset with long delays. However, once she had taken the 609 trolleybus to Highbury Corner and then changed onto a petrol bus, Ruth managed to pass the time away by reading a copy of the *Sunday Pictorial* which somebody had left behind on their seat. The front page made grim reading, for it not only carried reports about the disastrous landing of British paratroopers at Arnhem, but also an extremely disturbing article about the skeletons of Allied bodies that had been un-covered in the jungles of Burma.

Ruth shivered at the thought of Tom coming to such a fate, and quickly turned the page to read about the government's plans for the demobbing of soldiers returning home at the end of the war, and the paltry increase of seven shillings a week they were offering to men below the rank of sergeant who would be serving in the Japanese campaign. Ruth threw down the newspaper angrily. Seven meagre shillings! Was that the best they could offer to men such as Mike? Seven shillings for risking their lives in the steaming hot jungles of the Far East? By the time she had got off the bus and was met by Mike, she was so angry she could hardly talk. But she soon calmed down, and within a few minutes, the two of them were strolling hand-in-hand through the lush green fields of Victoria Park.

Although it was a grey, unsettled morning, they spent almost an hour on an old stone bench, watching the antics of the Home Guard drilling up and down relentlessly. Not far in the distance, they could see an RAF barrage balloon unit still on standby in case there came a signal from the Outer London defences to say that enemy aircraft were on the approach.

Once they had moved off again, Mike had some worrying news to pass on to Ruth. 'Grandad says someone told 'im Jerry's got a new secret weapon,' he said grimly. 'It's some kind of a rocket.'

'A rocket?' asked Ruth, puzzled. 'What does that mean?'

Mike shrugged. 'Search me,' he said. 'But they say it don't need no pilot, like the buzzbombs, an' yer get no warnin'.'

'It all sounds a bit far-fetched to me,' said Ruth dismissively. 'I can't imagine anything being more terrifying than the doodlebugs.'

'I shall still worry about yer,' said Mike, slipping his arm around her shoulders.

'I shall worry about *you*,' countered Ruth. 'More than you'll ever know.' She leaned towards him, and they kissed.

A short time later, they were sitting down to a meal with Cyril, who had cooked a Sunday beef roast. 'Don't ask me where I got the meat,' he said, as always tapping the side of his nose with one finger. ''Cos I won't tell yer!'

Ruth laughed, but was greatly impressed by the amount of trouble Cyril had taken to cook for them. Everything was done to perfection, especially the roast potatoes, which were crisp to the touch, but not overcooked, and the carrots had been steamed whole with just a hint of black pepper and mint to flavour them. For 'afters', as Mike and his grandad called it, he had made a rhubarb pie, which although in need of something more to sweeten it than saccharin tablets, was tender and succulent, and went down a treat with custard made from dried milk.

Once they had finished the meal, they all sat sipping tea in front of Cyril's proverbial fire. For hours on end they listened to his tales of Hackney in the old days, how when he was a young man the funeral hearse was always pulled by two black horses, which his own dad had kept tethered in what used to be the old carpentry workshop, now no more, 'thanks to that doodlebug with the fire in its tail,' said an embittered Cyril. One story that particularly appealed to Ruth was his description of how elegant the back streets of Hackney used to be in the old days. 'Fit for a king!' he called them. But the real shock came when Cyril announced that, as soon as Mike got out of the Army, he, Cyril, was going to retire.

Mike roared with laughter. 'Don't listen to 'im, Rufe,' he joked.' ''E's bin promisin' ter do it for the last ten years. Grandad won't retire 'til we carry 'im out in one of 'is own boxes!'

'Well, you listen ter *me*, smartarse!' countered Cyril. 'When yer *do* carry me out, yer'd better make sure it's in a better coffin than the one yer made fer poor ol' Ben Oakley. One of the 'andles come off before we even got 'im ter the crematorium!'

Now Ruth laughed with Mike. 'I can't see why you should want to retire, Uncle Cyril,' she said. 'You don't look anywhere near your age.'

Cyril's expression immediately changed. 'D'yer fink so?' he asked, vainly adjusting his toupee for the umpteenth time. 'D'yer really fink so?'

To reassure him, Ruth covered his hand affectionately with her own. 'You're a very handsome man, Uncle Cyril,' she said. 'You've got a lot of years ahead of you yet.'

Cyril positively beamed with pride. 'Fank yer, me dear,' he purred. And with a sniffing look across at Mike, he added, 'I can't imagine why a nice gel like you would want ter get mixed up wiv

301

a spiv like 'im!'

They all chuckled.

'Still,' said Cyril more seriously, 'the fact er the matter is that I've 'ad enuff er lookin' after dead folk. I've seen too much of it in this war, too much sufferin', too many tears. Whatever time I've got left, I want ter get the most out er bein' wiv the livin' – not the dead.'

Ruth and Mike exchanged a sombre look, then watched Cyril get up from his chair, and go to the French windows. 'Yer know,' he said, peering out into the garden below, 'a lot er folk take the mickey out of our trade. They fink we're a lot er bleedin' bloodsuckers, rubbin' our 'ands wiv glee every time we see anuvver customer comin' fru that door downstairs. But we ain't. We're only 'uman, ain't we? We've got feelin's just like any-one else. An' in any case, folk 'ave ter be looked after when they die. It's not a laugh-a-minute job, but somebody 'as ter do it.' He turned around to look at them. 'D'yer know wot I fink it is?' he asked. 'I fink people laugh at us 'cos we make 'em nervous. It makes 'em fink about themselves, about when it's goin' ter be *their* turn ter be carried out in a box. I mean, let's face it, we're all afraid er dyin', ain't we? But it comes to us all – sooner or later.'

For Ruth, Cyril's poignant words struck home only too forcibly. She reached for Mike's hand beside her, and held on to it.

''Onestly, mate!' said Mike, rebuking him. 'It's bein' so cheerful as keeps you goin'! Can we change the subject, please?'

Reminded that he was being too maudlin, Cyril

suddenly perked up. 'Sorry about that,' he said directly to Ruth. 'That's wot yer get fer livin' too long on yer own. I tell yer wot...' He went across to the battered-looking old upright piano, which was tucked away in an alcove. 'Why don't we 'ave a bit of a sing-song?'

'Oh Gawd!' groaned Mike. 'From the sublime to the corblimey!'

As Cyril opened the keyboard lid, Ruth got up to join him. 'I didn't know you could play the piano, Uncle Cyril,' she said eagerly.

'No,' called Mike. 'An' when yer 'ear 'im, yer'll know 'e can't!'

As soon as he sat down, Cyril started playing and singing 'Let the Rest of the World Go By', and within moments, Ruth was joining in. Mike clamped his hands over his ears, until Ruth suddenly came across and dragged him over to sing along with them. After they had joined in the chorus of a couple of songs, however, Mike could take no more, so he grabbed hold of Ruth's hand, and yanked her out onto the balcony.

'We can't just leave him like that,' said Ruth, scolding Mike. 'Besides, he's got a lovely voice, and he plays that piano really well.'

'Don't worry about Grandad,' Mike assured her. ''E'll sit an' play that fing all day if 'e 'as 'is way. 'E won't even know we've gone. Come on. I'll show yer the garden.'

He led her down the steep iron steps, which ended up in the small back garden below. Amongst the profusion of overgrown hollyhocks, there were weeds everywhere, and as they strolled around, Mike would occasionally sigh, and stoop down to pull some of them out. But Ruth could see what it all must have looked like before Mike was called-up, for there were splashes of colour everywhere, including late-flowering roses, a few dahlias, and a variety of shrubs which were clearly in need of some radical pruning.

'I put this down meself,' said Mike, pointing out the narrow path made of crazy paving. 'Took for ever an' a day, I can tell yer.'

Ruth admired his work, and strolled with him along the path. 'No air-raid shelter?' she remarked.

'Ha!' scoffed Mike. 'Yer'd never get Grandad in one of them fings! 'E'd sooner take 'is luck in 'is own bed!'

'Let's hope none of us has a need for one much longer,' Ruth said, forlornly.

They came to a halt at a broken wooden fence, which marked the boundary of Cyril's property, and the rear exit gate, which was used, as Cyril had once told Ruth, for carrying in and out late departed 'customers' from the Chapel of Rest. They paused awhile to listen to the old man still tinkling away on his joanna upstairs. In many ways, it was a wistful sound, a sad reminder to both Ruth and Mike that in a few days' time they would be parted again.

'I'm not comin' back 'ere, yer know,' Mike said, as he looked up towards the balcony from which they had just come. 'Goin' away's given me a new outlook on life. I don't want ter spend the rest of me years knockin' up boxes. I want ter try somefin' different.' He looked back at Ruth again. 'I haven't told Grandad yet. But 'e won't mind. In

304

fact, I fink 'e 'alf expects it. 'E's always supported me in anyfin' I've tried ter do. 'E taught me 'ow ter write all fancy, 'e encouraged me ter go off an' play football wiv me mates – an' 'e looked after me. All me life, 'e's looked after me. I can't imagine any mum an' dad doin' any better than 'e's done fer me.' He suddenly noticed that Ruth was staring straight into his eyes, so he slipped his arms around her waist, and kissed her.

'I don't want you to go,' said Ruth when their lips parted. 'Isn't there any way you can get out of it?'

Mike grinned. 'Not unless I desert,' he replied.

'Why not?' replied Ruth, without actually meaning it.

'Me? Desert!' He shook his head. 'Not on yer nellie!' he said firmly. 'I believe in this war.'

Ruth stood back and looked at him in astonishment. 'You believe in *war?*' she asked.

'I believe in gettin' rid er the gits who started it,' he told her. 'Until that 'appens, we don't stand a chance of a decent life.'

Ruth felt so much fear and anguish, she gently pulled away from him, and stared aimlessly out into the garden. 'You know, Mike,' she said, 'it isn't easy for us women, sitting at home, not knowing whether our menfolk are alive or dead. It's not easy to imagine what it's going to be like *if* or *when* they get home. I just don't know what I'd do if anything happened to you.'

'I'll tell you what you'd do,' he said, giving her a quick peck on the lips, 'yer'd find someone else, and start a new life ... no, I mean it!' he said, putting his fingers to her lips. 'Life 'as ter go on,' he continued. 'No one 'as the right to expect someone ter sit alone fer the rest of their days, just grievin' fer the past. Life is fer livin', Rufe,' he insisted. 'As it is, fings're goin' ter be bad enuff when the fellers come back an' find there ain't no jobs waiting fer them.'

'But what if they find that their women aren't waiting for them either?' asked Ruth. Even as she said it, she felt completely overwhelmed with guilt, for memories of her final moments with Tom on that railway platform before he left came flooding back to her, memories of promises she had made and not kept.

'Well now,' replied Mike. 'That's an interestin' question! I 'ope that don't mean yer won't be waitin' fer me?'

'Oh, I'll be waiting, Mike,' Ruth assured him. 'If there's one thing I can promise you, it's that. Just come home – that's all I ask.'

On Monday morning, Ruth received a letter from her mother. Although Bella spoke English well enough, her written language left a lot to be desired.

> *The Priory*
> *Ballard Close*
> *Chesterfield, 14/9/44*

My dear baby,
Just to tell you that I coming home at next weekend. I feeling so much better and now I want to get back and help you in the shop. I miss you and think of you all time.

Your Aunt Katya and Aunt Glinka send you many kisses.
Love from Mama.

PS. Please not to meet me. I get taxi from Euston station

Ruth put the letter down, relieved that at least her mother would not be returning home until the weekend, by which time Mike would have already left. Even so, she decided that it was now pointless to keep her relationship with him a secret, and that the moment Bella got home, she would tell her everything. However, when Ruth got to *Whitlock's* to open up that morning, there was another surprise in store.

'I'm sure you'll be relieved to know, miss,' said the police sergeant who had been investigating the break-in, 'that we've taken a man into custody in connection with the incident here the other evening. He'll be appearing at Highbury Magistrates' Court first thing tomorrow morning.'

Ruth's heart sank. After her encounter with Ted Simmons in the shop during the early hours of the morning before, this was the last thing she wanted. 'Who is he?' she asked, dreading the answer.

'A man called Simmons, Edward Simmons,' replied the sergeant. 'Sad to say, he's local. You probably know him. Lives just round the corner in Jackson Road.'

'Yes,' replied Ruth, sombrely. 'I know him.'

'We shall need you to come to the station in

307

Hornsey Road to make a statement.'

At that moment, the two newspaper boys, Dave and Phil, appeared, ready to start their morning deliveries. 'Blimey! What's going on?' said a wide-eyed Dave when he saw the two uniformed cops in the middle of interviewing Ruth.

''As there bin a murder?' asked Phil ghoulishly.

'Come back in ten minutes, please,' said Ruth, shuffling both boys back out of the shop.

'Wot about the papers?' asked Dave, burning with curiosity.

'Ten minutes!' She closed the door behind them, and turned back to the sergeant. 'How d'you know this man you've arrested is the one who is responsible?' she asked.

'Because he told us so,' the officer replied. 'He's given a full confession.'

Ruth was absolutely flabbergasted. Surely she had told Simmons the night before that she was not going to take any action against him, so why had he given himself up? 'So what has he confessed *to?*' she asked.

The sergeant exchanged a quick, puzzled look with his Special Constable colleague. 'To unlawfully breaking into your shop,' he replied, 'and stealing various items from your stock.'

'Well, surely that's of no consequence now?' Ruth asked, as she made her way behind the counter. 'We must have made a mistake. There's nothing missing from the shop after all.'

Again the sergeant and constable exchanged a puzzled look. 'Nothing missing?' asked the sergeant. 'But what about the Woodbine cigarettes – and the ginger beer?'

Ruth attempted a dismissive laugh. 'Ginger beer?' she said. 'The place is absolutely full of the stuff. I've got more than I can cope with. And as for the Woodbines – well, as you can see...' she turned around and showed the full stock of Woodbines on the shelf alongside the other cigarettes, 'Mrs Dapper must have miscounted the stock. The shelf was empty because we'd sold most of them. If she'd only taken the trouble to go into the back room, she could have replenished the stock on the shelf.'

'I see,' said the sergeant. 'Then what about the mess in here? Was that a "mistake" too?'

'Schoolchildren,' replied Ruth confidently. 'I believe your constable here suggested as much when you were last here.'

This time, the sergeant didn't bother to exchange a glance with his colleague. 'Schoolkids don't usually break into shops in the middle of the night,' he said heavily. 'They're usually in bed at that hour.'

Ruth shrugged. 'Anyway,' she said, 'no harm done. If you don't mind I'd like to forget about the whole thing now. So please accept my apologies for the trouble we've caused.'

The sergeant moved to the counter. 'So do I take it that you're not prepared to support a charge against Simmons?' he asked.

'What's the point?' replied Ruth. 'From what I hear, poor Mr Simmons has been having quite a lot of domestic problems just lately. I think he must have been very confused when he came to you.'

'So you're saying that you *won't* support a

309

charge?' asked the sergeant. 'Am I right, Miss Whitlock?'

'Yes,' replied Ruth firmly, looking him straight in the eyes. 'And if you please, Sergeant, my name is Madiewsky, not Whitlock.'

Once the two policemen had gone, Ruth breathed a sigh of relief, but all during the morning she couldn't get it out of her mind what Ted Simmons had done, how stupid he'd been, and how close he had come to being brought up before the Magistrates' Court and sent to prison. Even so, she was still not convinced that Simmons was out of trouble, and after Freda Dapper had relieved her for the afternoon, she made her way home with a heavy heart, her mind racing with the dread that the matter was not yet over. But when she turned the corner from Jackson Road, and started to make her way down the cul de sac, she stopped with a start when she saw someone in the distance, sitting on the coping-stone immediately in front of the 'end house'. 'Mrs Simmons,' she said coldly, as she approached. 'Would you mind telling me what you're doing here?'

The moment Ruth reached her, Rita stood up and growled, 'Yer dirty little cow! I'll get yer fer this! As sure as God eats little apples – I'll get yer!'

Chapter 16

Ruth's bust-up with Rita Simmons outside the 'end house' was the talk of the neighbourhood. Their stand-up row could be heard the length and breadth of both the cul de sac and also Jackson Road, with Rita castigating Ruth for accusing her husband of breaking into her shop, which Ruth categorically denied, by saying that she had told the police that there was no way that Ted Simmons could have been guilty of such a crime, and that the whole episode was nothing more than a complete misunderstanding. Needless to say, Rita refused to believe anything Ruth had said, and before storming off, she ranted and raved about Ruth and her succession of boyfriends, and how she had 'done the dirty' on the bloke she was supposed to be marrying. It took Ruth several days to get over the incident, and she was so upset that Mike wanted to go down to Jackson Road and 'sort out the old bag'. However, by the time it came to the last full day of Mike's leave, Ruth's only wish was to make as much of their final hours together as she possibly could.

On their last afternoon, Ruth and Mike decided to go 'up West', mainly because Mike was in nostalgic mood, saying that before he went he wanted to be reminded of what dear old London town looked like. And so for the best part of two hours they strolled, arm in arm, around the back streets of Soho, passing through Piccadilly and the covered-up plinth of the statue of Eros, which had long been removed for the duration of the war, and then through Leicester Square, where people were still queuing up to see *Gone With the Wind* outside the Ritz cinema, after nearly four years of it playing there to crowded houses. Then they made for Trafalgar Square, where the entrances to most of the government and Empire buildings there were protected with sandbags. On the way, Mike resented the fact that there were so many American GIs around with girls on their arms, but Ruth reminded him that most of them were only young blokes like himself, in a strange country, and miles away from their family and friends back home, and that these were probably *their* final few days before going off to risk their lives in some far-flung corner of the world.

A short while later they stopped to admire the view from Westminster Bridge. Below them, the River Thames was at full tide. The hundreds of windows in the imposing London County Council building were an odd sight, with the brief flashes of sun reflecting in the different panes of glass, all of which were protected from bomb blast by strips of sticky tape. They turned to look up at Big Ben as it struck the quarter hour behind them, and marvelled at the fact that the famous London landmark had managed to survive so many air raids. As it was a midweek afternoon, there was a fair amount of traffic around, with police cars hurrying in and out of the gates of Scotland Yard just behind them, and the sound of trains fracturing the air as their noisy metal wheels clattered on the rails as they made the sharp turn from the Victoria Embankment, and onto the bridge past the statue of Queen Boadicea. Ruth suggested that they move on, but Mike wanted to stay and savour the moment. As they peered out in silence towards the majestic dome of St Paul's cathedral in the distance, beyond the bend in the river, Mike suddenly said, 'I've left everyfin' ter yer in me Will.' He turned to look at her. 'It's as well yer know,' he said.

Ruth was utterly shocked. 'Your *Will?*' she gasped.

'Yeah,' replied Mike. He couldn't understand why she should be so surprised. 'When yer don't know if yer never comin' back, yer 'ave ter tie fings up, don't yer?'

'But Mike,' said Ruth, uncomprehendingly, 'you're a young man. You've got years before you need to make a Will.'

Mike grinned. 'That's not wot the Army fink!' he replied. 'This geezer, this officer come round an' gave us all these bits er paper. 'E said, it was just a precaution – just so's there were no problems *if* anyfin' 'appened to any of us.'

'I can hardly believe it,' said Ruth, in disbelief. 'Asking boys of your age to think about such mundane things.'

'No, Rufe,' said, Mike, slowly shaking his head. 'None of us blokes can afford ter put our 'eads in the sand. I mean, if anyfin' 'appened ter me, unless I told 'im, Grandad wouldn't know wot ter

313

do wiv all my possessions – not that I've got all that many. I've got nearly a 'undred quid in the Post Office, an' I've left yer a few uvver fings as well.' He drew close so that their noses were almost touching. 'I'd be very grateful,' he said, 'if yer could take care of me plants. Grandad wouldn't know 'ow. 'E always fergets ter water 'em.'

Ruth pushed her face into his shoulder. She felt like crying.

'It's no big deal, yer know,' said Mike. 'This sort er fing 'appens all the time in the Army.'

'I hate the Army!' she growled angrily. 'I hate *all* armies! They drag men down, they turn them into machines!'

Mike grinned. He loved it when she got angry, because her nose crumpled up, and her eyes were flashing like traffic lights. 'Yer can't do wivout 'em,' he replied.

'Oh yes, we can!' insisted Ruth. 'If there were no armies, no armies in any country in the entire world, *then* we could do without them.'

Mike shook his head. 'Don't you believe it,' he replied. 'When this war's over, there'll always be somebody somewhere who's spoilin' fer a fight.' He suddenly realised that all this talk of war on his final day was depressing her. 'Yer know somefin'?' he asked, trying to perk her up. 'I'm starvin'! Why don't we go back ter that British Restaurant we saw down Piccadilly way. We might get some bangers an' mash or somefin'?'

'No!' Ruth replied, emphatically. 'This is our last day together, and if we're going to eat, we're going to eat a decent meal. Come on!' She

314

slipped her arm around his waist. 'We're going home.'

Edie Perkins always preferred to go shopping alone; that way, she could take her time over choosing things, which wasn't possible when someone was with her. But today, she had no option, for Rita Simmons knew it was Edie's day for going up to Taffy Evans's fruit and veg barrow in the Holloway Road kerbside market, and for some devious reason or another, Rita had insisted on going with her.

'Come on girls!' called Taffy, whose familiar Welsh baritone voice sounded as if he was setting everything he said into song. 'Best King Edwards – penny a pound! Tell me where you can find better spuds at that price!'

'Give us a coupla pounds, Taff,' returned Edie, who was already searching around on his barrow for a decent green cabbage.

'An' wot about you, madam?' Taffy asked Rita, as he weighed Edie's potatoes up on his scales. 'I've got some beautiful cauliflowers. You look like a woman who could do with a good meal!'

Edie sniggered, but Rita was not amused. 'A pound er carrots,' she said, icily, 'two pounds er Cox's, an' two pounds er tomatoes. An' while yer at it, try not ter be quite so bleedin' funny!'

Edie glared at her, but Taffy took it all in good humour. Once he'd served Edie, tucked the vegetables in her string bag, and collected his money, he did the same for Rita.

''E's too clever by 'alf, that one,' complained Rita, once she and Edie were on their way again.

'I don't know why you keep goin' ter a bleedin' foreigner. 'Icks's is just as good down Seven Sisters Road.'

'Wales is not a foreign country,' countered Edie, as she inspected the other barrows and stalls as they moved on. 'In any case, Taff don't mean no 'arm. *An*' 'e's cheaper than Wally 'Icks by a mile.'

Rita grunted tetchily.

They two women made their way back slowly down Holloway Road and then, much to Rita's irritation, Edie wanted to stop at a furniture store to enquire whether they had any upholstery material in stock for her easy chair. But before they had even reached the front door of the building, Edie discovered why Rita had insisted on coming out with her. 'So who put 'er up to it then?' demanded Rita, bringing them both to a halt at the store entrance.

'What yer talkin' about?' asked Edie.

'That bleedin' Poley,' snapped Rita. *'That's* who I'm talkin' about. She told the coppers my Ted broke into 'er shop and nicked some fags. Was it you who tipped 'er off?'

'Rita!' gasped Edie, shocked. ''Ow can yer say such a fing? 'Ow can yer even fink it?'

'Well, I'm tellin' yer,' retorted Rita, unconvinced, *'somebody* did – an' once I find out who, I'll 'ave their bleedin' guts fer garters!'

'But I 'eard the coppers dropped all charges against Ted fer lack of evidence, that the 'ole fing was a mistake.'

'It was a mistake all right!' Rita said tersely. 'A mistake to accuse a poor innocent sod of some-

316

fin' 'e didn't do. Unless, that is,' she added pointedly, 'somebody wanted ter get their own back on *me*.'

Edie paused a moment, then in a fit of anger, she left Rita and stormed off into the store.

Shocked by her friend's reaction, Rita went in after her. ''Ang on a minute, Perkins,' she growled. 'Wot're *you* gettin' yer knickers all in a twist about?'

The little woman swung round angrily on her. ''Ow long 'ave I known you now, Rita?' she said. 'Firty, forty years? An' yet yer still treat me as though I'm a bit er dog-shit in the road.'

'Can I help you, madam?' said a bewildered young shop girl who came up to them.

'No!' bellowed Edie. 'We're just lookin'!'

The girl, totally taken aback by Edie's attitude, beat a hasty retreat.

'Now you listen ter me, Edie,' began Rita.

'No, Rita!' said Edie. 'Just fer once, *you* listen ter *me*, Rita Simmons!'

Around them, heads turned, as their raised voices unnerved the staff, and the few customers that were in the store.

'Fer yer information,' continued Edie, 'nobody told the coppers about Ted – not Rufe, nor me. If yer must know, it was Ted 'imself. An' yer know why?' She leaned forward, and glaring straight into Rita's eyes, lowered her voice. ''Cos Ted *did* break inter the shop that night.'

Rita scowled. 'What!' she said, through clenched teeth.

'Yes!' said Edie. ''E did it becos 'e was boozed out of 'is mind, becos 'e 'adn't the faintest idea

317

wot 'e was doin'. At least, that's wot 'e told me when I came round ter your place and saw all those packets er Woodbines on your dresser, an' the two empty bottles er ginger beer.' She suddenly turned around and saw people listening to every word she was saying. 'Wot're *you* all lookin' at?' she roared, her tiny voice booming around the sparsely stocked furniture showroom. The place cleared in a flash.

Thoroughly humiliated, Rita turned around, and made for the door. But Edie, her courage now to the fore more than ever before, rushed around to block her way. 'All these years I've listened ter you rantin' an' ravin' about absolutely any bleedin' fing! But yer've never looked at yerself, Rita. Yer've never asked yerself *why* yer don't like people, an' *why* people don't like *you*. Wot Ted did the uvver night was becos 'e was desperate, a cry fer 'elp. An' all becos er you, *you* Rita! All becos yer couldn't care a damn *wot* the world finks of yer.' She drew up close to Rita, and stared her out. 'Yer so bitter, yer even tried ter pin the blame on someone else. Wot sort of a person are yer, Rita?'

'I'm sorry, madam.'

Both women turned to see the store manager approaching them.

'Are you ladies here to buy anything?' the man asked, curtly.

'Maybe I am, an' maybe I ain't!' returned Edie uncompromisingly.

'Then if you have no business here,' replied the man, 'I must ask you to leave.'

Edie scowled at him. 'Don't worry, mate!' she

snapped. 'I wouldn't buy anyfin' in this dump if it was 'alf price summer sales!' With that, she turned, and swept off back to the entrance.

Rita, in a state of shock, slowly followed her out. When she got outside, she found Edie waiting for her.

'I just want ter say one more fing, Rita,' Edie said. 'I just want ter say that yer don't deserve ter 'ave a man like Ted. D'yer know why? 'Cos 'e 'ad the guts ter take those fags back, ter give 'imself up. Yer see, some people have a conscience, Rita, they know when they're in the wrong. Your trouble is that you could never fer one minute fink that *you*, the invincible Rita Simmons, could ever be in the wrong! When will yer learn, Rita? When will yer *ever* learn?' She turned, and walked off.

For several minutes, Rita stood there in the middle of the pavement, alone, and in a daze. All around her, people were going about their business, hurrying to catch a bus or a tram, stopping briefly to window shop, or just simply ambling along, taking the cool afternoon air. After waiting for Edie to disappear down Holloway Road, a tiny figure with her string bag swinging at her side, passing the entrance to the Tube station, and finally moving out of sight beneath the railway arch, Rita reluctantly started to make her own way home. But her mind was so full of the anger Edie had just thrown at her, that she couldn't concentrate on anything, not even the direction in which she was walking. How could Edie say all those things? she asked herself over and over again. Wasn't Edie supposed to be

319

her best friend? After all, they had known each other for so many years, had shared so many moments together, watched so many people moving in and out of houses down Jackson Road, exchanged opinions on them, criticised them. No, she told herself, as she came to an abrupt halt. It wasn't Edie who criticised. It was she, Rita herself, who did all the bitching, the doing the dirty on folk. And why? For what reason? The only answer she could give herself was, *Because they're there*. She moved on again, and without realising what she was doing, stepped off the pavement without looking to cross over to the other side of the road. Only by the grace of God did she escape being knocked down by an Army truck which came hurtling down the road, and skidding to a halt only just in time. Ignoring the curses and angry shouts of the soldier driver and his passenger, Rita continued on her way.

She crossed over the junction with Hornsey Road, and was about to head off towards Jackson Road, when once again she came to a halt. After a moment's thought, she turned back down Hornsey Road, until she finished up directly outside *Whitlock's*. She peered through the front window, but there was no sign of Ruth, only Freda Dapper, who didn't notice her because she was too busy serving the usual rush of kids who had just come out of school. As she looked inside, the big woman felt one brief moment of remorse at all the trouble she had caused, not only now, but over the years. But then, almost as though an electric light switch had been turned off again, she came out of her daze. 'Bleedin'

320

Poley!' she grunted, meanly to herself. Then she turned, and made off home.

Mike tucked into his plate of herrings with sour cream, boiled potatoes, and green beans. 'Interestin',' was his only comment, as he did his best to accustom himself to a taste he had never before experienced.

'In Polish it's called *Sledz Marynowany ze Smietana*,' said Ruth, eating with him at the kitchen table in the 'end house'. 'Mama says it's a popular dish in the Polish country villages.'

'Well, I'll take yer word fer it,' said Mike dubiously.

Ruth looked worried. 'You don't like it, do you?'

Mike realised that his cool response had hurt Ruth. 'That's not true, Rufe!' he assured her. 'It's just that I'm not used to this type er cookin', that's all. At 'ome, all that Grandad's ever given me is a roast on Sunday, leftovers on Monday, an' anyfin' we can turn our 'ands to fer the rest of the week. It's a long way from fish an' chips ter 'errings in sour cream,' he joked. 'But I promise, I *do* like it. It's somefin' yer can get used to.'

Ruth laughed. 'Mike Buller,' she teased, 'you're such an old fake!'

Now it was Mike's turn to look hurt.

Ruth elaborated. 'You know very well you can't wait to get back to that NAAFI canteen!'

He laughed with her, until they both realised the implication of Ruth's remark. 'I'll take your 'errings any day ter pie an' mash in the NAAFI,' he replied bravely.

They sat in silence for a few minutes, finishing off the bottle of white wine which Bella's aged aunts had brought over at Christmas, and which Ruth had used as part of the ingredients for the dish she had just cooked. 'You know,' she said, 'I'm beginning to feel we're like an old married couple – you coming home from work in the evening, me waiting for you with your slippers, a glass of wine, and dinner.'

'Well, it'll be the first time,' said Mike. 'This is the first wine I've ever drunk in me life. I was brought up on brown ale and bitter, remember!'

Ruth smiled back at him. But she was choked, and she found it difficult to swallow. The thought that this could be the last time they would eat together was churning over in her stomach and, as hard as she tried, she just couldn't get it out of her mind. From time to time, Mike watched her whilst she ate. He too felt an empty feeling in his stomach, and even though he really was getting used to the new type of cooking Ruth had taken so much trouble to prepare, he found it difficult to digest. 'Penny for 'em?' he asked.

Ruth looked up to find him smiling affection-ately at her. 'I was thinking about unspoken love,' she replied.

He looked puzzled.

'I never once heard my father tell my mother that he loved her,' she explained. 'Oh, I think he did – in fact, I know he did – but somehow, he must have always found it difficult to actually put it into words.'

'Is that why yer 'ated 'im?' asked Mike. 'Becos 'e couldn't *show* that he loved yer mum?'

'Hate him?' asked Ruth. 'I didn't hate my father. I just didn't respect him. You see, we had nothing in common. He only ever saw me as an object, an object that was there – sometimes placed at the table opposite him at dinner like you are now, or going to school, or going to work, or coming home from a dance late at night. He didn't know how to talk to me. He wouldn't have known what to say.'

'I knew a feller like that,' said Mike, during a pause in eating. "'E was a poofter, yer know, a pansy, didn't like gels an' fings, used ter work up the dairy. Anyway, I got ter know 'im when I was in the Scouts. 'Is name was Danny. We became quite good mates – nuffin' more than that, yer understand! The fing is, Danny 'ad a crush on this uvver bloke. Everyone knew 'er course, in-cludin' the bloke 'imself, *who*, as it so 'appened, was that way inclined 'imself. Trouble is, Danny never plucked up enuff courage to tell this uvver bloke 'ow 'e felt. Scared somebody might've shopped 'im, I s'ppose. But in a way, it was quite sad, 'cos some time later, I 'eard that this uvver bloke got killed when the *Hood* went down, yer know, that warship that got sunk up norf some-where.' He shook his head. 'Funny ol' world, ain't it?' He carried on eating. 'What about Tom?' he asked, quite casually. 'Did *'e* ever tell yer that 'e loved yer?'

Ruth looked up from her food. 'Yes,' she replied gloomily. 'He knew how to say that, all right.'

Mike looked up at her. 'Did *you* ever say it ter 'im?' he asked.

'Yes,' she replied.

'An' did yer mean it?'

'I suppose I must have done at the time.'

Mike smiled. He was grateful that she was being so truthful with him.

Once they had finished their meal, they went into the sitting room and pulled the sofa up in front of the fire that Ruth had lit earlier. It was still just light outside, so for the time being she didn't lower the blackout blinds. Then they snuggled up together on the sofa. 'What time is your train in the morning?' she asked, after he had given her a kiss.

'Ten o'clock,' he replied. 'But I don't want yer comin' wiv me.'

Ruth sat bolt upright. 'Oh, Mike!' she said, feeling hurt. 'Why not?'

'Becos there's no point,' he replied. 'It's better if I just go back 'ome ternight, then quietly disappear – no fuss, no panic.'

Now Ruth was really hurt. 'Well, thank you very much!' she said, springing up from the sofa. 'You're going away, I may never see you again, and all you can say is *no fuss, no panic!*' Clearly on edge, she left him and stomped across to lower the blackout blinds.

Mike immediately got up and went after her. 'Hey!' he said, turning her around to face him. 'I'd never've got 'ooked up wiv yer, if I knew yer 'ad a temper like this.'

'Well, if you feel that way—' she said, not seeing his smile.

But before she could say another word, he covered her mouth with a kiss. For a moment, she struggled, but then gave in, and threw her

324

arms around him. 'Oh Mike,' she said falteringly, as their lips parted, 'I can't bear this. The thought of you going away in just a few hours' time is more than I can–'

Once again he kissed her, this time more deeply. When they parted again, both were staring hard into each other's eyes. They remained like that for several moments. Then, with her eyes still on his, Ruth reached up behind her shoulders, and unclipped the hooks on her blouse there. Unwilling at first, he eventually reached up and cupped both nipples in his hands. With his help, she reached forward, and pulled his shirt out from his trousers. Then he waited whilst she undid all the shirt buttons. Once the shirt was thrown onto the nearest chair, he removed his vest, so that he was now bare-chested. When this was done, Ruth slipped out of her skirt, and let it fall to the floor. Both of them had already removed their shoes when they first came into the room. Now wearing only panties and bra, Ruth put both her hands onto Mike's shoulders, which was a signal for him to lean down and kiss her nipples, one by one. This he did for several minutes, using his tongue to arouse her even more. She then took hold of his hands, and slipped them round behind her shoulders. 'Are you sure?' he asked softly.

Ruth nodded.

He unclipped her bra, and that too fell to the floor.

Ruth reached across and turned off the table lamp. The only light now was from the dying flames of the fire in the grate. Mike was next. He slowly unbuttoned his flies, lowered his trousers, and kicked them off.

They were both now standing facing each other, dressed only in their underwear. Mike held out his arms, and she fell into them, sliding her own arms around his waist. Now fully aroused, Mike shuddered as he felt her nipples pressed up firmly against his chest. Gradually, he felt her hands sliding down his thighs. She responded accordingly. Now fully naked, they pressed their bodies together as tightly as they could. Then Ruth led him back to the fireplace, and they slowly sank to their knees on the rug there. They stretched out, facing each other, staring into each other's eyes, their hearts thumping madly with the beat of excitement. Ruth took the initiative. Turning Mike around, she laid him flat on his back on the rug then positioned herself so that she could lower herself down onto him. But as she was doing so, he suddenly sat up. 'No, Rufe!' he said, brusquely. 'We can't take the chance.'

'I want to,' replied Ruth, emphatically.

'You haven't thought this fru,' he said.

'I have, and I want you,' she insisted. 'I won't let you go, I won't let you leave me until we've had these moments together. Please, Mike.' She leaned down, and kissed him fully, deeply. 'I do so love you.'

Mike leaned back again. This time he helped her to slowly lower herself onto him. She sighed, and made only the slightest of groans as she felt him enter her. It was not the first time for either of them, so there were no unexpected concerns. The further she lowered herself, the greater the ecstasy, the warmth, the feeling that they were united in love at last.

When it was over, they lay there for several hours, clasped in each other's arms in front of the fire. Until it was time for Mike to go, they shared a cigarette together, and stared into the flames until the dying embers had all but vanished.

Although he had a train to catch early the following day, Mike did not leave the 'end house' until late that evening. At the moment of their final parting, neither said a word. They merely stood in the hall by the front door, gazing for one last time into each other's eyes. There was, after all, no need for words.

A kiss was all they needed to say goodbye.

Chapter 17

Bella looked so much better after her holiday in Chesterfield, Ruth thought. Clearly, she had been looked after wonderfully well by her aged Polish aunts, for when she came home the following weekend, she had more colour in her cheeks, her eyes were brighter, and she seemed altogether more optimistic about her own health. By Monday morning, Bella was back in Whitlock's again, irritating both Ruth and Freda Dapper by giving them instructions about what should and should not have been done whilst she had been away, and generally making a thorough nuisance of herself. Despite this, Ruth would still not allow her mother to return full-time to the shop, and much to Bella's intense annoyance, she was packed off back to the 'end house' each afternoon for a couple of hours' rest.

Before her mother's return, Ruth had agreed with Freda Dapper that it would be better if they said nothing about the events that had recently taken place, even though it was more than likely that one of the customers would chatter about it sooner or later. And as far as Ruth herself was concerned, she had decided not to tell her mother right away about her involvement with Mike, especially in view of what had taken place between them just a few days before. In fact, that final night alone with Mike, and indeed all their time together during that eventful ten days, had had a profound effect on Ruth, and she had no doubt that life without him was not going to be easy.

However, Bella was a shrewd woman, and during her convalescence being fussed over and cared for by Aunts Katya and Glinka, she had had a great deal of time to think about Ruth, and to speculate about what her complicated daughter had been up to whilst she was away. By the middle of the following week, her curiosity was getting the better of her, and as she sat on her usual stool behind the counter, sipping a cup of tea and watching every move Ruth made, she finally couldn't resist the temptation to start asking some probing questions.

'It must have been lonely for you at home, darling,' she said cunningly. 'Night after night, coming back to an empty house, having to cook for yourself. Were you able to make contact with any of the neighbours whilst I was away?'

Ruth was aware of what Bella was up to, and was prepared for it. 'I wasn't lonely at all, Mama,' she replied, teasingly. 'As a matter of fact, I had very little time to myself because I had *so* many visitors.'

Bella was not amused. 'That's not funny, darling,' she said. 'Are you still hearing from that boy?'

'Which one?' asked Ruth flippantly.

'The one who writes you so many letters.'

That was it, Ruth decided. She'd hoped that her mother would have calmed down a bit since she'd been away, but no. It was clear that, now she was back, the nagging was going to start all over again. 'As a matter of fact,' she said, quite boldly, leaving the old magazines she had been trying to make a display of in the window, 'Mike has just been home on ten days' leave. If you'd have come home a few days earlier, you could have met him. He said several times, he was sorry to have missed you.'

Bella got up from her stool, and went into the back room.

Ruth followed her in. 'You can't keep on like this all the time, Mama,' she said. 'Mike is a truly wonderful person. He loves me very much. And I love *him* very much, too. Remember, you once asked me to be truthful with you, and not to keep things from you. Well, I'm being truthful with you now, and I'm telling you what I should have told you a long time ago.'

'And what about Tom?' asked Bella, taking her

teacup to the sink there, and washing it under the tap. 'I suppose he's a thing of the past now?'

There were times when Ruth felt quite cold towards her mother, and this was one of them. It was so typically callous of her to say such a thing, so narrow-minded. 'That's not fair, Mama,' she replied, her voice cracking with emotion. 'I feel so bad about Tom, I really do. I feel so helpless, that there's nothing I can do to help him, no way I can tell him how sorry I am for what I've done.'

'But you're prepared to have a relationship with someone else without knowing for sure what has happened to Tom?'

Bella's cross-examination was beginning to irritate Ruth, so without pursuing the subject any further, she turned and went back into the shop. She had always known that this wasn't going to be easy, that was why she had dreaded this moment. But whatever happened, she would not allow herself to be bullied.

'Have you spoken to Father O'Leary about it?' Bella was calling from the open back room door.

'Father O'Leary,' replied Ruth, 'understands perfectly. As a matter of fact, I took Mike to meet him.'

Bella went silent, then after a long pause asked sceptically, 'Are you telling me that Father Tim has given his blessing?'

Ruth, at the shop window again, repeated, 'I said, he understands perfectly well.' In the hope that her mother would let it drop, she carried on with her work, but it was no surprise when, after a few moments, she found her mother standing just behind her.

'I went to see Dr Sharp this morning,' Bella said, sombrely. 'He said that with my condition, I have to be very careful. Apparently the death rate from severe angina these days is very high.'

Ruth stopped what she was doing. She'd been down this road before with her mother: blackmail disguised as heroic courage. 'I'm sorry to hear that, Mama,' she replied. 'It's odd, but you look so well.' She didn't mention that she too had spoken to Dr Sharp on the telephone that very morning, and his version of Bella's condition was somewhat different from the one she had just heard.

'Looks deceive,' said Bella weakly. 'Dr Sharp said I should be careful to avoid stress – any kind of stress.'

For her own kind of reason, this amused Ruth. But she was careful not to show it. 'Dr Sharp is absolutely right,' she agreed, turning round to comfort her mother. 'From now on, you must take everything quietly, no getting worked up about anything.'

Bella snorted. 'Not much chance of that.'

'Why's that, Mama?' asked Ruth.

Bella hesitated, stiffened, then went to collect her coat from the back room. 'I might as well go home,' she called. 'I'm getting tired.' When she returned, she was wearing her coat and headscarf. 'I'll see you later.'

Ruth went to her, and kissed her lightly on the cheek. Bella got to the door, opened it, but stopped. 'What religion is this boy?' she asked, as casually as she could manage.

Ruth tried not to smirk. 'He follows no

religion,' she replied. 'But he has a lot of faith.'

For a brief moment, Bella tried to work that one out. But she gave up, and left.

Over the next few weeks, Ruth scoured every newspaper in the shop for any information she could find about the war against the Japanese in the Far East. But try as she might, the only real news she could glean was that American forces were invading the Philippines amid fierce naval battles in the Pacific Ocean. With no word yet from Mike, her fears were that he would be subjected to the same kind of conditions in the jungle that Tom must have endured, and that could mean that it might be a very long time before she heard from him again, if ever.

Towards the end of October, however, she received a letter from her old fire-fighting mate, Mavis Miller, who told Ruth that as she had now managed to get out of the Fire Service, she had saved up enough cash to get herself a nice little place of her own in Blackstock Road, between Highbury Barn and Finsbury Park. By the tone of the letter, Ruth reckoned that Mavis was on to a lucky streak, and when in the same letter Mavis invited her to go and visit her, she grabbed the opportunity, for these days she felt quite isolated from feminine companionship.

The first week in November was turning out to be quite cold, with icy patches on the pavements in the morning and evenings, and the first signs of smog drifting down from the endless chimney pots that were pouring out thick black smoke from people's coal fires. On the evening of 5

November, 1944, and now that lighting restrictions had been partially eased, the Guy Fawkes celebrations were in full swing, and Ruth's view from the top deck of the number 29 bus that she was travelling on to Finsbury Park was of the intermittent flashing of fireworks which were lighting up the dark evening sky from practically every back yard en route. After getting off the bus at the entrance to Finsbury Park Tube station, Ruth had to walk the rest of the way to Mavis's flat, which was situated a good three hundred yards up Blackstock Road. Although it seemed to be a bit of a run-down area, it did have the advantage of being only a short walk from the Finsbury Park Empire, and the disadvantage of bordering the Arsenal Football Stadium, which had continued to be a mecca for devout fans throughout the course of the war.

Mavis's furnished bedsitter was situated above a dentist's surgery, and the first thing that hit Ruth when Mavis opened the street door was the stifling smell of ether. But her old friend's ecstatic welcome more than made up for that, and within minutes they were settled into two easy chairs in front of the coal fire in Mavis's tiny grate, smoking together, and chinwagging like mad. Ruth was amazed how good her old mate was looking and, more importantly, how tidy her room was looking, with a double bed against one wall and covered in a large pink eiderdown, a varnished gate-legged table and two chairs, and two cupboards on either side of the fireplace which contained Mavis's provisions, cooking utensils, and practically anything else she could

333

cram into them. 'I 'ave ter use the dentist's lav downstairs,' she said, 'but I use a jug an' bowl fer washin' up 'ere.'

'Mavis, you're so organised!' said Ruth, who, despite the sparseness of the room, quite envied the way Mavis had started to get her act together. 'Before you know where you are, you'll be an old married woman!'

'I bleedin' 'ope so,' replied Mavis, puffing hard on her fag. 'I told Charlie before 'e went back that if 'e don't make an 'onest woman er me when 'e comes 'ome again, 'e's goin' ter 'ave one big problem.'

Ruth's expression changed. 'Problem?' she asked, sceptically. 'You don't mean—'

Mavis roared with laughter. 'Nah!' she replied, assuredly. 'Nuffin' like that. I always make 'im wear somefin' when we're doin' it. I 'ave no intention of 'avin a bun in the oven from *anyone* 'til I've got a ring on me finger!'

Ruth's smile was forced. Mavis's remark had slightly unnerved her.

'It's all right fer men,' said Mavis. 'They 'ave themselves a good time, then leave us gels ter carry the can. In any case, if my mum an' dad ever found out wot I'd bin up to, they'd probably disown me.'

'Like Sweetie,' Ruth said wistfully.

Mavis sighed. 'Yeah,' she agreed. 'Like poor Sweetie.' She flicked the remains of her fag into the fire. 'Mind you,' she said, 'if I'd bin told I was goin' ter 'ave a muvver and farver like Sweetie's, I'd've refused ter be born! Did yer see 'em at Sweetie's funeral – all them crocodile tears? I felt like bein' sick! An' yer know wot I 'eard? I 'eard that after the funeral, they told everybody 'ow much they'd loved their daughter, an' 'ow much they was goin' ter miss 'er. Bleedin' 'ypocrites!! Yer remember 'ow they never so much as once come ter see 'er all the time we was workin' up the station. 'Ow they can live wiv theirselves after that, Gawd only knows!'

A few minutes later, both girls were sitting down to early evening 'tea', which Mavis had proudly prepared herself. Ruth found it a bit disconcerting to be eating a pair of grilled kippers on a Sunday evening, but considering that Mavis only had a small gas cooker tucked away behind a curtain on the landing outside, she had provided a very tasty meal, with boiled potatoes and thinly sliced bread and marge to go with the kippers, and tea from a gigantic teapot that her mum had given her.

'So tell me about your dentist,' asked Ruth, meticulously picking out the treacherous bones from her kipper.

''Im!' spluttered Mavis. 'Randy old sod! 'E's always popping up 'ere ter see if there's anyfin' I need. Strikes me it's not wot *I* need!'

Ruth laughed. Mavis hadn't changed one bit.

'Anyway,' Mavis dabbed her lips with her handkerchief, which she kept tucked up her dress sleeve, 'apart from that, he's quite harmless. On yer way out, I'll take yer in an' show yer his surgery. 'E likes me ter keep a spare key in case of emergencies!' She leaned across the table to Ruth, and lowered her voice. 'It's where 'e does all 'is pullin',' she joked. 'Teef that is!' Once again

335

she rocked with laughter at her joke.

Ruth laughed too, but was still busy with her kipper bones. 'So yer still 'aven't told me about *you*,' Mavis prompted, her mouth full of bread and marge. ''Ave yer 'eard from Mike at all?'

Ruth nodded. 'We spent ten days together.'

Mavis looked up with a start. 'Yer mean – yer've actually seen 'im?'

Ruth shrugged. 'Why yes,' she replied. 'The reason he was sent home from France was because they were posting him out to the Far East.'

'Oh, but that's wonderful,' said Mavis, beaming. 'Not that 'e's gone out East, but that 'e's okay. Like I told yer when we last met, the way Charlie was talkin' I 'ad a terrible feelin' Mike'd bin injured or somefin'.'

'No, thank God,' replied Ruth. 'In fact, we had ten glorious days together.'

'I bet yer did!' said Mavis lecherously.

Ruth smiled back weakly. She was embarrassed, so she quickly changed the subject. 'Mavis,' she said, putting down her knife and fork, 'd'you mind if I don't finish the kippers? I've had a bit of an upset stomach for the last couple of days.'

'Oh, Rufe,' said Mavis, concerned, putting down her own knife and fork. 'I fawt yer looked a bit pale. Yer not comin' down wiv somefin' are yer?'

'No, no,' said Ruth hurriedly. Although this was a perfect opportunity for her to talk over something that she couldn't really discuss with anyone else, she was reluctant to bring the subject up. 'I've just got a bit of a headache, that's all.'

To Mavis's intense irritation, from the neighbouring houses outside, they could hear the laughter of children as they let off fireworks around their bonfires. 'Little perishers,' she protested. 'Ain't they 'ad enuff bangs all fru the war!' But when she took a passing glance at Ruth, something didn't seem quite right. 'Is there somefin' yer want ter tell me, Rufe?' she asked, with uncharacteristic tenderness.

Ruth was surprised. 'No,' she replied. 'Why, should I?'

The other girl reached across and covered Ruth's hand with her own. 'Yer don't look yerself today. Yer look tired.'

'Don't be silly,' Ruth said brightly. 'I'm perfectly all right.' She got up from the table, collected her cigarettes from her handbag on the easy chair, and quickly lit one. When Mavis came across to join her, Ruth offered her a cigarette. Mavis took one, lit up from Ruth's and, for a few moments, they stood in silence in front of the grate, staring into the fire.

'So fings're goin' really well between you an' Mike, are they?' asked Mavis. 'Yer've changed yer mind – about waitin' fer Tom?'

'What's the use, Mavis?' said Ruth, agitated. 'I can't go on waiting for him for ever. I love Mike. I never thought it would happen like this, but it has, and there's nothing I can do about it.'

Mavis turned to look at her.

'He loves me too.'

Mavis smiled, but her expression changed to concern. 'Where does that leave yer,' she asked, 'wiv Tom's family? Do they know yet?'

'No,' replied Ruth. 'But I intend to tell them. I owe it to Tom.'

'An' wot about yer ma? Does *she* know yet?'

'Oh yes,' replied Ruth. 'She knows all right. I'm sure that at this very moment, she's trying to find a way to convince me that I'm doing the wrong thing, that I should wait until I actually see Tom's body returned home in a coffin before I get on with my life.'

Mavis put a comforting arm around Ruth's shoulders. 'We all 'ave ter do wot we 'ave ter do, mate,' she said. 'Life's a funny ol' fing. Nobody does yer any favours, when yer don't do wot they want.' She waited a moment, then asked tenderly, 'Did you an' Mike – you know?'

Ruth's immediate instinct was to take offence, to tell Mavis that she had no right to ask questions like that, that she was always making jokes about such things, and poking her nose into matters that didn't concern her. But as she looked at Mavis's lovely round face, with her shining auburn hair now longer than when she was serving as a firewoman, she realised that this was the reason why she had come here – to confide in her. She nodded mutely.

Mavis smiled, but not coarsely. 'I don't blame yer,' she said. ''E's a real smasher. I'd've done the same if it was me.'

'Mavis,' said Ruth, no longer holding back. 'I've missed my last two periods.'

'Oh blimey!' said Mavis, dismayed. 'Are yer sure?'

'As sure as I'll ever be.'

Mavis sighed. 'When did yer – I mean, when

338

did you an' Mike—'

'The night before his leave was up.'

'An' – yer didn't wear no protection?'

Ruth shook her head.

'Blimey, Rufe!' said Mavis. 'An' you're s'pposed ter be the clever one round 'ere.'

'No,' replied Ruth, flopping down into the easy chair. 'In this last couple of years, I haven't been at all clever.'

'Look, mate,' said Mavis, squatting down at Ruth's feet. 'Yer don't 'ave ter listen ter anyfin' *I* say. I mean, I'm no expert on all this kind er stuff, but the first fing I fink yer'd better do is ter go an' see a doctor.'

Ruth shook her head. 'I can't do it,' she replied.

'Why not?'

'Because my doctor is also my mother's doctor. Once *she* finds out, there's going to be all hell to pay.'

'This is *your* life we're talkin' about, not 'ers. But yer'll 'ave ter tell 'er sooner or later, so the sooner yer do, the better it'll be.'

Ruth was still shaking her head. 'I just don't know what to do, Mavis,' she sighed. 'I've been such a stupid fool, such an utter, ridiculously stupid fool. And yet I'm not sorry for what I did. At the time it seemed the right thing – the only thing to do. I wanted Mike so badly. I knew that if he went away and I hadn't taken this one opportunity, I'd never be able to forgive myself.'

Mavis looked at her as though she was mad, but then started to think hard. ''Ave yer 'ad any uvver symptoms?' she asked urgently.

'Headaches, nausea a few times – mainly in the

339

morning. There are some things I can't digest so well now...'

'If there *is* a kid on the way,' Mavis asked, talking right through her, 'd'yer want ter get rid of it?'

Ruth's reply was adamant and emphatic. 'No!'

'Right.' Mavis sprang to her feet. 'Then yer 'ave ter go to a doctor as soon as possible.' She hurried over to a small bedside cabinet and took out an address book. 'I know one,' she said, quickly looking up where he lived. 'I've bin ter 'im a coupla times meself fer a check-up. 'E don't know you, an' 'e won't care a monkey's.' She found his address in the book, then quickly scribbled it down at the top of an old women's magazine. As soon as she had done that, she tore it off, and brought it straight across to Ruth. ''Is name's Dr Benson,' she said, busily. ''E'll charge yer five bob fer a consultation, and no questions asked. But it's worf it, Rufe. As soon as yer know the position, then yer can make up yer mind where yer go from there.'

For a brief moment, Ruth stared at the scrap of paper, unsure what to do.

'Take it, Rufe!' insisted Mavis, shoving it at her. 'It's dang'rous ter take risks wiv yer body. Yer owe it ter yerself, ter Mike, *an*' ter wotever it is yer carryin' round inside.'

'Oh, Mavis!' Ruth took the scrap of paper, got up from the chair, threw her arms emotionally around the other girl's neck, and hugged her. 'You don't know what a relief it is for me to be able to talk to someone. You really are a good friend.'

'Well, don't speak too soon,' said Mavis. 'The way fings're goin', yer never know wot's just round the corner...'

As she spoke, there was the most enormous, terrifying explosion. They both screamed, and with the place shaking with the blast, glass shattering in the windows, and patches of plaster crumbling down onto them from the ceiling, the two girls dropped to the floor flat on their stomachs, and frantically tried to protect the backs of their heads with their hands.

'Christ!' yelled Mavis. 'Wot the 'ell was *that!*'

Despite the boast by the Minister of Supply, Duncan Sandys, that the V1 'doodlebug' menace was now effectively over, the risk of attack by the Germans' latest secret weapon had greatly increased since the first two V2 rockets had fallen in Chiswick in West London, and Epping in Essex. Although Islington had not yet fallen victim to one of these ruthless, silent monsters, the direct hit by a V2 on a row of terraced houses in Upper Holloway at the beginning of November 1944 caused damage not only to the immediate vicinity, but also to areas some great distance away. The fact that it came on the evening of Guy Fawkes Day was an irony that did not go unnoticed.

Ruth and Mavis were left shattered and in tears as they lay on the floor of the bedsitter, not knowing whether the whole building was about to collapse on top of them. The shop in Hornsey Road did not escape damage either, for yet again, the front windows were blown in and had to be boarded up, and the shelves were emptied of stock with the sheer vibration of the over-powering explosion, which occurred more than a mile away. And when Ruth got back home that evening, she not only found her mother a quivering mess, but also discovered the house itself with more windows shattered, and tiles off the roof. However, within minutes of the explosion, Edie Perkins and her beau, Harold Beaks, were out in the street in the dark, helping their neighbours to clear up the mess, and joining in the universal condemnation of the Nazi thugs and murderers.

It was therefore not the ideal time for Ruth to call on the doctor recommended to her by Mavis, but a few days later, she did manage to find her way up to the Edwardian terraced house in a Finsbury Park back street. It was an anxious time for Ruth. Despite her assurance to Mavis that she wanted to have the baby, there remained a nagging concern at the back of her mind that if she did go ahead and have it, it might cause an irreparable rift with her mother. The dilemma did not go away when, after only fifteen minutes' examination by the completely detached Dr Benson, it was confirmed that Ruth was indeed eight weeks pregnant.

'Forgive me Father, for I have sinned.'

'How long, child, is it since your last Confession?'

'A long time, Father.'

'And what *is* your Confession, child?'

Ruth hesitated. On her way to St Anthony's

Church, she knew only too well that it was not going to be easy for her to make her Confession to Father O'Leary, but it had to be done. 'Father, I'm to give birth to a child out of wedlock.'

After a deep sigh, there was a significant moment of silence from Father Tim on the other side of the grille in the Confessional. 'This is indeed a mortal sin in the sight of God, my child,' he replied, voice low. 'However, God is merciful, and He will forgive your sin if you repent, and pay penance.'

'I will, Father.' Now she had said it, now she had told the truth about what she had done, Ruth somehow felt that a great weight had been lifted from her shoulders.

'And what of the child's father?' asked Father Tim. 'Is he aware of your situation?'

'It's Mike, Father, and he's miles away,' replied Ruth. 'He's in great danger somewhere in the Far East. I have no idea how to contact him, or even if I'll ever see him again.'

'Then I shall pray for ye, child – even though ye have sinned.'

'Thank you, Father.'

'My child,' continued Father Tim, 'for your penance say three full Rosaries with the Sorrowful Mysteries. And pray to the Lord God to guide you through the difficult times ahead.'

'I will, Father.'

'Pray also for your mother, that she may be given the strength to bear the burden of this dark time.'

With the eerie sounds of shuffling feet on the stone floor of the church behind them, through the grille, Ruth could see the profile of the joyous man she knew, head now bowed down with grief.

'I'm so sorry, Father,' whispered Ruth.

The priest turned towards her and very quietly intoned the absolution: *'Ego te absolvo a peccatis tuis.'* And then, with the sign of the cross, *'In nomine Patris, et Filii, et Spiritus Sancti. Amen.'*

Ruth left St Anthony's and made her way in the dark down Hornsey Road. The bulb in her torch was beginning to flicker, indicating that she needed a new battery, so she turned it off, and followed the edge of the kerb by the light of a weak, watery moon. Amongst all the words Father O'Leary had used in the Confessional, none were more potent to her than: *'Pray also for your mother, that she may be given the strength to bear the burden of this dark time.'* No matter how hard she fought against her natural feelings, she could only think of the opposite, that somebody needed to give her the strength to cope with her mother when she told Bella that she was about to become a grandmother.

By the time Ruth got home, Bella had taken herself off to bed. Although it was still early in the evening, the last few days had been very trying for her, especially with the shock of the V2 rocket explosion in Upper Holloway Road, and the odd distance that seemed to be growing between her and her daughter ever since she had got back from Chesterfield. 'I've left some cold chicken for you on the kitchen table,' she said, as Ruth came into her bedroom.

'Thank you, Mama,' said Ruth, 'but I'm not

hungry.' She went across to the bed, and perched on the edge. 'Mama,' she said, 'I have to talk to you.'

'I was wondering when,' replied Bella, propped up with her pillows.

Ruth took hold of her mother's hand, and gently held it. 'You've got to understand something,' she said. 'You've got to understand that I love Mike – I mean, *truly* love him. And he loves *me*. You're going like him, Mama. He's so different. He's good at so many things. He can do carpentry, he knows all about plants, and d'you know something? His grandfather taught him how to do wonderful old-style handwriting.' She nudged up closer to her mother. 'He's a very special person, I promise you.'

'Have you promised to marry him when he comes home?' asked Bella astutely.

Ruth hesitated a moment. 'No, I haven't,' she replied.

'Why not?'

'Because he hasn't asked me,' replied Ruth. 'Remember, we only had ten short days before he went out East. Two people have to get to know each other really well before they make such an important commitment.'

'Tom was prepared to make such a commitment.'

'I knew Tom for quite a long time,' Ruth reminded her. 'I shall always be grateful that he proposed to me. But life has to move on.'

'Is that why you've stopped wearing his engagement ring?' asked Bella, determined to make Ruth's efforts more difficult.

'I sent Tom's ring back to his mother last week,' said Ruth. 'It belongs to his family now – not me.'

'So now you can move on?'

'Yes, Mama,' Ruth replied. 'I hope and pray that I can. But there's a problem.' She squeezed her mother's hand. 'I went to see Father O'Leary this evening. He gave me the strength to tell you what I need to tell you now.'

Bella pulled her hand away. 'When is it due?' she asked bluntly.

Ruth's eyes widened. Had she heard right?

'You're going to have a child, Ruth,' said Bella. 'I'm asking you when?'

Ruth stared her out for a moment. She had always known her mother to be shrewd, but this was uncanny. Almost in a state of shock, she asked, 'You – *know?*'

Bella's look was expressionless. 'I'm your mother,' she replied. 'I don't have to be told what I *already* know.'

Chapter 18

It was the best Christmas present Ruth had ever had. To receive a letter from Mike, the first since he had left London in September, was more than she had dared hope for. And on Christmas Eve! The moment she saw the photo-gram air-letter on the rug by the street door, with the address standing out in that wonderfully familiar Old

346

English script, she grabbed at it, rushed straight back up to her bedroom, perched on the edge of the bed, and read it voraciously:

Number 1, Sin City
Somewhere
Date? Don't ask awkward questions!

Hello, you,
Before I go any further I'd better tell you that as I write, I'm sharing a bed with at least five girls – well, there were five, the last time I counted them! Only kidding, Ruth! The only person I'd like to be in bed with right now is you. Mind you, you might find it a bit hot out here. Sometimes the temperature gets up to over a hundred degrees. The other day there was a terrific thunderstorm, and when it was over I saw a great big lizard drying off on a rock in the jungle. I thought I might bring him home as a pet for you. Can't wait to see him snoring on your rug in front of the fire!

The rest of the letter was mainly about the blokes he was with, and how, despite everything, they were all getting on well together. Here and there were hints of hardships but, as usual, the Army censor had had a field day deleting anything that might give a clue as to where the regiment were. By the time Ruth got to the end of the letter, however, she was left in no doubt about his feelings for her, and how he would be the luckiest bloke in the world if she decided to save herself for him until he got home. There was, however, one rather poignant footnote:

347

Of course, if I shouldn't get back, just don't forget me, because if you do I'll come back and haunt you!

I hope this gets to you by Xmas, and if it does, I hope you have a marvellous time with your mum.

I'll be thinking of you, Ruth. I just hope you'll still be thinking about me too.

Feel my kiss.

Mike xx

Ruth's eyes were welling up with tears as she put down the letter. Mike always seemed to write as he spoke, and as she read his words, she could see him standing before her, with that cheeky look and dark flashing eyes with the long eyelashes. But her thoughts now turned to only one thing. Now that she had an Army Post Office contact she could write to, how soon would she be able to get a message to Mike to let him know that he was going to be a father? Her first instinct was to rush to her dressing-table and find a pen and writing pad. But something made her hesitate. What if he *didn't* welcome the news? What if he was absolutely devastated to think that he might now be tied down for the rest of his life, and that she, Ruth, had tricked him into making love to her that night?

The thought crushed her, and her hand automatically went to her stomach. She was grateful that her twelve-week pregnancy was still slight enough for her to get through Christmas without too many searching questions. *'My goodness, we are putting on weight, Ruth.'* She could almost hear the snide remark being voiced over and over

348

again, especially from her father's tiresome cousin, Richard Whitlock, when he and his wife Nora came to the traditional Christmas Eve dinner that evening at the 'end house'. But first, she had something important to do, something that had been preying on her mind for some time.

There was no Christmas tree in the Phillipses' living room this year. All through the war years they had kept up the family tradition, but now that Tom was no longer around, there seemed no point. At least, that's how Pearl Phillips felt, for despite her initial confidence that her son was still alive, after a year of silence, it did now seem that the official line, *missing, presumed dead* meant exactly what it said.

Ruth was determined to pay her respects to the Phillips family, especially at such a sensitive time of year. That is why she had shut up shop at two o'clock, bought a potted scarlet poinsettia from a street seller in Holloway Road, and made the journey on foot up to the house in Camden Road. She was still feeling a sense of guilt over the way her rushed engagement to Tom had come to such a swift and complex end, and to compensate for this, she wanted to make it clear to the family that she did not have a callous disregard for the grief they must surely be suffering.

'Miss 'im? Yes, er course we miss 'im. The 'ouse isn't the same without our Tom. It never could be.'

Pearl's sad little dirge for her only son was

349

heartbreaking. From the moment Ruth stepped into the sitting room and saw the way Pearl put the plant next to a framed photograph of Tom on a small polished side-table, she found it difficult to cope. There was no doubt that Pearl had deteriorated a great deal since Ruth had last seen her several months before. This was particularly noticeable in the way she dressed, with no care or interest in how she looked. Even her hair needed a comb through it, and the carpet slippers she slouched around in seemed to be too big for her. It was a pathetic, distressing sight, and Ruth had no idea what could be done to ease the poor woman's suffering. Ken Phillips was no help. Most of the time he just sat in his usual armchair by the fire, puffing on his pipe, and doing a crossword puzzle in the *Daily Sketch*. It was left to Kate to make the tea, a job that she clearly hated doing, and when she finally persuaded her mother to sit down and talk to Ruth, she had to keep going back and forth to the kitchen to collect first the spoons, then the sugar, and then even the milk.

'Are you having people over for Christmas, Mrs Phillips?' asked Ruth. Almost as soon as she spoke, she realised what a futile question it was, for there was absolutely no sign anywhere of either a Christmas tree or decorations.

'Oh no,' replied Pearl. 'We always said that this year we'd keep ourselves ter ourselves. After all, when yer one short, there don't seem no point, do there? It'll be diff'rent next year though,' she said. 'When we're all back tergevver again.'

Ruth exchanged an anxious glance with both

350

Phillips and his daughter. But she had to wait until Pearl had left the room before expressing her concern. 'How long has she been like this, Kate?' she asked.

'She started to go downhill the moment that telegram arrived,' replied Kate. 'Whatever we say, whatever we do, she refuses to believe that Tom won't be coming home. The trouble is, when the war ends and that day comes, I think it'll kill her.'

Ruth didn't know what to say. She looked to Phillips, hoping he would be able to say at least something that would give some kind of hope. But he remained stolidly unresponsive. And so, in desperation, she turned to Kate. 'I hope,' she said, with difficulty, 'that I didn't cause too much distress by sending back Tom's engagement ring?'

'Why should it?' the girl replied tersely. 'Tom's dead, and you've got someone else – so what difference does it make?'

'That's enough now, Kate,' said Phillips, without looking up from his crossword.

They were practically the only words he had spoken since Ruth had arrived, but she was grateful for them.

'Well, it's true, isn't it?' replied Kate. 'Just look at her. Shows how much *she* cares whether Tom's dead or alive!'

'That's not true, Kate,' snapped Ruth. 'I was in love with your brother. I'm as upset as all of you about what's happened to him.'

'How do you know how we feel?' Kate raised her voice angrily. 'What would you do if Tom suddenly walked through that door right now?

Would you still tell him how much you *loved* him when you're obviously carrying another man's baby?'

'Kate!' growled Phillips, slamming down his newspaper. 'That's enuff now!'

Even though she knew what Kate was saying was true, Ruth was deeply wounded by the girl's outburst.

'It's true, isn't it?' insisted Kate, who was now so emotionally charged, she was prepared to say anything. 'You never intended to marry Tom. That's why you sent his ring back.'

Phillips got up from his chair. 'Kate!' he roared angrily. 'Go an' see if yer muvver's all right!'

But Kate was determined to finish what she had to say. 'What are you so afraid of, Dad?' she said defiantly. 'Tom's gone. *Somebody's* got to stand up for him.'

'I won't tell you again!' warned Phillips.

Kate hesitated, looked from her father to Ruth, turned and left the room, slamming the door behind her.

Ruth was devastated. She couldn't believe the harsh outburst she had just been subjected to. 'I'd better go,' she said, getting up from her chair.

'No,' said Phillips, coming across to her. 'Please don't go. Yer mustn't listen ter Kate. Sometimes she's a stupid little cow – she don't know wot she's sayin' 'alf the time. She's upset,' he said, attempting to appease Ruth. 'She's bin upset ever since we got that telegram. No one's ter blame. It's *'er* problem, not yours.'

Ruth was puzzled. 'Problem?' she asked. 'Why should it be a problem?'

'She feels guilty,' said Phillips. 'Not about you, but about 'erself.' He went to collect his smouldering pipe from the ashtray on the small table beside his chair. 'Just before Tom went away, she 'ad one 'ell of a bust-up wiv 'im. She told 'im 'e was a fool ter get 'imself involved wiv someone like you.'

Ruth sighed deeply. She felt crushed. 'What's the matter with her?' she asked. 'What have I done to her that's so wrong?'

Phillips finished relighting his pipe. 'She's jealous of yer, Rufe,' he replied. 'It's as simple as that.'

For Ruth, the man's remark was like a bombshell. 'Jealous?' she replied, in disbelief. 'Of *me?* But she's Tom's sister!'

'It's *becos* she's 'is sister,' replied Phillips. 'Kate's always looked up ter Tom as a kind of a hero. 'E could never really do anyfin' wrong in 'er books an' she always wanted 'im ter feel the same about 'er. So when someone comes along an' takes the attention away from 'er, well, Kate's a funny girl, just like 'er mum, too emotional. I fink the problem was always that she couldn't bear ter fink of losin' a bruvver that she'd spent all her life wiv.'

Ruth was overcome with guilt and puzzlement. With this brief and rare visit to Tom's family, all her good intentions seemed suddenly to have misfired. This was Christmas Eve, a time of goodwill and understanding. And yet, as she stood in the middle of this soulless sitting room, the very idea of Christmas seemed to be a million miles away. After a moment of deliberation, she

353

said, 'Mr Phillips, what Kate said is true. I *am* going to have a baby.'

Phillips hesitated only briefly. 'Yes, I know,' he said. 'We all know. Who is he?'

'Someone I met by accident,' Ruth replied with great difficulty. 'But I swear to God we didn't get together until after I knew about Tom. He's in the Army – out in the Far East. I have no idea if I'll ever see him again.'

'I 'ope yer do,' said Phillips. 'It wouldn't be fair if it 'appened all over again. Look.' He went to her. 'No matter wot my family fink, from now on yer must make yer own life.'

They exchanged a weak but understanding smile. 'Goodbye, Mr Phillips,' she said, shaking hands with him. 'I hope no Christmas will ever be as bad as this one for you.'

The man took her hand. 'You know somefin', Rufe?' he said. 'I'm sorry fer wot's 'appened ter Pearl's boy. But I'm also sorry that *you'll* never be part of this family.'

It was almost dark when Ruth left the Phillipses' house. Despite the fact that it was now bitterly cold, she was deeply grateful to be out in the fresh air again.

The glistening white angel on the top of Bella's Christmas tree was brought out every year at this time. It was an annual event, just like the traditional Polish Christmas Eve dinner that Bella had given at the 'end house' every year since she first married Harry Whitlock. Before the war, the lush green pine tree with lighted candles clipped to each of its branches had always been a sight to behold; the neighbours had made a special point of strolling down the cul de sac just to catch a glimpse of it through the tall windows of the Whitlocks' front room, but ever since the introduction of the blackout in 1940, only the dinner guests themselves had the privilege of marvelling at the wondrous spectacle. Despite the war, the lighted candles were still there, and so were the little boiled sweets wrapped up in paper and tied to the branches, each of them vying for pride of place with the other decorations that had been locked up in the cupboard under the stairs since the same time last year.

Bella's guests were also traditional. Her aged aunts, Katya and Glinka, were there as usual, down from their cosy nook in Chesterfield, and Harry Whitlock's favourite cousins Richard and Nora, who were never favourites with Ruth. However, this year, at Ruth's suggestion, there were two additional guests – Edie Perkins from next door and her gentleman friend, Harold Beaks. From the moment she arrived on Harold's arm, Edie was beside herself with excitement, and was so made up with trinkets from Woolworth's that she looked as though her rightful place was up there amongst the other decorations on the Christmas tree.

The main tradition of all was, of course, the meal itself, and Bella always stuck to that rigidly. She had spent all day preparing the Polish delicacies, and Ruth had great fun watching Edie's face as she tackled dishes which included a clear beetroot soup called *barczsz*, followed by cold jellied haddock cooked in breadcrumbs, powdered egg, and onions, and boiled in a muslin cloth. There were also lots of different vegetables, and an endless selection of different types of salads, followed by another soup made from dried mushrooms. The table looked beautiful, laid with a white lace tablecloth, and, as usual, one chair at the table was kept free, in respect for Bella's late husband.

'Don't they never eat turkey at Christmas in Poland?' Edie asked, pulling a face as she swallowed a lump of jellied fish.

'Only when they can afford it,' replied Bella, amused.

Whilst Ruth poured everyone glasses of vodka, provided by Katya and Glinka's black-market contacts, Harold tucked into what was his clear favourite – the dessert, a diamond-shaped pastry containing poppy seeds, honey and raisins, and also boiled in a muslin bag. Harold had always had a sweet tooth, and he drooled when Bella and Ruth described how, before the war, they always had a chocolate torte to round off the Christmas Eve meal.

It was immediately after the ritual breaking of the *oplatek*, a thin pastry inscribed with the sign of the cross, that Ruth suddenly found herself at the mercy of Richard Whitlock's feeble humour. 'My goodness!' he said predictably. 'We *are* putting on weight, aren't we, Ruth? I know someone who's been eating far too many marshmallows!'

Ruth waited for him to finish laughing at his own joke. 'Marshmallows,' she countered, 'are usually better off in the stomach than in the mind.'

To Richard's disapproval, his wife Nora sniggered. She had long had to endure his humour, and she loved it whenever he got a taste of his own medicine.

At that moment, Bella exchanged some words in Polish with her two aunts, who were sitting alongside her at the table, but Ruth immediately scolded her. 'Now Mama,' she said, 'you know it's the rule only to speak in English when we have guests.'

'Aunt Katya was saying,' explained Bella pointedly, 'that the extra weight suits you.'

'Oh,' said Ruth, flattered, replying to them in Polish. 'Thank you, Aunts.'

'It always amazes me wiv all this rationin',' said Harold, already slurring his words after two glasses of vodka, ''ow there are so many fat people around.'

Edie kicked him under the table.

Aunts Katya and Glinka immediately checked their own rather ample waistlines.

'Maybe it's not only the food that does it,' said Richard, avoiding the temptation to look at Ruth. 'For some people, that is.'

Ruth ignored his remark.

'I was so sorry to hear about your young man,' said Nora, who had a pretty, long face, but was alarmingly thin. 'Is it true that he's out in the Far East, and that you haven't heard from him?'

Ruth flicked a glance at her mother, who deliberately looked away. 'Yes,' she replied. 'The last his family heard was that he's missing, presumed dead.'

Edie kept her head down, and held Harold's

hand under the table.

'I suppose that means there's no hope?' asked Nora.

'Not necessarily,' said Richard, before Ruth had a chance to answer. 'There are quite a few stories in the newspapers these days about men at the front being given up for lost, and then they suddenly turn up after their relatives have been notified.'

'D'you think that's possible, Ruth?' Nora asked eagerly.

'His family think not,' replied Ruth. 'It's been too long.'

Nora sighed. 'What a miserable Christmas it must be for them all,' she said. 'And you too, you poor girl.'

Ruth smiled at her. 'Thank you, Aunt Nora,' she replied gratefully.

'For many people,' said Bella poignantly, 'there's no Christmas at all.' She turned a wistful look towards her elderly aunts. 'Especially in the old country.'

Katya and Glinka, whose grasp of the English language was still minuscule even after living in Chesterfield for so many years, sat in silence, aimlessly staring at their plates. Their minds were miles away, with those members of their family and friends who might have survived so far living under the tyranny of a ruthless invader, quietly praying to themselves that it would not be long now before their ordeal came to an end.

Richard Whitlock broke the lengthy silence that followed. 'I wonder what Harry would say if he were here tonight?' he said, unconsciously seeing the empty chair on the opposite side of the table, without actually looking at it.

'I think he'd be very proud of his wife *and* his daughter,' said Nora. 'I know, because he told me so – several times.'

No one was more surprised to hear that than Ruth. During the years when she was growing up, never once did her father show her anything but disapproval.

'Oh, Harry had his faults all right,' admitted Richard, 'but he was always devoted to his family, *all* his family.' He turned his attention directly to both Bella and Ruth. 'I remember the first time I heard him speaking in Polish – before you were born, Ruth. I couldn't believe it! I mean, I always knew that he had a good ear for the *sound* of foreign languages, but he seemed to pick it up so quickly – and so well!'

Bella smiled and nodded gently to herself.

'When I asked him how he managed it,' continued Richard, 'he said, "When my child's born, I want it to know that it's just as much Polish as English." Old Harry was a funny bloke at times, but he always cared for the people who mattered most to him in his life. Trouble is, half the time he didn't know how to say it.'

Ruth found herself looking up at her father's ashes in the casket on the mantelpiece.

'Well,' said Edie, who was herself now beginning to feel the effect of the vodka, 'let's 'ope this is the last Christmas we shall all have ter go round in the blackout.'

'Hear, hear!' agreed Nora.

'And let's 'ope,' she continued, pointedly ad-

359

dressing herself directly to Ruth at her side, 'that when the boys come 'ome again, they'll be able ter pick up where they left off, that they'll find everyfin' the same as when they left.'

Ruth, one hand discreetly on her stomach, returned Edie's affectionate look.

Richard stood up, and held his glass out towards the empty chair. 'To absent friends,' he said, offering a toast.

Edie had to help Harold to get up as everyone echoed Richard's words: 'To absent friends!'

Before they had a chance to sit down again, Glinka, who at eighty-four years of age was the younger of the two sisters by just eighteen months, broke into an old Polish folk song. In a clear, unfaltering soprano voice, she sang in Polish of 'the better days to come, the land of bright skies and blue rivers', and of 'the golden time when loved ones will meet again'. It was the most beautiful sound Edie had ever heard, so much so that when they all put down their glasses and linked hands in a traditional show of unity, tears slowly trickled down her face.

For the rest of the evening, everyone remained at the table enthusiastically chatting and exchanging memories and anecdotes with one another, until just before eleven o'clock, when it was time to leave for midnight Mass.

St Anthony's Church looked most beautiful. The whole place was lit with candles everywhere, the flickering flames reflected not only high up onto the church eaves, but also onto the eyes of the Virgin Mother's plaster statue, which seemed to spring to life with joy and follow the movements of every person who approached with an offering. And when Bella's party arrived, Edie, although not a Catholic herself, was particularly impressed by a magnificent tableau of the night before Christmas, made by children from the nearby Catholic school.

The pews, as usual for this annual celebration of the Eucharist, were filled to capacity, the women's heads covered with scarves, their menfolk at their sides, and children struggling to contain their excitement at the chance of being allowed to stay up so late, and also at the prospect of what Christmas presents they might be getting later that morning. Bella and Ruth sat in one pew near the rear of the church. On either side of them were Richard and Nora, also non-Catholics, Katya and Glinka, and Edie and Harold. They were an odd combination, but united by the beauty of such a memorable occasion. Most of all, of course, it was the music of the Mass itself that made this such a joyous event, with the choir of mainly female voices, joined, by the deep, rich baritone of one of the regular male singers and, in the absence of a church organ, accompanied by one of the talented elderly parishioners on an old upright piano. The *Kyrie*, the *Gloria* and the *Sanctus* had never sounded more beautiful. And when, near the end of the Mass, some of the congregation approached the altar to receive Holy Communion from Father O'Leary, Edie held Harold's hand. For her, who usually only ever went inside a church for weddings and funerals, this Christmas Eve had turned out to be one of the most memorable of her life.

Back at the 'end house', Ruth lay in bed, thinking about all that had taken place on that extraordinary Christmas Eve. It was now the early hours of the morning, and outside, Christmas Day was still shrouded in dark. There really was a lot for her to dwell upon, especially that sad encounter with the Phillips family up in Camden Road, and the antipathy shown her by Tom's sister, Kate. She kept asking herself if it really was possible for someone as young as Kate to be so obsessed with her brother, as Phillips had suggested? Was it really possible that Kate could be obsessed to such an extent that she was actually jealous of anyone with whom her brother might fall in love? It was a strange and puzzling situation. And then she thought about her mother's Christmas Eve dinner downstairs, the food, Edie and Harold giggling together on two glasses of vodka each, and dear Aunts Katya and Glinka, and that lovely song, so full of hope and joy.

And what of her father's cousin, Richard, and his nasty little allusions to how much weight she had put on? Did he suspect? she asked herself. Did he know about Mike, and that she would soon be a mother? Of course he did, she decided. Whatever else Richard was, he was no fool. She had no time for him, no time for him at all. He was a troublemaker, always trying to suggest that he had done so much for his late cousin, when he hadn't, in fact, ever done anything at all. Nonetheless, he had made her think again about her father. Was it really true that Harry Whitlock had loved them both, her mother *and* herself? Was the man Richard had described *really* her father, he who had spent his life disapproving of every single thing she ever did? *'He always cared for the people who mattered most to him in his life. Trouble is, he didn't know how to say it.'* Richard's words echoed around her mind. They made her question her entire relationship with her father. Had she underestimated what he thought of her, she wondered, or was she just as much to blame as him, closing her mind to him because he expected her to live by the same principles as himself?

It was becoming perfectly obvious that sleep would elude her for some time, so she got out of bed, went to the window, and raised the blackout blind. Christmas Day was there all right; she could see it out there in the dark, in the constantly restless moonlight, which popped in and out of the clouds, briefly flooding her room with a silvery glow, only to plunge the world into night again a moment later. From time to time, she could see her own reflection in the glass panes of the window. But the more she stared, the more she could see two more images standing behind her. Mike and Tom were there, both of them beckoning to her, forming a perfect triangle between the three of them. But only two images could remain, and as the moon dipped in and out of the clouds yet again, one image gradually withdrew into the cold dark night, leaving only Ruth and Mike standing there, reflected in the mirror of a great big world on the brink of an uncertain future...

363

Chapter 19

Theresa Marika Daisy Buller was born in the 'end house' at just after three o'clock in the afternoon on Wednesday, 20 June 1945, almost exactly six weeks after the end of the war in Europe. Theresa was a couple of days late, but when she finally arrived, she duly let the world know that she was a force to be reckoned with! The middle-aged midwife, who had the misfortune of possessing only two front teeth, said that Theresa was clearly going to be an obstinate child because she never stopped kicking her feet when she tried to bath her. How the dear lady came to that conclusion was anyone's guess, but she was efficient enough, and even stayed around for several hours after the birth, just to make quite sure that both Ruth and her mother knew how to cope with a newly born child.

After weeks of anxiety about how her mother would take to the actual birth, Ruth was astonished to see how thrilled Bella was when the baby finally arrived. The first time she held the child, tears of joy streamed down her face, and she kissed the poor little thing all over its face and head so many times, it was a wonder it was able to come up for breath. And it was clear right from the word go that, despite the fact that Theresa did have an English father, Bella was determined that her grandchild should get used to the sound of the Polish language as soon as possible. Therefore, morning, noon, and night Ruth could hear cries of *'Piekna! Piekna!'* from her mother as she drummed it into the child that she was the most 'beautiful' baby in the whole wide world.

The naming of Ruth and Mike's daughter was a joint effort. Although he did not as yet know about the birth, in January, Mike had received a letter from Ruth to tell him that she was pregnant, and that the birth was expected somewhere around the second week in June. As soon as he read the letter, Mike was over the moon, and he immediately asked his sergeant if someone could get a message back to Ruth to tell her so. Since then, Ruth had received several letters pestering her with questions to be answered after the baby's birth: who did the baby look like, what was the colour of his or her eyes, and did he or she suck their finger the same way Mike did when he was the baby's age? The choice of name he left to Ruth, but his only request was that, if the baby was a girl, one of the names should be Daisy, after his late grandma, who had been so good to him. Ruth readily agreed, and chose Theresa after her favourite saint, and Marika, which was her mother's middle name.

The greatest joy of all for Ruth was to know that Mike was thrilled at the prospect of becoming a father; in his letters, he wrote about the great times all three of them would have together after he came back home and he and Ruth were married. The only concern for Ruth now, and it was a very real one, was that it had been quite some time since she had last heard from Mike.

During the second week in July, and with her mother and Freda Dapper now looking after the shop again, Ruth decided to take young Theresa along to Hackney, to introduce her to her great-grandad.

Cyril wept when he saw her. 'She's Daisy all over again,' he said. 'Livin' image! Got her mum's pretty chin though – oh yes!' But within minutes of holding the baby in his arms, he found that he had a wet lap. 'Just like yer dad at 'is age, ain't yer?' he informed little Theresa. 'Only got ter look at poor ol' Cyril an' yer turn on the waterworks!'

Ruth laughed. She loved to see the two of them together. It somehow felt as though Mike was much closer. 'Have you heard from him, Uncle Cyril?' she asked hopefully.

The old man's expression stiffened. 'Not since April,' he replied, with a worried sigh.

'D'you think there's any significance?' she asked, watching his reaction carefully.

'Nah,' said Cyril, handing the baby back to her. 'Yer know wot the Army's like. It's probably their bleedin' Post Office again. Always gettin' 'eld up wiv red tape or somefin'.' When he caught Ruth's eye, he realised that she didn't believe a word he had said. 'Ter be 'onest, Rufe,' he said, 'I just don't know. I phoned the Army's so-called information line the uvver day. They told me ter get on ter the War Office. Nobody knows nuffin' – or don't want ter know. Typical of this bleedin' country!'

Ruth cradled Theresa in her arms. 'I suppose the only comfort we have is that if anything *had*

366

happened to him, they'd have let us know.'

Cyril shook his head. 'Nuffin's 'appened ter 'im, Rufe,' he assured her. 'Yer can take my word fer that. Mike knows 'ow ter take care of 'imself.'

Then Cyril went off to make the tea, leaving Ruth to change the baby's nappy. She found it difficult to concentrate, for the old man's reaction had left her uneasy. Despite his attempts to reassure her, he had only reinforced what she herself had been dreading for the past couple of months, that something *had* happened to Mike, and that it was only a question of time before they heard about it. As she looked down at little Theresa, lying flat on her back on her lap, waving her arms and kicking her legs in the air to make it as difficult as she could to have her nappy changed, Ruth could feel that old sense of foreboding that had bedevilled her and the Phillips family during those long months of silence from Tom.

'Did Mike tell yer I'm givin' up the business?' said Cyril, as he came back into the room with the teapot.

'You spoke of it when I was here before, but I wasn't sure if you were serious. Mike said you wanted to give it up one day, but I didn't think it would be so soon.'

'War's over now,' he said, at the table pouring two cups of tea. 'I've seen all the stiffs I want ter see – not that I ever wanted ter actually *see* 'em!' he joked. 'Comes a time when yer want ter get on an' do all the fings yer've never 'ad time ter do in yer life, like goin' round the boozer ter 'ave a pint or two, or play a game er darts wiv some of me

367

mates. An' I've bin promisin' Daisy's cousin Lil fer years that I'd pop over an' see 'er in Peckham. I mean, Peckham's not a million miles away, is it? It's only on the uvver side er the river.'

Ruth finished pinning up Theresa's nappy, then cradled her upright in one arm. No, she thought to herself, Peckham wasn't a million miles away, and Cyril had earned the right to do whatever he wanted in his old age. God knows he had worked hard enough for it all his life. 'What will you do with the business?' she asked.

Cyril put a cup of tea in front of her on the other side of the table. 'Sell it, I s'ppose,' he replied. 'I might let Jimbo 'ave it. 'E an' Mike used ter work tergevver down the workshop. 'E loves the work. 'Im an' 'is two boys'll probably make a better go of it than *I* ever have.'

'I doubt that,' said Ruth.

'Anyway,' said Cyril, 'Mike wants ter move on, an' I don't blame 'im. Yer can't make yer fortune knockin' up boxes fer stiffs all yer life, nah, that's a mug's game. 'E's got brains, that boy. 'E'll put 'em ter good use all right, 'speshully now 'e's got you an' little Miss Muppet 'ere ter look after. Mind you,' he took a sip of his tea, 'it ain't goin' ter be easy. When the boys come back 'ome, there's goin' ter be a lot er trouble.'

'How d'you mean?' asked Ruth.

'Most of 'em're goin' ter expect ter get their ol' jobs back. An' when they find that somebody else's got 'em, there're goin' ter be a few fireworks, I tell yer, 'speshully fer the blokes comin' back when the war out East's over. It's bin bad enuff demobbin' this lot from VE Day.'

Ruth took his point, and was concerned. 'D'you really think things are going to be that bad, Uncle Cyril?' she asked.

'Sure as God made little apples,' he replied. 'An' I dread ter fink wot's goin' ter 'appen when the blokes find their 'ome lives've bin turned upside down. Bleedin' murder, if yer ask me!'

Again Ruth took his point. Ever since the end of hostilities in Europe, there had been worrying reports in the newspapers about the number of men returning home from the front to find that their wives or girlfriends had either gone off with other men, or had found their menfolk so changed that they couldn't bear to live with them any more. Consequently, domestic violence, and even murder, had been on the increase. Theresa was beginning to grizzle, so Ruth got up from the table and tried to soothe her by gently rocking her to and fro.

'What will you do with this place, Uncle Cyril?' she asked. 'Will you stay here or find somewhere else to live?'

'Gawd knows,' he replied. 'I'll face up ter that when Mike gets 'ome, an' you two decide wot yer goin' ter do.'

'You wouldn't like to live out in the country somewhere?'

Cyril nearly had a fit. 'The country!' he gasped. 'Blimey, wot would I do in the country? Scare the life out er me livin' wiv fields all round me, no people ter talk to. No, I'm London born an' bred. 'Ackney's my patch, an' this is where I stay. But I'm tellin' yer, the war may be over, but mark my words, we're in fer a bumpy ride ahead!'

Old Cyril's words were turning out to be more prophetic than anyone might have imagined, for as soon as the euphoria of VE Day had died down, it quickly became evident that the hardships of war were being replaced by the hardships of peace. Instead of an immediate end to rationing, there were more shortages than ever, especially with food. Queues seemed longer for even the most basic items such as vegetables and cooking fat. Ruth was breastfeeding little Theresa, but whenever she tried to buy their own meagre ration of two pints of fresh milk each for herself and her mother, which was supposed to be sufficient to last a whole week, she had to get up early in the morning to be first in the queue at the local dairy. Fortunately, neither she nor her mother took sugar in their tea, so they usually swapped their weekly ration for cheese with Edie next door, who was then able to satisfy Harold's sweet tooth, especially now that he had virtually moved in with her.

Matters were made no easier by the calling of a General Election on 26 July 1945. For the first time in years, everyone was talking politics again, and this meant hot tempers and angry opinions flaring up amongst the customers in the shop, in the queues, and on the wireless. Ruth was amazed how people seemed to know how to put the country to rights, even if they had no concrete ideas about how to increase or abolish the rationing system, or find new homes for people who had been bombed out during the war. In some ways, it had been an ugly campaign, with crowds cheering or jeering the wartime Prime Minister, Winston Churchill, wherever he went. Whether they were grateful to him or not for his morale-boosting role in helping the British people to survive the war, he was defeated at the ballot box, and the Labour Party was swept into power, with Clement Attlee forming the first post-war government. When she heard Churchill's resignation speech on the wireless that evening, Ruth couldn't help reflecting back to those extraordinary moments only a few weeks before, when the ecstatic crowds outside number 10 Downing Street on the evening of VE Day had repeatedly yelled out for their hero, *'We want Winnie! We want Winnie!'*

Ever since Theresa's birth, Ruth had agonised over whether it would be a wise decision to take the baby to see the Phillips family. Her previous visit there had been so traumatic that she was reluctant to open up old wounds, if there were any. But the more she thought about it, the more she came to the conclusion that it might just be too much for poor Pearl Phillips to take. The decision was made easier for her when, at the beginning of August, she received a rather upbeat letter from Kate:

127A Camden Road
N7
3/8/45

Dear Ruth,
I thought I would write to tell you that Mum and Dad have arranged a special service for Tom at their

371

church on Sunday evening. It was the vicar's idea, and now that we know we shan't be seeing Tom any more, we thought it would be the next best thing to having a funeral. But it's not going to be all sobs and tears. Mum's promised to behave herself, and we've told her that it's just a way of saying goodbye to him.

If you feel like coming, we'd all love you to be there – you and your baby, if you'd like to bring her. It's at 6 o'clock at St Barnados in Hillmarton Road just off Caledonian Road. Do you know it? Anyway, if you can come, just turn up. Some of our relatives will probably be there, but don't let that put you off!

Ruth, please forgive me for the way I treated you when we last met. I had no right to talk to you like that. I know you loved Tom, and it's no fault of yours what's happened to him.

Please come!
Love, Kate

St Barnados Church was barely half-full, and most of the congregation who were there were asked to fill the pews towards the front. Ruth arrived just as the service was starting, so, with Theresa in her arms, she tried to make as inconspicuous an entrance as possible, sneaking around the back to the far aisle, and sitting alone in a row of empty pews halfway down. She hadn't been in an Anglican church for a long time, and she was pleasantly surprised. In many ways it was just as beautiful as St Anthony's, except that the ceiling seemed to be more arched, and the stone slab walls a duller grey. But the thing she loved most were the vases of flowers, which seemed to be in profusion all over the place, and complementing them delightfully was a long red carpet which ran right down the centre aisle from the entrance, and up towards the altar.

As soon as she sat down, it was time to get up again, for the vicar had announced the number of the first hymn, 'All Things Bright and Beautiful.' It was during this that heads in the front pew turned around to take a look at her, and her baby, including Kate, who smiled and waved. Ruth knew none of the people there, but wondered how many of them knew who she was, and if they did, how they would react when they saw her there with another man's baby. One couple in particular, a middle-aged man and woman, craned their necks to glare at her, but when they saw that she had noticed them, they quickly looked back at their hymn books.

After several prayers, a reading from the Bible by Ken Phillips, and two more hymns, which Ruth later heard were particular favourites of Tom's, the vicar discreetly climbed the steps up to the pulpit to give the address. He was a middle-aged man, with very little or no hair, but Ruth thought he had a lovely face, which, from where she was sitting, seemed to be permanently flushed. Once he had talked about Tom's life, his strong commitment to his family, and the sacrifice he had made for his country, he touched on the general mood in the country, and the difficult times that lay ahead.

'Sadly,' he said, 'Tom is no longer with us. But when the others who have survived this terrible war *do* come home, what will they find waiting for them? They'll find a land torn apart by grief and despair, and loved ones who have prayed each night that they would return unharmed. And when they meet again after, in some cases, years of parting, will they still recognise those they left behind? Will they hold them in their arms and thank God for keeping them safe while they were gone? Or will they see no more than perfect strangers, who only existed once in their imagination?'

Ruth listened to this with intense interest. *Perfect strangers*. Is that really what the men will find when they get home? she asked herself. Is that what Mike will find? Is that what *I* will find when I lay eyes on him again after so long?

The vicar wound up the service by asking the congregation to pray for Tom's soul, and for his family, relations, and friends who were going to have to continue on their long journey of life without him.

Once the service had come to an end, Ruth was joined by Kate and her mother. 'Oh,' gushed Pearl, the moment she set eyes on little Theresa, 'yer little darlin'!' Ruth willingly passed the baby to her, and felt the anguish as tears welled up in the poor woman's eyes. 'She's so like *you*, Ruth,' said Pearl, adding poignantly to the baby, 'an' I bet yer look like yer dad too!' Theresa, who had been so good all during the service, was now getting irritable, so Pearl quickly handed her back to her mother. 'Wasn't it a lovely service,' she said. 'I felt as though Tom was right there wiv us, agreein' wiv every word the vicar said.'

'I'm sure he was,' agreed Ruth. 'He would have been very proud of what you've done for him today.'

Pearl beamed, and leant forward to peck Ruth on the cheek. 'I want yer ter know,' she said, softly, 'that I'd've bin a very proud woman to 'ave 'ad you fer me daughter-in-law. I only 'ope whoever yer settle down wiv knows that yer worf yer weight in gold!'

Just then, Pearl was whisked away by the vicar, who wanted her to talk to some of her relatives.

'It's not been an easy day for her,' said Kate, as she watched her mother go. 'She got a parcel from Tom's regiment yesterday. They sent back some of his personal belongings that he left behind at his base camp. The only definite thing we've been able to find out is that he went missing whilst he was out on a mission in some jungle in Malaya. Apparently, he was the only one of his unit that didn't get back.'

Ruth felt quite distraught. 'Didn't anyone go back to try to find him?' she asked.

Kate shook her head. 'Officers don't allow their men to do that sort of thing,' she replied. 'Not in places like that.'

Ken Phillips came across with the middle-aged couple who had glared at Ruth during the service. 'Rufe,' he said heartily, 'this is my sister, Mary, an' 'er 'usband, Phil.'

'How d'you do?' Ruth said with a forced smile, holding out her spare hand to the woman.

The woman shook hands, and with an equally forced smile asked, 'Nice baby. What's 'er name?'

'Theresa,' replied Ruth.

'Who's the farver?' asked the woman's husband.

Ruth was taken aback to be asked such a

question by someone she didn't even know. 'Her father's name is Mike, Mike Buller. He's in the Army – in the Far East.'

'When's 'e comin' 'ome?' asked the woman.

Ruth was irritated to be asked so many questions. 'Who knows when *any* of our boys will be getting home?' she replied, with a fixed but polite smile.

'Well, we all know one of 'em who *won't* be, don't we?'

To Ruth, the man's remark was some kind of accusation, and she didn't like it at all. But before she had a chance to reply, Kate quickly intervened. 'Tom used to stay with Auntie Mary and Uncle Phil,' she said. 'He always said they were like his second mum and dad.'

''E used ter confide in us,' said the woman, who was stolidly refusing to make eye-contact with Ruth. ''E told us all about you an' 'im plannin' ter get married.'

'It was quite a surprise when we 'eard yer'd found someone else,' said the man.

'It was quite a shock to me,' countered Ruth, 'when I was told Tom was dead.'

The man and woman swung each other a look. 'Dead?' asked the man, surprised. He turned to Ken Phillips. 'Did they actually confirm that Tom was dead?'

'Missin', presumed dead,' said the woman, before Ken could answer her husband's question. 'The Army always says that ter cover themselves.'

'Tom's dead, Auntie,' insisted Kate. 'If he was still alive, he'd have been home long before now.'

'Don't you be so sure, young lady,' said the

376

man, correcting her. 'Nuffin's proved 'til there's concrete evidence.'

'What more evidence d'yer need, Phil,' asked Phillips, joining in the exchange for the first time. 'If the Army fink 'e's dead, then that's that.'

'*Fink!*' said the man. 'That's the key word, Ken – *fink*. Everyone draws conclusions, then go about their lives as though nuffin's 'appened.'

Ruth now found it difficult to contain her irritation with these people. 'I'm not sure what you mean, Mr —,' she said. 'I don't see what else we can do with our lives when we're told the facts.'

'There are no facts, young lady,' insisted the man. 'Assumption. Nuffin' more than assumption.'

'Who knows?' said the woman, clearly getting out of her system everything that she had been bottling up for some time. 'If we didn't all rush inter fings, fings might be diff'rent.' Then with a passing look at Theresa, who was now fast asleep in Ruth's arms, she added, 'Still, it's just as well dear Tom ain't 'ere. The shock might've killed 'im off anyway.'

Having said their piece, Auntie Mary and Uncle Phil moved quickly off, and joined the queue of people who were slowly shuffling out of the church.

'Yer mustn't pay no attention ter them, Rufe,' said Phillips. 'Their trouble is that they was far too close ter Tom. They can't bring themselves ter believe that 'e really 'as gone.' He put a comforting arm around Ruth's shoulders. 'Don't worry,' he said, 'yer've done the right fing. You just carry on wiv yer life the way yer want.'

It was a beautiful summer evening when Ruth left the church and made her way back home pushing Theresa's pram down Caledonian Road. With the blackout restrictions now lifted, in a few hours' time the streets would no longer fall prey to the dark of night. Like everyone else, Ruth found it such a relief to know that the clouds of war had finally passed. But after having to endure the ignorance of people like Auntie Mary and Uncle Phil, it came as no comfort to her to know that in both war *and* peace, there would always be narrow-minded types like them around, people who assumed the worst, without ever knowing the best.

When Ruth got home from Tom's church service, she found Edie Perkins and Harold Beaks having a glass of rhubarb wine with her mother. Although she was delighted to see them, she couldn't make out why they all seemed to be in such high spirits.

'Edie and Harold are getting married!' gushed Bella. 'Isn't it wonderful?'

Ruth looked at the happy couple, sitting coyly side by side on the sofa in the living room. 'Oh, Edie,' she said, going to her, and giving her a big hug and a peck on the cheek. 'I'm so happy for you! And you, too, Harold! I must say, it's about time too!'

Edie giggled like a small schoolgirl, and Harold's face crumpled up shyly. ''E popped the question ter me while I was makin' me Yorkshire puddin',' she said. 'I was so shocked, I nearly didn't put in me dried egg!'

Their laughter woke up Theresa, who was still in her pram in the hall outside. Bella rushed out to attend to her, and returned a moment later with the baby in her arms. *'Piekna, Theresa! Piekna!'* If calling the child 'beautiful' over and over again was her way of getting her to sleep, she clearly had to think again.

Ruth was quite prepared to let her mother take over. After her encounter with the Phillipses' relatives, it had been a long evening. 'So, Edie,' she said, flopping down onto an armchair near her, 'when's the big day, and where? Are you going to be in white?'

'Oh, my goodness no!' exclaimed Edie, quite flushed. 'We're gettin' married up the Registry Office. It's only fair to our uvver 'alfs.'

'We fawt it might be a bit insensitive ter do wot we've boaf done before,' explained Harold, reverentially. 'Seein' as 'ow Edie's a widow, an' I'm a widower. An' in any case, Edie ain't exactly a young woman any more.'

Edie was outraged. 'An' you're not exactly a young man eivver, 'Arold Beaks!' she countered in a flash.

Harold immediately put his arm around Edie's shoulders, and gave her a quick apologetic hug.

'Anyway,' said Edie, 'we've decided ter do it on my birfday – September the first.'

'How romantic,' said Ruth.

'It was 'Arold's idea,' said Edie, glowing with excitement as she briefly stole a glance into his eyes. ''E's a very romantic person. Ain't yer, dear?' Harold lowered his gaze shyly. 'What about this

379

then?' said Edie, suddenly flashing her engagement ring to Ruth. ''Arold bought it in Woolworf's,' she boasted proudly. 'I chose it meself.' Even as she spoke, she couldn't help reflecting inside on that wedding ring she had gawped at so many times in the window at Samuels', the jewellers in Holloway Road. 'Wot d'yer fink then?' she asked.

Ruth took a close, admiring look at the ring. 'It's absolutely lovely,' she said. 'I can tell you two are going to be very happy.'

'We *are* happy,' said Edie, turning again to Harold. 'Ain't we, dear?'

'Ra-*ther*,' replied Harold, who hadn't stopped beaming since Ruth had entered the room.

They all waited whilst a train rumbled across the bridge above the house. As soon as it had passed, Bella said, 'Edie and Harold have asked if we know some place where they could hold the reception. I told them they can have it here.'

Ruth did a double-take. Knowing how much her mother treasured her privacy, she couldn't believe she had made such a generous offer. 'Here?' she asked. 'In this house?'

'Why not?' replied her mother. 'Edie has always been such a wonderful friend and neighbour to us. It'll be fun.'

Ruth was astounded.

Edie fidgeted uncomfortably. 'It's just that I don't 'ave much room left in my place these days,' she said, 'not now I've let the two top rooms ter them nurses from the Royal Northern. I must say it's very kind er yer boaf. It'd certainly 'elp us out of a pickle, wouldn't it, 'Arold?'

Her fiancé nodded.

'An' we won't be much fuss, I promise,' continued Edie. 'I mean, there won't be more than a dozen or so people comin', an' I fawt if I can lay me 'ands on some extra coupons, I could give 'em all some 'am an' salads or somefin'.'

'We'll be very proud to have you here, Edie,' Ruth assured her. 'And to do anything we can to help.'

'You're a coupla gems – boaf of yer!' said Edie. 'Ain't they, 'Arold?'

Again he nodded.

'The only fing is,' said Edie, a little tentatively, 'I was wonderin' whevver I could call on yer ter 'elp me wiv somefin' else?'

Ruth flicked a quick look at her mother. What were they letting themselves in for now? she wondered.

'It's Rita,' said Edie. 'Yer see, as yer know, I 'aven't really bin on talkin' terms wiv 'er fer quite a time now. She was just gettin' too much fer me, puttin' me down, an' bossin' me around. But when I got ter finkin', well, the fact is, she an' me've known each uvver a long time now. She used ter be about the only person I 'ad ter talk to.' She sighed. 'The trouble is, despite the way Rita's treated me these last few years, I don't fink I could bring meself ter get married wivout askin' 'er ter the weddin'.'

Chapter 20

On Monday, 6 August, the day after Bella and Ruth had agreed to let Edie and Harold use the 'end house' for their wedding reception, the American Air Force dropped an atom bomb on the Japanese city of Hiroshima. The effect was devastating, not only for Japan, but for the entire world; for the people of Islington, it meant that the war in the Far East was virtually at an end.

As soon as she had heard the news on the wireless, Edie rushed out into the street, desperate to speak to anyone who knew what was going on. 'An *atom* bomb? What's an *atom?* What's so special about it? What does it mean?' These were the questions that everyone was asking, unaware that the splitting of the atom had led to the production of the most powerful bomb in history, a single bomb that had just wiped out an entire city, together with nearly all of its civilian population. It was a bomb that could and would end the war at a stroke. It was a bomb that would change the course of any future war. But to Ruth, the implication had an even greater significance. It meant that all those boys fighting the Japanese out there in the Far East would soon be home. And that would surely have to include Mike. All she hoped now was that they would get him home as soon as possible, so that he and Ruth could be reunited, and so that he could see his baby daughter before she grew any older. And she hoped that it might even be possible for him to be there when Edie and Harold held their wedding reception at the 'end house'.

'So wot's all this about a weddin'?'

It wasn't very often that Rita Simmons paid a visit to Whitlock's, but when she did, she made quite sure that her presence was felt.

'I got an invitation ter Edie Perkins's weddin',' she growled. 'Wot's she fink she's up ter at 'er age?'

'Yes, isn't it wonderful?' replied Bella, who was there with Ruth, Theresa in the pram, and Freda Dapper. 'To think that she has found love all over again after so many years.'

'Who's she kiddin'?' said Rita, with her usual lack of compassion. 'She's got 'erself mixed up wiv some randy ol' sod who's just lookin' fer a slap an' tickle, an' yer call that love?'

'Harold Beaks is a very nice man, Rita,' called Ruth, who had just finished breastfeeding Theresa at the back of the news rack behind the counter. 'I think they're going to be good for each other.'

'Are they now?' said Rita bitterly. Her large frame had great difficulty in manoeuvring between the various shop displays. 'Well, if she's goin' ter do it,' she said, approaching the counter clutching Edie's invitation card, 'she should just do it, wivout all this showin' off.' She strained to read the wording on the card, but without her glasses, she had to hold it out about half an inch from her nose. *'Reception at the End House, Annette Road, by courtesy of Mrs B. Whitlock.'* She lowered the card, and looked up at Bella. 'Fancy now,' she said, with her customary sneer. 'Edie's got it made fer 'er, ain't she? Yer'd never get me 'avin' me weddin' reception in someone else's 'ouse.'

'Then I take it you won't be joining us?' asked Bella dismissively, returning to her book-keeping.

'I din't say that, did I?' returned Rita, quick as a flash. 'If she wants me there so bad, I s'ppose I'd better come.'

'I'm sure Edie would quite understand if you couldn't make it, Rita,' Ruth said mischievously. She came out from behind the counter and returned Theresa to her pram. 'I mean, I'm sure she understands what a busy woman you are.'

Freda tried her best not to giggle.

Rita knew they were making fun of her. All her instincts told her to fight back, to show them that none of them were any match for her. But these days, she found it difficult to muster any of her former fighting spirit. The energy had gone, so had the will. In the old days, she could have given as good as she got; if anyone had so much as said one word out of place to her, she'd have had their guts for garters. But nowadays, she only had to walk into a shop to find out what people *really* thought of her. Not that she cared a brass monkey's, of course. But the only trouble was, she was getting older, and the jibes were beginning to hurt.

'So may I tell Edie that you and your husband have accepted her invitation?'

After drifting away in her mind for a second or two, Rita was brought back into focus by the sound of Bella's voice. 'Wot?' she said, floundering. 'Wot d'yer – oh no. Not Ted. 'E can't come. 'E'll be on nights. 'E 'as ter do a lot er nights at work these days.'

Ruth exchanged a puzzled glance with Freda.

'Maybe one of your children could come with you?' asked Bella. 'Edie says she knows them all.'

'No!' snapped Rita, soon back to her old self. 'I don't need no one ter 'old *me* up! If Ted can be out on 'is own night after night – so can I!' She turned, and lumbered back towards the door. 'Oh, by the way,' she called out. 'Yer can tell Edie that if she's expectin' a weddin' present then she'd better let me know wot she wants. That is, *if* she can spare enuff time ter break away from 'er fancy man!' She turned, but the moment she had left the shop and closed the door behind her, she suddenly peered back in again. 'Tell 'er, wotever she chooses,' she bellowed, 'it'd better not cost more than five bob!'

The war against Japan was now officially over, and Wednesday and Thursday of the following week were declared a public holiday. This meant that once again street-parties were hurriedly organised, with everyone chipping in to help: the men setting up trestle tables from the local church hall along the middle of the road, hanging bunting and flags out from the windows of houses on either side of the road, and collecting chairs from as many households as could spare them, and the women getting together to make sausage rolls, Spam sandwiches, potato fingers, chocolate oatcakes made with cocoa, different

385

flavoured jellies, and blancmange made with dried milk. Bella, together with the owner of a toy shop in Holloway Road, provided nearly two hundred balloons, and in just three or four days, kids from all over the neighbourhood had made hundreds of paper hats and decorations to give each street the feeling that a great victory celebration was about to begin.

On the evening before the first day of the public holiday, Mavis Miller turned up at the shop looking for Ruth. Bella told her that Ruth was at home, and when Mavis got there, she found her in the middle of bathing Theresa in an enamel bowl in the kitchen. Ruth was delighted to see her old friend again, but she was not so pleased when she heard the news Mavis had brought. 'He's alive, Ruth.'

Puzzled and confused, Ruth asked, 'Who, Mavis?'

Mavis was grave-faced. 'Tom,' she replied. 'Tom Phillips.'

Ruth was completely taken aback. 'How d'you know?' she asked, falteringly.

'Charlie,' replied Mavis.

For some reason this irritated Ruth. 'Oh, for God's sake!' she snapped. 'How is it that Charlie seems to know the whereabouts of every single soldier in the British Army?'

'He saw the lists,' Mavis answered frankly, trying not to show how hurt she was by Ruth's attitude.

'Lists?'

Mavis found it both painful and difficult to answer. 'The lists of deserters.'

The more Ruth heard, the more she found it all difficult to understand. 'Mavis,' she asked, as rationally as she possibly could. 'Are you telling me that Tom – is a deserter?'

'Charlie says Tom was in some regiment attached to the Fourteenth Army in Burma.'

'Burma!' exploded Ruth, finding it impossible to take in what Mavis was telling her. 'The Army told the Phillips family that he'd gone missing somewhere in Malaya.'

Mavis shook her head. 'All I can tell yer is wot Charlie told me 'e saw. Tom's name *was* on that list, Rufe.'

Ruth couldn't think straight. She wrapped Theresa in the towel, picked her up, and gently rocked her in her arms.

'I know Charlie's only in the Medical Corps,' said Mavis, following Ruth out of the kitchen, 'but they all talk amongst themselves about the blokes on these lists.'

Ruth, with Theresa in her arms, went straight into the sitting room. 'I find this so incredible,' she said, 'that I can only think there must be some mistake. Tom would never desert. He comes from a strong religious background. His family would never get over the shock if they knew he'd done that.'

Mavis drew close to Ruth, and gently turned her and Theresa round to face her. 'There's no mistake, Rufe,' she said solemnly. 'Believe me.'

Ruth lowered herself onto the sofa. 'But if it's true,' she asked, 'if Tom *is* on the run somewhere – where is he?'

Mavis sat down beside her. 'That's somefin'

387

you've got ter fink about, Rufe.'

'Me?'

'For all we know,' Mavis said, with a look of real concern, 'Tom may well be back in this country.'

Ruth was stunned and waited for the implication to sink in. 'Why should *I* be worried by–' She stopped. 'You think Tom could harm me because of...' Both of them looked down at Theresa cradled in Ruth's arms. She was grizzling, and on the verge of crying.

'Ter be a deserter, Rufe,' said Mavis, clearly trying to warn her, 'yer 'ave ter 'ave nerves er steel. But Charlie says some of 'em go right over the top.'

'What d'you mean?' Ruth asked.

Mavis hesitated before she answered. 'They *can* go over the top. From wot Charlie says, some of 'em can be really twisted – an' dangerous.'

Ruth now felt real uncertainty within. 'You think *I'm* in danger from Tom?'

'Not exactly,' Mavis said unsurely. 'But after wot 'appened ter Sweetie, yer can't afford ter take chances.'

Ruth got up, and started to pace around the room in an attempt to pacify Theresa. 'What do you expect me to do? Lock myself in at night just in case Tom comes back and gets angry because I thought he was dead, because I've had a child by someone else? It's too silly for words. Tom isn't like that. He's a kind, sensible person. He'll understand, I know he will. He'd never try to harm me.'

Mavis took a packet of fags from her dress pocket, and lit two of them simultaneously. 'I

388

want ter tell yer somefin', Rufe,' she said, her voice solemn and intense. 'Tom once made a pass at me.'

Ruth turned, and just looked at her.

'I know yer won't believe me,' continued Mavis, 'but it *did* 'appen, I swear ter God it did.' She came across and offered one of the fags to Ruth. But Ruth shook her head. ''E tried it one time when 'e come up ter the station ter pick you up. I told 'im yer was still out on a call, so 'e 'ung around 'til yer come back.' She stubbed the second fag out into an ash-tray on a small table beside the sofa. 'I know I shouldn't tell yer this, 'speshully after all yer've bin fru, but I can tell yer that when 'e tried it on, an' I told 'im ter piss off, 'e turned really nasty on me.'

'What?' Ruth gasped. 'What did he say?'

'It's not wot 'e said,' replied Mavis. 'It's wot 'e *did*.' She took a draw on her fag. 'First of all, 'e raised 'is fist ter me. "*Silly bitch!*" he said. Then 'e pushed me in me chest wiv boaf 'ands, an' I fell over.'

Ruth found it difficult to take all this in.

'Luckily,' continued Mavis, ''e didn't 'urt me, but when I saw 'im go, I fawt if I'd tried ter tell 'im wot I fawt of 'im, 'e'd've – well, I don't know wot 'e might've done.'

'Did anyone else see this?'

Mavis shook her head. 'I know it's 'ard ter believe,' she said, 'but most er the blokes were eivver upstairs, or out the back doin' an equipment check.'

Once Mavis's story had sunk in, Ruth stiffened. 'No, Mavis!' she snapped, firmly. 'I'm sorry, but

I can't believe any of this. Tom isn't that kind of person. He's kind, and considerate, and would never hurt anyone, let alone a friend of mine. I don't know what happened between the two of you, but you're wrong about him. And as for him being a deserter, if you don't mind my saying so, I think your Charlie's a bit of a mischief-maker! Now if you'll excuse me, I've got things to do.' Clutching Theresa tightly in her arms, she turned, and quickly swept out of the room.

Dumbfounded and hurt, Mavis watched her go in disbelief.

The street celebrations had been going on all day. With more than twenty long trestle tables for the tea-party set up from mid-morning onwards, practically every back street in Islington had been sealed off to traffic. The order of the day was 'enjoy yourselves', and that's what everyone intended to do. The preparations had started the night before, and by the time the festivities had started in earnest, the residents of Jackson, Annette and Hornsey Roads were worked up into a state of sublime exhilaration. It all began with a dozen or so kids marching down the street, using dustbin lids as hastily improvised musical instruments. Then came a fancy-dress parade of mums, dads, aunties and uncles, and anyone else who cared to join in, all of them draped with the flags of the Allied countries who had won the war. Even Ruth joined in, leaving little Theresa with Bella to watch from the pavement as, draped in the Polish flag, she waved and shouted as loud as her lungs would allow.

Never in all her life had she let her hair down so dramatically in public. Edie and Harold were there too, although with tensions beginning to surface between the Western powers and the Soviet Union, Edie was at first a little unwilling to allow herself to be used as a standard bearer for the Communist hammer and sickle flag.

In the afternoon, the kids had a whale of a time, playing every street-game that had ever been devised, including an endless egg and spoon race (using table-tennis balls), Musical Chairs, to the accompaniment of local resident Gladys Wilmot, who had kindly provided her upright piano for the two-day celebration, Blind Man's Buff, and the noisiest sing-song the neighbourhood had ever heard. The tea-party itself was just as rowdy, and by the time the kids had finished, they had thrown nearly every bit of the leftovers at each other in a wild food-fight. But who cared? They and their mums and dads, brothers and sisters, could now sleep safe in their beds at night. From now on, no one would have a care in the world, because the war – all parts of it – was truly over at last!

'Wot does VJ mean?' one of the more senile neighbours, named Granny Hobbs, asked Tub Trinder, just as one of the kids had showered him with a couple of spoonfuls of raspberry-flavoured jelly.

'Wot d'yer fink it means, yer silly ol' cow?' he growled back. 'Victory over Japan!'

'Japan?' asked poor old Granny Hobbs, somewhat confused. 'But I fawt we was fightin' the Germans?'

There was no answer to that, so Tub sighed in despair, and continued to fend off the hail of jelly that was still being directed at him.

It was true, however, that with two major national celebrations taking place within just three months of each other, VJ Day should have come as something of an anti-climax. But not a bit of it! By the time it was growing dark, the adults were only just getting into their stride, and the singing, dancing *and* drinking were still to come!

Ever since word had got around that Edie was getting married to Harold Beaks, Edie herself had blossomed. The grumbling had died down, the flat-soled shoes had been replaced by semi-high-heels ('seconds' from Barratts shoe shop, therefore needing fewer ration coupons), and the imitation fox-fur stole bought by her late husband had been taken out of mothballs, and given a few airings. These days, she was hardly ever seen without a perky little black straw hat with a bird's feather stuck up the side. As she and Harold curved their two bodies to the strains of a tango, their expressions rigid with determination to show their skills off to the admiring onlookers, Edie positively purred with newfound pride. She was in love, she had her man, and she wanted the whole world to know it.

'Edie!' spluttered Ruth, almost speechless with admiration. 'Where on earth did you learn to dance like that?'

Edie's face, streaked with sweat, lit up. 'Ooh, yer should've seen me in me young days,' she replied, coyly. 'I used ter go to a dance school up

Camden Town. I was always known as the princess of the quick-step.' She turned to Harold, who was sitting at her side amongst a group of women neighbours. '*You* used ter go ter dancin' lessons too, din't yer, dear?'

'Regular as clockwork,' replied Harold, squeezing her hand affectionately.

'Well, I thought you were wonderful!' said Bella. 'Both of you.'

Just then, they all jumped as a child let off a firecracker nearby. This in turn woke up Theresa in her pram, who then began screaming.

'Stupid little sod!' Edie yelled at the child, who, when he saw the look of anger on her face, beat a hasty retreat.

'Good job Rita ain't 'ere!' called one of the women in the group. 'She 'ates the bleedin' fings!'

'You're right!' Edie called back. 'Yer should've seen 'er in the air-raid shelter – used to scream 'er 'ead off every time a bomb went off.'

'Well, I can't say I blame her there,' said Ruth.

'Where is Rita anyway?' asked another woman in the group. Edie's expression changed. 'Gawd knows,' she replied.

'Is everything all right between you now?' asked Ruth.

''Ow would I know?' shrugged Edie.

'But she says she is coming to your wedding,' said Bella.

'Is she?' asked Edie. 'Well, if she is, she ain't told me. It's got RSVP on that invitation card,' she said airily. 'That means yer s'pposed to reply – in writin'.'

'Maybe she's got uvver fings on 'er mind, dear,' suggested Harold diplomatically.

'Well, that's up ter 'er,' retorted Edie. 'If she wants ter come, she can come. But I ain't goin' down on bended knees fer 'er!'

Rita stood at her first-floor bedroom window, looking out through the white lace curtains at the street-party now in full swing below. After nearly six years of the blackout, she found it strange to see bonfires burning on the street corners, coloured Christmas tree lights draped high across the road, and candles and paraffin lamps glowing brightly in the late evening of what had been a beautiful mid-August day. Behind her, Ted was tidying himself up. He had already shaved and had his wash-down at the kitchen sink, and he was now putting on a clean shirt, and the grey flannel trousers that he kept for best. Rita ignored – or pretended to ignore – what was going on behind her back, keeping her attention focused only on the street below.

'Ain't yer goin' out there then?' Ted asked, as he pulled up his braces. 'Sounds like everyone's 'avin' a good time.'

'I don't feel like it,' replied Rita dourly.

Ted carried on dressing. 'Yer don't get many chances like this,' he said. 'VE, VJ Day. Only come once in a lifetime, I 'ope!' He stopped what he was doing, only too aware that Rita was in another of her dark moods. He went across to her. 'Cheer up,' he said. 'It might never 'appen.'

'It's already 'appened,' replied Rita, still without turning. 'It's appened over an' over again.'

394

'Fer Christ's sake, Rita,' he said, turning away again. 'Don't let's start goin' fru all that again!'

Rita turned round. 'Why not?' she asked. 'D'yer fink I'm blind?'

'I dunno wot yer talkin' about,' said Ted, sitting on the edge of the double bed, and putting on his shoes.

'No?' she asked, standing over him. 'Then tell me why you're puttin' on a clean shirt, yer Sunday trousers, the good shoes I bought yer before the war? Don't try an' tell me you're toggin' yerself up like this just ter go outside ter the party?'

Ted tied his laces. He didn't have to look up at her to know that she was scowling at him, resenting every single thing he did. 'I'm going ter the boozer, Rita,' he said calmly. He looked up. 'I'm goin' ter spend the evenin' wiv people who enjoy my company.'

'You mean, who enjoy a little bit on the side as well!'

Stone-faced, Ted asked, 'Wot're yer gettin' at, Rita?'

'Yer *know* wot I'm gettin' at!' she snapped.

Ted sighed, leaned forward, rested his elbows on his knees, and ran his fingers wearily through his short, heavily greased hair. 'If I live ter be a 'undred,' he said, anticipating yet another confrontation with her, 'I'll never understand yer, Rita.'

'Who is she?' Rita asked relentlessly. 'An' don't bother ter deny it, becos I know diff'rently.'

Ted slowly looked up. 'Yer fink I'm knockin' some gel?' he asked.

'I'm no fool, Ted,' Rita replied, for once without raising her voice. 'I don't go round wiv me eyes closed.'

Ted got up, took the dog-end from behind his ear and lit it. For a brief moment he looked around the dreary room that he had shared with Rita for so much of their lives. There was almost nothing he liked about the place. It had Rita's style and personality stamped all over it, right down to the pathetic little dressing-table between the windows, which was overcrowded with bits of make-up – powder, lipstick, and face cream that he had never once seen her use. And the drab brown eiderdown, and the walnut-wood double wardrobe, that she had insisted on buying in a junk shop years ago. But that was Rita. Do her own thing, and to hell with anyone who thought differently. Rita – queen of the junk shops! Oh God! How he hated himself for even thinking in such a way. He turned to look at her. 'I'm not goin' wiv anyone, Rita,' he said quietly.

'Yer expect me ter believe *that?*' she growled.

'I don't expect *you* ter believe anyfin', Rita,' he replied. 'All I know is that when yer get somefin' fixed in yer mind, yer won't let go of it.' He drew closer to her, but when he reached out to gently touch her hair, she resisted. Ted sighed. 'Just look at yer,' he said. 'Yer've just let everyfin' go. Oh, I don't just mean the way yer look, yer size 'as never bin a problem wiv me. No, it's wot yer've become, Rita, inside *'ere.*' With one finger, he pointed to his forehead. 'Yer've just given up wiv me, wiv the kids, wiv Edie, wiv all the people yer know, but most of all wiv yerself.'

He went to the window and stood there, staring out aimlessly. 'Fing is, it's not all yer fault, I know that. I'm just as much ter blame. I should never've let yer get this way.' He pulled on his dog-end, and turned to look at her on the opposite side of the room. As he looked, her hair still in net and curlers, the same old drab summer dress wrapped around her huge frame, he reflected on what she had once been. 'D'yer know somefin', Rita?' he asked. 'D'yer know wot I fawt when I first saw you all them years ago? I fawt, this is not only one of the most smashin'-lookin' gels I've ever seen, but also one of the nicest. Wot 'appened to us, Rita? Wot 'appened?'

He went to the wardrobe, collected a short-sleeve pullover, and put it on. Then he collected his flat cap, which was hanging on a hook behind the door. 'So wot're we goin' ter do about it, gel?' he said, the feeling of despair cracking through his voice. 'I don't know why yer can't believe me when I tell yer that there's no one else in my life, and there never 'as bin. But, if it *should* ever appen, *if*, then it'll only be becos I know there's no way I'm ever goin' ter be able to get fru ter you.'

For one brief moment, their eyes met. But hers were the first to look away. Ted put on his cap, and in deep despair, calmly left the room.

Rita remained exactly where she was until she heard the street door open and close downstairs. Then, after a moment or so of deep thought, she eventually moved. She sat down on the dressing-table stool, and reluctantly plucked up enough courage to look at herself in the mirror. There were a million questions going through her mind, as she studied the tired, bloated face she could see there. Quite unconsciously, her hands found the jar of face cream on the table in front of her. Her eyes still fixed on herself in the mirror, she unscrewed the top, dipped her fingers into the cream, and gently started to apply some of it to her cheeks. Soon, her entire face and forehead was covered with it. But the moment she had finished, she noticed that something odd had taken place. She leaned forward to take a closer look. What she saw were two dark eyes highlighted by a mass of white. But they were glistening in the reflection of the glare from the solitary overhead light bulb. Like water in a country pond, her eyes were filled with tears. And those tears were beginning to overflow, slowly seeping their way down her rounded, cream-covered cheeks.

The party outside was now in full swing. Midnight came and went, but no one seemed to notice. The kids, finally knocked out by the sheer exhaustion of a hectic day, simply fell asleep either in their mum or dad's arms, or in any spare corner they could find. For the adult residents, however, the party went on, and with the bonfires crackling on the corners at each end of the road, a mass sing-song turned into a dance, and the dance turned into a 'hokey-cokey'. This was where Edie came into her own, for she knew every movement and every word of them – and what with that and the combination of several strong gin and tonics, she was clearly having the time of her life.

Ruth and her mother watched from kitchen chairs on the pavement nearby. After quite a long spell of tears and baby tantrums, little Theresa had finally gone to sleep. 'I think I'll take her back now, Mama,' said Ruth. 'With a bit of luck, she'll sleep through until her next feed.'

'All right, darling.' Bella herself was beginning to flag. 'I'll stay just a few more minutes to help with the washing-up.'

After saying a weary good night to everyone, Ruth slowly eased Theresa's pram through the still inexhaustible crowds of revellers, and gradually found her way back into the cul de sac. Once she'd let herself in at the front door, she quietly lifted Theresa out of the pram, and gently held her against her shoulder. 'Come on, little lady,' she said, softly. 'You're too young to be going to parties like this.' With Theresa in her arms, she carefully climbed the stairs, and went into her bedroom.

It was a wonderful feeling for her to be able to turn on the light again without having to rush over to lower the blackout blinds. But once she'd laid Theresa on the bed, she did go across to draw the pretty floral patterned curtains that her mother had made shortly after VE Day. She took a few minutes to undress, and clean her teeth at the wash-stand. When that was done, she tiptoed back to the bed and switched off the lamp. She soon had Theresa snuggled up close to her, and whilst she lay there, she talked to her baby as though she understood every single word her mother was saying. 'Oh my darling,' she sighed.

'If only your daddy were here now. When are we going to see him again, little one? When?' She gently pressed her cheek against Theresa's, then kissed her softly on the forehead. The constant daily fears were plaguing her again, fears that she might never see Mike again, and that her baby would never see its father. 'When your daddy comes home,' she said tearfully, 'you two are going to be such good friends. I bet you'll even be able to talk to him in Polish!'

As Ruth lay there, trying to get off to sleep, she was suddenly distracted by a movement on the stairs outside. 'Mama!' she called. 'Is that you?' There was no reply, so she imagined that the sound she had heard had come from the late-night festivities still going full-blast in the streets outside. She leaned her head back on the pillow again, and closed her eyes. In her mind's eye, she could see Mike – Mike laughing, Mike grinning at her, Mike smoking, writing, weeding in the garden up at Hackney. Lying there in the dark, Ruth felt a smile bloom on her own face. He was there with her, lying beside her, caressing her. 'Oh Mike,' she sighed. 'I do love you so much–'

Before she could even reflect on another word, a hand sprang out of the dark and clamped down over her mouth. She had no time to scream, and her struggling was useless, but she was still able to protect Theresa by hugging her tight into her arms. Ruth's heart was pumping loud and fast, and although she found it hard to breathe, she soon realised that it was impossible to defend herself against the tall, menacing figure in the dark. Then came silence. Whoever he was, she could hear him, she could feel his warm breath on her face as he leaned down close over her. For God's sake, she asked herself, tucking her baby's face as tight as she could between her breasts, who *was* this monster? What did he want?

'Move – an' I'll kill yer!'

As soon as she heard the voice – *that* voice – it told her all she needed to know.

Chapter 21

Even in the dark, Tom Phillips's voice was unmistakable. The only difference was that it had become gruff and hoarse, which, for Ruth, only heightened her feeling that she was listening to a voice from the dead. But Tom Phillips was real enough. Perched on the edge of her bed, his outline seemed to her to be overpowering and grotesque, as though a massive human form had suddenly stepped out of the grave. Alone and helpless, his hand clamped over her mouth to stifle any sound, all she could do to protect herself was to pull the bedclothes up as far as she dared without suffocating her baby.

'For ever an' ever.' Tom's voice was barely audible as it drifted towards where Ruth was propped up against her pillows. 'Remember, Ruth? Remember that touchin' farewell on the platform at King's Cross? *"For ever an' ever."* Is that wot yer mean by promisin' ter wait fer me?'

'How was I to know you were alive, Tom?' Ruth

asked, her voice cracking with emotion. 'Your family said you were dead, we *all* thought you were dead – that we'd never see you again.'

Tom grunted. 'Sorry ter disappoint yer all,' he said. 'As yer can see, I'm very much alive.'

Ruth heard the rustle of the eiderdown as he leaned towards her. 'You promised ter wait fer me. Why didn't yer wait fer me, Ruth?'

Ruth felt all the blood drain from her body. Yes, she asked herself, why *hadn't* she waited for him? After all, he did propose marriage to her, he did buy her an engagement ring, he did say he loved her. And she had told him that she loved him, too. But if that was true, why couldn't she have waited until they had absolute confirmation that his body had been found? She had betrayed him for another man, and this was the result. He was here to take his revenge, and there was nothing she could do about it.

'I wanted to wait for you, Tom,' she replied trembling with fear. 'I wanted to believe that one day you'd come back.'

'But I didn't, did I? So when the cat was away, the mouse just 'ad ter play?'

'No,' she insisted. 'It wasn't like that.'

'No?' he asked sceptically. 'Wot *was* it like, then, Ruth?'

Ruth suddenly felt the movement of her baby as Theresa tried to free herself from her mother's tight grasp. What could she say to this man, who had left as her future husband, and now returned as a man who was intent on revenge for all the pain and hurt he had suffered? He was right. Her mind was bursting with guilt. It was true: she had played whilst he was away. 'It was a long time, Tom,' she pleaded. 'I waited, I promise you, I *did* wait. But when there was no word from you, no word at all for so many months, I feared the worst – we *all* feared the worst. That's why, when someone came along...'

'I know,' said Tom, sounding quietly under-standing. 'Yer don't 'ave ter explain ter me. I know exactly 'ow yer felt. I s'ppose I knew that before I went away. Wot was it yer said?' He leaned closer. '*"For ever's a long time."* That's wot yer said, wasn't it, Ruth? An' wot else was it yer said? *"When I say I want to save myself for you, that doesn't mean I don't want you."*'

Ruth felt herself shrivel up inside. 'I didn't mean that, Tom,' she pleaded. 'It was different then. We were together, and I thought we were always going to be together.'

At that moment, Theresa started to grizzle.

'Poor little baby,' said Tom. 'Want yer dad, don't yer?' He stretched out his hand, and tried to touch the baby's face.

'No!' Ruth panicked, shielding Theresa from him with her body. 'Please don't touch her.'

'Ruth!'

Tom leapt up from the bed as they suddenly heard the sound of Bella calling from downstairs. 'Not a word! I'm warnin' you!' He scurried across the room to hide behind the door.

Ruth was shaking all over, as she heard her mother coming up the stairs.

'Are you awake, darling?' called Bella, quietly peering into the room.

Ruth was breathing so hard, she found it diffi-

403

cult to answer, for her thoughts were concentrated on Tom, who was concealed just a few feet from where her mother was standing. 'I – I'm all right, Mama,' she called back nervously. 'Theresa woke up, but she's quiet now.'

'I'm not surprised,' said Bella, coming across to her. 'I'm afraid it looks as though the party outside is going to go on all night.' With the door left open and the light shining in from the landing outside, she leaned over Ruth and the baby. 'Can I get you anything, darling?' she asked. 'I could make you some cocoa. It won't take a few minutes.'

'No, Mama,' Ruth replied, breathlessly. 'We're perfectly all right. I'm going to give her a feed in a little while.'

'My poor darling,' replied Bella, with a sigh. 'It's not easy being a mother, is it?' Now that she had become a grandmother, Bella's attitude towards Ruth had changed. Gone were the recriminations, the fears about Ruth's former ways. The baby had brought them together, there was no doubt about that, and the relationship between Bella and her daughter had become warm, supportive, and caring.

Bella leaned forward and kissed Ruth on the forehead, then she lightly kissed Theresa too. 'Good night, my darlings,' she said. 'Sleep well – both of you.'

Then to Ruth's intense relief, she left, closing the door quietly behind her.

Ruth lay there, waiting until she had heard her mother's bedroom door open and close. For several moments there was an eerie silence.

Gradually she plucked up enough courage to peer over the top of her bedsheets, straining to see when Tom would emerge again from the dark. But the room remained quite still. 'Are you there?' she called, her voice low and uncertain. 'Tom?' She waited a few more moments, then cautiously sat up in bed, still clutching little Theresa in her arms. She slowly made her way across the room to the door, where, in one swift movement, she turned on the light switch.

The room was now flooded in light. But there was no sign of Tom.

Mavis Miller loved her new job. Serving behind the counter in the women's lingerie department at the North London Drapery Stores was right up her street, because every time a new consignment of silk stockings came in, she was able to grab a pair for herself before the hordes started queueing for them. However, she did find it difficult to handle the ration coupons, which were still a requirement, despite the war in Europe having been over now for nearly three months. Being an old gossip herself, she did love to stop and have a chinwag with her customers, many of whom she got to know quite well, and was soon on first-name terms with. She hadn't set eyes on Ruth since that awful occasion when she had gone round to the 'end house' to tell her about Tom Phillips being alive and on the run. It was therefore quite a surprise when she saw Ruth making straight for her from the first-floor entrance whilst she was serving one of her regulars. Once the customer had gone, Mavis turned to Ruth. But after their last meeting, she still felt a little hurt and uneasy.

'Hello, stranger,' she said tentatively. 'How's things then?'

'He *is* alive,' said Ruth, coming straight to the point. 'You were right, and I was wrong. Please forgive me.' She looked as though she hadn't slept all night.

Despite what she had told Ruth, Mavis was truly shocked to hear that it was true. 'Hang on a minute,' she said, coming from behind the counter and giving Ruth's arm a comforting squeeze. 'I'll just get someone ter cover fer me.'

A few minutes later they were talking together in front of the windows on the stone floor landing outside. There were only a few stragglers in Sussex Way below, but just beyond it, Seven Sisters Road, still bedecked with flags and bunting from the VJ celebrations, was absolutely brimming with shoppers.

'But 'ow did 'e manage ter get in?' Mavis asked, careful to keep her voice down whilst people passed in and out through the swing doors.

'He used the spare key,' replied Ruth wearily. 'He knew we keep it under a flower-pot outside the front door. He saw me use it once when I'd forgotten my own key.'

'He must've scared the daylights out er yer,' said Mavis. 'Yer should've gone round an' got the cops straight away.'

Ruth shook her head. 'I was more scared for Theresa than for myself.'

Mavis was worried. 'Yer fink 'e might've 'urt 'er?' she asked.

'I don't know.' Ruth shuddered. 'He was so strange, so ... different. I think he's so angry about what I've done, he could be capable of doing anything.'

Just then, two women shoppers came up the steps and, without more than a passing glance at either Ruth or Mavis, made their way through the swing doors marked *Women's Clothes & Lingerie*. Mavis waited for them to go, then drew closer to Ruth's side. 'So 'ow did yer leave it when 'e went?' she asked. Even though her voice was no more than a whisper, it still echoed up and down the stairwell.

Ruth sighed despondently. 'We left it nowhere,' she replied. 'Whilst my mother was still in the room, he just vanished – into thin air.'

'Yer mean, 'e didn't say anyfin' about comin' back ter see yer again?'

Again Ruth shook her head. 'But he will.'

Mavis tensed. ''Ow d'yer know?'

Ruth turned to look at her. 'Because he has unfinished business, Mavis.'

Mavis took a packet of fags out of her pocket, offered one to Ruth, and took one out for herself. 'Sounds ter me as though 'e's gone bonkers,' she said, as they lit up.

'Hardly surprising,' said Ruth. 'When you think of what those boys have been through...'

'Maybe so,' said Mavis. 'But not all of 'em desert.'

Ruth looked down through the windows. Two young women, who couldn't have been much more than teenagers, were each pushing a pram with a baby in it. In those few split seconds, she

407

wondered who they were, where they came from. She wondered whether they were in the same kind of predicament as herself; whether, when their first boyfriends returned home, they would also have to explain why *they* hadn't waited. And then what? Anger, tears, frustration, disbelief? War certainly knew how to turn lives upside down.

'Er course, yer'll 'ave ter go ter the cops,' said Mavis, her voice coming out of the blue.

'Pardon?' Ruth looked up to find Mavis staring at her. 'Oh – no,' she said, disorientated. 'I won't do anything like that.'

'But why not?' pressed Mavis, incredulously. 'If 'e's on the run from the Army, they'll be wantin' 'im fer a court martial or somefin'. You know as well as I do wot 'appened ter poor ol' Sweetie. When these blokes come back, they can't see straight. Nine times out er ten they're dang'rous.'

'No, Mavis,' said Ruth, shaking her head. 'He's suffered enough already. As long as he doesn't harm me or my baby, I don't want any part in getting him into any more trouble.'

'Rufe,' said Mavis, trying to reason with her, 'Tom's in deep enuff trouble as it is. If 'e goes any furver, they'll lock 'im up an' frow away the key.'

Ruth was still shaking her head.

'Be reasonable, Rufe!'

Before she could continue, an elderly woman came out through the swing doors with a little girl, who looked like her granddaughter. 'It's a waste of time, in't it?' she said to both girls. 'There's nuffin' ter buy really. I can't wait fer the day when we can get somefin' decent – an' wivout these ruddy coupons!'

Ruth and Mavis agreed by nodding with a smile as the old lady and the chirpy little girl with her made their way slowly down the steps.

'Wot about 'is family?' asked Mavis. 'D'yer fink they know?'

'I doubt it,' Ruth replied. 'If he's on the run, then I imagine he's trying to keep out of sight.'

'Which means 'e must be 'idin' out somewhere?'

Ruth sighed. 'Who knows.'

A woman customer came briskly out through the swing doors, and clattered downstairs. As she did so, the sound of a gramophone record of Vera Lynn singing 'Yours' filtered through from the department where Mavis worked.

'Yer've got ter tell 'em, Rufe,' said Mavis, sliding a comforting arm around Ruth's waist. 'Yer've got ter tell Tom's family. This is somefin' yer can't afford ter keep ter yerself.'

'They'll never believe me, Mavis,' replied Ruth. 'I'm not even sure I believe it myself.'

'They'll 'ave ter believe it, Rufe,' insisted Mavis. 'Tom belongs ter them, not ter you. It's up ter them ter sort 'im out. Don't yer understand, in 'is present frame er mind, 'e could do anyfin'. Charlie says all these blokes ought ter be put in some kind er place when they can be kept an eye on. They need close care an' attention.'

'Tom needs *love* and attention, Mavis,' said Ruth. 'And that's something I can never give him. And, sadly, neither can his own family.'

Ruth made her way back slowly to the shop along

409

Hornsey Road. Fortunately, Bella always relished the opportunity to look after the baby whenever her daughter was out, so Ruth made no great effort to rush back. She wanted time to think, to work out what options she had for dealing with Tom's sudden and dramatic return home. The first thing she had to consider were Mavis's fears that Tom's mental state could make him dangerous. But *how* dangerous? she asked herself. Everything depended on how jealous he might feel, about Mike, and about their baby. Would he really harm any of them? No, she decided. Despite what had happened to him, Tom was basically a kind, loving person; he would never even hurt a fly. And yet, time and time again the doubts began to creep in. That voice. Oh yes, she recognised it all right, but she couldn't deny that there was something different about it. She thought about not being able to see his face, and wondered what it looked like, and how it had weathered all the pain and suffering he had clearly endured over the past year of living rough in the jungles of a foreign land. Try as she may, Ruth couldn't help feeling absolutely astounded by the fact that, if Tom had indeed deserted, as Mavis and her boyfriend had suggested, then how had he managed to find his way home from such a great distance, from the other side of the world.

She came to a halt and found she had reached the corner of Jackson Road. Pausing for a moment or so, she took a passing glance at the place where, only the night before, the VJ party had been in full swing. And just along the road, she could see the corner of the Annette Road cul de sac, where only a short while ago, Tom Phillips had come back from the dead to change her life for ever.

Bella was feeling tired. She had spent most of the morning dividing her time between serving customers in the shop, and looking after her grandchild. Ever since baby Theresa had been born, Bella had become a doting grandmother, rushing to stand in for Ruth every time she needed to go out somewhere on her own, and dismissing any thoughts in her mind about having a granddaughter who was, in the eyes of the law, illegitimate. But, although she was still only in her fifties, Bella was not getting any younger, and the combination of coping with a baby which spent a lot of the day screaming its head off, together with struggling to keep a heart condition under control, was sometimes quite a strain. For various reasons, today had not been easy. Despite Freda Dapper's help, there had been an endless stream of customers who had complained about the lack of sweets, the shortage of cigarettes, and the frustration they felt with the new government which seemed to be making no efforts to bring about the end of rationing. Nearly everyone who came into the shop grumbled about the hardships of war continuing right on into the peace. They wanted relief from gloom and shortages. They wanted to see things that they could buy, back in the shops again.

By the time Ruth returned from her morning

out, Bella had had enough, and felt just about ready to drop. As soon as Freda left work around four in the afternoon, Ruth urged her mother to go home too and get some rest, but Bella said that she needed to talk something over with Ruth, something that had been preying on her mind for some time. 'I think it's time to sell up,' she called from her chair in the back room, just as Ruth had managed to get the baby off to sleep in her pram.

Ruth was taken completely by surprise. 'Sell up?' she asked incredulously, going in to join her mother. 'D'you mean – the shop? You want to sell this shop?'

'Yes,' replied Bella. 'I think we've gone about as far as we can go.'

Ruth sat beside her. 'I don't understand, Mama,' she said. 'What do you mean?'

'I mean,' Bella said, 'that all this is now too much for you and me. When your father was alive, it was a business to be proud of. But what with the war, and the way things are now, we should be thinking about doing less work, not more.'

'The way things are,' repeated Ruth. 'D'you mean because of what's happened, because of me and the baby?'

Bella shook her head. 'No, no,' she said reassuringly. 'It's something I've had on my mind for a long time. Why do we need to work the long hours we've put in these last few years? Why shouldn't we just put our feet up and start to enjoy life?'

'I'm so sorry, Mama,' said Ruth, trying to

comfort her. 'I never knew you felt this way.'

'Oh, I'm not unhappy or anything,' Bella assured her, 'but I think there comes a time when you know you're ready to stop.' She took a causal look around the room, which was piled high with crates and boxes, stock that was still waiting to be opened; a parlour table that was covered in paperwork. 'When your father first brought me here, it was so exciting, such a great adventure. I learnt how to do stock-taking, balance the books, choose the right things to sell. But most of all I learnt about England, about English people, about who and what they really are.' She looked back at Ruth again. 'But it's no longer an adventure,' she said wistfully. 'Now, it's just living from one day to the next, listening to what people think, what they hate, what they expect. Our shop is no longer a place where the neighbours can meet and buy the things they want to buy, it's a place where they come to grumble and complain.'

'But that's what being English is, Mama.' Ruth made a little joke of it. 'Grumble and complain, yes – but it's only a way of getting something off their chest.'

Bella shrugged. 'All I know is, I've come to the end of my time working here. Of course, if you feel like staying on, I shall transfer the property into your name.'

'No, Mama,' Ruth protested.

'What difference does it make?' asked Bella. 'I've left everything to you in my Will. What you do with it all will be entirely up to you. At least the "end house" will be a wonderful place for you and Theresa to live. And Mike, of course, if and when he ever gets home.'

Ruth's expression changed. The very mention of Mike's name had sent her stomach churning, for it immediately reminded her of the dilemma facing her over Tom. Was this the right moment to tell her mother that Tom was still alive? 'Mike *will* get home, Mama,' she said, standing up.

'It's been a long time since you heard anything, darling,' said Bella. 'In the newspapers it says that most of our soldiers who've been fighting out East are already beginning to return home.'

'He's coming home, Mama!' insisted Ruth.

'You still believe that, despite what happened to Tom?'

Ruth shuddered. 'Tom is different, Mama,' she said, with anguish. 'If the War Office say he's dead, then we must believe them.'

'Do *you* believe them?' asked Bella.

Ruth slowly turned to look at her. Bella had that look in her eyes, the look that revealed so much about what she was trying to work out in her own mind. 'As far as *I'm* concerned,' Ruth said forcibly, 'Tom is in the past. My future is with Mike.'

Once Bella had gone home, Ruth set about unpacking some of the stock in the back parlour. The job seemed to take for ever, mainly because of the usual rush of late-afternoon customers who wanted to collect their evening newspapers before the shop closed. At least the kids were on summer holiday from the school down the road, so she didn't have to worry about them crowding into the shop for a bottle of Tizer, a couple of bars of liquorice, or any boiled sweets that might still be available in the jars lined up on the shelves behind the counter. But even when she had closed up shop for the night, there was still some paperwork to do, and the contents of the cash till to be balanced up and locked away in the back parlour safe. Apart from this there was also little Theresa to be attended to, for not only did her nappy smell to high heaven, but she was getting close to her six o'clock feed.

It was therefore nearly seven o'clock when Ruth locked up and got away from the shop. When she finally managed to wheel Theresa's pram out into Hornsey Road, there were the first signs that the claustrophobic heat of the day was gradually giving way to a cool breeze. With the fresher air caressing her cheeks, Ruth was able to move at a brisk pace. Although it was a bright evening, with the sun low in the evening sky and casting deep lengthening shadows the pavement beneath the Holloway Road railway bridge was already shrouded in gloom, so much so that Ruth felt compelled to increase her pace. But before she had reached the halfway mark, she slowed down again, disturbed by the figure of a man entering from the far end. She had no idea why she should feel unnerved. It was due in part to the fact that there was no one else around and the smell of urine from the men's public toilet was overpowering in the enclosed space. As the figure came closer, Ruth wanted to turn round and hurry back, but something told her to keep on walking. It was only when the man came into full view that she finally recognised that it was

Tom Phillips. She came to an abrupt halt; she was shaking from head to foot. Without saying a word, he stopped directly in front of her. In the only natural light that was left beneath the bridge, Ruth could see that his features were rough and drawn, drained of all colour, his eyes piercing and blank. With her heart thumping hard, and her legs feeling as though they were about to give way beneath her, she tried to open her parched lips to say something. But before she could do so, Tom moved on, and swept straight past her. By the time Ruth had plucked up enough courage to turn and look over her shoulder, he had gone.

The moment Ruth walked through the front door of the 'end house', she knew something was wrong.

'Ruth!'

Ruth turned with a start as she heard her mother calling to her from the sitting room. 'Mama?'

'In here, darling!'

Once she had made sure the baby was still sleeping in her pram, Ruth went into the sitting room, where she was surprised to find her mother with Edie Perkins and Harold Beaks. 'Oh, hallo,' she said, a bit taken aback. 'Is anything wrong?' Edie was dabbing her moist eyes with a handkerchief.

'It's very sad,' said Bella. 'Poor Mrs Simmons.'

'Mrs Simmons? Rita?' asked Ruth, puzzled. 'Why, what's happened to her?'

'Ted's walked out on 'er,' said Edie, being

comforted by Harold on the sofa.

'Walked out on her?' echoed Ruth.

'It 'appened after the party last night,' sniffed Edie. 'If I know Rita, she must've 'ad a bust-up wiv Ted, an' when 'e went off ter the boozer, 'e didn't come back.'

Ruth sighed. After all she'd been through that day, this was more than she could take. 'How do you know all this, Edie?' she asked. 'You two haven't talked to each other for ages.'

'The nurse told me,' said Edie. ''Er next door neighbour fawt somefin' 'ad 'appened when she saw Rita's front door open. So she dialled 999, and got the ambulance. They found Rita lyin' on the floor in 'er bedroom, moanin' and groanin', 'er face all covered in face cream.'

'She'd taken 'alf a bottle of aspirins,' said Harold. 'If yer ask me, she's lucky ter be alive.'

'But she *is* still alive?' asked Ruth.

'Apparently she's already back home,' answered Bella.

Ruth was now utterly bewildered. 'What!'

'They just pumped 'er dry,' said Harold, 'an' sent 'er back 'ome again. After all the 'ard times they 'ad durin' the war, the doctors don't take too kindly ter people who try ter do away wiv themselves.'

''Speshully when they've tried doin' it before,' said Edie darkly.

Ruth's mind was now so shattered that she didn't really know what more she could say. 'Well,' she said, 'Edie, you're her best friend. Don't you think you should go round and see if she's all right?'

417

But Edie was shaking her head vigorously. 'I couldn't do that,' she replied emphatically. 'I just couldn't.'

'But why not?' asked Ruth. 'I know there have been problems between you and Rita, but the two of you have known each other for a long time. I'm sure if anyone could help her, you can, Edie.'

Edie was still shaking her head. 'I couldn't, Rufe,' she said. 'I just couldn't. I'm too scared.'

'Scared? But you told me that after what you said to her, you'd never ever be scared of her again.'

'Yer don't understand.' Edie tried to explain. 'It's not her I'm scared of. It's me. Yer see, I've 'urt 'er an awful lot. After the fings I said to 'er, she'll find it difficult ter fergive me.'

'That can't be true,' said Bella. 'She's coming to your wedding.'

'Maybe she is,' said Edie. 'An' maybe she's not. But whatever appens, I'd never forgive meself if I went round there ter see 'er, an' I 'urt 'er all over again – 'speshully after all she's goin' fru wiv Ted.'

For one brief moment, Ruth felt as though she was going out of her mind. Try as she may, she couldn't understand Edie's attitude to Rita. One minute they were the best of mates, the next they were at each other's throats. Human relationships, she said to herself – why do they always have to be so complicated? 'I'm sorry, Edie,' she said, 'but I really don't see what else you can do. If you really can't bring yourself to go round to see Rita, then how are you going to know if she needs any help?'

Edie dried her eyes, then exchanged a look with

418

Harold. 'We'd know,' she said sheepishly, 'if somebody else went for me.'

Ruth had no idea how she had managed to get herself into this ridiculous situation. Surely she had enough problems of her own, without getting involved in an extraordinary love-hate relationship between two totally different people, who both had their own reasons for needing each other. As she plodded her weary way to the end of the cul de sac, her eyes were all over the place, searching the front gardens, the pavements on either side of Jackson Road, and as far down Annette Road as she could see in the rapidly failing evening light. After her terrifying experience beneath the railway bridge no more than an hour before, her nerves were tingling with fear and apprehension. What was Tom Phillips up to she kept asking herself. Why was he trying to terrorise her like this? What did he want of her? She wondered how long all this would go on. How could she find him? she asked herself. How could she soothe his hatred and bitterness? Would she be able to prevent him from harming both herself and her baby? Questions, questions, questions – all with no answers. Oh God, she sighed. If only Mike were there to support her.

In Jackson Road, she made straight for Rita's house. She slowed down as she drew close, mainly to check first if there were any lights on in the house. The thought had occurred to her that if Rita had tried to commit suicide again, she would have no idea how to cope with it. To see the remains of a dead person lying in the debris of bomb damage during the Blitz was one thing, but finding a neighbour dazed and unconscious on her own floor from an overdose of pills was quite different. Ruth had even more doubts as she approached Rita's front door. After all the trouble and unpleasantness the big women had caused both Ruth and her mother, why on earth should she come to her rescue? Wouldn't it be better for her to just do away with herself, so that everyone around her, including her husband Ted, could be left in peace? Even as the idea occurred to her, Ruth felt ashamed of herself. What she had agreed to do was not for herself, it was for Edie. Edie cared, and that was good enough for Ruth. Even so, she still feared the worst. Had she really done it this time? Poor Rita. Ruth suddenly felt extremely sorry for the woman.

The moment of truth came when she knocked on Rita's front door. It was troubling enough to find that there were indeed no lights on in any of the rooms either downstairs or upstairs, and when she found herself standing on the front doorstep without response for what seemed like an eternity, Ruth began to feel the first signs of panic. In desperation, she finally crouched down, opened the letterbox with her fingers, and called out: 'Rita! Are you in there?' To her absolute shock and astonishment, the door immediately swung open, and the passage light was switched on.

Standing there, like a vision from hell, eyes blazing, hair in curlers and net, was Rita. 'What the bleedin' 'ell d'yer fink *you're* doin'!' she roared.

Ruth immediately straightened up. Totall₃
flustered, all she could mutter was, 'Are you all
right?'

'Wot're yer talkin' about?' yelled Rita. 'Wot
d'yer take me for? Er course I'm all right!'

With that, she slammed the door in Ruth's face.

Chapter 22

It was good to hear music in the open air again.
When she was a small child, Ruth had often been
taken to Finsbury Park by her mother. The thing
she loved most, after feeding the ducks on the
lake, was going to the old bandstand to watch a
military band concert. She would tap her small
foot and join in the music as soldiers in bright
scarlet tunics and gold epaulettes played everything from 'The British Grenadiers' and 'The
Blue Danube' to some of the most popular tunes
of the day. During the war, however, all that had
come to an end, and apart from the RAF barrage
balloons floating high in the sky on the Seven
Sisters Road side, the park had remained quiet
and peaceful.

For Ruth, today should have been just as peaceful, for the war was now over, and strolling with
Theresa in her pram through the gradually
restored flower gardens was like turning the clock
back to the time when her mother had done
exactly the same thing with her. Unfortunately,
this was no ordinary Sunday afternoon, at least

for Ruth, for she was convinced that, amongst all those happy smiling families who were enjoying the warm sunshine so much, was someone watching her, someone who was intent on making her life as tense and as nerve-racking as he possibly could. Her only salvation now was Mavis and her boyfriend, Charlie, who had arranged to meet her in the old café near the lake.

The café itself had been boarded up for so long that it was now in need of urgent repair and decoration, and although very watery tea was available at the self-service counter, the only snacks on show were packets of Smith's crisps and a few slices of plain cake made with dried eggs and dried milk. Fortunately, the place was fairly deserted, for most people were taking advantage of the afternoon sun, and sitting either at tables outside or on the nearby grass. It was therefore quite easy for Ruth, Mavis, and Charlie to talk together at one of the tables in the corner, without being overheard.

'Phillips is a sick man,' Charlie told Ruth as he watched her sipping her tea. 'Like so many of the blokes out in those jungles, he must have seen some pretty gruesome sights.'

Meeting Charlie Raynor for the first time had been quite a surprise for Ruth. Not only was he good-looking, with blond hair that was beginning to grow after years of a regulation Army cut, but he was also intelligent and well-educated. 'When you say sick,' she asked, 'are you talking about his body or his mind?'

'All I can tell you,' said Charlie, 'is that working

in the Army Medical for so long, I've seen a lot of blokes like him. The things they were asked to do was just too much for them. Of course, the Army will always do their best to keep it all quiet, but some of the blokes they've got locked away have just quite literally gone to pieces.'

Ruth thought about this for a moment. 'And you think this is what has happened to Tom?' she asked.

Charlie flicked the ash from his cigarette into a tin ash-tray on the table. 'When I saw his name on that list,' he said solemnly, 'I remembered what Mavis had told me about him. So I got a mate of mine to do a bit of poking around for me – strictly off-limits, you understand.'

'What did you find?' asked Ruth directly, clutching the baby in her arms, whilst at the same time juggling with her cup of tea.

Charlie was reluctant to continue.

'Go on, Charlie,' urged Mavis. 'Ruth's got a right ter know.'

Charlie took a deep pull on his cigarette. 'There was this medical report,' he said. 'February of last year. Written by the MO of his unit out in Burma.' He hesitated. 'Something happened,' he continued. 'Phillips was out with a patrol. Something happened.' He stopped again.

'Please tell me, Charlie,' pleaded Ruth.

Although still reluctant, Charlie went on: 'They got ambushed. The Nips came down on them and...' He hesitated. 'The whole patrol got wiped out. All of them except Phillips – and one other.' He looked up to see Ruth's reaction.

'Go on, please,' she said calmly.

'The Nips caught up with them,' continued Charlie. 'They executed the other guy, but Phillips got away.' Again he looked up, first at Mavis, then at Ruth.

Mavis leaned across and placed a comforting hand on Ruth's arm. The baby was making laughing sounds, so Ruth put down her cup, and snuggled their two faces up together.

'As far as I can tell from looking at his records,' said Charlie, 'Phillips disappeared from his unit some time after that. Before he went, he was treated for malaria, dysentery – and shock. But after what happened to him out there, the worst part has to be his state of mind.'

Ruth's eyes automatically checked over the empty restaurant. Then she stood up, and with Theresa clasped in her arms, she peered out through the café window at the crowds of people milling around, children playing games with their families, young couples strolling hand in hand, groups of women just talking to each other, laughing, joking. But what she was really looking for was the anguished face that had confronted her beneath the railway bridge. All her instincts told her that Tom was out there, a lost soul, searching for something that he would never be able to have. And as she clutched Theresa even closer to her heart, the guilt gradually started to overwhelm her.

'How could I have betrayed him?' she said aloud, staring out through the open window as though she was talking directly to Tom himself. 'He trusted me, and yet I betrayed him. Why? After all he's been through, struggling to survive

424

in what must have been a living hell – and yet I couldn't wait for him. Why?'

'Becos yer couldn't love 'im,' said Mavis, who joined her at the window. 'Becos yer was bein' trufeful ter yerself.'

'But not truthful to him,' replied Ruth, her voice cracked with emotion.

'Fallin' in love is like that, Rufe,' she said, her arm around Ruth's waist. 'Someone's always bound ter get 'urt.'

Ruth put Theresa back in her pram.

'You can't take chances with this bloke, Ruth,' said Charlie, stubbing out the remains of his cigarette. 'Somebody's got to turn him in.'

'I can't do that, Charlie,' insisted Ruth. 'Even if I wanted to, which I don't, I don't know where to find him.'

'At least tell the cops yer've seen 'im, Rufe,' begged Mavis. 'Once they know 'e's on the loose, they'll keep an eye open fer 'im.'

'You can bet your life they're already doing that,' added Charlie. 'The Army must have notified them, and there's bound to be a warrant issued for his arrest.'

Ruth felt her insides falling apart. 'I can't do it,' she said, her face contorted with anguish. 'Tom loves me. I once loved him. It's not his fault that the whole world seems to have turned against him.'

'He could kill you, Ruth.' Charlie's stark warning jolted her. 'He could kill you *and* your baby.' Charlie got up from the table, and stood directly facing her. 'Even if he hadn't deserted, his mind must be so twisted about you that he can't see

425

straight. If you want to take my advice, then at least tell *somebody* what's going on. Because if he *is* out there watching you, like you say, then it sounds to me as though he's absolutely determined to get you.'

A little later, with Charlie's words still ringing in her ears, Ruth made her way home along Isledon Road. As she pushed the baby's pram briskly past the Astoria cinema, there was a long queue of hopefuls waiting to get into the second house Sunday showing of the popular new Bing Crosby, Bob Hope film *The Road to Utopia,* so she quickened her pace self-consciously, just in case there were any prying eyes amongst them who were taking more than a passing interest in her.

'*Tell somebody.*' Try as she might, she just couldn't get Charlie's words out of her mind. She knew exactly what he meant, and she also knew that she was trying to avoid doing it. She had to tell the Army that she had seen Tom, and that for his sake as much as for the safety of her baby and herself, they had to take him into custody before it was too late. So why wasn't she doing just that? she asked herself. Why wasn't she making her way straight to the police station in Hornsey Road to get their protection? The predicament she was in was so bewildering that she felt like screaming out loud with frustration right there in the middle of the road. Even though the lives of both her baby and herself were in danger, she just couldn't do it. She blamed herself for what had happened. She had betrayed Tom once, and she just couldn't do it again.

426

As she walked, her eyes fixed firmly on the pavement, she suddenly felt overwhelmed by a wave of deep despair. Coming to an abrupt halt, she closed her eyes, and covered them with one hand. There were tears just waiting to fall, but they held back obstinately. In the darkness of her mind she could now see only Mike. He was smiling, drawing close. She could feel his lips pressed against hers. He was caressing her, loving her. *'Stop worrying,'* he was whispering in her ear. *'Nothin's ever as bad as it seems. Don't worry, I'll soon take care of this nut-case for yer.'*

'Oh God!' cried Ruth, stretching out unconsciously to touch him as if he were really there. 'Help me, Mike! Please help me!' But his image disappeared as quickly as it had come. Her tears were finally set free, gradually trickling down her face through her fingers.

'Are you all right, miss?'

Ruth leapt back with a terrified start, but when she uncovered her eyes, she saw that an elderly man had stopped immediately in front of her. 'Oh yes,' she replied, flustered, embarrassed. 'I'm quite all right, thank you.'

'If there's anything we can do to help?' asked the man's elderly wife, joining them.

'Oh no,' insisted Ruth, quickly wiping away the tears with her fingers. 'I'm just a bit tired, that's all.'

'I'm not surprised,' said the woman, peering down into Theresa's pram. 'They're quite a handful, aren't they? Especially at this age. Hallo, little beauty.'

Theresa gurgled and broke into a huge smile as

the woman pulled a funny face at her.

Ruth waited for the elderly couple to go before she moved on. By then, she had retrieved Theresa's dummy, and put it back into the child's mouth. A few moments later she was passing a row of tall terraced Edwardian houses which had been badly bomb-damaged during the early days of the Blitz, but still seemed to be partly occupied. She hardly noticed them. But just as she was passing the final house in the terrace, immediately alongside a great gap where the rest of the terrace had once stood, she was startled by a voice calling to her.

'Ruth! Up here, Ruth!'

She swung around, and looked up at the house. Her blood turned to ice as she saw Tom Phillips standing at a top-floor window waving to her. Her immediate instinct was panic, to make off as fast as she could, but before she had gone even a few yards further along the bombed-out gap in the terrace, she brought herself and the pram to an abrupt halt. Fired with the knowledge that she at least now knew his whereabouts, she turned around and made straight for the house. Once she had parked the baby's pram in the small bare front yard, she made her way up the stone steps leading to the front door. She wasn't surprised to find it unlocked, and so, with great trepidation, she went inside.

The house was a wreck. Although the structure was still standing, so much plaster had come down from both the passage walls and the ceiling that the wooden slats beneath were clearly visible. She picked her way over the rubble, avoiding the pools of stagnant water which had formed right the way through to the back garden. Everything smelt of dust and decay and cats' and dogs' urine. She poked her head only briefly into the ground-floor room on her right, for it too was no more than a pile of rubble, but it did get her wondering why Tom would want to choose such an unlikely place to hide out. Going to the bottom of the stairs, she called out, 'Tom! Are you up there?' Her voice sounded dull and lifeless in the gloom, and as it reached the top of the stairs, it seemed to provoke a fall of dust. Before attempting to go upstairs, she took one final look outside to make sure that Theresa was quite settled in her pram. When she was satisfied that it was safe to leave her alone for a few minutes, she trod carefully up the creaking broken staircase.

'Tom!'

By the time she had reached the first-floor landing, Ruth's voice had become more shaky and shrill. The lack of response had already made her feel that it had been a mistake to enter the house alone, and when a section of banister suddenly fell away as she started to climb the final flight of stairs, everything inside her urged her to get out of the place as fast as she could. But a steely determination took over. She had to have this out with Tom once and for all, and until she did, she would continue to live in fear of her life.

'Tom!' she called again, this time with irritation. 'Where are you? Why won't you answer me?'

She reached the top-floor landing. There were two doors, one to her left, the other to her right;

she chose to investigate the latter first. She knew immediately that it was unlikely Tom was in this room, for the door opened with some difficulty, mainly because of the small pieces of rubble that were wedged up against it on the inside. The room itself must once have been a kitchen parlour, for there was an empty tin of Spam on a table there, and two plaster-filled saucepans on the open oven-range. Fortunately, the force of the bomb blast had blown out the windows, which at least allowed some fresh air to decontaminate the foul smells of mouse and rat droppings. For one brief moment, she went to what had once been a window, but was now no more than a great hole in the wall. She felt quite queasy as she stood there, gazing down through a sheer drop to the small garden below, where a completely buckled Anderson shelter was partially buried beneath a pile of earth, rubble, and rubbish.

On the landing outside, she nervously made her way towards the door of the second room where she had seen Tom at the window, and where she was sure he was now waiting for her.

'Tom,' she called, then stretched out her hand, and slowly eased the door open.

Even though there were clear signs that someone had been bunking down there, the room itself was deserted. Now she was really scared. Going through her mind was the possibility that she had imagined the whole thing, that what she had seen up at the window was no more real than the image of Mike that had come to her during those few lost seconds of despair. How could anyone live in such appalling conditions? she asked herself. This place wasn't fit for a rat, let alone a human being. But just as she had convinced herself that she had worked herself up for nothing, she smelt something burning, and noticed a half-smoked cigarette smouldering on a heap of plaster. Her newfound confidence deserted her immediately, and she gasped at the sound of Tom's voice calling to her from the landing below.

'Ruth! Down here, Ruth! We're waitin' fer yer!'

Utterly panic-stricken, Ruth rushed for the door. *We?* What was he talking about? *Oh my God!* Her worst fears were realised when she burst through the half-open door of a room downstairs on the first landing.

''Allo mate!' said Tom, standing at the open window, with a huge grin on his face. 'Just look who we've got 'ere.'

To Ruth's horror, he was cradling little Theresa in his arms. 'No!' she yelled, lunging straight at him.

But before she could reach him, he turned and threatened to throw the baby out through the window. 'I wouldn't if I was you,' he warned.

Ruth held back. 'Tom,' she said, overcome with fear and distress, 'why are you doing this to me? What do you want?'

He stared her out for a minute, his expression a mix between calm reason and madness. 'I want us ter be friends, Ruth,' he said, his eyes soft and pleading. 'I want us ter be friends just like we used ter be. You, me, and now...' he looked down at the baby in his arms, 'our little gel.'

431

Ruth went quite cold. Although his back was turned to the window and the light was shining in her eyes, it was the first chance she had to really see his face. Gone were those fresh good looks, the bright eyes, the full, thick lips, and the friendly expression. In their place was a face lined with tension, tormented eyes. She couldn't help recalling the happy times they had spent in each other's company, that glorious day in the back garden of the Phillipses' house in Camden Town, when they had kissed under the apple tree. Everything had seemed so idyllic, so perfect then. But now, as she looked at the unstable soul before her, holding her baby, filling the air with menace, she couldn't recognise him. To her he was no more than a perfect stranger. 'Theresa is not your girl, Tom,' she said, her voice cracking with emotion.

'Oh but she is,' he replied brightly. Then looking at the little bundle in his arms, he asked, 'Yer are, ain't yer?'

In one swift movement, Ruth again rushed at him. This time she reached him before he had time to turn to the window, but as she did so, he managed to get his arm around her neck, and hold it in a vice-like grip.

'No, Rufe,' he said calmly, clutching the baby with one arm, and Ruth with the other. 'This little gel is the one we should've 'ad – you an' me.' He pulled Ruth so close that his face was almost touching hers. 'Why didn't you wait fer me, Rufe?' he asked. There was pain and sadness in his voice. 'D'yer know wot it was like sittin' out there in that stinkin' 'ole, finkin' about yer,

432

dreamin' about yer, knowin' that you were my reason – my only reason – fer stayin' alive?' His voice was now a mere whisper. 'If it wasn't fer you, I wouldn't be 'ere now. I found my way out of that graveyard just so that I could be wiv yer. I walked, I swam, I worked my way on every boat I could get on, just so that I could get back ter you, back ter the only fing that I ever wanted in the 'ole wide world. Ask me 'ow I did it, Rufe. Ask me 'ow I found my way inter one bleedin' country after anuvver, lyin', cheatin', beggin' – just ter be wiv you. An' yet – yer couldn't wait fer me. Why, Rufe? Why?'

Until he had loosened his grip on her throat, Ruth was convinced that he was going to do away with her there and then. Before she could answer, she backed away. 'I loved you, Tom,' she said hoarsely. 'I swear before God that I *did* love you. But...' she tried to swallow, but her throat was too sore, 'I – I thought I'd lost you! We all did. I thought I'd never meet someone else that I could love as much as I loved you, but I did.' Scared, and with tears streaming down her face, she watched him look down in bewilderment at the baby in his arms. 'Give her to me,' she pleaded, arms outstretched. 'I beg you, please give my baby back to me.'

Tom looked up at her. Now there was a dark, threatening look in his eyes.

'Give yourself up,' Ruth whispered. 'It's the right thing to do, the only thing. People care for you. *I* care for you. You need someone to look after you.'

This angered him. His face hardened, and he

433

turned again to the window.

'No, Tom!' she begged, sobbing. 'If you love me, then please give me back my baby.' She stretched out her arms, and slowly moved towards him.

Bella looked at the clock on the mantelpiece. It was after five o'clock, and she knew something was wrong. Ruth was always home at this time to feed the baby, and the fact that she had been gone for so long was beginning to concern her. For a while now, Bella had been pacing up and down in the sitting room, constantly peering out of the window to see if there was any sign of her daughter and the pram coming down the cul de sac. Twice she had been out into the street and sat waiting anxiously on the coping-stone by the front yard gate. Again and again she checked the clock with her watch. Yes, something was definitely wrong. She decided to try once more outside.

The August early evening sun was still quite warm, although the earlier heat was gradually giving way to a soft breeze that rustled the leaves on a young poplar tree in one of her neighbours' front gardens. She went first to the middle of the road to see if she could see any sign of Ruth and the baby anywhere at all in the whole length of Annette Road, for she knew that if Ruth had been walking with friends in Finsbury Park, as she had said, they would more than likely approach from Roden Street at the far end of the road. However, apart from one or two kids playing hopscotch on the pavement in the distance, the road was absolutely clear.

Bella went back to the coping-stone, her mind seized with anxiety. Had they been knocked down by a car, or taken ill in the park? All these thoughts were now plaguing her. She sighed. Oh God, what a time these last few years had been – losing Harry, the war, Ruth's relationship with Mike Buller, the baby. It was a lot for someone like Bella to take in, especially after all she had gone through herself, knowing that her own motherland had been ripped apart, and the loss of contact with any of the family and friends she had left behind.

And yet, every time she thought about it, only one name kept coming to mind: *Tom Phillips*. Why? People had often told her that she was psychic, and the fact that his body had never actually been recovered was something that had always troubled her. Several times it had crossed her mind that should Tom still be alive, then what would happen if he came home, only to find that while he was away, his fiancée Ruth had had a child by another man? She shuddered. It was a situation too awful to even contemplate. But then, it was a possibility that couldn't just be ignored. It was a problem that was going to face many men when they eventually came back from that terrible war to find betrayed love and broken homes. Was it any wonder that when they returned home and found that their loved ones had become nothing more than complete strangers, there would be so much bitterness amongst them, so much hate? Hope was the only thing that had kept those boys alive, and if that had now been taken away from them, what was left?

'Mama!'

Bella sat up with a start as she heard Ruth's voice. Shocked to see the distressed state her daughter was in, Bella rushed down the cul de sac to meet her. 'Darling!' she cried, throwing her arms around her, trying to comfort her. 'Tell me, tell me! What is it? What's happened?'

Ruth burst into tears, and couldn't speak. All she could do was to take Theresa out of the pram and hug her tight. 'Oh, Mama!' she cried. 'What am I going to do? What *am* I going to do?'

Bella threw her arms around both her daughter and her granddaughter. 'It's all right, darling,' she said, gently stroking Ruth's hair in an effort to calm her down. 'Tell me, just tell me what's happened?' In many ways, it was a futile question, for she suspected she already knew the answer.

Kate Phillips was a solitary kind of person. She had very few people that she could call her friends, and those she had found her too introverted and narrow in her outlook on life. In many ways, it was a pity that she had been just too young to be called up for any kind of public service during the war, for it would have helped her to learn how to get on with people, helped her to break her claustrophobic ties to the family. Thanks to her father, she had managed to get a job as a clerk in the Housing Department at the Town Hall, but even there, she kept herself to herself. She got to work at nine in the morning and left at five-thirty in the evening. It was a ritual she was prepared to adhere to. Anything that happened between those hours didn't seem to matter to her at all. Therefore, it was with some surprise that, just as she was leaving her office on Monday evening, she found Ruth waiting for her on a bench seat in the main entrance of the Town Hall. 'Ruth?' she called, as Ruth came across to meet her. 'What are you doing here?'

'He's alive, Kate,' said Ruth. 'Tom's alive. I've seen him.'

'What!' gasped Kate, totally shocked.

'I didn't want to tell you,' said Ruth. 'I wanted to keep it from you. But I can't do so any longer.' Even though she lowered her voice, it still echoed in the vast entrance hall. 'He's run away from the Army, Kate,' she said, with urgency.

'Run away?' Kate was still in a state of shock. 'You mean – he's a deserter?'

'Yes,' replied Ruth. 'He apparently went missing in February of last year, and gradually found his way back home from Burma.'

'Burma!'

'Yes, I know,' said Ruth. 'I know it sounds incredible – but that's what he did. God knows how. I can hardly believe it myself.'

'And I don't believe it either!' said Kate loftily, turning her back on Ruth and moving off.

Unaware that someone had been watching and listening to them both unnoticed from nearby, Ruth followed her. 'It's true – you *must* believe me! I tell you, I've seen Tom with my own eyes. He's ill, Kate! The Army are looking for him, and any moment now the police are going to start

437

asking you and your family a lot of awkward questions.

Kate came to an abrupt halt, and swung round on her. 'You're a liar!' she snapped angrily. 'My brother's dead, and you're just trying to smear his name so that you can have a smooth ride with your fancy new boyfriend.'

'That's not true.' Ruth was distressed by Kate's reaction. 'I haven't heard from Mike in months, so I don't even know if he's alive or dead. But Tom is very much alive, and he's a very sick person.'

'How dare you!' snapped Kate. 'It's not enough for you to promise to marry my brother and then go off and have another bloke's baby. Oh no! You have to blacken his name, you have to call him a coward. Well, he's not! And I think you're the most despicable person for even suggesting it.' She turned, and swept off down the Town Hall steps.

'He tried to kill me.' Ruth's voice brought Kate to another abrupt halt. Ruth slowly came down the steps to her.

'On VJ night, he broke into our house,' Ruth told her. 'He got into my bedroom – and threatened me. Me *and* my baby. I thought he was going to kill me. If it hadn't been for my mother coming in, I don't know *what* would have happened. Then he approached me again – when I was out on my way home with the pram. He just stopped in front of us, and stared. It was frightening, Kate. He looked – so ill.'

Kate was shaking her head. 'I still don't believe you,' she said, but her expression showed a mixture of emotions.

'Yesterday afternoon,' Ruth went on, 'I saw him again. He called to me from the top window of a bombed out house in Isledon Road. I left the baby in her pram outside, and went in to see him. I wanted to tell him that I was sorry for what had happened, and to try to explain.'

Once again, Kate shook her head in disbelief.

'He took my baby,' Ruth said, her voice shaking with emotion. 'He talked to her as though she was his own, as though he was never going to part with her.' She hesitated. 'When I tried to take her from him, he very nearly killed me.'

Kate's lips twisted with anger. 'May God forgive you for what you've just said!'

Without another word, Ruth pulled back the top of her blouse, and bared her neck. 'Does *that* look as though I'm lying?' she roared. 'Well – *does* it?'

Kate looked at Ruth's neck. It was swollen, and bruised black and blue.

'Whether you believe me or not, Kate,' said Ruth, her voice cracking, 'I'm telling you that your brother *is* alive, and if someone doesn't help him soon, something terrible is going to happen.'

Although they sat next to each other on the bus all the way from the Town Hall to the Nags Head, Kate spoke not one single word to Ruth. But what Ruth had told her had completely stunned her, and if she was going to believe the harrowing story Ruth had told her, then the only way she was going to be able to know the truth was to speak with Tom herself. But as the bus tumbled its way along Holloway Road, the one thought going through Kate's mind was that Tom *was* dead, and the only reason Ruth had made up such a preposterous story was because of her own guilt. Because if it was true, if Tom *was* alive and hiding out in that house, then why hadn't Ruth gone straight to the police? It wasn't enough to be told by Ruth that she didn't want any harm to come to him. After all, why should *she* care when she had a man and a baby of her own? Even after they had got off the bus, and made their way briskly towards Isledon Road, the doubts remained. Until then, and despite the bruises on Ruth's neck, Kate was not prepared to accept what Ruth told her.

Once they had left Tollington Road and crossed over Hornsey Road into Isledon Road, it was only a few minutes' walk to the house where Ruth and her baby had been confronted by Tom. As they passed the Globe pub on their right, old Bessie was already thumping out her early-evening medley of music-hall songs; the two bars inside were clearly quite crowded, since some of the drinkers had spilled out onto the pavement outside.

Kate allowed Ruth to lead her past the gap in the bombed terrace of houses which was now nothing more than a building site. But as they drew close to the house where Ruth had seen Tom, she gradually slowed down and came to a halt. Several navvies were perched high all over the masonry and brickwork, hammering away at what remained of the house, which already had no roof or top floor, and which was clearly in the

440

final stages of demolition.

'Is this it then?' asked Kate sceptically, speaking for the first time since they had left the Town Hall.

There was nothing Ruth could say. She was too shocked, aware that everything she had told Kate would now be dismissed out of hand. All she could do was to look up forlornly at the gradually widening gap in what had once been an elegant row of houses.

After Ruth and Kate had gone their separate ways, a middle-aged man emerged from the shadows of a public air-raid shelter on the opposite side of the road. He crossed over, and before moving off, Ken Phillips took his own lingering look up at the remains of the house, which had stirred such disbelief in his own daughter's mind.

Chapter 23

Edie Perkins looked smashing. Well, at least that's what her beau Harold Beaks thought when he saw her coming down the stairs on the morning of their marriage at the Town Hall Register Office. And everyone else thought the same for, with Bella's help, she had saved up enough clothes coupons to buy a short-sleeved, below the knee, light grey taffeta dress from Selby's department store in Holloway Road, and decked out in a little pom-pom hat in matching grey, and

441

a half-veil, Edie really did look the cat's whiskers.

The ceremony, such as it was, was short and sweet, and as Edie and Harold's guests only numbered fourteen people, plus two kids and little Theresa in her pram, there was very little fuss in getting them all there and back. The one exception was Edie's Uncle Arthur, who was so old and deaf that Edie's spivvy married nephew, Felix, was heard to mutter that *'one more change of underpants, and the ol' boy'll be ready fer the knacker's yard!'* However, Uncle Arthur wasn't the only person who didn't hear a word the Registrar said, for most of the male guests present were so bored, they switched off before the wedding rings had even been exchanged. Nonetheless, the females present lapped it all up, with the exception of Bella, who had always strongly disapproved of any marriage ceremony outside the Church, specifically her own Roman Catholic Church. The only regret for Edie was that, despite the fact that Rita Simmons had accepted the wedding invitation, she had failed to turn up. Edie had tried to put a brave front on it by saying that it would be a far happier day without her, but throughout the ceremony, her eyes constantly flicked towards the door, to see if Rita was there.

For such an austere post-war period, the wedding reception at the 'end house' was a triumph of determination over an incredible shortage of practically every type of food that should have been available for a wedding breakfast. However, the buffet table in the kitchen looked magnificent. Between them, Bella and Edie had made a spread fit for a king – and queen. Amongst the favourites were cold homemade sausage loaf, sliced ham, Spam (of course), Egg Champ made with dried egg, potatoes and runner beans, beetroot and white cabbage salad, and a mixed salad of lettuce, tomatoes, celery, cucumber, and spring onions. For dessert there was a fruit trifle and several plates of sweet biscuits, some bought, some home-made. But the *pièce de résistance* was, without a doubt, the eggless fruit cake decorated with white icing sugar bought from one of Edie's friendly neighbours who was clearly 'in the know'. The cake itself was made by Bella, and the moment Edie saw the inscription, *Edie and Harold* in blue on top, she burst into tears; it was, she said, the first time anyone had done anything like that for her in her entire life.

When it was all over, and everyone had moved into the sitting room, Harold was forced to get up to make a speech. 'Dear relatives, friends, an' neighbours,' he began, tentatively, doing his best to ignore the jeers and jibes of the men, and Felix in particular. 'On be'alf of, of...'

'In case yer've fergotten,' yelled Felix, to gales of laughter, 'yer wife's name's Edie!'

'On be'alf of Edie and meself,' continued Harold, ignoring the teasing, 'I want ter fank yer all fer comin' ter support us on this – our speshul day.'

Everyone cheered, applauded, and thumped the side of their chairs.

'Most of all, er course,' continued Harold, turning to Bella and Ruth, 'I want ter fank our 'osts – or should I say our 'ostesses...'

'Yer was right the first time, 'Arold!' called Gladys, one of his neighbours from the street he used to live in before he moved in with Edie.

More laughter.

'Wot's 'e say?' asked a bewildered Uncle Arthur, with one hand cupped over his ear.

Felix filled him in. 'Uncle 'Arold says 'e's lookin' forward ter gettin' 'is leg over wiv Auntie Edie ternight!' he joked, again to gales of laughter.

'Don't be so disgustin', Felix!' scolded his wife, Rose, who was having a fag with a couple of Edie's neighbours from Jackson Road. 'That's uncalled for.'

'I 'aven't done that sorta fing since yer Auntie May died,' said Uncle Arthur, who was clearly in his own twilight world.

'Never mind, dear,' said Rose, at his side, patting his hand. 'Yer've still got time.'

'Yeah,' called Felix. 'But only just!'

More roars of laughter, which now woke up Theresa in her pram.

Harold again tried to continue, but he now had to compete against Theresa yelling her head off. 'I want ter fank Bella and Rufe,' he said, having to shout, 'fer lettin' Edie an' me use their place fer this do, an' also fer the trouble they've taken in gettin' all this grub tergevver.'

Cries of, 'Hear, hear!'

Ruth was unable to calm Theresa, so she lifted her out of the pram, and started nursing her.

Harold was now so flummoxed, he didn't know what more to say.

'Go on, dear,' whispered Edie. 'Get a move on!'

'I can't,' said Harold. 'I've forgotten wot I'm

444

s'pposed ter say.'

Edie sighed impatiently. 'Oh Gawd,' she said. 'Yer 'opeless!' As she got up, Harold immediately sat down. 'Wot 'e was tryin' ter say,' she said, 'is that we're lucky ter 'ave such good pals and neighbours as Bella an' Rufe 'ere'

Rumbles of agreement all around.

'I've known 'em boaf now fer a good many years,' she continued, 'an' I tell yer this much, yer won't find better people if yer search from one side er London ter the uvver!'

Again, agreement all around, but not from Theresa who yelled her disapproval.

'Times ain't been easy fer 'em,' Edie went on. 'In fact they ain't been rosy fer any of us. That bleedin' war – it nearly knocked the daylights out er our little neck er the woods. I don't know about you lot, but there were times when I fawt we weren't goin' ter get fru it all.'

More rumbles of agreement from around the room.

'In fact, I'd almost given up wonderin' wot it'd be like ter 'ave the lights on again wiv no blackout down, an' if someone 'ad told me this time last year that it wouldn't be too long before we could buy whatever we want in the shops wivout the coupons I'd've told 'em they was stark, bleedin' bonkers. And now I know that's exactly wot they are!'

Laughter all round. Ruth was struggling to calm Theresa.

'But jokin' apart...' continued Edie.

She was interrupted by a loud knocking on the front door outside. Bella sprang to her feet, and hurried out to see who it was.

Edie waited for her to go, then continued: 'But jokin' apart, the only fing that kept us from goin' down was the fact that we all stuck tergevver – fru fick an' fin. Our little neighbour'ood,' she said, with tears in her eyes, 'was all part of one big 'appy family...' She had hardly got the words out when Bella came back into the room. With her, clutching a brown paper parcel in her hand, was Rita.

'Evenin' all!' called Rita brightly, seemingly unaware that everyone was just staring at her in total silence. 'Sorry I'm a bit late.'

Conscious of the hostility around the room, especially amongst the neighbours, Edie went straight to her. ''Allo, Rita,' she said diplomatically. 'Fank yer fer comin'.' She pecked Rita lightly on the cheek.

''Ere,' said Rita, shoving at Edie the parcel she had brought for her. 'This is yer present. It's a pair of pillowcases. They're brand new, never bin used. I've 'ad 'em in me chest er drawers since I got married.'

'Fank yer very much, Rita,' said Edie. 'It's very good er yer. We're just 'avin' a drink. Come an' sit down.'

Gladys and Rose cleared a place for Rita on a kitchen chair at the side of Uncle Arthur.

'Wot'll yer 'ave ter drink, Rita?' asked Harold.

'My usual!' she blurted, taking in Bella's room, which to everyone around her seemed to be the only reason she had turned up.

Harold went off to get her drink.

The uncomfortable silence continued, until

Uncle Arthur, quite shamelessly looking at the way the cheeks of Rita's huge rump were bulging over the sides of her chair, suddenly said, 'I bet it's a long time since yer 'ad *your* legs up!'

The place erupted.

For a brief moment, Rita glared angrily at them all. But then, gradually, her face cracked into a grin, which then broadened as she also shook up and down with laughter at the old boy's remark.

The party went on until well after midnight. The sing-songs were so loud, Bella was afraid that the neighbours might complain, until she remembered that most of their immediate neighbours were in the room anyway, singing along with everyone else. Even Rita had joined in, but despite the fact that her voice sounded like a fog-horn, it proved a just punishment for Edie's nephew Felix, who had to partner her in a duet of 'My Old Dutch'.

Edie and Harold were first to leave. Even though they were only spending their honeymoon night in their own upstairs bedroom next door, they departed like young lovers, hand in hand, glowing with joy – and from several glasses of booze.

Fortunately, several of the wedding guests had got together and done the mountain of washing-up, but by the time everything had been put away, everyone had gone, and Theresa was tucked up safely in her cot upstairs, all Ruth and Bella wanted to do was to flop down into the two armchairs by the fireplace.

'It's odd, isn't it,' said Ruth, wearily kicking off her shoes, 'when you think of all the years we've

447

known Edie, and now here she is a happily married woman all over again.'

'It's wonderful,' agreed Bella. 'If ever a person deserves a new start in life, it's her. But I must say, if I live to be a hundred, I shall never understand that extraordinary woman.'

'Rita Simmons, you mean?'

Bella nodded. 'Coming in so late like that, ignoring the wedding ceremony, and turning up just as some people were thinking of leaving. She seems to be a woman of so little conscience.'

'I don't think it's anything to do with conscience, Mama,' said Ruth. 'Rita's a sad, totally self-absorbed woman. It's no wonder her husband's left her. I'm just amazed he didn't do it a long time ago.'

'Marriage is not easy, darling,' said Bella. 'For some it takes a whole lifetime to get to know the person they've chosen to live with. You'll understand that yourself when Mike comes home, when you have to start thinking about two people instead of just one – or in your case, two people and one baby!'

They laughed gently together. Behind them, the clock struck the half-hour.

After a moment of silence from both of them, Bella asked, 'Where do you go from here, darling?'

Ruth looked across at her. Now that the excitement of Edie's wedding was over, the old anxieties were returning. 'Where *can* I go?' she sighed. 'Each day I live on tenterhooks, waiting to see if the postman is going to bring me a letter from Mike, or even just a scrap of news from

448

someone to tell me that he's all right. I can't tell you how desperately I need him, Mama. I can't tell you how much I want to hold our baby up for him to see, for him to hold her in his arms, to see the look in his eyes, to know that all three of us are at last together. This *waiting* drives me mad – the uncertainty of not knowing when or whether I'm going to see him again.'

'What about Mike's grandfather?' asked Bella. 'Perhaps *he's* heard something by now?'

Ruth shook her head. 'When I went up to see him last week, all Uncle Cyril knew was what we had both heard some weeks ago, that Mike's battalion had finished active duty – wherever they were – and that they were about to be posted home.'

'Well, he's probably on a troopship on his way back home right now.'

'Oh God,' sighed Ruth, 'I do hope so. I really do hope so. Every time I step out through that door, I get an awful feeling in my stomach that I may never get home again. The fact that I haven't seen or heard anything of Tom since that awful Sunday afternoon in Isledon Road only makes it worse. I know he's out there somewhere – waiting for me. Again, it's the not knowing that's so agonising.' She leaned her head back in her chair, and closed her eyes. 'Oh, Mama,' she said despondently, 'you've no idea what it feels like to know that there's someone out there waiting to kill you.'

'If you believe that,' said Bella, 'then you should go to the police.'

Ruth opened her eyes and looked across at her.

449

'I just can't do it,' she said, shaking her head. 'Once they catch him, he'll go to prison. I don't want to be the one who's responsible for doing that to him. Not after all the agony he's gone through – and is *still* going through.'

In some ways, Bella admired her daughter for her stand. But no matter how noble and humane her reasons, Bella was more concerned with Ruth and Theresa's safety and well-being than with respecting Tom Phillips's sensibilities. 'What about Tom's sister?' she asked. 'Have you heard from her since you told her that Tom is alive?'

Ruth shook her head. 'There's no point,' she replied. 'The moment I saw them demolishing that house, I knew that neither Kate nor anyone else was going to believe me. All I can hope for now, Mama, is that Mike gets home as soon as possible. He's about the only person who can help me now.'

After Bella had turned in for the night, Ruth poured herself a small glass of brandy from the remains of a bottle that was left over from the wedding party. Then she turned off the light, curled up on her chair, leaned back and closed her eyes again. The weight of the past few months was now telling on her. How could she cope with looking after a baby, she asked herself, and the endless fear of being struck down by a man who had lost his reason? What with that, and the knowledge that both her mother and Mike's grandfather were talking about selling up their businesses and starting a new life, she felt as though she was drowning, and struggling to come up for air.

Ruth had dozed off, and was awoken by the sound of the clock on the mantelpiece striking the hour. She sat up, yawned and stretched, then, noticing that she hadn't quite finished the brandy in the bottom of her glass, she drained it and returned it to the small table where several empty beer bottles were left from the party. She felt wretched, not only tired, but thoroughly worn out. She more or less shuffled her way back across the room, but before she left, she went to collect her packet of cigarettes from the mantelpiece. As she did so, her eyes were drawn to the casket containing her father's ashes. Half-asleep, and floundering in the dark, she found herself talking to the casket as she had done on many occasions before, as though to her father himself.

'Would it be too much to ask you to help me, please, Papa?' she said, with a touch of irony. 'I've never asked you for many favours, but I'm in trouble, and if *someone* doesn't help soon, well ... who knows.' She turned, and started to move off. But before she had gone more than a few steps, she stopped, and looked back at the casket. 'Tell you what,' she called quietly. 'I never meant all those things I said about you. And I think you liked me a lot more than you ever dared admit, despite all the things you used to say. So why don't we call a truce? I'm scared, Papa. More scared than I've ever been in my entire life. And I have no one here I can turn to. So please help me. I promise I'll pay you back somehow, if you'll just do – *something.*'

She paused briefly to curtsey and cross herself

451

at the small plaster-cast statue of the Virgin Mary on the wall, then left the room.

A few hours later, Ruth awoke with a start to hear someone banging hard on the front door outside. It took her a long time to focus on what was going on, for she had had a terrible night with Theresa, answering the baby's demands for a feed, changing her very soiled nappy, and spending the best part of an hour trying to get her back to sleep. What made it worse now was that it wasn't dark any longer, but broad daylight, which meant that it must be late, although she hadn't heard her mother leave the house to go to the shop just before seven o'clock. She rubbed her eyes, threw back the bedclothes, checked that Theresa was still sleeping in her cot, and fumbled around trying to put on her dressing-gown. It was only whilst she was doing so that a terrible thought suddenly occurred to her. Suppose it was Tom Phillips banging on the door down there? He must know she was alone in the house when her mother went to the shop first thing every morning, and this would be a perfect opportunity for him to get to her again. The first thing she did was to hurry to the window, where she peered discreetly around the curtains.

'*Ruth!* Are you up there?' The man stepped out onto the front yard path, and looked up at her window. It was Harold Beaks from next door.

Ruth quickly opened the window. 'What's the matter?' she called. 'What's going on?'

'Yer'd better get down 'ere!' Harold shouted back.

'Why?' called Ruth. 'What's wrong?'

'Just get down here!' he yelled. 'It's important!'

Ruth's heart started to thump hard. What now? As she put on her carpet slippers, all sorts of anxieties started to crowd her mind. Was it Tom? Had he done something terrible? Had he tried to break in again or something? No. That was impossible because she herself had removed the spare key from the flowerpot near the front door. So what else could it be?

Her legs nearly gave way as she hurried down the stairs. Although she had had no time to comb her hair or look at her face before opening the front door, she knew only too well that she must look a complete wreck, especially after a sleepless night with Theresa. 'Harold!' she cried, as she unlocked the front door. 'What is it?'

'Yer'd better come wiv me, young lady,' he said, his face stern and mysterious.

'Where?'

'Next door.'

'Why?'

'Edie needs yer.'

'But Harold,' she protested, 'it's early in the morning. I've only just got up.' She was absolutely astounded when he suddenly grabbed hold of her hand, and without allowing her time to close her own front door, dragged her out into the street and straight into Edie's place next door. 'Harold!' she yelled. 'What the dickens are you playing at?'

The new Mrs Beaks, still in her honeymoon nightgown, net and curlers, was waiting for her in the front passage.

'Edie!' Ruth pleaded. 'What's this all about?'

Edie was unable to say a word. Tears were streaming down her face. 'In 'ere,' she said, slowly easing open the door of her front parlour.

Ruth looked first at Edie, then at Harold. She was totally bewildered. Doing as she was told, she went quietly, cautiously into Edie's parlour.

Someone was waiting there, his back to her. He turned. ''Allo you,' he said, with a grin.

Ruth screamed, and flung herself straight into Mike's arms. The more they hugged each other, the more the tears filled her eyes. 'Oh God!' she gasped, over and over again. 'I can't believe it! I just can't believe it! I thought I'd never see you again! I thought ... oh God!'

Edie peered into the room. But it was all too much for her, for she too was sobbing her heart out. So she quickly closed the door, and left them to it.

When Ruth opened the door of her bedroom, Mike followed her in with his heart beating fast. What he had been through during the war in the jungles of Malaya, he reckoned, was nothing compared to this. *This* was clearly going to be one of the most nerve-racking experiences of his life.

Ruth went to the baby's cot, and gently lifted her out. 'Theresa,' she said, 'I want you to meet your daddy.' She was beaming as she handed the bundle to Mike. 'Mike,' she said, 'this is your daughter, Theresa Marika Daisy Buller.'

Before taking the bundle, Mike wiped his hands on his trousers. His eyes were bulging out of their sockets as he stared down at the tiny figure he was holding. 'Blimey!' he said, shaking like a leaf. 'Ain't she a dot!'

Ruth laughed. 'All babies are tiny,' she said. 'They do grow bigger, you know.'

'Yeah,' he replied. 'But she's over two months, ain't she? I still fink she's a dot.'

As she watched him delicately holding the baby's fingers with his own, Ruth felt as though her whole body was about to burst with joy. She didn't want to laugh, she didn't want to cry, she just wanted to savour the moment, a moment she would remember for the rest of her life. 'You can kiss her if you want,' she said. 'It's allowed.'

Mike leant forward, and gently kissed his daughter on the nose. ''Ow-de-do, Theresa,' he said proudly. 'Pleased ter meet yer!' As he spoke, the baby seemed to laugh out loud, and then grabbed Mike's own nose. ''Ere – wotchit, mate! That's my 'ooter!'

Ruth was deliriously happy, and later, when they went back down to the sitting room, Mike was still clutching the baby in his arms as though he was never going to let her go. Once he was settled comfortably beside her on the sofa, Ruth had her first real chance to look at him. She was amazed how well he looked, a little thinner than the last time they had met and made love right there in the very place they were sitting, but sun-tanned a deep bronze colour, as though he had been on a holiday to the seaside. It was so good to see him in civilian clothes again, even though they were baggy. 'If this is what they give you for demob,' she teased, 'they needn't have bothered.'

'Ha!' said Mike, the baby sucking hard on his little finger. 'Yer should've seen wot some of the uvver blokes got. In comparison, mine's Savile Row!'

Ruth immediately started questioning him about all that had happened to him since he went away, asking how difficult it must have been to fight in all that heat? But Mike was not very forthcoming about what kind of active service he had been involved in, and he kept to himself the horrific sights he had seen, and the atrocities committed by the Japanese troops on innocent civilians in the steaming hot jungle. Ruth soon realised that this was neither the time nor the place to plague him with any more questions, and she made a conscious decision not to pursue it until he had settled down again into civilian life.

'So?' Mike asked. 'Your place or mine?'

Ruth was puzzled. 'What are you talking about?' she asked.

'We're a family now,' he said. 'We've got ter find somewhere ter live tergevver. Grandad said we could move in wiv 'im if we like. It could only be fer a time though, now 'e's set 'is 'eart on movin' out.'

'I'm sure my mother wouldn't object to us living here,' replied Ruth. 'Especially under the circumstances.'

'Yer probably right,' said Mike, looking around. 'There's a lot more space fer three than my room.'

'It wasn't the space I was talking about,' Ruth told him. 'There's another reason. Something –

important. Something I've got to tell you about.'

For the next hour or so, Mike listened grim-faced as Ruth described the horrors she had gone through ever since she had discovered that Tom Phillips was still alive and stalking her. He found it as hard to take in as she had, especially as he knew of blokes just like Phillips who had practically gone off their heads trying to cope with jungle warfare, and the nightmare of fighting an enemy that had no code of conduct when it came to the treatment of prisoners-of-war. Once Ruth had finished telling him all she knew, he handed the baby back to her, lit up a fag, and went to look out of the window. Ruth's description of how Tom had nearly killed her not only worried him, but also got him thinking. 'D'yer 'ave any idea where 'e's 'idin' out?' he asked.

'That's just the trouble,' replied Ruth. 'He has this knack of disappearing into thin air. I never know when he's going to turn up and scare the daylights out of me. But I don't want the police brought into this.'

'We don't need any coppers,' replied Mike, in one of his rare moments of seriousness. 'Leave this ter me.'

This set alarm bells ringing for Ruth. 'No, Mike!' she said, hastily settling the baby into her pram, and going to him. 'I don't want you involved. I don't want you putting yourself into any danger.'

'Look, Rufe,' he said, with intensity. 'If you fink I'm goin' ter just sit around an' wait fer this nut-case ter get is 'ands on you *an'* our kid, then I'm

457

tellin' yer right now, it just ain't on!'

'Mike,' she said, 'Tom isn't a nut-case. He's a very real person who's suffered so much hurt and pain. The last time I saw him before he went away, he was one of the kindest people on earth. That's why I loved him – or *thought* I loved him. But when I saw him again in that terrible house...' Fraught with guilt and anxiety, she leaned her head against Mike's shoulder. 'You should have seen the look in his eyes. He's like a fly caught up in a spider's web. He just doesn't know how to find his freedom.'

'I won't let 'im 'urt yer, Rufe,' said Mike.

She looked up at him with a sense of true relief. 'I know you won't,' she replied. 'That's why I thank God for bringing you back to me. But it wouldn't be right for me to forget that I am partly to blame for what's happened. So I can't just close my eyes and forget that he exists. All we can hope for now is that he'll forget all about me, and try to find someone who can help him to start his life all over again.

They kissed.

Over Mike's shoulder, Ruth caught a glimpse of the casket containing her father's ashes on the mantelpiece. She smiled, and hugged Mike as tight as she could.

Despite the many reservations Bella had had about Ruth's reckless relationship with another man, the moment Ruth had brought Mike into the shop, her spirits were immediately raised, and she embraced him like her own son. But, as always, her enthusiasm was tempered by practicality. 'The first thing you must both do,' she insisted, as she rocked the baby back and forth in her arms, 'is to go and see Father O'Leary. Now that you're together, you owe it to Theresa to give her the protection of a marriage blessed by God.'

Ruth exchanged a brief grin with Mike. 'You mustn't forget, Mama,' she said, half-teasing her, 'Mike isn't a Catholic.'

'Yes, I know,' replied Bella impatiently, 'but I'm sure Father O'Leary can take care of all that. It's just a question of getting converted.'

Ruth sighed. She had been through all this before with her mother, and now, with all the other problems she was having to face up to, it would drive her mad to have to go through the whole thing again. 'Had it occurred to you, Mama,' she said, 'that Mike might not *want* to convert?'

Bella was horrified. 'Then how are you going to get married if he doesn't?' She gasped. 'Oh God! You don't mean you'd go to the Register Office?'

'Well, it was good enough for Edie and Harold,' Ruth reminded her.

'Edie and Harold are not young people!' snapped Bella. 'Besides, they've both been married before.'

'Of course, the other thing we haven't considered,' said Ruth mischievously, turning to grin at Mike, 'is that Mike might not *want* to marry me.'

'Yeah, that's a point,' agreed Mike, playing along with her tease. 'I shall 'ave ter give it some serious consideration.'

Bella's eyes widened with horror.

'On second fawts, 'owever,' Mike said casually, 'I've already made up me mind, so I don't really 'ave ter consider anyfin', do I?'

Bella's eyes were popping out of her head with anxiety.

'Don't you worry, Ma,' said Mike, going to her and putting a reassuring arm around her shoulders. 'If your daughter agrees ter tie the knot wiv me, I'll be the proudest man in the 'ole wide world!'

The bell above the shop door tinkled, and a customer came in.

'Kate!' cried Ruth, immediately going to her. 'What's happened?'

'Can I speak to you?' she said tensely. And aware that Mike and Bella were watching her, she added, 'Alone.'

Ruth threw a quick look at Mike, who was puzzled. 'It's all right,' she said, 'I'll only be a minute,' and immediately followed Kate out into the street.

'I've seen him,' said Kate, the moment she and Ruth were alone.

'Who – Tom?'

Kate nodded. She looked as though she'd been through some kind of terrible ordeal, for her face was pale and ravaged with anxiety. 'He followed me after I came out of the pictures up at Camden Town last night,' she said, her voice cracking with emotion. 'I couldn't believe it was him. I still can't believe it.'

'Oh, Kate,' said Ruth, trying to comfort her. 'I tried to tell you. God knows, I *did* try.'

'We walked around the streets together,'

460

continued Kate. 'It seemed like hours. Even though it was dark most of the time, every time we passed a light in a shop window, I could see his face ... it was so – changed. I just didn't recognise him.' She struggled to contain her tears. 'He told me everything. It sounded ... terrible.'

'What he's had to go through,' said Ruth, 'is more than any mortal person should have to endure. He needs all the help we can give him.'

'He wants to see you.' Ruth froze. 'He wants me to take you to him.'

'Why?' Ruth asked warily.

'He wants to talk to you.'

'The last time we met, he tried to kill me.'

'He said he never meant to. He said he was upset – because you had your baby with you.'

Ruth shook her head. 'I can't do it, Kate,' she said sorrowfully. 'I'm afraid of him. I'm afraid of what he might do to me, especially now that Mike's back home again.'

Kate's expression hardened. 'So that's him, is it?' she asked bitterly, glaring towards the shop.

Ruth nodded. 'I can't do it, Kate,' she repeated. 'Please don't ask me to.'

'You just said he needs all the help *we* can give him,' said Kate. 'If you mean what you say, then you should give him a chance. He says he'll give himself up if you'll just let him talk to you.'

Ruth stared at the girl. Could she believe her? she asked herself. Could she really believe that Tom had come to his senses, and was now prepared to sacrifice his freedom, just so that he could talk with *her?* And if they met, what would

461

he want to talk about? Would he want to tell her that he now understood why she hadn't waited for him, and that he wouldn't stand in the way of her having a life with another man? Or was he using his sister as a way of drawing Ruth into some kind of trap, where he would finally take his revenge, and finish off what he had started to do in that wretched bombed-out house?

'Do you trust him, Kate?' she asked.

'He's my brother,' the girl replied.

'That's not enough,' said Ruth. 'Tom is not the person he was. Even you have to admit that. If he tried to kill me, would you be able to stop him?'

'He won't try to kill you.'

'How do you know?'

'Because he doesn't love you any more. Because he wants to get on with his own life.'

For a brief moment, Ruth thought seriously about what Kate had said. Then she took a casual look to see if Mike was watching her from the shop window. 'Let's go,' she said.

But as they started to move off, Mike came out from the shop. 'Where yer goin'?' he called.

'It's all right, Mike,' Ruth replied hastily. 'I've got something to do. Be back later!'

'If there's somefin' wrong, I'll come wiv yer,' Mike called.

'No, Mike!' Ruth called back, suddenly panicking. 'Wait for me. I shan't be long!'

As he watched Ruth and Kate hurrying off down towards Holloway Road, Mike was more than a little curious. Why was Ruth rushing off in such a hurry? he asked himself. He didn't like it. He didn't like it at all.

Chapter 24

After a direct hit by a V1 flying bomb in August 1944, the Gaumont cinema had now been closed for more than a year. Although it had only opened its doors for the first time seven years before, in its heyday the majestic building had been a mecca of screen and stage entertainment, and one of the most popular and lavish venues in London. Ruth therefore found it an odd place for Tom Phillips to hide out in. However, when she got there, she found that the grand cinema was a shadow of its former self for, although the bold exterior and shell of the building had somehow managed to survive any obvious serious damage, the luxurious, traditionally styled interior had been completely gutted.

By the time Ruth arrived at the theatre with Kate, she was full of forebodings. The problem was, she didn't entirely trust the girl, who had become a strange, distant type of person, whose obsession with her brother was still, to Ruth at least, a source of disquiet. And why had Tom chosen to rise up from the dead only to his sister, but not to their parents? And why did he now want Kate to bring Ruth to see him, when on three previous occasions he had chosen to make his presence felt in a far more frightening way?

'Are you sure this is the right place?' Ruth asked nervously, as she followed Kate to the back of the building, where they had to squeeze through a gap in the wooden fence.

'This is the place,' Kate assured her, once they had reached the far side.

For a moment they paused to look around; all the windows and exits in the building had been boarded up.

'It looks a bit dangerous,' Ruth said. 'And what if someone finds us here?'

'There's no one here,' insisted Kate. 'There's no building work going on, and there probably won't be until they decide what to do with the place.'

A few minutes later, they were inside what had once been the auditorium; now open to the sunlight, it contained a tangled mess of iron girders, fallen masonry, plaster, and electric cables and bits of lighting battens dangling help-lessly from the ceiling. They entered from behind the stage area, and once they'd found their way around what was left of the safety curtain, Ruth found it an incredible sight to look out on to the sea of beautiful rose-pink seats, which were now almost entirely buried beneath a mountain of rubble and debris. 'This way,' called Kate, as Ruth followed her out through one of the exits, down a relatively intact flight of stone stairs, and into a vast underground space that was once used as a patrons' waiting area, now strewn with debris, and lit only by a shaft of light coming through a hole in the concrete ceiling. 'He's in there,' said Kate, indicating one of the few doors that had not been blown off its hinges.

'Aren't you coming with me?' Ruth asked warily.

Kate shook her head. 'It's you he wants to see,' she replied, 'not me.'

Reluctantly, Ruth made her way towards the door, conscious of the sound of her feet crunching unevenly on glass and other debris. Now, more than at any time since she had agreed to come to meet Tom Phillips, she was overwhelmed by a feeling of deep unease. But she had come too far to turn back now, and by the time she had plucked up enough courage to push open the door, she was ready to face up to whatever lay in wait for her inside.

'Ah! There yer are, Ruth!' called Tom, who was clearly visible by the light of a hurricane lamp set on a badly scarred desk, the floor around him littered with rubble and discarded, sodden paperwork floating in several inches of water. His feet were perched up on the desk, fag in mouth, fingers locked behind his neck. 'Welcome to the Gaumont, Holloway. Seats at all prices!' He got up from his chair, and offered it to her.

Ruth remained with her back to the door. 'No, Tom, thank you,' she answered firmly. 'Kate said you wanted to see me.'

His shadow crept across the wall behind him as he slowly came towards her. 'She's a good gel, my sister,' he said. 'Finks the world er me.'

'What are you doing in a place like this, Tom?' she asked compassionately. 'How are you managing to live? How are you managing to eat, to sleep in this filthy hole?'

'You don't 'ave ter worry about me, Ruth,' he said, unsmiling. 'There are plenty er ways ter survive in this world. I *know*. I've 'ad plenty er practice this last year or so.'

Ruth was still standing near the door. 'What do you want of me, Tom?'

He took a step towards her. 'I want yer back, Ruth.'

A cold chill shot through her entire body.

'I didn't ask ter go ter war,' he said. 'But I did. And then they robbed me. They robbed me er you. I felt cheated. I don't want ter be cheated. Yer my gel – an' I want yer back.'

Ruth watched him very carefully, watching for any move that would jeopardise her ability to escape from the room. At this moment, all she could think of was Kate, no doubt listening outside the door, enjoying the way she had enticed her to this bizarre meeting with her brother. 'You know that's not possible, Tom,' she replied courageously. 'You know that I've moved on. I didn't plan it that way, but it's happened now, and there's nothing we can do about it – you *nor* me.'

To her relief, he turned around, and moved away with his shadow. 'Did I tell yer about wot 'appened ter me when I was out there in the bush, wiv me mate? Before I got picked up by our patrol?'

Ruth found it difficult to look at him.

'It was these Nips, yer see,' he said. 'We got caught in this ambush – me an' me mate.' He paused and she looked up. His face was totally impassive. 'They tied us up to these big palm trees. This Nip officer spoke English. 'E wanted ter know 'ow many men there were in our patrol.' He paused, and pulled on his fag. 'We wouldn't

466

tell 'im,' he said.

'Please, Tom,' begged Ruth. 'Don't.'

'They cut Rick down,' Tom continued, ignoring her pleas. 'Rick was the uvver guy – me mate – they cut 'im loose from the tree. They made 'im kneel down in front er me. I could see the look in 'is eyes.' He hesitated, and pulled on his fag again. 'Then they bent 'is 'ead forward, and this uvver bod comes up be'ind wiv this – *fing* – this great big curved sword.'

Ruth closed her eyes, and covered her ears. It was the wrong thing to do, for she suddenly found him wedged behind her, between her and the door, which he closed with his back, his arm locked around her waist. 'Then they sliced off 'is 'ead, Ruth,' he said, without emotion. 'Right there, while I watched 'im, while I watched the look in 'is eyes.'

'*Please*, Tom.' Ruth was close to tears.

''Is 'ead dropped on the ground, right by me feet.'

Ruth cringed with horror at what he was telling her.

'An' yer know wot the Nips did next?' he continued, increasing his hold on her. 'They left me. They just upped an' left me there wiv Rick's 'ead on the ground in front of me.' He gradually released his hold on her. 'I spent the 'ole night like that. In the mornin' I fawt it was all just a nightmare – but it wasn't. Some Burmese kid found me, and cut me loose. An' then I got back ter me unit.'

When he had finished his story, tears were streaming down Ruth's face. 'Oh God, Tom!' she

467

cried. 'I'm so sorry.'

'Yes,' he replied, without expression. He flicked the remains of his fag into a pool of stagnant water on the floor. 'But I have a lot ter fank yer for, Ruth,' he said. 'When I was tied up all that time, the only person I could fink about was you. You got me fru that night, Ruth. Without yer I'd've just – given up.' He came from behind to face her. 'D'yer know wot I fawt about all durin' that time, Ruth?' he asked. 'I fawt about that time when yer come ter see me off on King's Cross station – the way yer looked at me when we said goodbye. *For ever and ever.* That's wot yer said, wasn't it, Ruth?'

'I know, Tom,' cried Ruth. 'I *know!*'

'Yeah,' said Tom. 'But wot yer *don't* know, Ruth, at least, I don't *fink* yer know, is that I believed yer. I still believe yer. An' I still love yer.' He drew close. 'But, like they say, it's time ter move on.' He moved closer, and leaned towards her. Ruth cringed, but he persisted, waiting for her to respond. When she eventually did, he gently kissed her. 'G'bye, Ruth,' he said, softly, the kindness returning to his eyes, a kindness that Ruth remembered with such affection. 'Be seein' yer.' He leaned forward for one final kiss, but as he did so, the door sprang open, and Mike burst into the room.

Taken completely by surprise, Ruth yelled out, 'No, Mike – no!'

It was too late. Ignoring her pleas, Mike grabbed hold of Tom by the scruff of his neck, and hit him hard with a right upper-cut. Tom went flying, toppling backwards, but somehow managing to stay on his feet. Mike immediately went after him.

'Don't!' begged Ruth, desperately trying to hold him back. But while she was doing so, Tom came at him, and landed Mike a heavy blow on his face which sent him sprawling into a pool of water on the floor.

Ruth's scream brought Kate hurrying into the room. 'Christ!' she gasped. 'What's going on?'

Ruth rushed to Mike's side. The blow he had taken from Tom had completely felled him. 'Mike!' she cried, frantic with panic, trying to revive him. 'What have you done, what have you done?'

Not satisfied that with his superior strength he had knocked Mike unconscious, Tom was so enraged that he picked up a heavy lump of wood, and raised it high in the air, ready to bring it crashing down onto Mike's head.

'No!' yelled Ruth and Kate, both of them determined to shield the fallen man from Tom's savage attack.

But Tom was equally determined, and he positioned himself as close to Mike as he possibly could. However, just as he was about to bring down the piece of wood he was brandishing, a voice boomed out from the open door.

'Tom!'

He froze, and both Ruth and Kate turned to look.

It was Ken Phillips. 'Don't do it!' he said. Then he quickly went across to Tom, and stretched out his hands. 'Give it ter me.'

Tom stared in bewilderment at him.

469

'Please – *son*.'

All eyes were on Tom as he hesitated, looked down at Ruth, then reluctantly handed over the lump of wood.

Phillips took the wood, and threw it across the other side of the room. Then he moved closer to the boy, and in the flickering shadows of the hurricane lamp, he said, 'Come on, son. Time ter come 'ome.'

Rita Simmons didn't like drinking on her own, but as she now had no alternative, for the past few weeks she had taken to nipping round the Globe for a quick one soon after opening time in the evening. Although Bessie hadn't yet arrived to start pounding out her regular medley of popular sing-songs, the public bar was still quite full, mainly with builders and demolition workers who were pulling down the rest of the bomb-damaged houses further along Isledon Road. The difference about Rita tonight, however, was that, for once, she had discarded her net and curlers, and, as she was wearing a pretty floral-patterned summer dress that she hadn't worn in years, she really looked very nice. But then, as she had been alone for some time now since Ted had walked out on her, just lately, Rita had had a lot of time to think, not only about how she looked, but about how she could start putting things right in her life. She was under no illusions, of course. She had come to realise that life gives no favours away, and that if you want to better yourself, the only person who can do it is yourself. But where could she start? Where could she start to pick up the threads of a normal life again, start putting right all those things that she had messed up so disastrously? At the moment, she hadn't a thought in her head about *what* she could do, but since she had made a conscious decision not to play around with any more bottles of aspirins, she knew that she had to begin somewhere.

''Allo, Rita.'

Rita didn't have to look to see who it was who had joined her. After all, it was Edie who had asked her to come and have a drink with her. 'Well sit down then if yer goin' to,' she snapped. But the moment she said it, she regretted her tone of voice. 'I'm glad yer could come, Edie,' she said, even attempting a welcoming smile.

'Fank yer,' said Edie. 'Just like ol' times.'

'I got yer usual all ready,' said Rita eagerly, sliding a glass of gin and tonic across the table to her.

'Ooh – lovely!' said Edie, taking a sip the moment she got her hands on the glass.

'Yer sure 'Arold, I mean, yer 'usband, yer sure 'e don't mind yer comin' out wivout 'im?'

'Er course 'e don't, silly!' said Edie. ''E ain't me jailer!'

'Well,' said Rita, 'I was wond'rin' – seein' as 'ow this is yer 'oneymoon an' all.'

Edie leaned closer, and whispered into Rita's ear. 'Me an' 'Arold've bin on our 'oneymoon fer a good time now,' she sniggered.

They both roared with laughter.

'Wot about the Poleys?' asked Rita, once they had settled down and each taken a gulp of their drinks. 'Got over all their problems, 'ave they?'

471

''E came 'ome, said Edie, with a sickly smile.

Rita swung a look at her. 'Who?'

'Rufe's boy.'

'Yer mean – er kid's farver?'

'Oh, 'e's so lovely, Rita,' said Edie. 'Yer should meet 'im. 'E's got such beautiful eyes.'

'I imagine it wasn't 'is eyes that got 'er in the family way!' splurted Rita, showing that old ways die hard.

Edie's response was a weak smile.

'Sorry,' said Rita. 'I didn't mean that like it sounded.'

Edie was astonished to hear her old sparring partner being so apologetic. She couldn't remember how many years it had been that Rita had talked as though she had barbed wire in her mouth, but now it sounded as though she was at least trying to develop a softer side to her nature. How long it would last, however, was another question, but for the time being at least, she was feeling much more relaxed in Rita's company. 'Rufe said that her mum's finkin' about sellin' up,' she said.

Rita did a double-take. 'Sellin' up?' she asked, with incredulity. 'Yer mean the shop? *Whitlock's?*'

'That's right,' said Edie. 'Rufe says her mum wants more time to 'erself. Can't blame 'er really. I mean, er on yer legs all day in that job. And yer still not finished when yer lock up fer the night. All that paperwork an' fings.'

'*Whitlock's* goin',' lamented Rita. 'After all these years. It's the end er the world! Where am I goin' ter get my Ted's fags from now on?'

There was an awkward silence, as both women

472

realised what Rita had said.

'Not that 'e cares where they come from,' she added hastily. 'Wherever 'e is now.'

Edie looked to left and right to make sure no one was overhearing them. ''Aven't yer got *any* idea where 'e's gone?' she asked.

Rita shook her head. ''Aven't seen 'im since 'e walked out on me on VJ Day. Can't say I blame 'im really.' She took a quick sip of her own gin and tonic. 'I never made fings easy fer 'im.'

'Wot 'appened, Rita?' asked Edie, aware that she was treading on dangerous ground.

Rita considered this for a moment. 'I drove 'im out,' she replied. 'I told 'im I knew about 'im 'avin' a fancy piece.'

''*As* 'e?' asked Edie.

'No idea,' replied Rita. 'Trouble is, when 'e was always out round the boozer night after night, I reckoned that 'e was round there wiv, well, *someone*. I never fawt fer one minute that the reason 'e went out so much was becos er me.'

Edie waited a moment, then asked her: 'Wot would yer do if 'e came back?'

For a moment, Rita didn't answer. Too much was swirling through her mind, too many incidents were plaguing her, like all the times she had belittled him in public, by calling him weak, only interested in himself and his booze, too many hurtful attacks on him both as a husband and as a father. Every time she thought about him, she felt a wave of guilt and anger, anger at her own bombast and stupidity. In all the years she had known Ted, she had criticised him, ridiculed him, and even yelled at him in front of their kids. Never once did she praise him for any of the good things he had done for both her and their family. Never once did she show that she thought he was someone worth knowing. Never once did she show that he was someone worth – loving. 'If 'e came back,' she said, 'I'd probably go and cry me bleedin' eyes out.'

'But would yer take 'im back?' repeated Edie.

Rita turned and looked at her. 'Wor der *you* fink, Edie?' she asked.

At that moment, Bessie had opened up the keyboard of her old Joanna, and the next minute the whole pub was resounding to a rousing sing-song of 'My Old Man Said Follow the Van'. As usual, Rita and Edie joined in with the rest of them, but after the first chorus Edie excused herself and scuttled off to the Ladies. But Rita, now sitting alone again, and bellowing out the words of the song for all she was worth, had no idea that she had been set up. Whilst her attention was drawn to Bessie, who had moved some of the crowd at the bar to do a knees-up, somebody had joined her at her table. When she turned back, she found Ted sitting opposite her. Her face was a picture – shock, astonishment, joy, and finally tears. She tried to say something to him, but he merely put his fingers to his lips, and urged her to carry on singing with him.

As she made a discreet getaway from the pub, Edie purred with satisfaction. A job well done, she told herself.

Mike was feeling pretty sorry for himself. Although he had never exactly thought of himself as Joe Louis, he had at least always been able to give as good as he got. But that punch Tom Phillips had landed on his face was so powerful, he felt as though he'd been hit by a lump of iron. In fact, he now had such a bad cut over one eye that Ruth had had to rush him across the road to the Royal Northern Hospital where he was given two stitches.

'If you're going to come back to Civvy Street and start your own personal war,' said the cocky young doctor who had attended him in the Out-patients' Department, 'then may I suggest that you pick on someone your own size!'

Mike was not amused. After he and Ruth had left the hospital and made a quick call back at the shop so that Ruth could tell Bella what had happened. Then Mike said that if he was going to move into the 'end house' with Ruth, then he'd better get back to Jessop Place to collect some of his things. Ruth agreed, but once she'd fed the baby, and left Bella and Freda Dapper to keep an eye on her, she insisted on taking Mike back to Hackney in a taxi.

On the journey there, Mike was still stunned, not only by the iron fist that had nearly knocked the daylights out of him, but also by the know-ledge that he was not nearly as tough as he thought, a fact that actually quite pleased Ruth. 'I'd sooner you were all brains and no brawn,' she teased. 'But as a matter of fact, I think you actually have both!'

Despite Ruth's loving care, Mike still felt a bit sour when he thought that he'd come through a war out in the jungles of Malaya relatively

475

unscathed, only to come home and get roughed up in a punch-up, which he himself had started.

'I still don't know how the hell you suddenly turned up like that,' said Ruth. 'D'you mean to say you followed Kate and me after we'd left the shop?'

'Yeah,' groaned Mike, irritably. 'Dope that I was.'

'But why?' asked Ruth. 'When I was going off with Kate, why did you think that anything was wrong?'

'Come off it, mate,' replied Mike. 'It's not 'ard ter put two an' two tergevver – not even fer me. Once yer mum told me who that gel was, I knew somefin' was up. Trouble is, I nearly lost yer in the crowds up 'Olloway Road. By the time I caught up wiv yer, yer'd already gone inside that pitture 'ouse. Mind you, I didn't 'ave ter use much brainpower ter work out where yer'd gone to.'

'Yes,' she said. 'But it was a pity you had to attack Tom like that. It wasn't necessary.'

'Wasn't necessary!' spluttered Mike. 'If I 'adn't bin there, 'e could've frottled yer!'

'No, Mike,' she said, soothing him. 'He was just trying to say goodbye.'

'Ha!' grumbled Mike, making the most of his injury. 'That's a funny way ter say goodbye! Anyway, who was this uvver geezer I saw when I come to?'

Ruth sighed, and leaned her head on his shoulder. 'That was Ken Phillips,' she replied forlornly. 'He's Tom's father – his stepfather really. He's an odd man – thinks more about his

476

vegetable allotment than his family. Well, that's what I thought until he turned up in that cinema. Kate said that soon after she knew that Tom was alive, she went straight to her father and told him. It sounds as though he had an inkling of what had being going on, more than I thought.'

When they got to Jessop Place, Mike was furious when his grandad saw that his grandson had got himself a black eye. 'I always told yer ter cover wiv yer left 'ook,' said Cyril, laughing his head off.

'It's not funny, Grandad!' protested Mike. 'I've got two stitches over my eye. I could er got blinded.'

'Get orff!' returned Cyril. 'Just fink wot Nelson did wiv one eye!'

Whilst Mike went up to his room to collect some of his clothes, Ruth waited in the parlour with Cyril. 'You must be sad Mike's leaving,' she said, 'especially when he's just come home after being away for so long?'

Old Cyril shook his head, and poked the fire that despite the fine weather was blazing in the grate. 'Not really,' he said. 'Mike's always bin an independent sort er boy. An' in any case, I'm gettin' too old, too fixed in me ways ter 'ave 'im 'angin' round me all day. Anyway, 'e's got a crackin' gel of 'is own ter look after now – *two* crackin' gels! It's about time 'e took on a bit er responsibility!'

Ruth strolled out onto the balcony with him. Down below, the garden was beginning to look overgrown, and that lush fresh green that always heralded the start of a new season was already showing signs that it was preparing itself for the autumn. Spread out before them, the rooftops and spires of the city were now bathed in a burning red glow from the dying rays of the sun.

'It's a funny ol' place Lond'n, in't it?' Cyril said, wistfully. 'I mean, when yer fink of all it's bin fru over these past few years, there it is, still out there, puttin' on a new face, an' ready ter get up and start all over again.' He paused a moment. There was a great deal on his mind. 'I'm not goin' ter enjoy leavin' this place, yer know. Oh, I know I've got ter move wiv the times, an' be practical. But d'yer know 'ow long I've lived 'ere? Forty-two years come next December. I remember when me an' my Daisy moved in. It was Christmas, but there weren't no snow. Mind you, it din't look much from the outside – after all, if yer startin' up a business wiv stiffs, it's not the look er the place that counts, is it! But when we come up 'ere...' He sighed. 'Wot a view! Daisy fell in love wiv the place right away. And when young Mike come ter live wiv us, it seemed as though we'd got a family of our own fer the first time. I mean – just look at it! The country 'as trees, an' fields, an' cows and sheep an' all that sort er fing, but Lond'n, well, there's somefin' speshull about chimney-pots, an' pavements, an' rows er shops, an' mums yellin' at their kids out in the street. An', I'll tell yer somefin' Rufe. When I come out 'ere in the morning, nuffin' out there ever looks the same. Every day there's somefin' different.' He smiled gently to himself. 'Oh yes,' he said. 'I shall miss this place all right, that's fer sure. It ain't easy parting from an old mate.'

Ruth put her arm around his waist.

'Yer'll take care of my boy, won't yer?' he asked. ''E's pure gold.'

'Of course I will,' replied Ruth.

'An' if 'e don't care fer you an' that youngster er yours,' he added, ''e'll 'ave me ter reckon wiv!'

Mike came into the room, lugging a huge suitcase. 'Now don't ferget ter water my plants,' he said to his grandad. 'If I find any of 'em die while I'm away, there'll be trouble.'

Cyril winked at Ruth. 'Depends on 'ow long yer goin' ter be away,' he replied.

A few minutes later, Cyril was downstairs, helping them to get some of Mike's things into a taxi. Although he was clearly putting a brave face on it, it was a day he had been dreading for a long time.

'Right then,' said Mike, giving the old boy a hug. 'Be seein' yer then.'

'Course,' said Cyril huskily. 'Any time yer passin'.' Once Ruth had given him a warm farewell kiss and a hug, he slammed the taxi door behind them, and they were off. He watched the taxi until it had finally disappeared down the long stretch of Mare Street. Then he turned, and went back inside to water the plants.

The Phillipses' house on Camden Road was, like a flower, blooming in the morning sunshine. Not that it was a particularly attractive house from the outside, but its grey bricks and sloping tiled roof had a nobility and elegance about them that made it look a more expensive property than it actually was. Ruth had always liked the house

479

itself, but admired it far more than the family who lived there. However, the Phillipses had had more than their share of trials and tribulations, and that is why she was calling on them, the day after the 'drama' in the poor old Gaumont. She had persuaded Mike that, for obvious reasons, it would be better if she went alone, and so, after leaving him to look after the baby for an hour or so at the 'end house', she made her way on foot to the Phillipses' house which, after this visit, she was never likely to see again.

'Tom spent the night in 'is own bed fer the first time in over two years,' said Pearl Phillips, whose eyes were still red from crying all through the night. ' 'E said it's the best night's sleep 'e's 'ad in a long time.' As she spoke, she was staring out through the kitchen window into the back garden, where she watched every movement Tom was making, as he ambled amongst the profusion of well-kept flowerbeds. 'I 'ope they don't take 'im away too soon,' she said forlornly. 'If they'd just leave 'im wiv us fer a bit, I'd take really good care of 'im.'

'Kate,' said Ken Phillips, who was standing with his daughter and Ruth watching Pearl protectively from nearby. 'Take yer muvver inter the sittin' room. I want a word wiv Rufe.'

Kate nodded. 'Come on, Mum,' she said, gently.

The woman offered no resistance, and like a small child, allowed her daughter to lead her out of the room.

'The poor woman,' sighed Ruth. 'It must have been a terrible shock for her.'

480

'Ter be 'onest,' said Phillips, 'I don't fink she really understands wot's 'appened. When we brought Tom home yesterday afternoon, she treated 'im as though 'e'd just come from work at the end of the day. She's 'ad so many munffs of worryin' about whevver 'e was dead or alive, I reckon she can't really take anyfin' in any more.'

Ruth looked out at Tom in the garden. 'He looks as though nothing has happened,' she said quietly. 'As though he's at peace with himself at last.'

'I wouldn't say that,' replied Phillips, joining her. 'But I fink 'e's given up worryin' about wot's goin' ter 'appen ter 'im.'

'What *is* going to happen to him?' Ruth asked.

'I'll turn him in.'

Ruth swung him a startled look.

'It's the only fing, Rufe,' said Phillips, with obvious pain. 'Tom needs care, the sort er care we can't give 'im in 'is own 'ome. They won't be 'ard on 'im. And anyway, if we tried ter 'ide 'im, it would only make fings worse. Besides, the police came 'ere lookin' fer 'im the uvver day,' he said. 'I knew where 'e was at the time but I didn't fink the time was right. I wanted ter give 'im a chance ter get fings off 'is chest, an' sort fings out. Mind you, I'm not sure if 'e'll *ever* do that, but at least 'e deserves the chance.'

They continued to stand there in silence for a moment or so. It was a strange feeling for Ruth to be there, looking out at the man she had once loved, had once promised to marry. But she reminded herself that Tom wasn't really a man, he was still just a boy, even though what had

481

happened to him out there had robbed him of his formative years, and replaced it with a future that would be laced with memories of sheer horror. 'When did you first know that he was–'

'Still alive?' replied Phillips. 'You told me.'

She turned to look at him. *'Me?'*

'The day you came to meet Kate up at the Town 'All. I was just comin' out er my office. I 'eard everyfin' yer said. I even followed yer boaf ter that 'ouse down Isledon Road. I know Kate fawt yer was makin' the 'ole fing up, but *I* didn't.'

'But why didn't you tell me?' asked Ruth.

'Because,' said Phillips, 'until Kate told me that Tom 'ad made contact wiv 'er, and asked 'er ter bring yer ter see 'im, I still couldn't be sure. Ter be 'onest wiv yer, I've bin in two minds about 'im ever since 'e went missin'. But I always 'ad this 'unch that 'e was alive.'

'What do you mean?' she asked.

Phillips hesitated. 'I never really believed that 'e was dead,' he said, with some anguish. 'Don't ask me why. I s'ppose it was just instinct. But the funny fing is, I've 'ad an awful lot er time ter fink over these past few munffs. I've bin finkin' about wot that war did to our lads, and 'ow they're goin' ter be able ter cope wiv some of the fings they've 'ad ter put up wiv, and 'ow 'usbands an' wives are ever goin' ter be able ter settle down when they're all tergevver again. War's one fing, gettin' over it's somefin' quite diff'rent. But if there's one fing I've learnt, it's that, although Tom's really Pearl's son, not mine, I *do* feel fer 'im more than I've ever fawt possible.' He turned to look at her. 'Does that make sense?' he asked.

Ruth nodded sympathetically. 'When will they come for him?' she asked.

'I'm goin' ter phone 'em after yer've gone,' he said practically, without emotion. 'Why don't yer go out an' see 'im?'

At the end of the garden, Tom was smoking a fag, one hand idly hanging on to the branch of the apple tree beneath which he and Ruth had once embraced. As she approached, he turned to look at her. 'I wasn't goin' ter 'urt yer, yer know,' he said.

'I know, Tom,' she replied, as she reached him.

'I'm sorry about yer bloke,' he said awkwardly, looking away. 'When 'e went fer me like that, I 'ad ter do somefin'.'

'It's been a terrible time for you, Tom,' she said compassionately. 'And for all of us. I never wanted to hurt you, either. If things had been different, I would have waited for you – for ever.'

'"For ever and ever,"' he said dreamily. 'There's no such fing really – is there?'

'Oh, but there is,' she replied, now feeling confident enough to draw closer to him. 'D'you remember this tree? How we stood right where we are now, holding each other tight? It seems a lifetime ago. We were different people. But I *did* love you. I *still* love you – and always will. But it is different now.'

As she leaned forward and kissed him gently on the cheek, for one moment, Tom stared at her, puzzled and confused. Seeing her standing there was bringing back memories of their times together, the way they had held hands when they strolled, the way he used to run his fingers

483

through her soft dark hair, and the kisses that seemed to hold for ever. But she was right, he said to himself. They were different people now. But it didn't mean that there could never be a future without her. What was it everyone kept saying to him: *'Time to move on now, Tom.'* '"Time to move on,' he murmured.

Ruth smiled warmly, affectionately at him. 'Goodbye, Tom,' she said.

'Goobye, Ruth,' he replied.

She slowly made her way back towards the house. She didn't want to turn back to look at him, for she wanted to hold on to the memory of those last few precious moments they had spent together.

Chapter 25

The Orange Luxury coach station in Parkhurst Road was absolutely brimming with people. Not surprising really, for not only was it a fine Sunday morning, but for most people, it was also the last beano of the season. Most of the 'gang' from in and around Jackson Road were there, including Ruth, Mike, Theresa, and Bella, Edie and Harold, Rita and Ted, Tub Trinder and his missus, daughter, son-in-law, and granddaughter, and everyone who had booked their place on the outing with the people who ran the darts club at the Globe pub. Several crates of booze were loaded into the hold beneath the seats, followed by several baskets of sandwiches, cakes, lemonade and a few off-the-ration sweets for the kids. As most of the seaside resorts had been out of bounds for holidaymakers during the war, beanos had also been restricted, but now they had at last been reintroduced, the excitement amongst the day-trippers was almost at fever-pitch, and most of the male passengers started boozing from the moment the coach left the station.

The road to Clacton-on-Sea was via the East End, but once the driver had taken the coach past Romford, there were several detours into the countryside, mainly to allow the men to have what the ladies somewhat coarsely referred to as 'their piddle stops'. Tub Trinder was first to rush off the coach when it made its first stop alongside a rather muddy wood; he told everyone that he had been bursting to go ever since he got on. Eventually even Edie needed to take a break, but she immediately got into trouble when she was bitten on a delicate place by a persistent fly, whilst she was crouching in the long grass out of sight of the others.

For Ruth, this outing was idyllic. The idea of going down to the sea for the day with her future husband, baby, and mother was something she would not have even dreamed about just a few months before. But here she was, cuddled up to Mike at her side, Theresa wrapped up on her lap, her mother sitting directly behind nattering happily with one of the neighbours, and the rich green of the countryside just rolling past the windows as they drove. The worst part was the endless sing-songs, for although they created a wonderfully happy atmosphere, they just seemed to go on and on, getting louder and noisier as they went. However, what with that and the countless bottles of bitter and brown ale that were consumed, by the time the coach finally reached Clacton, nearly all the passengers were so exhausted, they found it difficult to keep awake.

Once they had alighted in front of Clacton Pier, however, they perked up and decided to go their separate ways, some to find the nearest fish and chip shop, others to sort out the nearest pub. As it was now late September, the holiday season was beginning to wind down for some of the promenade shops were already boarded up. Even so, there were still many attractions left for the families, especially the amusement arcades which never seemed to close, not even during the war, and which were adored by kids of all ages. In no time at all, most of the female members of the party were sporting KISS ME QUICK hats, whilst the men either went for mock coppers' helmets, or straw boaters. Leaving Rita and Ted behind to tackle the first candyfloss anyone had seen since before the war, Edie and Harold strolled off along the front, and despite the fact that they had now been married for three whole weeks, they held hands as they went, blissfully unaware of anything or anybody they passed on the way.

Ruth and Mike plumped for a stroll along the pier. Everyone knew that Ruth had a very specific reason for wanting to do this, which was why she was carrying with her a brown paper carrier bag, and so after Mike had paid the sixpence each admission fee for Ruth, himself, and Bella, they quickly assembled Theresa's push-chair, and found their way through the entrance turnstiles. On the other side, they stopped for a cup of tea at one of the small open-air cafés.

'Haven't been ter this place for donkey's years,' said Mike, lighting a cigarette. 'Last time I come 'ere, some bloke caught a fish up the end that was there so small, it looked like a tiddler. One mouthful, an' it was gone!'

Ruth laughed. 'My father used to go fishing here,' she said. 'He loved the place. Isn't that so, Mama?' she asked pointedly.

Bella smiled and nodded. 'The last time I came here with him,' she said, 'we sat in two deck-chairs overlooking the sea at the end of the pier for nearly two hours. It was so freezing cold, he walked all the way back here and bought me a knee blanket. I still have it at home. He used to spend hours just staring into the sea. For him it was like a second home. I think if he had lived long enough to retire, he would have sold up and moved down here.'

'Would yer 'ave liked that, Ma?' asked Mike.

Bella shrugged. 'Who knows?' she replied. 'A woman follows her man wherever he wants to go.'

''Ear that?' said Mike, immediately turning to Ruth. 'Yer mum's got the right attitude!'

'No, Mike,' returned Ruth. 'We are *not* going to emigrate!'

Bella, who had Theresa on her lap, looked up

with a start. 'Emigrate?' she asked fearfully.

'Don't worry, Mama,' Ruth said reassuringly. 'Mike saw this advertisement in the newspaper. They're offering cheap passages ter people ter emigrate ter Australia. It's a ridiculous idea.'

'Why?' asked Mike. 'We're only young, an' Australia's a young country. Besides, who wants ter 'ang around waitin' 'til the queues die down an' the ration books are frown away? There are no prospects in this country left fer people like you an' me.'

'Not now,' insisted Ruth, 'but there *will* be – one of these days.'

'One er these days is right,' grumbled Mike. 'An' one er these days I could win the pools, except I'll be too old then ter spend the money!'

Bella smiled. Despite the fact that her future son-in-law would most probably be taking her daughter away from her to the other side of the world, in the short time she had known him, she had got to like him enormously. It wasn't surprising, for, from the moment they had met, they had developed an excellent rapport. Although they were from different cultures, religion, and social backgrounds, Bella found Mike to be not only honest and sincere, but also someone who frequently made her laugh with his East End banter and his determination to make a good life for Ruth and their baby. And Mike also liked Bella, despite not being able to understand what she was saying in her Polish accent half the time. As they spent more and more time in each other's company, Mike felt that for the first time in his life, he had a mother of his own he could turn to.

A few minutes later, they started the slow stroll along the pier. Mike led the way, walking briskly ahead, with Theresa wrapped up warmly in her push-chair. There was quite a cool breeze blowing against them, and so Ruth and her mother walked arm-in-arm to keep warm. Ruth loved the crisp fresh coastal air, the smell of salt, the spray from the waves as they crashed against the firm steel struts of the old pier, which had obstinately defied the bullying of two world wars. She felt free, free as the air she was now breathing. She had a man whom she loved to the depth of her soul, a baby daughter she idolised, and a newfound relationship with her mother that had transformed her whole attitude to family life. So *this* was what she had been searching for, during these past few tumultuous years – a family that she could truly call her own.

'Would you really think about going to Australia?' asked Bella, still pondering what Mike had just said.

'Of course not,' Ruth replied emphatically. 'England is our home. I'd feel strange going off to live thousands of miles away. Mike doesn't really mean what he says. It's just that he gets very depressed about the way things are going. The other day he asked me why he should have ever fought for a country when the only reward is endless queues outside the Labour Exchange, shortages of everything in the shops, and long faces at the government's hollow promises. I said, "No matter how bitter you feel towards any government, you should never allow them to force you away from the country you've fought so hard for.'"

'You don't have to worry about me, you know,' said Bella, quite out of the blue. 'I wouldn't mind if you decided to go.'

'Don't be silly, Mother,' said Ruth.

'No, I mean it,' said Bella. 'If I was young, I'd do the same thing. Remember, I left Poland to come here with your papa. When you're married, if you love someone, you'll travel to the ends of the earth with them.'

After that, the subject was not discussed again by any of them. Even so, what Bella had said struck a chord in Ruth's mind, for she suddenly remembered how, before he was posted abroad on active duty, Tom Phillips had once discussed the possibility of them both emigrating to either Australia or Canada. However, his reasons were somewhat different from Mike's, for in those days he had pined to get away from the claustrophobic atmosphere of life with his family in Camden Road. And as she and Bella strolled along the pier, high above the waves which were breaking recklessly against the struts, their cheeks blood red, and hair flapping wildly in the wind, she couldn't help feeling a sense of relief that Tom did not have to face a court martial, and was now being looked after in an Army mental rehabilitation centre somewhere in the West Country. Her only hope now was that one day he would be fully recovered from the traumas he had suffered during the war, that he would forgive her for what she had done, and that he would be well enough to settle down with a wife who would give him all the love and care that he so desperately needed.

When they reached the end of the pier, they could hear music from a piano playing in what must have been, before the war, a small open-air stage. There were dozens of elderly people sitting around in deck-chairs, watching, tapping their feet in time to the music, and humming the songs from the times when they were young, and falling madly in love.

'D'yer wanna park down 'ere?' called Mike, coming to a stop at a secluded spot overlooking the sea. 'If so, I'll go an' grab a coupla chairs.'

'No, Mike!' Ruth called back. 'It's too chilly. Just give Mama and me a few minutes to do what we came for, then we'll go.'

Mike gave the thumbs-up sign, and wandered off with Theresa in her push-chair.

Ruth felt a warm glow as she watched the two of them go off, Mike chatting excitedly to the baby as though she understood every single word he was saying. Then she and Bella moved on to the farthest edge of the pier that they could find. Ahead of them was the vast expanse of open sea, now grey and wild under a threatening sky. Ruth dug into the carrier bag she was holding, and took out the casket containing her father's ashes. But when she offered it to her mother to scatter, Bella declined. 'No, darling,' she said. 'This is between you and Papa now.'

'No, Mama,' objected Ruth.

'No, darling,' insisted her mother, holding up the palm of her hand. 'This is what I want. This is what *he* would have wanted.' With that, she took the empty carrier bag from Ruth, moved away, and went off to watch from the secluded cover of a wind shelter nearby.

For a moment or so, Ruth just stood there with the casket in both hands, staring out to sea. In those few strange moments, her entire life seemed to be flashing before her. No matter where she looked, she could see her father's face reflected in the water beyond. But for the first time he looked different, totally different, because he was smiling at her, and for one fleeting moment she felt she could hear him talking to her: 'Well, if you're going to do it, Ruth,' he was saying, 'then get on with it. God knows, I've had to wait long enough!'

Long enough? Long enough for what? Ruth wondered. And then she reminded herself why she had told her mother that she wanted to come here today, today of all days, the anniversary of her parents' wedding all those years ago, and why, ever since her father had died, she had resisted the idea of casting his remains out onto the waters of his beloved sea.

She turned briefly, and saw Mike watching and waiting with Theresa just a short distance away. Mike smiled, and waved. Ruth smiled, and gently waved back. Then she turned to her mother, who blew her a kiss.

'All right, Papa,' she said, moving back to look out to sea again. 'You kept your side of the bargain, and now I'll keep mine. Thank you for bringing Mike home to me. Thank you for my baby, and thank you for giving my life back to me.' She slowly opened the casket, and shielded

492

the ashes inside from the wind. But as she did so, as if she had suddenly turned off an electric light switch, the wind disappeared immediately, to be replaced by a soft, cool breeze.

'Goodbye, Papa,' she said, holding the casket out over the water. Gradually she scattered the ashes out to sea, where they settled down onto the dull grey surface, until they started to undulate with the waves, and drift majestically out to sea.

Ruth felt her mother's arm slide round her shoulders, and for several moments the two women just stood there, one head leaning against another, watching the ashes of a past life now slowly drifting off on the outgoing tide towards a seemingly endless horizon.

The publishers hope that this book has given you enjoyable reading. Large Print Books are especially designed to be as easy to see and hold as possible. If you wish a complete list of our books please ask at your local library or write directly to:

Magna Large Print Books
Magna House, Long Preston,
Skipton, North Yorkshire.
BD23 4ND

This Large Print Book for the partially sighted, who cannot read normal print, is published under the auspices of

THE ULVERSCROFT FOUNDATION